the SeaRch for
WaLLaCE
wHippLe

tHe SeaRch fOr WaLLaCE wHippLe

DONALD SMURTHWAITE

DESERET BOOK COMPANY
SALT LAKE CITY, UTAH

Library of Congress Cataloging-in-Publication Data

Smurthwaite, Donald, 1951–
   The search for Wallace Whipple / Donald Smurthwaite.
      p.   cm.
   Summary: Having been challenged by his bishop to keep a journal, sixteen-year-old Wally records the ups and downs, the joys and fears, of his sophomore year in high school.
   ISBN 0–87579–830–6
   [1. High schools—Fiction. 2. Schools—Fiction. 3. Conduct of life—Fiction. 4. Mormons—Fiction. 5. Diaries—Fiction.]
   I. Title.
PZ7.S664827Se   1994   93–46245
[Fic]—dc   CIP
                                                  AC

Printed in the United States of America
10   9   8   7   6   5   4   3   2   1

*For my family—Shannon, Emily, Kelly, Christopher
and Kevin—and for any kid who has ever felt a little
out of place at a stake dance.*

*Special thanks to a couple of good friends
Richard Romney and Kathleen Lubeck.*

CONTENTS

CHAPTER 1

tHe
CHaLLenGE

FRIDAY, AUGUST 31

Call me Wallace. Wallace F. Whipple. Some years ago—never mind how long precisely—having little or no money and nothing in particular to interest me . . .

Oh, what's the use? It will never work. I have 200, blank, white pages to fill, and I may as well be trying to float across the Pacific Ocean in a leaky rowboat. This is impossible. I can't even plagiarize 200 pages, much less fill them up with stuff about me. Nobody has to tell me that my life is boring. It's a fact that I deal with every day. It's not like I'm writing the memoirs of Wallace F. Whipple, all-universe basketball player, or Wallace F. Whipple, the famed medical researcher who cured the common cold, baldness, and facial blemishes. I'm just a kid, and sort of an ordinary one at that. Who in the world is going to care about the life and times of a 16–year-old guy in Oregon?

This is, of course, Bishop Winegar's fault. There I

1

was in his office, just telling him about my life during my birthday interview. He's listening mostly, nodding occasionally, asking a question now and then. We go on that way for about a half hour, and then he reaches into his desk and pulls out a journal. An empty journal as it turns out, the one of the famed 200, blank, white pages.

"Wally, I'd like you to have this," Bishop Winegar explains. "You're going through some very exciting times in your life now, and I think keeping a record of them would be good."

Whoa, Bishop. Are we talking about the same human being here? Good ol' Wally Whipple? Exciting times? The last exciting thing that happened to me was two years ago when I got sick on a roller coaster and my friend, Lumpy Felton, had to carry me off over his shoulder.

Exciting? No way. You've got me mixed up with someone else, like a rock star or a famous athlete.

"You'll be able to look back in a year and see the choices you've made, how they've affected you, and how you've grown, Wally. So I'd like to present this to you, with your promise that for one year, you'll diligently keep a journal. Next year, we'll review how it worked, during your birthday interview."

Well, he's the Bishop. What can I say? Only one thing. Okay. That's it. Okay. Bishops have never steered me wrong.

"I know that you're probably thinking that your life isn't that interesting. But just start with the basics. Write down who you are, the way you feel about things, what worries you, and what makes you happy. Stick with those kinds of things. You'll start to become comfortable and gain a better grasp of the things that should go into a journal after you've been writing for a few months. You might even look at this as an adventure, a means of discovering yourself. A search, for a special young man named Wally Whipple."

He handed me the journal. I smiled the way you do for class pictures. All teeth and no feeling. I felt like someone had just handed me a dozen of my Aunt Margaret's holiday fruitcakes, each of which weighs approximately fourteen pounds, and told me to run a few miles. Thanks, Bishop Winegar. I'll do it because you want me to, not because I have much of a story to tell.

Oh well. Let the search for Wallace Whipple begin.

SUNDAY, SEPTEMBER 2

One page down. One hundred and ninety-nine left. Progress, I guess. Today is fast Sunday. We're home from church and I expect we'll eat in an hour or so. It seems like the right time to sit down and take on this journal thing again. The basics. That's where Bishop Winegar said I should begin. Let's get real basic.

Name: Wallace Fremont Whipple, Jr.

Age: Sixteen, but very mature. And confident. Yep, that's me. Mature and confident.

Occupation: Student, most of the time. Trying to act like a normal human being the rest of the time. Bright future as a professional basketball player.

Hobbies: Reading the classics, such as sports biographies and the sports page; music, especially listening to my collection of tapes by the masters—Tony Bennett, Perry Como, Mel Torme, and others who are old enough to be my grandfather. Strange, I know, but at this point, I choose to blame it on an aberrant gene.

Social Life: Unless you count taking my sister to the roller rink, it's nonexistent. Glenda Ferguson did have a crush on me in the 7th grade, but it all ended tragically when I saw her sharing French fries with Brad Knight one afternoon at Hamburger Bob's. An ugly chapter in my life from which I am still recovering.

Physical: Tall (6'3" and growing), slender (actually, "skinny" is a more accurate description of my 130–pound frame), brown hair, brown eyes. When I look at myself in the mirror and hold my head at the right angle and comb my hair just so and smile jauntily, I sometimes almost think that I'm sort of ruggedly handsome. I started to shave in the 7th grade, though, which was a real status symbol.

I do not, however, wear glasses, white socks, or shirts with more than one pizza stain on them. I have my dignity, you know.

Acquaintances: My close confidant is the aforementioned Lawrence "Lumpy" Felton, who came by his unusual nickname when his little brother couldn't quite pronounce Larry.

Family: Father, Wallace F. Whipple, Sr., the successful hardware department manager at the Aisles of Value store; Mother, Pamela Whipple, simply world-class at everything; Siblings, five-year-old brother, Chuck, who is extraordinarily awesome, and fourteen-year-old sister, Natalie, whom I acknowledge as a blood relative only on rare occasions.

Activities: Church, of course. Scouts, where I'm almost an Eagle. And shooting hoops on the driveway, my most favorite activity of all. And, in case my journal should ever fall into the hands of my parents, I do dabble in homework. Occasionally.

Long-term Goals: Getting a basketball scholarship, being able to dunk in a year, going out on a date before receiving a mission call, and getting through high school without doing major brain cell damage. And maybe getting a job at Hamburger Bob's, so that I can eat there even more than I do now. Be all you can be, that's my motto.

Well, that's it. Wally Whipple at a glance. What you see is what you get.

Natalie, my demure, sweet, sister, is bellowing that dinner is ready. Session Two of the journal is coming to a close. I am now through slightly more than one percent of this, and it hasn't been too bad.

Now, if I can only think of what I'll write about tomorrow.

MONDAY, SEPTEMBER 3

Let it be known: I fear no man. Reckless is my middle name. Sort of.

Case in point: I am always the first in line for the family flu shot. I laughed my way through the spook alley last Halloween. Further proof? When Rich Larsen split his lip playing basketball at church, it was I who very calmly took off my gym sock and shoved it in his mouth to control the bleeding. No Nerves Whipple.

Sure, Wally. Then why are you as jittery as gelatin about starting high school?

Because of this: Tomorrow I will be in school with kids who drive cars. They hold good jobs, like at the Spiffy Shine Car Wash. They date. Some date a lot. They take college entrance exams. Sometimes, when they go out to a restaurant, they order salad, just like your parents do. True, they are only teenagers, but they are almost human in many ways. Am I ready for this? Can Wally Whipple make the jump to marginal adulthood? Lumpy called today. Our conversation went like this:

LUMPY: "So are you nervous about tomorrow?"

ME: "Surely you jest! What is there to be nervous about? Ha! Cool Hand Whipple here. Ha, again! You amuse me, Lumpy. You are totally and amazingly wrong. Ha!"

LUMPY: "You sound really nervous."

ME: "I am."

What if I come home everyday and do six hours of homework and still can't keep up? What if my teachers think I have applesauce where billions of brain cells functioning in perfect rhythm should be?

What if the boys choir teacher asks me to sing a solo? I can't sing!

What if some 230–pound gorilla who plays nose guard on the football team, who has hair on the palms of his hands and has a locker next to mine, says, "Hey, punk! I don't like da way ya look. You get outta dis hallway before I rearrange your face"?

What will I do if an outstandingly gorgeous senior cheerleader says hello to me? Does that mean she wants to go out? Does that mean she wants to get to know me?

What if, what if? My goal tomorrow will be basic. You know, something along the lines of the goal of most single cell life forms. I want to survive. Simply survive.

WEDNESDAY, SEPTEMBER 5

Day One at Benjamin Franklin High School is over. And I lived to tell about it.

Oh, I did see one hulking football-player-type near my locker in the hallway and for a tiny fraction of a second had visions of being twisted like a pretzel around the school's flagpole, but you know what? He ignored me! Completely. Was I ever relieved. I *love* being a nobody.

Not that there wasn't one near disaster.

I need to explain something. I can't sing. I mean, rocks rattling in a paint bucket sound better than my singing voice. I was even an outcast in Primary at singing time. I miss notes by margins that are usually reserved to describe distances in outer space. But as a tenth-grader, you have your choice of three whole electives—wood shop, art, and boys choir.

My wood shop skills are roughly equivalent to those of a termite's: everything I touch turns to sawdust.

And when I draw people, they're stick figures. That gives you an idea of my art ability. My little brother, Chuck, draws better than I do. Rembrandt can rest easy.

Lumpy, who knows me well, said I should sing in

the boys choir. "There are about eighty guys in it and you can lip-synch the whole year. Just show up on time and look sincere and earnest. You'll pass the class on punctuality alone," he counseled. "In wood shop and art, you have to make things and then show them to the teacher. Then you get graded on them and that's where you're in trouble."

He wasn't trying to make me feel bad, he's just my best friend and knows my limitations. So I took choir. The problem started when Mr. Ashbury asked each of us to sing a few lines in front of the whole class. That's when the anxiety attack hit. One by one, each guy gets up and sings a bit of a song. Mr. Ashbury would nod, make a few notes, then tell him where to sit in the choir.

Immediately my mouth went dry and I started to quiver. This was my worst nightmare come true. Lumpy looked at me with horror. He's sat beside me at church and knows what my singing voice is like. What would happen? I'd be thrown into wood shop, a choir exile, where I'd be doomed to making cutouts of geese in flight for the entire year. Mr. Ashbury was moving through the class in alphabetical order at a quick pace. I looked at the clock and it seemed each minute was an hour. I wondered if this was something I should say a prayer about. I decided immediately, that yes, it was okay to pray because of the stark terror I was feeling. I prayed.

Lumpy's turn came. He has a nice singing voice and Mr. Ashbury smiled as Lumpy went through a verse of "America the Beautiful."

"Very nice, Larry," Mr. Ashbury gushed.

We were into the middle of the alphabet. Fifteen minutes left in class.

A half-dozen other guys sang. They all sounded like Pavarotti. Five minutes.

I prayed again.

We were into the *Ws* now. Vince Walton sang . . . I looked helplessly at Lumpy. Take all the time you need, Vince. Please. Rats, he's done. My whole life is passing before me. Mr. Ashbury is calling my name. I stand slowly on wobbly legs.

"Wally . . . are you set? How about 'My Country 'Tis of Thee'?"

I nod sickly.

I gulp and take a huge breath. Mr. Ashbury pounds out the intro on the piano. I open my mouth. It is dry, very dry. The first note bounces around in my head but then evaporates when . . . this is true . . . the bell rings!

Mr. Ashbury looks sad. "We're out of time. We'll finish next class. Wally, why don't you go take a place with the tenors."

"Tenors? Oh sure, tenors. Yes, I'm a tenor, Mr. Ashbury. A tenor all the way. I've always thought of myself as a tenor. A tenor is what I will be."

He ignores my babbling. Not wishing to press my luck, I grab my books and escape to the safety of the hallway.

Lumpy is in awe. "You dodged one, Wally."

"I know. I think praying helped. By the way, do tenors sing high or low?" I asked.

"High," Lumpy said, shaking his head.

Anyway, so I'm a tenor. And really happy to be one.

FRIDAY, SEPTEMBER 7

My schedule at school looks like this:

First Period: Choir.

Second Period: Social Studies, with Mrs. Aparicio. This class should be okay, since I've always liked social studies.

Third Period: Gym. Mr. Timmins, the varsity basketball coach, is the instructor. Big break. He'll be unable to ignore the awesome, raw athleticism I intend to display. By the time the year is over, I will have him drooling at the prospect of having me play for him next year.

Fourth Period: Lunch. Best part of my day.

Fifth Period: English, with Mrs. English. I'm not making this up. That's her real name. And teaching English is her real job. Frankly, I'm nervous about this one. Word at school has it that Mrs. English is to tenth grade composition what Attila the Hun was to defenseless villages.

Sixth Period: Math. Algebra this year, with Mr. Herk. He wears pocket protectors and those fat, black glasses that went out about the year 1971. Plus, he wears a tie wide enough to double as a tablecloth.

Seventh Period: Health. I hope they don't make too much of eating right, although I must say that I ate from all the major food groups today—ice cream, pizza, fries, and chocolate.

That's it. My day in review. I hope I can survive it for a year.

SUNDAY, SEPTEMBER 9

I have this theory about parents, especially those

with teenagers. I think that every so often they all get together late at night for a secret meeting in someone's garage, where they plot things they can do to keep us out of trouble. One of their best moves is to keep us exhausted so that we don't have any energy left to mess around at all. I can hear them talking.

Parent #1: "Little Jimmy is going out for the wrestling team. That will sure take it out of him. Wrestling is wonderful for that, you know."

Parent #2: "Yes, and we can count on the teachers for two hours of homework each night, although I would like to see that bumped up to three or four hours."

Parent #3: "I agree, Fran. We've found having a job after school is very effective—something like unloading freight trucks or moving pianos."

Parent #4: "I've always felt that if they go to bed doing anything less than praying for death and bandaging bloody stumps, then you haven't completely drained their energy reserves. You've got to have their tanks on empty every night."

And so it goes, until they have figured out a routine that is guaranteed to keep us kids exhausted. I can see it now. Lumpy calls on a Friday night and half-heartedly suggests, "Let's go get crazy over a milkshake at Hamburger Bob's." And I feebly answer, "Like to, Lump, but I have just enough energy left to finish cleaning the garage for the third time this week. Family first, you know." And Lumpy mumbles that he's really too tired to go anyway and that maybe an evening of watching "M.A.S.H." reruns is all he's up for.

The reason I bring all this up is that tomorrow

seminary starts. *Early morning* seminary! We don't have "release time" in Portland, so we all meet at the church at 6:15 A.M. That's "A.M.," as in the morning. Very early in the morning. Some, in fact, may argue it's still night. They'd be right, too.

Our course of study this year is the Book of Mormon, and I'm looking forward to that. Four years from now, I'll be on my mission, and I'm not exactly a world-class student of the scriptures. Like, I know the Old Testament is the big one, but after that I'm a little shaky. My problem is this: It's just that, well, starting my day that early will be tough. I'm not a "morning person." In fact, I've always considered myself as sort of a "mid-afternoon type."

Journal update: Only 191 pages left. Bishop Winegar asked me at church today how the journal was coming. I told him pretty well, it wasn't so bad after all. He smiled, the way bishops do when something turns out right.

MONDAY, SEPTEMBER 10

So, how well can a day go that begins with your father leaning over your bed and saying, "Son, it's 5:30. Rise and shine"?

It wasn't that bad, really. I like my seminary teacher, Brother McNair. And I've already figured out that if I take the Book of Mormon a piece at a time, slow and steady throughout the year, I can finish reading it. And by the time I got to school today, I was wide awake, ready to lip-synch my heart out for Mr. Ashbury.

But there is more. Today is the day that I think plain-old-vanilla-flavored Wally Whipple fell in *like*.

Yes, *like*. Like as in G-I-R-L. Until now, girls were just sort of there. I mean, I knew they existed but didn't take much notice of them. True, there is Natalie, my sister, but judging half of the human race based on her would not be fair. I would remain, eternally, a bachelor. However, today, my awareness of girls leaped to uncharted territory.

Lumpy and I were in the back row, halfway searching for a couple of two-by-fours to prop open our eyes, when she walked in. Tall, slender, with light brown hair and dark brown eyes. I stopped talking to Lumpy and just sort of stared. Glenda Ferguson turned to dust in my memory. My throat went dry and my stomach went knotty, and *for some reason,* my heart started to thump.

Lumpy waved his hand in front of my eyes. "You okay, Wally?"

I nodded and croaked something from deep inside my soul. "Uhhh." Then Lumpy noticed her.

She took a seat on the row ahead of us and quietly arranged her books on the arm of the chair.

It wasn't just the way she looked. It was her smile, the way she carried herself. Suddenly, I wanted not to be Wally Whipple, but Wallace—strong, mature, manly. I wanted to be a professional athlete, a surgeon who can operate on two patients at the same time, a man who quietly works to help the needy and bolster the weak. Honest, these are the things I thought. Being in *like* can do funny things to you.

I really paid attention in class, especially during introductions. I found out her name is Julie Sloan, and that she just moved here from San Diego. She's in the Fourth Ward, one of three that feeds into our seminary class. She is a sophomore and also attends Benjamin Franklin, two huge breaks for me. I began to feel really good about life and my relationship with Julie Sloan. Julie Sloan. Julie Sloan Whipple. Sounds good. Get hold of your emotions, Whipple. She doesn't know you from the dust bunnies under your chair.

My turn came. I rose and cleared my throat. Very suave. "Hello, I'm Wallace Whipple." I stopped for effect and gazed around the room, displaying my most confident smile. "I like many things, I have an interest in them all." Dumb, Wally. An interest in them all! My suave exterior began to crack and peel like paint on an old barn. "What I mean to say is, that my interests are berried. I mean varied." Giggles from around the class. I began to feel warm. "Such as sports and athletics," I groped. Dumb, again. "And I'm very happy to be sitting here today." Whipple, how could you? You're standing. "And I like the Book of Mormon, which is slightly smaller than the big one, you know, the Old Testament."

My clever way of showing her—I mean, the entire class—that I have a spiritual side. "Anyway, I'd like to make friends with you all." Better sit down after saying something that made a little sense. I forced a smile and slumped back down in my chair. I was fading and was almost to the point where I had decided to become a hermit the rest of my life. Then she, Julie Sloan, someone whom I had known for all of fifteen minutes but who had already crashed the top ten list of the important people in my life, turned and smiled. "I hope we can be friends, Wally."

Now, I could be wrong about this, and I don't mean to jump to any conclusions, and I know it's dumb to even think it, much less write it, but the fact remains she did talk to me and maybe, just maybe, she *likes* me, too.

WEDNESDAY, SEPTEMBER 12

Okay, so Lumpy and I are sitting next to each other in the bleachers in the gym waiting for P.E. class to begin. Mr. Timmins—Coach Timmins—stands before the class in his snappy white gym teacher's outfit and announces that Mr. Leonard, the cross-country coach, wants a few words with us.

Mr. Leonard steps in front of us and clears his throat. "Men, we have a problem and I need your help. No, your school needs your help. Only six men from the sophomore class turned out for cross-country. That isn't enough to field a competitive team."

He's disappointed that only six guys showed up for cross-country? Ha! I've seen those guys. They all look like the poster child for starving orphans. Tall. Thin as a bean pole. Deathly pale. All legs and bony arms. And man, do they ever work! I talked with one guy in choir who runs cross-country. For warm-ups, he says, they run three or four miles. Then they run across town and up mountains, fording raging streams and swimming through deep lakes for their real work-out.

No way. Not me. Nevertheless, I get this funny

feeling that Mr. Leonard has taken note of my 75–inch frame, most of which is legs, with a certain longing.

"Some of you men may be champions and not even know it," he says, looking at me. I wiggle nervously and try not to make eye contact. "If you plan to go out for basketball, for instance, you'll be in the best shape of your life. Those full-court wind sprints at the end of practice will be like a stroll to the corner mailbox for you. Think of it. The best shape of your life."

I glance at Lumpy, who is six inches shorter than I am and about thirty pounds heavier. His nickname fits him. His eyes are fixed on Mr. Leonard. "Best shape . . . " he mumbles. He is wavering, I know.

"Don't do it, Lumpy," I whisper. "Those guys run until their tongues scrape gravel. Be strong, Lump!"

Mr. Leonard is now so close that we could shake hands. "So, how about it, men? Do we have people here who are willing to work hard and show their true colors? Are any of you equal to the test? Who here, would like to be able to say, 'I HAVE CONQUERED!'"

Lumpy's hand shoots up. I cringe. He looks at me and blurts, "I bet Julie Sloan likes athletes!"

And before I know it, my hand is in the air, too. For the woman I *like*.

"Wonderful, men. Come to the cross-country room tomorrow after school."

What am I getting myself into?

THURSDAY, SEPTEMBER 13

I cannot believe how tired I am. The Parents'

Conspiracy has claimed me as one of its prisoners. They win. No contest. I surrender.

Yes, Lumpy and I took on our first cross-country practice today. I have zillions of muscles whose existence I was blissfully unaware of until now, all sending constant electrical blips of pain to my cerebral cortex. And as the other guys on the team cheerily reminded Lumpy, me, and two others hooked by Mr. Leonard's rah-rah speech, the day *after* the first workout is even worse.

Dad thinks it's great that I'm on the cross-country team. Anytime a child is sweating and tired, the father is happy and figures he is doing something right. Dad says cross-country running will build my character. Mom is also happy that I have one more thing to do. (I'm not fooled by her sweet, caring exterior. I'm convinced she's the head of the Conspiracy.) Natalie is mortified. "That's a dweeb sport. Why didn't you go out for football? That would be exciting." As if getting blindsided by a linebacker is exciting. And what position could I go out for in football, given my noodle-like physique? Goal post? My little brother, Chuck, on the other hand, says he'll be my cross-country coach and together we'll win some races. I think the world needs more Chucks.

Second chapter of First Nephi, then some homework before dragging my aching body into bed.

I wonder if Julie even knows there is a cross-country team?

SUNDAY, SEPTEMBER 16

It's well after 10 P.M., but I can't fall asleep, so

scribbling in my journal seemed like a good thing to do. Beats counting sheep.

I'm sitting in bed, with a little lamp next to me. Chuck is across the room from me, zonked out and unaware of how complicated my life is becoming. What's on my mind? This and that. Lots of things and nothing.

School. It hit me for the first time, that I have a chance to fail at something. Let's face it, up to this point, things have been easy. I've been gliding on cruise control. I know where my next meal is coming from, and I have never had to worry about where I'll lay my head at night. But now . . . I could finish 800th in my cross-country race. I could blow a class or two. It's possible that kids at school might point at me as I pass down the hall and snicker because of the way I look or because of something I said in class. **Horrible thought for the day:** Maybe I turned out for a dweeb sport because I am one.

I'm in two worlds. Mom and dad tell me I'm special, and yet, some hot number at school can turn me to dust just by giving me a crusty look. How do you stay special at home or in church and still be cool at school? Do you just choose one path and hope the other works out in some miraculous way? Is this what the bishop was trying to tell me about the choices I'd soon be making in my life? Less than a month into it, I've concluded one thing already: Being sixteen is not easy.

WEDNESDAY, SEPTEMBER 19

"You've got to talk to her!"

This is Lumpy's advice to me regarding Julie Sloan, given to me over the phone.

"She doesn't even know you exist."

"Yes she does. She talked with me on the first day of seminary."

"And hasn't since."

"Well, I'm the rugged, quiet type. I need to grow on people."

"*Mold* grows on people. Look, I know you. You'll worship her from afar and never say a word to her. In the meantime, some other guy will make a move and you'll be peach fuzz. I have a plan and you need to hear it."

"I don't want to hear your plan," I protested, dying to hear what it was.

"It's simple. We don't sit in the back at seminary, but in the front, near the door. When class is over, we do not make a quick escape, but instead, we mess around with our books until Julie comes by. At just the right moment, you look up and say, 'Hi, Julie. How's it going?' Do that, and it will be like you're concerned about her. She'll think you're sensitive. Girls like sensitive guys."

"Do you think it will work?"

"Wally, you're just saying hello. You're not proposing. That will come later, like next week."

"Funny, Lump."

"Then, you'll do it tomorrow?"

"Yeah. I'll do it. Anything to get you off my case. I'm doing this for you, not me, Lumpy."

"Right, Wally."

"Right, Lumpy."

THURSDAY, SEPTEMBER 20

Dad got me up at the usual time, which is to say before the chickens have opened their eyes. I have to admit I was a little excited because today was when I planned to put The Move on Julie. Concerned, I told myself. You've got to act concerned. On the road to a long-term relationship, concern is the expressway to the heart. Lumpy might know what he is talking about, although we stand even in the number of dates we've gone on, 0–0.

Today, I told myself, you are sophisticated. You are a man of the world, couth and experienced. In control of any situation, even if it means talking to a girl.

I decided to take no chances. I brushed my teeth longer than usual. And even though it had been only three days since I had shaved, I shaved again. Then I splashed on some of Dad's aftershave. It smelled good. My confidence was soaring. I splashed on some more. I practiced holding my head at the right angle so that my ruggedly handsome features would be impossible to miss. With great relief, I noted that I had exactly the same number of zits as the night before, meaning no new blemishes had attacked during the night. This was going to be a morning to remember, of that I was certain.

I got in the car with Dad and we headed toward seminary. He looked at me curiously when I climbed in but said nothing. Maybe he was noticing my new attitude. He did roll down his window part way even though it was cool outside, so maybe what he was really noticing was my aftershave.

We picked up Lumpy who climbed in and sniffed

the air. We got out at the church and walked toward the seminary classroom. "You smell good," Lumpy said. "It reminds me of the smell in my dad's hospital room when he had his appendix taken out."

"Thanks. Part of the new me. A guy who is in control."

We were the first to arrive, and we took the chairs closest to the door. So far, so good. Julie walked in a couple of minutes later, and I very coolly pretended not to notice her. She, very coolly, pretended not to notice me, too. That's okay, I reminded myself; merely one of the quirks of *like*. It felt good to know that I was catching on fast. The lesson began, about Nephi and his brothers returning to Jerusalem for the plates of Laban. I really got into it and almost forgot about Julie and our plan for getting acquainted.

Brother McNair looked at his watch and announced that it was time to quit. We had our closing prayer. Lumpy poked me in the side and gave me a quick thumbs up.

This is it. A magic moment dead ahead. Remember, you've got on aftershave. You can do anything.

The kids in the class stood and gathered their belongings and trudged out the door while Lumpy and I lingered. Julie grabbed her books and began walking toward the door. She looked great. Seeking inspiration, I whispered, "Julie Sloan Whipple" to myself. Go with the flow, Whipple. She was five feet away.

I casually reached for my books—and knocked them on the floor. My confidence dissolved like sugar in the rain. The books landed at Julie's feet. I frantically bent over to pick them up and banged my head hard on the desk. I had wanted to say something to show concern, but instead, I was battling to stay conscious. This was worse than singing a solo in choir!

Julie looked concerned though. I stood up and opened my mouth—and nothing came out!

"Are you okay, Wally?" she asked.

I nodded my head and then sort of gurgled something like, "Geretsy sklim der book und fall down."

Lumpy heroically tried to salvage the situation. He turned to Julie, who looked as though she didn't know whether she should laugh, cry, or just feel pity for the person who by now had firmly established himself in her mind as the King of the Klutzes.

"Vocalitis frigidalis," Lumpy hastily explained. "Wallace here has a rare medical condition that sometimes flares up at the most inopportune times. It has to do with his membranes and the way the saliva glides over them. Very rare. Right, Wally?"

"Lurper vood cough und lapse," I mumbled, struggling to keep from going into shock.

What a time for me to speak in tongues!

Julie's expression changed, her soft brown eyes shone with sympathy. "Oh, I'm sorry. I hope it's not too painful. It must be a terrible thing to deal with." She cautiously walked around me as I bent over a second time and fumbled for my books. She stopped and looked back at Lumpy. "By the way, do you smell anything peculiar?"

"No, nothing," he answered nervously. "Certainly not anything like aftershave."

She glided out the door, and Lumpy and I were alone. "You didn't do so good," he said, sadly.

"I don't want to talk about it. I'm going straight from here to a foreign country like Nepal or Wyoming and live my days out, hermit-like."

"Look at it this way. She'll always remember you, Wally."

"That's exactly what I'm afraid of now."

"After this, your day can only get better."

It turned out, he was right. My quota of disasters for the day was filled before 7 A.M. Now there is only one thing to do, close my journal for the day and turn off the lamp. I will do just that, but very carefully.

Vocalitis frigidalis! Why me?

FRIDAY, SEPTEMBER 21

Chuck, my little brother, is one person I can count on in times of turmoil.

I got home from cross-country a little earlier than usual. Chuck was sitting outside, waiting for me. He had on his little tennis shoes, his sweat pants, and his basketball shirt. "Shoot some hoops, Wally?"

"Maybe. I'm really not in the mood, though."

"What's wrong?" Chuck, with his radar-like sensitivity, had honed right in on the fact that all was not right. I rarely tell him no when he wants to shoot baskets.

"It's hard to explain. I want someone to be a friend, and it's not working out."

"We're friends, Wally."

"Yeah. I know. Pals forever."

"We're pals because you're nice to me. Are you nice to the other boy?"

"Maybe I haven't done so good in that way. I've

been trying to impress her in other ways. That's usually what you think of first, but it doesn't always work."

"Her?"

"Yeah. 'He' is a girl."

"If I want someone to like me, I'm nice first. It always works."

"Always, huh? Maybe you're on to something. I need to be nice first. You gotta be nice."

"Can we shoot hoops now?"

"Sure. But only if you don't dunk on me."

Chuck is right. When all the layers are peeled off, about the only thing you have left is how nice you are. Not how you look, not how you talk, not who you hang out with, not even how smart you are. It's how nice you treat others. Wally Whipple needs to pump some more nice into his act. Chuck told me so, in a very nice way.

SUNDAY, SEPTEMBER 23

I'm slowly getting over my belly flop with Julie. From long experience being a geek, I know the stages of mortification. First comes total embarrassment, next humiliation, followed by intense brooding.

Then you realize that the train is leaving the depot with or without you—what I mean is, the sun keeps coming up, the world still spins, life goes on. Lick your wounds, and get with the program, Whipple. Anyway, I'm ready to move out of the intense brooding stage.

Church was good. The main speaker was Chad Keller, who is leaving next week for a mission in

Alberta, Canada. It's funny. I never really thought of Chad as a missionary because he's not much older than I am. I mean, he used to bless the sacrament when I was a deacon. We used to go to Mutual together. But there he was, in his new suit and crisp white shirt, telling the whole ward that while he'll miss his family and friends, he's excited to begin his mission.

All of this tells me something. BIG HINT: In three or four years, I'll be the guy in the new suit and white shirt. I hope I'll be looking forward to my mission—and be as prepared as Chad is.

The biggies this week:

1. First English paper due on Thursday. Topic: "Through the Eyes." Mrs. English told us to write something through the eyes of someone or something else. My paper is on what I would do if I were invisible for one hour. Weird, huh?

2. First cross-country meet on Tuesday. Do I ever have the butterflies!

3. Scouts. I'll be teaching some of the 12–year-olds first aid.

4. Math test on Friday. I was worried about algebra but got a most excellent break. I sit next to the class genius, Edwina Purvis. Whenever I don't get it, which is pretty much twice per class, she leans over and whispers something to help me understand, or she stays a minute after class to explain things. Is that nice, or what?

Almost a month into high school, no mortal wounds. Almost two weeks of cross-country, and I haven't fallen into a heap in the locker room.

And, ta-dah! Almost twenty pages into my journal,

and I'm beginning to think I just may fill up every last page in it.

TUESDAY, SEPTEMBER 25

I have to admit it. I thought a lot about the cross-country race last night. I need to be prepared—just in case I win. So I stood in front of the mirror in the bathroom and practiced how I would hit the tape. After about fifteen minutes, I decided to do so with my head down but my arms raised in triumph. I also decided that I would immediately turn around and congratulate the next few runners coming in. Humble in victory. I would deflect all praise to my teammates the next day at school. "They were an inspiration to me," I'd say. Gracious in winning. That would be me. In the newspaper interview, I would thank Coach Leonard who spotted in me the raw material of a great champion.

Only trouble is, I didn't get a chance to use my routine. You don't get the opportunity when you finish 37th, as I did. And by the time I staggered across the finish line, all I wanted to do was sit down in a nice grassy area and get my heart rate down to about 2,000 beats per minute.

Thirty-seventh! Yuck. That's not even mediocre. On the bus trip over to the course, Coach Leonard tried to motivate us. He asked each guy what his goal for the race was. Some said they wanted to win. Some were more modest and said just finishing was their goal. When Coach Leonard asked Lumpy, he thought hard for a few moments and said he just didn't want to get nauseous.

For me, the race was over after one hundred yards. There were about sixty-five of us—it was a five-way meet. The starter pointed the gun in the air and fired. All at once, it seemed everyone was sprinting, legs and elbows flying in all directions.

I wanted to stop and shout, "Hey, slow down! We've got a long way to go!" Of course, I didn't, so I just tried to keep up. Half a minute into the race, I was thirty yards behind. It was miserable. I felt like a grizzly bear had dug his teeth in and latched onto my side and that weights were attached to my arms and legs.

Chuck and Mom were there. (Natalie was not. "Me! Go to a cross-country race? No way. What if some of my friends were there?" was her overall reaction.) They couldn't have cheered any more if I were in the Olympics. It could have been worse, though. Lumpy got off to a slow start and then tailed off. He finished 51st, although he avoided getting nauseous.

I talked about the race with my dad tonight. He heard the disappointment in my voice and told me not to worry, that I had attained my goal of finishing. He also said that there was nothing wrong with finishing 37th, as long as I had given it my best.

He's right, but I wonder if he understands completely. When you do sports, your whole self is on the line. And you get an instant reading on how you stack up. Winner or loser. First place or fiftieth place. Trying your best or not hardly trying at all. Plus, it's all so public. Guys at school know. ("Hey, Whipple! Heard you finished 37th. Really smoked 'em, pal.") People at church know. Your family, too. And when you're confronted with reality, you'd much rather say, "Yeah.

First place. Tough race, but I handled it," rather than admit you finished 37th and felt like throwing up after the first mile. So is it selfish to want to be a winner? And still I wonder . . . will I ever be a champion, at anything?

THURSDAY, SEPTEMBER 27

I handed in my first English paper today. All at once I had this anxiety attack, right near the end of class.

Fear of failure reared its ugly head once again. I thought, "Hey, you're sixteen years old. You should be writing about world events, the intricacies of the U.S. economy, cold fusion. Instead, you've written a paper about being invisible. I took my time at the end of class, wondering if I should turn my paper in or start over and get docked a grade for being late.

"Wally, I don't have your paper yet, do I?" Mrs. English asked. She's an older woman, in her late 30s at least, and she wears those little reading glasses on the tip of her nose. She was peering over them at me, kind of like an owl ready to pounce on a helpless field mouse.

"Uh, no, Mrs. English. I've got it done, but I'm sitting here thinking that maybe it's not, well, mature enough to turn in. It's about being invisible. Pretty dumb, huh?"

"It sounds very creative to me. I'd like to look at it. I'll make you a deal. If the paper is not up to standard, then I'll return it for you to do over, and there will be no penalty."

"Really? That's fair. That's more than fair. That's decent, Mrs. English."

Boy, was I surprised. I didn't think she was the kind of teacher who gave anyone a break. Maybe there's more to her than what hall talk has.

In the meantime, all I have to do is sweat until she returns my paper.

SUNDAY, SEPTEMBER 30

I have a friend in Fourth Ward named Amy Hassett. She used to be in my ward but moved a year ago. I saw her in the hall at church today and suddenly felt a surge of boldness. After the preliminaries ("Amy, how ya doin'?"), I very coolly asked, "Say, Amy, what do you know about this new girl in your ward . . . Judy . . . Judy Loan, or something like that?"

"Oh, you mean Julie Sloan. Well, we've been doing some things together, and she's really nice. I think she likes it here in Portland, although she thinks it rains too much." And on she went, telling me all that I wanted to know about Julie.

I got an earful in the next two minutes.

Julie moved here from California because her dad got a job transfer. He manages an insurance company office.

She plays the piano.

She plays tennis.

She likes to dance.

She's a good student.

She doesn't have a boyfriend. NOTE: The door is wide open, Whipple. Waltz on through. Seize the moment.

And, as Amy says, Julie is nice. I need to call Lumpy. We have to plan our next move. I've got a really good feeling about things. I can hardly wait to show Julie how nice I really am.

CHAPTER 2

OcToBer

TUESDAY, OCTOBER 2

Another cross-country race. Another finish in the middle, among the faceless horde. This is hard work and no glory. Maybe I should have gone out for football. Yuck! I can't believe I wrote that. Lumpy and I keep reminding ourselves how much character we're building and how someday we will be better citizens of the world. And for the record, I have run every step of every race, and Lumpy has yet to get nauseous.

THURSDAY, OCTOBER 4

Let's see, how about a headline?
Whipple Dazzles Hardboiled English Teacher
Bright Future Predicted for Young Writer
Whipple Nominated for High School Pulitzer Prize
What brings on this sudden surge of self-confidence? Mrs. English handed back our essays today. I

was cowering in the corner wondering what grade I got and if she would remember our bargain and just let me try over again. She handed the papers back, folded. I gulped as she gave me mine, without a hint on her face about how I'd done. I glanced around to make sure that no one else in the class could take a peek at my paper and then folded it open, ever so slightly. I peered just inside the fold and noticed a lot of red ink near the top. I felt like someone had punched me in the stomach. What a lousy idea, writing about being invisible. Why hadn't I written as though I were someone who really counted, like a world leader or Clyde Drexler?

Then I opened it all the way. At the top of the paper was an A.

Me? An A from a teacher who would have marked down William Shakespeare! How could this be?

The note at the bottom said, "An excellent effort. Creative and fresh in its approach. You have a wonderful ear for dialogue and a nice feel for words. Good-work, Wally."

I laid the paper across the top of my desk, just in case anyone did take a look. An A from Mrs. English is nothing to be ashamed of.

I'm not sure, but I think maybe English is going to be my favorite subject in school this year.

SATURDAY, OCTOBER 6

Cross-country was brutal yesterday. We warmed up by running four miles, then Coach Leonard had us run to the top of a nearby hill called Mt. Tabor. And that wasn't all. When we got back, he said he was concerned about our ability to finish strong, so we did some wind sprints. The way he said it, you'd have figured that wind sprints were a treat, like "Wow, are you guys ever lucky! We're going to do some wind sprints! Isn't that terrific!" Who knows what comes next week? A run to Canada? San Francisco and back? Maybe a little jog to Florida. I am sure my mother recruited Coach Leonard into the Parents' Conspiracy Movement.

Lumpy and I agreed that we deserved something for just getting through the week. We talked about going to the football game that night, but decided that sitting in a wet stadium for two hours and cheering while people run into each other didn't really sound like fun. We talked about a movie, but figured we'd fall asleep before it was over.

So we decided on the old standby—Hamburger Bob's for milkshakes.

We talked about school, we talked about sports, we talked about church, and finally got around to Julie. I told him what Amy had passed on to me.

"Good intelligence. What are you going to do now?"

"I don't know. Play tennis, I guess."

"You've never picked up a raquet in your life," Lumpy reminded me.

"Well, I could learn."

"And by then it will be summer and any chance that you had of going out with Julie will be long gone."

"I could learn to play the piano."

"You?" Lumpy asked with more cynicism in his

voice than I thought was necessary. "You don't even know the difference between an oboe and a sonata."

"I do, too. An oboe is long and it makes a deep sound like OOOBBBOOOEEE. And a sonata is like a nap that you take in the afternoon."

"Wally, get real! You've got one choice. It's not tennis, and it's not anything to do with music. You've got to go to a dance. And ask Julie to dance and not just stand around and try to act cool."

A dance! I think I'd rather jog to Florida and back. Dances are like a whole different culture to me. I don't understand the way people move. I don't understand how you know what part to move. I don't even understand how you ask a girl to dance. And I'm sure that Tony Bennett is never played at stake dances.

"How am I going to learn to dance? Who can teach me?"

Lumpy looked thoughtful. "Well, let's see. Not someone you want to impress, because you'll come across like a dweeb. You want it to be someone who doesn't know you very well and who could care less about you socially."

We looked at each other, and something very much like inspiration came over us. "Natalie!" we chimed in unison.

Natalie, my dance instructor? In a way, I'd rather crawl to the top of a mountain made of crushed glass. But . . . the thing about her is, she can dance. I don't know where she picked it up, but she has all the moves on a dance floor. Natalie has been going to stake dances for the last four months, since her fourteenth birthday. Although I've never gone to one ("I have a ton of homework, tonight, Mom"), she comes home and you can tell she's been out on the dance floor all night just by the way she looks, like, she's so pleased with herself. Learning to dance would be faster and easier than learning to play the piano or becoming a tennis star. My path seemed clear, broken glass and all. Wallace Whipple will learn how to dance. For the girl he likes.

"When's the next stake dance?"

"Next Saturday night."

I gritted my teeth and fairly snarled, "I'll be there."

MONDAY, OCTOBER 8

I love my sister, Natalie. Deep down, way deep down, I truly love her. No matter that we're complete opposites in everything. I still love her, despite the fact that she is stubborn, demanding, self-centered, and often rude. She does have a few good qualities. For example, she dresses well, always looks cute (except first thing in the morning when she gets up), is generally kind to Chuck; and I once saw her help a frightened kitten down from a tree. Given time, I'm sure that I will recognize other fine traits in her character, and I need to continually tell myself that at least we have the same parents in common, if nothing else.

She is an original. In the third grade, she was asked to write down what she wanted to be when she grew up. All of the girls put down what you'd expect at that age—a teacher, a mommy, a nurse, a ballet dancer.

Then there was Natalie. She wrote that she wanted to own a mall someday. Third grade! I remember

Mom and Dad looking at each other after reading her answer. "Do you suppose we have a problem in the making?" Mom asked, shaking her head.

Yes, I did ask Natalie if she would help me learn a few steps so that I could go to the stake dance this weekend with some experience. I asked her after family home evening, when she was in her room. I knocked on the door and asked her in the nicest way possible. I told her it was about time for me to stretch a little and try a few things that were new and different, like going to a stake dance.

She scrunched her nose. "Are you serious? You're not going to embarrass me or anything, are you?" she asked. "I have an image to protect, you know."

I explained to her that, no, I didn't want to embarrass her. In fact, I told her, I'd even stay at the opposite end of the dance floor all night. That seemed to appease her somewhat.

"Will you promise not to tell anyone, who doesn't already know, that we're related?"

I said, yes, I would promise.

"What's in this for me?"

I thought that might come up, and I was prepared. I told her I would take her next turn for doing the dishes.

She thought it over for about five seconds. "Make it twice, and you've got a deal."

I told her okay. Dishes twice, and she would teach me to dance.

"Then you'll get the lesson on Thursday night. Dad works late and Mom has a stake Young Women's meeting. I'd rather not do this when they're around. But only for an hour. Not a minute more."

My cross-country meet is Thursday, and I know I'll be tired. But I didn't want to upset what thus far had been a delicate yet successful negotiation. I told her Thursday was fine. Sometimes, you've got to know when to compromise.

I hope I did the right thing. I guess I'll find out come Thursday. On the bright side, after spending an hour with Natalie on Thursday, asking Julie Sloan for a dance should be a piece of cake.

TUESDAY, OCTOBER 9

Got up early. Went to seminary. Went to school. Got by. Ran cross-country, went eight miles. Walked home. Studied. Played with Chuck for ten minutes. Dropped into bed at 8:36 P.M., after writing in my journal for about three minutes. Dead tired.

(This is the way I thought my entire journal would read. I am one-seventh of the way through, and I figured I was due for an entry like this. Good night!)

WEDNESDAY, OCTOBER 10

Today I worked on my confidence. To make a big impression on Saturday night, I'll need to be confident.

So, when I got up this morning, I looked at myself in the mirror and for an extra minute practiced a rakish grin. Yes, I could be described as having chiseled features, I decided, despite the presence of a couple of new zits.

I shaved again. My whole face, not just the upper lip.

I thought about the brilliant future I had as a writer/basketball player.

And I had this vision of me on the dance floor Saturday night, a study in rock and roll funk—people standing aside just to watch the tall, ruggedly handsome, newcomer "get down."

Confidence. Very important to a teenager ready to plunge into a life-altering experience, namely, his first stake dance. And Wallace Whipple has it. At least, I think he does.

THURSDAY, OCTOBER 11

Yes, I've had better days. How bad was it? Let's put it this way. I have lived approximately 5,900 days in my life, and off the top of my head, I'd estimate that about 5,893 were better than today. Where did I go wrong? A case could be made that my first tactical error was getting out of bed. But I did, although twenty minutes late.

That meant I wasn't on time for seminary.

Then my ride to school was late, so I was tardy by fifteen minutes.

In math, we got a test back. Mr. Herk handed it to me while softly clucking his tongue—not a good sign. My grade was a C-. I looked helplessly at the girl genius, Edwina Purvis, who also couldn't believe that I had bombed that bad.

In social studies, Mrs. Aparicio asked me a question in front of the whole class and I gave the wrong answer. Mrs. Aparicio is so nice that she never tells a student he or she is wrong. Until today. "Wally, that's not right."

In P.E., we started wrestling. I hate wrestling. How can I show Mr. Timmins my raw athletic ability while sprawled on a grimy mat filled with harmful bacteria while trying to hold onto some stranger's sweaty body?

Then there was the cross-country meet. I finished 42nd out of fifty runners. I just didn't have it. Even Lumpy, who is to running what a school bus is to an Indy 500 car, was only a few feet behind me at the finish line, and he was closing fast. Actually I'd like to quit cross-country, but if I did, I know I'd get **THE TALK** from my dad.

ME: "Dad, I'm quitting cross-country."

DAD: (putting the newspaper down on his lap) "Is that so, Son? Gosh, it seems a shame to me. All the work you've put in, and now you're thinking of just walking away from it? But, you do what you think is right."

ME: "Dad, what I think is right, is that I quit. I'd have more time to study."

DAD: "Well, Son, I think when you turned out for the team, you were committing to the coach and your teammates that you'd be there the whole season. They're counting on you. But, it's your decision, and you do what is right."

ME: "My decision is to quit, Dad."

DAD: "Son, in life you'll find many difficult obstacles to overcome. Cross-country today, maybe a college class or a job, tomorrow. It's been my experience that turning your back on a challenge never pays off in the long run. You're old enough to make your own decisions, though, and I know you'll do the right thing."

ME: "Dad, I think my decision is that I'll quit."

DAD: "Okay, Son. But you know, Whipples are not quitters. When the going gets tough . . . "

ME: " . . . the tough get going, I know. Dad, I think I'll stick it out. You've really helped me to see things differently."

DAD: (picking up his newspaper again) "Well, Son, I think you're doing the right thing, and you've certainly been your own man on this one. I respect that. And I think cross-country *is* building your character."

ME: "Thanks, Dad."

DAD: "Anytime, Son."

Then there was the dance lesson with Nat. Let's face it, it's tough to take a dance lesson from your little sister.

But the stake dance is only two nights away, and I had already done the dishes twice for her. And I really do want to change some things in my life . . .

Anyway, Mom and Dad are gone, all according to plan. Natalie and I push a chair and the sofa back in the family room. She puts on some music, clenches her jaw, and says, "Let's get this over with."

"What kind of music is that?" I ask innocently.

"Don't you know anything?" she snorts. "That's only the most gnarly group in the universe, Jaded Electorate. And the song they're singing is 'Ruin, Ruin, Ruin.' It has a really good message."

Chuck creeps into the room and cuddles up on a corner of the sofa. I'm glad to see him, because I need some moral support, and it's a cinch it won't come from Natalie, whose compassion meter is stuck on zero.

"Okay," Natalie says, businesslike. "Let's get basic. Songs have what is known as a beat. It's the part you can sort of feel."

"Like the boom or the thump?"

"Yeah. Anyway, what you want to do is move when you hear the beat."

"Move what?"

"Move whatever seems right. Like your arms or your legs or your head . . . or all of them. Try it. This song has a good beat. Even you can't miss it."

I try timing my moves to the beat. It is hard work. It seems that I'm always struggling to keep up. I don't really know what part to move. I sort of jerk my body around a bit. Natalie looks at me, and I can't tell what she is thinking. I put a little more into it. It's not so bad, maybe I'm a natural, I think. Natalie continues to stare at me. I need some feedback . . . any kind of feedback. I'm tired. My body hurts from running in the meet and my head throbs.

"How'm I doin', Nat?"

"You look like a wounded stork trying to take off in bad weather."

I stop dancing. Good old Natalie. Never sugar-coats anything.

"That bad?"

"Yep. Let's take it from the top. Now, there's this thing called the beat, and it's the part of the music you can feel, like the DA-BOOM, DA-BOOM . . . " I had to hand it to her, she really can move, but I couldn't get the feel of it.

Then, exactly one hour after we started, she announced that it was time to call Cindy, one of her obnoxious friends. Natalie almost ran out of the room, leaving me to push the furniture back then crumple on the sofa next to Chuck.

"Was I that bad, Chucker?"

"You aren't very good. I think you should do the hokeypokey. We're learning it in kindergarten. It's easy."

"Right, Chuck. The hokeypokey. Good dance, but only a complete nerd would do it at a stake dance."

So, I still can't dance, and all I have to show for my efforts is a pair of dishpan hands.

FRIDAY, OCTOBER 12

Today was normal. Nothing big or exciting. After yesterday, I was glad that today was a snore.

Coach Leonard did call a team meeting today before cross-country practice. "Gentlemen," he said, "As you all know, our sophomore team has a record of three wins and six losses. This is not up to my standards, and I must believe, not up to yours, either."

He stopped pacing and faced our team. "We have some runners here with great potential, but they are not fulfilling it." (Is it my imagination, or is he again looking right at me?) "I ask myself, is it lack of conditioning? No, it's not lack of conditioning. Is it lack of ability? No, it's not lack of ability. Is it lack of heart, then, the lack of the will to win? I think, Gentlemen, that perhaps it is."

He told us that we wouldn't have a workout that day, at least not one that he had planned. My heart began to soar. He told us he wanted us to design our own workout and think about our performance thus far. He wanted us to conduct a gut check, to renew our commitment to the team and winning.

Then Coach Leonard said he was going home, he wouldn't even ask us where we ran. He knew that he could count on us to give our all in practice, and that after today, we'd be a better, more united team. With that, he pulled his car keys out, walked to the parking lot, which was in full view, and drove away.

The mood on the team was serious. A couple of guys said they'd run to the top of Mt. Tabor—twice. Another guy said he would run to Wilson High and back, clear across the city. A group of others agreed they'd run fifty laps on the track.

Lumpy and I were quiet, thoughtful. We hadn't contributed much to the team. We knew we could do more. We both instinctively knew what we had to do for our workout. We jogged for ten minutes, long enough for everyone else to get into their workouts, then we made for that great physical fitness training center, Hamburger Bob's. Time for a gut check? What better place than Bob's? Hey-hey!

"Best practice we've had yet," exulted Lumpy, between bites of a double cheeseburger, smothered in onions.

"I think we've been working too hard and that's why my legs turn to rubber during meets," I said agreeably, while knocking off my second taco.

"You still going to the dance tomorrow?"

"Yeah."

"Have you learned how to dance yet?"

I tried to look irritated. "Sure. It's not exactly rocket science, you know. Just move to the beat and let yourself go. I've got a certain natural rhythm, maybe from all the basketball I've played. I have some real animal moves, Natalie said."

"I bet you don't ask Julie to dance. When the big moment comes, I bet you get nervous and don't do it. You're a big chicken."

"You doubt me?" I said, attempting to sound wounded.

"Yeah, I doubt you."

"Come to the dance and see for yourself."

"Okay."

I was surprised. Lumpy hasn't been to a dance, either. But he probably figured this was the time for him to make some changes, too. We finished off our food, then headed back to the locker room, hoping no one would notice the onions on our breath.

Now my problem is this: By slightly exaggerating my dancing ability (okay, by telling what could be construed to be a major lie), I've got myself into a fix. I'll have the terrible choice of either losing face with my best friend or once again coming off looking like someone who's a few bricks short of a full load with Julie.

I hope life gets easier when I'm an adult.

SUNDAY, OCTOBER 14

Mis·er·a·ble, adj., from French and Latin roots. Being in a pitiable state of distress or unhappiness (as from want or shame).

Pitiable. Distressed. Unhappy. That about describes it. I'm talking about the dance.

Oh, it started all right, maybe even good. But it didn't take long for things to unravel.

Lumpy's dad drove us to the dance. We got there
about an hour after it started, figuring it was cool to
be a little late. I wore my best slacks, a dress shirt, and
a loud sweater that my Aunt Ludene gave me a year
ago for Christmas that I hadn't the nerve to wear until
now. I checked myself out in the mirror before leaving and decided I looked good. I had shaved, just for
the heck of it, and dabbled a little aftershave on, even
though it stung. The old self-image was on the rise.

We checked out the cultural hall. Yes, a dance.
About one hundred kids, loud music, and a few chap-
erons looking as though it were all a painful experience for them. I tried to figure out the beat and
tapped my foot. Lumpy spotted a table with refreshments, and we decided to saunter over and get a little
quick energy. I scanned the crowd—there was
Natalie, who must have noticed we'd arrived, because
she was moving to the opposite side of the room. A
couple of other guys from my priests quorum were
out dancing. I saw my friend, Amy, who waved to
me. I was feeling good. Then I felt even better. I spotted Julie talking with a couple of her friends, not far
from the refreshment table where Lumpy was plung-
ing a handful of potato chips into dip.

"She's here, Lump," I whispered.

"Oh, yeah. I see her. This is great dip," he mumbled, his mouth filled with chips. "I didn't know they
had food at these things. You going to ask her now?"

"Naw. I need a little time to hit my stride."

Trying to figure out what moves I could copy, I
watched some kids dancing. I nodded my head to the
rhythm as best I could. Maybe there was more to
music than Sinatra. I kept an eye on Julie, hoping that

nobody else would ask her to dance. Everything was right. I felt good, loose. This is sweet. "Be cool," I said softly. "Your time has arrived, Whipple. Go for it."

"Okay, Lumpy. This is it. Next dance."

"Awesome. Have some dip. It will give you courage."

"Ha! You think I need courage? Not me. I'm ready."

The song ended. The next one came on. It was a slow number. I don't know how to dance slow. For slow dances, you actually have to touch somewhere, and I had not counted on having to really hold a girl while I danced. Being a couple of feet away made dancing seem less scary.

"Well, Wally? It's the next song."

"I can't dance slow, Lump."

"You're going to wimp out."

"Next fast number, I promise."

The slow number ended, and just as it did, Julie disappeared through a door.

"She's gone, Wally. Your big chance, and you blew it." And then he made a chicken noise.

I hate Lumpy's chicken noise.

"She'll be back," I said, with more certainty than I felt. For the next ten minutes, I kept a nervous eye on the door. Nothing. Maybe she had decided to go home because nobody was dancing with her. Maybe she'll go home and tell her parents she hates Portland. And it's all my fault because I can't slow dance.

The music stopped. Then it started. Then Julie walked in.

I looked wildly at Lumpy. "Now!" I almost shouted, as if charging into battle. I shuffled toward her. She looked up. She smiled. A smile! Life was good!

"Hello, Julie. I was wondering if you'd like to dance. With me, that is."

"Sure, Wally."

Wally! She called me Wally! She knew my name! I'd never heard it pronounced quite that way. W-A-L-L-Y. Not even from the lips of my own mother had I heard "Wally" spoken so wonderfully.

I escorted her out to the center of the cultural hall. I moved my feet, then my arms. Julie started to dance. I couldn't believe it! I was dancing! Me, Wally Whipple, dancing with a pretty girl, almost like I was a real teenager! I put my right foot in, then pulled it back out. Then I put my left foot in and pulled it out. Then I shook it a little. I shot a look at Lumpy, who had momentarily paused in his eating to watch this historic event, the coming out of Wally Whipple, Teenager.

Julie was all smiles. "Wally . . . "

I put my right arm in and put my right arm out . . .

"Aren't you doing a variation of . . . "

I shook it all about. Dancing was a piece of cake. The kid is a natural.

" . . . the hokeypokey?"

DISASTER! I had been doing the hokeypokey without realizing it! The color drained from my face. I felt as though I were going to pass out. My legs and arms turned to limp spaghetti. My high-flying self-image slammed back to earth with the force of a meteor hurtling in from outer space. "Baa, er, yes, it's ah, I guess, I was sort of, urd . . ."

"I think it's cute."

CUTE! She thinks it's cute! Long live the hokey-pokey, the dance of romance! And if she thinks it's cute, it only stands to reason that she must think the person who's doing the cute thing is cute also. Julie thinks I'm cute! I like being cute!

The song ended, much to my dismay. I could've danced all night. I knew what the prince felt as he whisked Cinderella around the floor. Julie thinks I'm cute. She almost said so. Cute is a very good start. Julie Sloan Whipple said I'm cute!

"You don't even look tired, Wally."

"Oh no. Me, tired? I'm on the cross-country team. I'm in the best shape of my life," I said, making a mental note to run my legs off for Coach Leonard next meet.

"You run cross-country with your medical condition and everything?"

"Yes. I mean, no. See, my condition is so rare that it only hits me every few years. Like once in a decade, pretty much like a solar eclipse. You just happened to catch me on a bad day at seminary, that's all. And it only lasts a short while. It's not really as serious as Lumpy described it."

"Well, I really respect cross-country runners. They work so hard and get so little credit."

She thinks I'm cute and she RESPECTS me! Whoa, this is too much. Not only would I run my heart out for Coach Leonard, I would WIN the race for the woman I like.

I got her back to the sidelines and thanked her. "We'll have to dance again," I said, very coolly.

"I'd like that."

I walked on air back to Lumpy, who was still at

the refreshment table. "Weren't you doing the hokey-pokey out there?"

I didn't bother to answer. I wanted to enjoy this moment, savor it forever. Reflect upon it again and again. Julie thinks I'm cute, and she respects me.

Was I reading too much into things? Nah, no way. I walked out to the couch in the foyer and sat down. One dance more, maybe two, before the night was over. That would be enough—for starters. I must have sat there for twenty minutes. Looking back, they were among the most excellent twenty minutes of my life. Too bad it didn't last.

Lumpy rushed into the foyer. "Wally!" he hissed. "You'd better come in here and see who's dancing with Julie. You've got a problem, man."

My stomach did a flip-flop. Someone else dancing with Julie? Who? I'd turn the jerk into tomato puree. I rushed to the doors, parted them, and glared in. Through the darkness, I saw Julie near the middle of the floor, dancing slowly and looking very content as Joe Vermeer led her around the floor.

And there was no mistake about it, the look on her face told me that she was definitely in *like*.

Joe Vermeer.

I must stop writing now. *Joe Vermeer*. Of all the guys in Portland, why Joe Vermeer?

MONDAY, OCTOBER 15

I read over what I wrote yesterday. I've thought about it calmly and maturely and decided not to worry about Joe and Julie.

Why *should* I worry? Joe Vermeer is only the senior class president.

Ha! Me worry? Joe Vermeer is only the starting wide receiver on the varsity football team.

No worries at all. Joe Vermeer is only a perennial honor roll student, and although he's never said it, will someday have his pick of med schools.

Why worry? Joe Vermeer is only the coolest person I've ever known. It comes naturally to him. I really believe that some people are born cool, born with style. People like Joe. He couldn't do anything klutzy, even if he tried. It isn't in his constitution.

So, Julie. You have your choice of Joe Vermeer or Wallace Whipple. Let's see, this will take about two seconds. The envelope please . . . and the answer is . . . Joe. Julie's only a sophomore like me. Couldn't Joe just grab his scholarship and head off to BYU and find someone from California or Utah to date?

You're overreacting, Whipple. One dance, that's all you saw. It's not like they're on their way to the temple. Be logical. Reason things out.

Okay. I am rational. I have reasoned things out. Stepping back from the situation, there is only one conclusion: Julie is nuts about Joe. I just know it.

Oh, well. I know what I can do. Devote my life to service. I'll start by serving a mission. Then another. I'll accept four church callings and excel at all of them. I'll grow old, never marry. People will whisper, "Wonderful man, that Brother Whipple. Too bad he never found the right one . . . " Little will they know that I found the right one and lost her while still a tender youth. I'll serve three more missions and then move to a third-world country where I'll help people dig wells, build homes, churches, hospitals, schools, anything . . . to forget.

Fast forward thirty years: Just in case I do marry and have a daughter . . . and she comes home with a guy just like Joe, and he wants to talk with me. And I know exactly what's coming. He is going to ask to marry my daughter. And you know what? I'm thrilled because the guy is All-American, a returned missionary, he's going to make bazillions of dollars, and he's crazy about my kid, and I can hardly wait to have him in the family.

Joe Vermeer!

I can't compete with him. He has it all. He never has to look in the mirror at just the right angle to be ruggedly handsome because, he *is* ruggedly handsome—all the time, from all angles.

And he's never had a zit in his life.

I can't stand him.

On the other hand, he's always nice to everyone and says hello to me at seminary even though I'm only a lowly sophomore.

What does Julie see in Joe?

Everything. That's all. Everything.

Julie Sloan Vermeer. Sounds good. Too good.

Joe will be a famous surgeon, or the president of the United States someday, and I will have only two skimpy thoughts to hold onto. One, he said hello to me in seminary. Two, I danced with his wife before he did.

Why Joe? Why Julie? Joe and Julie. Not Julie and Wally.

Reality check, Whipple. Don't let your imagination

run wild. It's not over yet, the most optimistic part of my brain says. Yeah. Sure, says the realistic part.

Natalie came to my door after church. "I saw you dancing," she says.

"Yeah, I danced."

"The girl you were with was cute."

"Yeah. She's sort of cute."

"Do you know her?"

I let out a long sigh. "No, I guess I don't."

And probably never will.

WEDNESDAY, OCTOBER 17

Today:

1. Bumped into Joe Vermeer on the way out of seminary. He meets across the hall with the seniors. He looked at me, cocked his head, and said, "Hey."

2. Didn't think about Julie once. (Okay, the truth is I thought about her maybe three dozen times.)

3. Helped plan a service project at Young Mens. Winterizing Sister Lawson's yard. She's a widow in our ward with a huge place to keep up.

4. Shot hoops in the dark with Chuck, who has yet to make his first basket, but never seems too bothered. I asked him if he minds never making a basket and he said, no, he just pretends they all go in. He may be on to something there.

5. Taking a cue from Chuck (see #4 above), I think I'll pretend the last half of Saturday night never happened.

FRIDAY, OCTOBER 19

The Parents' Conspiracy had the best of me

tonight. Sleep. I want to sleep, for long, uninterrupted stretches. True, it is Friday night, the time when a teenager's heart should be racing in anticipation of life's finer things, such as pizza, football games, pizza, movies, school dances, pizza, and more pizza. But all I want to do is sleep. "You look tired tonight, honey," Mom said sweetly to me an hour ago. Sure, Mom. Pretend you don't know. You probably hosted the chapter meeting tonight.

I did have a talk with Lumpy today during warmups for cross-country.

"What's your next move with Julie?"

I told him my next move was to go on a mission and forget about females.

"C'mon. You danced with her. She said you were cute. You've got a start on things. Don't let Joe intimidate you. Forget the fact that he's superior to you in every conceivable way. Are you a man or a mouse?"

I told him I was neither. I was a geek, which is somewhere in between, although more toward the mouse side.

"It's not like Joe has declared his everlasting devotion to Julie. Next fall, he'll be gone. So long competition," Lumpy wheezed as we ran up a hill in the rain.

Soon we were trotting by the varsity football team's practice field. Somewhere out there in that mass of beef was my rival, popping his pads and making harsh, guttural football sounds. While I, I was running—a natural, flowing, sweet expression of athleticism, known to humans from primordial times.

"I'm still going to go on six missions and devote myself to a life of service. Speaking of which, we are meeting at Sister Lawson's house tomorrow at ten to clean up. Be there, Lump," I panted.

"Okay. Don't give up on Julie, yet. Like, I've heard of cases where a really good-looking girl falls for a guy way below her. Sometimes they even get married."

I guess that comment was meant to lift my spirits, but it didn't do the job.

Chuck is sound asleep and something is tugging at both my eyelids. It is only 9:15 on a Friday night, and I am sixteen years old and ready for bed. Can you believe it? I'm sure my parents are overjoyed.

I'm glad Bishop Winegar talked me into keeping this journal. That way, when I am a parent, I will have a written record of all of my parents' successful tactics to use on my own children.

SUNDAY, OCTOBER 21

A good time at Sister Lawson's yesterday.

Wait! What am I saying? If this diary should ever fall into the hands of another 16–year-old, I would be hauled before the Teenager Police.

T.P.: "Okay, Whipple. You have been charged with admitting to a good time while doing work. How do you plead?"

ME: "Guilty."

T.P.: "Admitting to the enjoyment of work is a serious violation of the Teenager's Code. Think what might happen if adults heard you. It would ruin a perception that has taken decades for us to cultivate. You'll give teenagers everywhere a good name. Soon, we'll be *expected* to work and enjoy it. The consequences would be disastrous."

ME: "But it was a service project . . . "

T.P.: "Silence! You are sentenced to spend four years confined to a couch in front of a television set where you will be required to consume an endless supply of chips and soft drinks!"

Anyway, there we were, all the youth and our leaders, in Sister Lawson's yard—raking leaves, putting on winter fertilizer, washing windows, pruning bushes, and cutting the grass for the last time until spring.

I *liked* the way I felt after we finished. It didn't seem like work. Maybe because Sister Lawson was so grateful. She even cried. Honest, I'm not selling out on my generation, but I will remember the feeling I had for a long time.

Extra Note: I hardly even thought about Julie today. Am I getting over my broken heart?

Extra, Extra Note: Chuck told me he thinks his first basket is coming soon. I hope he's right. We all need a boost . . .

MONDAY, OCTOBER 22

There I was, in Mrs. English's English class. The bell had just rung. Mrs. English was shuffling some papers on her desk, getting ready to teach. It was almost dead quiet, with all of us trying to stay awake after lunch.

The door flew open. Boom!

There was the sound of boots. Large, heavy boots. Clomp . . . clomp . . . clomp. Every head in the class turned. A huge guy, our age, wearing long, pointy boots, denim jeans, a western shirt, and carrying a real cowboy hat in one hand, was making his way toward Mrs. English. The guy looked like he was straight out of a John Wayne movie. I mean, he could have been leading a cavalry charge over the ridge to save the circled-up wagon train. I was thinking his name had to be Billy, or Tex, or Rex, or Lex . . . He's got a horse, I know it. I looked for hay behind his ears.

He moseyed his way up to the desk. Even Mrs. English seemed to be surprised by this sudden aura of sagebrush, saddles, and yippie-yo-ki-yay in her classroom. Clearing her throat, she asked, "May I help you?"

Twenty-six pair of eyes stared intently at the second coming of Wyatt Earp. He pulled a piece of paper from his shirt pocket, a new student slip. "Howdy, ma'am. Muh name is Orville. Orville Burrell, and I'm fixin' to transfer into your class here. Come from a ranch near Heppner." He glanced nervously around the room.

Mrs. English smiled. "Well, Orville, we're glad to have you here." Noticing his anxiety, she added, "We're all friendly folks. Make yourself at home. There's a seat on the second row, right in back of Wally."

Orville twitched a little smile. "Thank you, ma'am. I guess it shows that I'm as jumpy as a long-tailed cat in a room full of rockin' chairs."

The class tittered. Orville marched down the aisle. Clomp, clomp, clomp. He eased into the desk in back of me and tapped me on the shoulder. "Howdy, Wally. Pleased to meetcha."

He put out his hand and we shook, amid the buzz from the other students. "Howdy, Orville."

Why I think this, I'm not sure. But I have this king-sized, blue-skied, big-mountain feeling that Orville and I just might become friends.

TUESDAY, OCTOBER 23

What do you know? It's been more than a week since the disastrous dance. I feel fine and don't even think much about Julie. I think I'm handling this in a very mature fashion, way beyond my years. I may even go to another stake dance and really cut loose on the hokeypokey, just to show there's no hard feelings. Grace under pressure. I can handle defeat. No problemo. I repeat, no problemo. I've made the adjustment, one hundred percent. Let the best man win. And like Lumpy says, it's not like Joe and Julie are engaged or anything.

Joe and Julie. Has a nice ring to it. Wallace and Julie. Sounds awful. I sometimes wonder why my parents didn't name me Jason or Lance or Brian or Chris or some other socially acceptable name. Joe and Julie. I wish them the best. Being an all-around basic sort of hero, a gentleman, a man with a heart as big as Alaska . . . Oh, what's the use? The only reason I haven't been thinking of Julie is because I've been trying hard not to. And I don't even look her way in seminary. A half-dozen missions still sounds like the way to go.

Seminary. I had a great day this morning. I've kept up on my reading. What I don't understand, Brother McNair has the knack of explaining. And what I do understand, he adds something more. This stuff will be useful when I'm on my multiple missions.

I saw Joe coming out of class. He was walking down the hallway to the door. He looked at me and nodded and said, "Hey." I looked at him, slouched a little, tried my hardest to look cool, and said back, "Hey." I saw Julie at the door. She smiled at Joe and they walked out together. Hey.

Thursday is the last cross-country race—the city meet. Twelve teams, each with their top seven runners. My goal is to finish in the top sixty. Hey.

Lumpy's season is done. He didn't finish among the top seven on our team, so he doesn't get to go to city. On one hand, I feel a little sorry for him. He ran hard (though slow), only missed one practice (Hamburger Bob's), and lost just five pounds. On the other hand, he did achieve his goal of never getting nauseous during a race.

Let's hope I do as well on Thursday. The top sixty doesn't sound tough, but I'll have to run my best race to get there. Just another in a long string of challenges I'm facing right now. What can I say?

Hey.

WEDNESDAY, OCTOBER 24

Mom is worried that I'm going to be a social misfit. Tonight she said something like, "Isn't there some nice girl that you'd like to go out with? You and Lumpy could double. You know, you're getting old enough to mix in a little. I think that Wanda Fenwick is really a nice girl. So polite and dignified. Such a lady."

Wanda Fenwick! No, Mom. No way. Wanda is the daughter of a friend of Mom's, and I know they spend lots of telephone time talking about their socially backward children and how they might get us together. Wanda likes horses. She has long, shiny hair, a long face with big teeth, and I've seen her—this is true—pawing the ground with her feet.

Take her on a date to a rodeo, bring along a feed-bag of oats that she can nuzzle, and it will be a perfect evening—for her. No, Mom. A huge, capitalized NO, with about twelve thousand exclamation points behind it.

I'd better find some safe way to show my parents that my hormone system is working fine, and that I am in fact a normal, male teenager.

Hmmm. Joe and Julie are a pair. And I get matched up with Wanda Fenwick. I have only one thing to say: Nay.

THURSDAY, OCTOBER 25

Dateline: Portland, Oregon. Wallace Whipple, a heretofore unheralded runner from Benjamin Franklin High School, today astounded friends, coaches, and opponents by finishing forty-third in the city cross-country meet at Jackson Park . . .

YES! This is true. I finished forty-third! Can you believe it?

Strategy. That's what did it. All season long, my strategy was this: start slow, then level off. Try to save energy by not running too hard in the beginning. But my strategy didn't work well. Once, in fact, Coach

Leonard told me he didn't understand how someone with such long legs and great form could run so slow.

Anyway, today at the city meet, I changed my plan. I took off like a shot. I was in about the top ten for half of the race. Just tooling along, and it wasn't until near the end that I really got draggy. Other runners passed me in batches, but still, I managed to finish almost in the middle of the pack. My mom and dad—let's face it, they were there ardently hoping that I wouldn't bring shame on the family name—went nuts when I came around the last corner. Chuck was a wild man. Yelling my name, jumping up and down. Lumpy even put aside the foot-long hot dog he was chomping on in order to cheer, which amounts to a tremendous sacrifice for him.

I fooled everyone. I have achieved something in cross-country. I'm average, and does it feel good! Maybe next year I can progress to above average, and after that, who knows? Maybe I'll make it all the way to pretty good.

And best of all: I WILL NOT HAVE TO RUN AN-OTHER STEP FOR MR. LEONARD FOR TEN MORE MONTHS!

FRIDAY, OCTOBER 26

Whipple's Life at a Glance:

1. Tryouts for tenth-grade basketball team on November 13. This day is circled on my calendar. In heavy red. With exclamation points.

2. Seminary party coming up in a week for both classes. This probably means an evening watching Joe and Julie hang out together.

3. There's a guy with a locker about three down from mine. He is a senior named Les Lorris, and he's big, with one eyebrow running clear across his forehead, and teeth that look like they were cut out on a jigsaw. He runs around with a girl named Roni who has virtually no chin, and is to makeup what the Pacific Ocean is to water. Lately, Les has been giving me more. More of a hard time, that is. (Does he think I want to steal Roni away from him? Ha!) It started with snide glances and has progressed, no, make that regressed, to crude remarks about how I walk, talk, look, act, breathe, etc. You get the picture. I don't know how to handle it, other than to wish aliens would capture him some night and transport him to their planet where he would live out the rest of his life under a bell jar as part of a scientific experiment.

4. I asked my mom if she remembered ever having liked someone in high school. She said yes, it happened several times. I didn't feel so weird about liking Julie when she told me that. Parents must have had feelings, too, when they were younger.

5. Natalie decided to try out for cheerleader at her junior high. This means endless conversations on the phone with her girlfriends, countless hours in front of the mirror to practice facial expressions, and although I don't quite get the link, at least thirty-seven trips to the mall and four new outfits.

6. I'm out of gas and ready to call it quits. Bedtime.

SUNDAY, OCTOBER 28

I got a call yesterday from Brother McAllister,

Bishop Winegar's executive secretary. The bishop wanted to see me before priesthood meeting this morning. When I got there, we talked for a few minutes, then he asked me if I would serve as priests quorum secretary. I told him sure.

"How's the rest of your life, Wally? I know you ran cross-country, and I assume basketball is just around the corner."

"Well, I sort of ran cross-country, Bishop. I don't think I'll ever be in the Olympics. But basketball does start in a couple of weeks."

"Great. I'm sure you'll make the team. I've seen you play on the ward team and you're a good player. Anything else we need to talk about?"

I'm not sure why, but it just sort of hit me. "How do you know if someone is getting mature or not? Lately, I've been thinking a little bit about being mature. At school, I see guys driving cars, practically engaged to girls, driving to Seattle for rock concerts. My worry is that I still feel like a kid—and maybe I should be doing more mature things in my life, like shaving more than twice a month."

Bishop Winegar sat back in his chair. Then he gave me an answer I didn't expect. "I guess, Wally, that the way I determine if someone is maturing is by how much they think about others."

Not fast cars? Not rock concerts in Seattle? Not reading from heavy books like Shakespeare or Louis L'Amour? Is that the answer?

"That's about it, Wally. How much you think of others and maybe whether you want all people to succeed. My definition wouldn't go much beyond that, Wally."

Thinking of others and wanting them to succeed? That's an idea I'll have to think about.

TUESDAY, OCTOBER 30

Halloween tomorrow. Thinking it would be the mature thing to do, I volunteered to take Chuck trick-or-treating this year. Natalie has said little about her plans, but just guessing, she will meet with friends at someone else's house and sneak out to go trick-or-treating. Of course, Natalie is not very mature yet.

Chuck is great at Halloween. He can never be your basic trick-or-treater and always comes up with something awesome for a costume. He is original, never anything from a store. Last year, he went as a chimney. When he was three, he was a basketball. This year, he is going as a box of corn flakes. No kidding. He thinks these things up by himself, too.

He told Mom about three weeks ago what he wanted to be. Mom found a big cardboard box and she and Chuck painted it white. After a couple of days, they got out some more paint and fixed it up just like a corn flake box. This is a true story. It's great to walk around the neighborhood with Chuck and watch the adults go nuts when they see him. And you should see the candy he hauls in! Mountains of it. He probably gets twice as much per household as a normal kid dressed up in a store-bought outfit. When he gets home, Chuck spreads his candy out on the kitchen table and categorizes it.

He separates Class A candy, the stuff he likes the most; Class B candy, which he likes less; and Class C candy, which he doesn't like at all. He eats the Class A candy and shares it with the whole family. Class B candy, he gives to his friends. And Class C candy, he gives to Lumpy, who is almost moved to tears to be remembered by Chuck on Halloween. I can hardly wait to go out with him tomorrow night.

Chuck is way cool. I should take lessons from him. He may be the only kid cooler than Joe Vermeer in all of Portland. Maybe he's the Whipple who should be trying to get Julie Sloan's attention.

CHAPTER 3

NoVemBer

THURSDAY, NOVEMBER 1

Lumpy and I were sitting in the cafeteria today, chowing down on our international menu—French fries, pizza, and chili—when we heard the clomping of cowboy boots from halfway across the room.

Hello, Orville.

"You boys mind if I pull up a stump next to you?"

"Not at all. You're welcome at my campfire anytime," Lumpy said.

Orville cocked his head and looked at Lumpy. "That's a tad corny, even for a cowboy."

"Must have heard it in a movie," Lumpy apologized.

Orville eased down next to me. "So you're Wally, the guy from English class. Who's your sidekick here?"

"Lumpy Felton," I nodded.

"Pleased to meetcha, Lumpy. Mighty peculiar handle, though."

"Lawrence is my real name."

We all chewed on our food for a minute. Orville was working on three hamburgers and a big carton of milk. "The grub here ain't nothin' to make a whup about, is it?"

"No, but you eventually get used to it, as soon as it kills your taste buds. You said you were from Heppner?" I asked.

"Yessir. We got a ranch there, about ten miles out of town, a little toward Irrigon. Lived there my whole life. Ain't hardly been no farther up the road than Pendleton. Ranchin's about all I know."

"Why did you move to Portland? This isn't exactly a cattle town," Lumpy said.

"Two years ago my mama died, and my dad hasn't been the same since. I think every biddy thing around the ranch reminds him of Mama. So he took to mopin' and lettin' things go a bit. I've got an uncle here in Portland who runs a feed and garden store. Jesse's his name. Uncle Jess can see what's happenin', so he calls up my dad and says, 'Come to Portland and give yerself a change of scenery. You can let your older boys run the ranch, and you can work for me for as long as you like.' Anyway, my dad, he turns it over in his head for a spell and one day just looks up at me and says, 'Orville, I feel like a grasshopper in an anthill. Let's go to Portland and see what it's like in the big city.'

"Now, I know my dad. He left it up to me, but all the while I knew he was pullin' for me to throw in with him. So I told him, why, yes, I'd come to Portland with him and we'd make a go of it together. I could tell he was mighty pleased."

"It must not be anything like your ranch."

"You're dead right about that, Wally. I don't reckon I'll ever get used to wakin' up and hearin' the sound of traffic. And I do miss my friends and animals. And, present company excepted, the folks here aren't all that friendly. They seem to be a little on the standoffish side."

"The kids here are mostly okay, they just don't know how to act around . . . "

"A cowboy, Lumpy. Thanks. I'll take the compliment anytime."

The bell rang, and it was time for Mrs. English's English class. "You headed my way, Orv?"

"You know I am."

"Then let's mosey on up to English class."

"Mosey? You got real cowboy potential," he said, a huge grin on his face. And together, we made our way out of the cafeteria and "moseyed" up the stairs toward class.

FRIDAY, NOVEMBER 2

One of Natalie's friends, Stacey Sullivan, came over tonight. Stacey is also trying out for cheerleader, and they're practicing together, which basically means they stand in front of the mirror and tell each other how good they look.

Even as I write, I can hear them in the bathroom as they pose in front of the long mirror on the door. What follows is a verbatim transcription of their conversation.

Natalie: "How do I look when I hold my head this way?"

Stacey: "Oh, wow, that's the look. Cute. Seriously. How about me?"

Natalie: "Oh, wow, you know you look good."

Stacey: "How is the back of my hair? I want it to look really good."

Natalie: "It looks good. How does my hair look?"

Stacey: "It looks good, really good, and I don't think it will fall out when you jump around and stuff."

Natalie: "But do you think it might, seriously?"

Stacey: "Well, it might, but it might not, so I think you should just go for it. Seriously."

Natalie: "Are you serious?"

Stacey: "Yeah, I'm serious. What if I mess up in front of all those people? I'll die. I'm serious."

Natalie: "You won't. You're good. Seriously. Now what about that first step I showed you? How does it look?"

Stacey: "It looks good. You know what we should do tomorrow? We should go to the mall and get some exercise there by walking around. Seriously. We need to get into better shape."

Four more weeks until the cheerleading tryouts. Four long weeks. Four tedious weeks. Four weeks where every other event in the Whipple household will pale by comparison. Four weeks of misery for us all.

Seriously.

SATURDAY, NOVEMBER 3

Tonight was the seminary party at Brother McNair's house and I had a good time. I liked the food, which always racks up big points with me. We had a lot of laughs, and Brother McNair has a great house. All the ingredients were there for an awesome evening. Yet right now I feel one thing more than anything else.

Confused.

It started off when Brother McNair announced that the first activity in the evening would be a scavenger hunt around the neighborhood. He said that we'd be matched in pairs. I very coolly glanced across the room toward Julie. What if . . . what if Julie and I were paired as a team on the scavenger hunt? Oh fate! Hand me sweet grapes on a silver platter! I would dazzle her. I would at once be cool, smart, funny, nice, kind, trustworthy, loyal, helpful, friendly, courteous . . . you get the picture. That night, she would lie down at home and think before dozing off, "I really like Joe, but I can't get Wallace Whipple out of my mind." And from there, who knows?

Let's do this in slow motion. Brother McNair walks to the middle of his family room. He has everyone's name in a basket. He raises the basket high in the air. Then with a smile, he pulls the first name out and reads it . . . Julie Sloan!!! He raises the basket again. His right hand fishes around the cards. One of them has my name on it. I need a break! Please, please . . .

I start making deals with my conscience. I will try to sing in Mr. Ashbury's class. I will no longer make fun of my sister, except when she really deserves it. I will wash the dishes without protest on my assigned nights. I will go on a mission and engage in good works throughout my life. I will pay my school library fine . . . if I can be paired with Julie.

Brother McNair's hand is on the card. My future is

riding on this. I close my eyes. The tension is unbearable. He is opening his mouth. The answer is . . . the answer is . . .

Lumpy Felton!

I am crushed. Foiled again. Batting zero in the game of love. I want to join the French Foreign Legion until I am old enough to start the first of three or four missions.

I sidle over to Lumpy. "Trade you. Trade you anything. My entire collection of baseball cards. My tenspeed. Natalie as a throw in," I plead, desperation in my voice.

"Naw, I don't think so," he says. "Everyone knows Brother McNair picked Julie and me out of the basket. It would be pretty obvious what you are up to. You've got to be more subtle, Wally."

"Yeah, right. Subtle. Maybe you've got a point," I said, my mind spinning wildly. "At least do this. Talk me up. Tell her how I want to help starving people in the third-world nations. And that I'm spiritual, too, and that I have a great little brother, and that I'm really nice. Stuff like that. Okay, Lumpy?"

Lumpy looked a little pouty. "Of course I will. I'll go to bat for my bud. You didn't really need to ask, Wally. I can be cool, too."

Brother McNair is still drawing names. Suddenly, I hear mine.

"Wally Whipple . . . and . . . Joe Vermeer! Okay guys, you're a team."

At this point, I'd rather be teamed with any number of people in the world, past or present. Ivan the Terrible comes to mind.

Joe walks over to me. "Hey."

"Hey, Joe."

He looks around the room, seemingly unconcerned that he has just been joined to a super nerd such as myself. But I'm not fooled. He'll hang around with me for a couple of minutes and then dump me for someone more befitting his high social standing. "Let's win this thing, Wally."

At least he knows my name.

"Yeah. Let's win."

"The way I've got it figured," Joe says, "is that everyone around here will head to all the houses on this street. They'll get the first two or three things on the list, then they'll start going to houses that have already been hit by other teams. If we want to win, I think we should head out a few blocks. Work the new territory. We lose a few minutes at the beginning, but we'll make up for it later. It'll be sweet, Wally. I like winning."

"Sounds okay, Joe."

And that's what we did. And that's how we finished the scavenger hunt fifteen minutes ahead of the next closest team. The Vermeer/Whipple ticket smoked the opposition.

What's so confusing about this? I had a great time with Joe. Here he is, all-world in everything—popular, the star scholar and athlete, and my chief rival for Julie's attention. I expected him to treat me like overripe fruit all night. Instead, he made me feel like an equal. His pal. A contemporary.

Do you get it, Whipple?

You expected him to be one thing and he turns out to be something different. That's why I'm confused. Could it be that I did a little judging when I shouldn't have? Could it also be that I didn't want to like him because he's beating my act with Julie? I guess the answer is obvious.

Now get this. At the end of the party, Joe looks at me and says, "Need a lift home, Wally?" Lumpy and I had come to the party like most sophomore geeks. A parent drove us. So I tell him, yeah, a ride home would be nice. A few minutes later, Lumpy and I get into his car along with Julie, and Joe takes us home.

I walk through the front door. Natalie is sitting slumped over one end of the couch, apparently worn out from a long day of being cute and adorable.

"How'd you get home?" she asks, yawning. "Wasn't Dad going to pick you up?"

"Joe Vermeer drove me home," I said casually.

"Joe Vermeer! Do you think he saw me? Are you serious?" she said, a look of intense disbelief mixed with panic, spreading across her face.

"Yeah. I'm serious," I said, trying to look like it was no biggy. "Didn't I mention that Joe and I are pretty good friends?"

SUNDAY, NOVEMBER 4

It rained today. After church, I came up to my room to write in my journal. Some people let the rain get to them, but not me. It's comforting to hear it tapping against the window. And the big gray clouds are like a huge blanket draped over the city, letting us know it's time to slow down and just think about things.

Thinking is what I've been up to this afternoon. There were lots of testimonies today. Brother

Seversen, a really nice guy in his 60s, who had a birth-day, and his kids came to visit him from all over the country. Sister Macabee, a widow who lives in a small apartment that is barely furnished, telling how thankful she is for everything she has and knows. Brother Mayhew, a man who doesn't say much, but who talked today about his son who is on a mission in France. And the little kids who all stand up and say "I know the Church is true. I love my mom and dad . . . "

The rain. Being at home. Those testimonies. I'm not exactly a spiritual giant, but things seem so right today. I'd like to feel this way all the time.

MONDAY, NOVEMBER 5

Basketball season starts in less than two weeks. In order to gain even the slightest competitive edge, I have started to run again a bit. A couple of miles on Saturday, and three times after school last week, I ran the stairs on the football field. It is not fun. I have a theory about running. In ancient times, when man only had rocks or primitive spears to help him catch his game, running was okay because it was necessary to bring down the hairy beasts that became supper. Now, however, humans run for far less crucial reasons than in ancient times.

Even though I'm not what most people would term an avid runner, I am an avid basketball player, and if running will help me to improve, there is but one choice.

I finally talked with Lumpy about Saturday night.

"Julie's really nice," he said.

"I know she's really nice. But were you able to talk about your best friend?"

"Yeah, no sweat. I told her lots of things about you, some of them even true."

"Like what?"

"Like you're a good writer."

Good writer. I like that. Writers are sensitive, intelligent, and very wealthy.

" . . . and that you're related to royalty."

"What?"

"No big-time royalty, just that a great uncle was a grand duke of Australia. And I told her you were a good tennis player and dated tons of girls."

"Anything else, Lump?" I asked, my stomach churning.

"No . . . that was about it. Except for the part about you helping to support your parents, both of whom are blind."

"Lumpy!"

"Lighten up, Wally. All I told her was you are a good guy and a good friend. What else does she need to know about you?"

The answer, I think, is nothing. At least for now.

TUESDAY, NOVEMBER 6

Report cards are coming out in two weeks. I know grades are important because when you apply for college, they start checking back to at least your second grade report card. This is how I'll stack up.

Boys Choir. I feel good about this one. Lumpy has assured me several times that all you have to do is show up and look earnest and you're a shoo-in for an

A. True, I do not sing in choir, but I have refined looking earnest to an art form.

Social Studies. Mrs. Aparicio is a super teacher and I seem to do better in classes that I like. Call it a B with a chance to raise it before the year is out.

P.E. Good attitude, and I've survived wrestling and square dancing. An A for sure. Take it to the bank.

Health: Just a gut feeling, but I think a B. Get it? Health? A *gut* feeling?

English. The big surprise in this year's scholastic lineup. Mrs. English's reputation is such that I figured it would be sheer luck if I pulled in a C. But what can I say? She loves me. She loves my work. Dare I say it? Credit Whipple with a big Ace in English.

Math. I'm hoping for a B. And that because of the girl genius, Edwina Purvis, for whom I'd like to do something nice, sometime, like buy her roses or invite her to eat tacos with Lumpy and me at Hamburger Bob's.

Not bad for the first quarter in high school. Right? My earlier worries about not being able to hack it have all but disappeared.

Note about my brother: Chuck brought home a mouse's paw from kindergarten today with instructions about microwaving it from the teacher. Microwaving kills the germs. Mom wasn't crazy about the idea, but she went along with it anyway. Natalie beebopped into the kitchen after school and peeked into the microwave, I think expecting something sweet. We had to almost pry her off the ceiling. Chalk one up for Chuck.

Note about Orville: I told my mom about Orv and his dad and she got all choked up. She said we need to have them over for dinner soon. Good sign for Orville because once you crack the Whipple home for dinner, it pretty much means a lifelong invitation to stop by for a meal anytime. It's one of the reasons I love my mom.

Note about Les Lorris, super turkey lips: He's still making rude comments whenever he sees me. I wish he'd just go away. Like to Outer Mongolia.

THURSDAY, NOVEMBER 8

Basketball tryouts dead ahead. I'm still running the stairs and mentally getting ready to dazzle my coach who is sure to be astonished. Just the beginning of a long and glorious professional athletic career.

Natalie is practicing hard for cheerleader. (Long hours in front of the mirror, calling her friends, mixing and matching clothes, etc.) Her lack of interest in doing what cheerleaders do (bouncing around, doing cartwheels, and cheering) is notable. Tonight at dinner, Dad asked her if she was learning any new routines or gymnastic moves in preparation for the tryouts. Natalie looked at him as if he didn't have a clue.

"Well, isn't it important to know how to do a cartwheel or a handspring?" he asked.

Natalie thought about it for maybe three-tenths of a second.

"Get real, Dad. The most important thing to do is look good. And I already know how to do that."

Dad looked at Mom with a funny expression and just shrugged his shoulders.

The thing is, she's probably right.

SUNDAY, NOVEMBER 11

The subject for today, again, is maturity.

You see, I haven't quite figured it out. I've been thinking about what Bishop Winegar told me—that maturity is how much you think about others and want them to succeed.

Let me see. Natalie and her cheerleading. What I hope is that she gets up in front of the student body and suffers a spontaneous outbreak of acne as she begins her routine, even though she has your basic flawless complexion. A chant begins to swell in the masses huddled in the bleachers. "Zits! Zits!! Zits!!!" Natalie gets all flustered, falls to the floor as loud laughter breaks out. Humiliated, she runs crying out of the gym, humbled in a way that she has never experienced. From that day on, she becomes a new and better person—more caring, loving, sharing—never thinking of herself. Is that what Bishop Winegar meant?

Naw. I doubt it.

What I think is, Bishop Winegar means I should hope that Natalie succeeds. That she ends up a cheerleader and is a good one at that. Not only should I wish for her success, but I should probably try and help her. Like, give her a male's perspective about what makes a good cheerleader. True, she would probably resist my offer to help and say something like as long as she looks good, all the guys will vote for her anyway. But I should at least make the effort, if I'm a mature guy.

This is difficult. It's not natural. It goes against the theory of sibling rivalry. I envy Nat, in a way. She moves so effortlessly among people. She can meet someone, and they can be best friends in ten minutes. Me? Feeling comfortable in a group is about as easy as turning around an aircraft carrier. Still, the idea of helping her is a tough one to swallow.

Nevertheless, Wallace Whipple will do the noble thing. How can I dream about helping out third-world nations if I can't help my sister? I will not make fun of her when she stands in front of the mirror practicing various looks for the occasion. Nor will I torment her when she makes her thirty-eighth trip to the mall to look for the right clothes. I will take a sincere and earnest interest in her venture and be supportive and positive.

I hope all this works. I hope I end up more mature when it's all over. Because if I don't, I'll feel like I wasted a lot of energy with nothing to show for it.

TUESDAY, NOVEMBER 13

At seminary today, Julie came in and looked around for a place to sit. There were about a dozen vacant seats in the classroom, but after looking things over for a second, she waltzed over and sat down right next to me. Can you believe it? She looked right at me and said—now get this—"Good morning, Wally!" Good morning! How did she think of it? And at the end of class she looked at me again—that makes twice today alone—and said, "Have a nice day." Maybe she likes me a little. A miniscule ember glowing in her heart that could burst into a raging wildfire someday.

The rest of my day should have gone so well. I was only about half-mental in school. Mr. Herk asked me to put a problem on the board and I messed it up royally. And then Mrs. English said we're going to start a unit on poetry, which I can't handle, because every poem I've ever read is about love, dying young, or dying young while in love. She even said we'll be writing the stuff during the next week or so.

And then came the biggest letdown of the day: basketball tryouts. I showed up for them, all right. Along with forty-three other guys. I had no idea so many would turn out. Mr. Ackley, the coach, didn't really know what to do with so many players.

What this meant was two hours of the thumb drill. Mr. Ackley had us crouch down in the defensive stance with our arms in the air. He'd blow his whistle and point his thumb in a direction. Then we'd kind of crab shuffle wherever he pointed. Left. Right. Backward. Forward. I've been doing this drill since the fourth grade. After that, we did baseline wind sprints. Isn't there more to athletics than running?

Maybe Coach Ackley is trying to weed the wimps out. But Wallace Whipple will not let wind sprints and thumb drills derail his basketball career. I got home from school at seven, dog tired. My mom looked at me with a twinkle in her eye and sweetly asked, "Tired, honey?"

The Parents' Conspiracy is working in the Whipple household.

WEDNESDAY, NOVEMBER 14

Okay, I tried it. I really did. And our conversation went like this:

ME: "So, Natalie, how is cheerleading going?"

HER: "What's it to you?"

ME: "Just wondering. I hope you're doing okay with it."

HER: "Well, of course I am. But why are you asking? You're never nice to me."

ME: "I was just concerned. I want you to . . . (gritting my teeth, groaning inside) . . . to succeed."

HER: "That's a laugh. Seriously. You probably really want me to fall on my face in front of the whole school. Or get zits the day of tryouts."

ME: (Caught, but nonetheless trying to look hurt.) "No way! I can't believe you would even think that!"

HER: "Did Mom or Dad tell you to be nice to me?"

ME: "No! All I want to do is see you . . . (trembling inside, stomach turning) make the cheerleading squad. Honest. And if I can help, let me know."

HER: "I don't believe you. I think Mom is making you be nice as punishment for something. I know you, Wally, and this isn't like you."

As I said, I tried. I think both of us have a way to go before we reach the next level of maturity.

By the way, we did more thumb drills and wind sprints. Six guys didn't show up for the second day, which means only thirty-eight are left.

FRIDAY, NOVEMBER 16

News flash! Stop the presses! A major announcement is at hand. Sources close to the president say . . .

I actually got to touch the ball at practice today! We did the thumb drill and wind sprints, of course, but for twenty glorious minutes, Coach Ackley had us form three lines at each end of the gym and dribble the basketball the length of the floor. We passed it to the next guy in line and he dribbled back. The old leather felt good in my hands. Who knows . . . someday Coach Ackley may even let us . . . do I dare say it? Shoot the ball at the hoop!

Basketball is not turning out the way I imagined. I'm sure that Michael Jordan didn't start out this way.

SATURDAY, NOVEMBER 17

I was half asleep on the couch this afternoon, dozing and watching a football game on TV. Only Mom and I were at home, and she came in and sat on a chair by the couch.

"Watching a little baseball, Wally?"

Despite being the mother of a gifted, athletic son, Mom has never figured out the difference between sports, although after watching Chuck and me on the driveway all these years, she can now pretty much recognize a basketball.

"It's a football game, Mom, but I'm not really into it."

"Oh, that's right, football," she said with a smile. "And you're not really into it. Well, that's good, Wally. I think you should relax more. I know how hard you've been working at school."

We sat for a minute and watched the game. One team scored on a long pass. "Now there's a play. Did you see how far he had to go to score that home run?"

"Yeah. A long way. That was a nice catch."

"It certainly was," she said, thinking she'd scored

a coup by mentioning a home run. I was getting the strong impression that Mom wanted to do more than talk sports with me. The feeling was confirmed a couple of minutes later when she very casually said, "You know, Wally, I was talking to Mrs. Barkle . . . "

I knew what was coming. Mrs. Barkle is a neighbor who lives four houses down from us. She is the mother of Viola Barkle, a girl who occasionally babysits Chuck.

" . . . and she mentioned that Viola sits home almost every weekend. Can you believe that, Wally? A cute girl like Viola. She is a little socially uncertain it seems, and Mrs. Barkle is worried."

Saying Viola is a "little socially uncertain" is like saying that Alexander the Great did his time in the military. Somewhere in this world there is probably a man for Viola, but it definitely is not me! Perhaps a Russian shot putter would do. But not Wallace Whipple. We are not a good match. Oil and water. Sugar and vinegar. Braces and salt water taffy.

"And I think Viola is so sweet and dignified . . . "

Viola dignified? Not exactly the word I would use to describe her. Of course, maybe I'm just prejudiced because I'm thinking about the way she looked with a huge jawbreaker in her cheek, the time she whipped every boy in the 7th grade in arm wrestling.

"She seems to like you, according to Mrs. Barkle. Maybe you should think about taking her out on a double date with Lumpy and one of his friends. I think the experience would do you good."

This is one of the most effective weapons in the parents' arsenal of guilt armaments. "It will be a good experience for you." So would a root canal, in some circumstances, but just the same, no thanks. Some experiences I prefer to avoid.

"I worry that you don't show enough interest in girls, Wally."

Girls, I'm interested in. No worries. If Mom only knew I'm thinking of proposing to Julie, as soon as we go on our first date. It's just that I'd never thought of Viola as a girl. That's hard to do when you know she could beat you up if she ever took a mind to do it. I was wide awake now and not liking the direction our conversation was taking. I needed out, desperately.

"Look, Mom, another home run! Did you see that?"

She looked at the television set in time to see a running back gain three yards.

"Oh yes, a home run. Very nice."

"I'll think about Viola, Mom, trust me, I really will. I know she's a nice girl, but with a mission and college coming, I don't want to get way ahead of myself and get overly committed with a girl."

"Okay, Wally. It's nice that you're looking so far into the future." She got up and left, much to my relief.

Dodged a bullet, I'd say. First Wanda Fenwick, now Viola Barkle. Mothers are wonderful, and there are very few things I would not do for my mom. But, going out with Viola Barkle is in that category. All I can say is that it's a good thing that our society does not by custom permit mothers to be matchmakers. Viola Whipple? It doesn't sound right. Not nearly as good as Julie Whipple, that's for sure.

SUNDAY, NOVEMBER 18

Thanksgiving is Thursday. At church today, there were some pretty good talks about showing gratitude for our blessings. I know I should, so here goes.

What Wallace Whipple Is Grateful For

I am grateful for my family. No doubt about it. Even Natalie. Definitely, Chuck. I'm glad I have a dad who is hardworking and who cares about us. And I'm glad I've got a mom who keeps us all headed in the right direction, with never a complaint.

I'm thankful for being a church member and priesthood holder.

Teenagers everywhere will wonder if I'm selling out, but I appreciate the chance to go to school, get an education, and choose what I want to do. Beats being born somewhere else and automatically knowing you'll be holding a wooden plow, following a musk ox around a dusty piece of land for fifty years of your life.

I'm thankful for friends like Lumpy, Mickey, Mel, and, maybe, Joe Vermeer, too.

I'm grateful for Bishop Winegar, Brother Hansen, Brother McNair, and the other teachers and leaders I have.

And a bunch of other things, such as my jump shot, which I hope someday to show off before the appreciative eyes of Coach Ackley.

To all the people I know and love, Happy Thanksgiving, and may we be friends and family forever.

There.

MONDAY, NOVEMBER 19

A complete and utter disaster today. A shock, a blow, a major setback. At age sixteen, I am facing ruination.

My report card came today. It did not turn out the way I had hoped.

Choir. The certain A. The grade padder. Had Mr. Ashbury going from here to the moon and back. Earnest. Sincere. Attentive. And for all that, he gave me a D.

A D! I'm not a Rhodes Scholar, but I've never had a D in my life. Why? This guy is supposed to be the original doughboy when it comes to grading. And here I am, staring at my report card, one sour note away from failing. Maybe there's a mistake. Somewhere the report card computer went "pffft," and all the A's were turned into D's. I'll go in tomorrow and the choir will be in an ugly mood. "No grade, no sing," we'll chant when Mr. Ashbury walks in. "Straighten out or we walk."

That's not all. English class, a B. Math, a C. Social Studies, another B. In P.E., my one and only A. Thank heaven I'm a finely honed athlete.

What do I do? My grade point average is 2.6, which is not going to get me into Harvard. My parents will not be pleased. Where did I go wrong?

TUESDAY, NOVEMBER 20

I did not sleep well last night. My mind was scampering along about a bazillion miles an hour, trying to figure out where my once-promising high school career went. Could it have been cross-country and always feeling worn out? No. Could it be church activities? No. Could it be the adjustment to high school? No. The problem is the one that I faced in the mirror this morning when I did my mid-November shave. Me!

I approached Mr. Ashbury on the outside chance that the computer had creamed my grade. No one else had complained. In fact, everyone in the choir seemed to be in a good mood, no doubt the product of getting a nice grade. Anyway, I dawdled a little after class was over, then slowly made my way toward Mr. Ashbury, who was gathering sheet music from his piano.

"Uh, Mr. Ashbury, I'd like to talk about, well, my grade," I sputtered.

He smiled ever so pleasantly and took his glasses off. "Sure, Wally. What is there to talk about?"

"I got . . . " I drew closer to him, hoping no one else would hear. " . . . a D. Is that the right grade?"

"It most certainly is. You didn't think the computer made an error did you?" he said, with what I thought was an inordinate amount of cheerfulness. Did he enjoy ruining the careers of bright, young high school students?

"I guess, um, I was hoping . . . "

"Wally. How many times did you actually sing in choir this fall? And I don't just mean mouthing the words."

"Not many."

"Like never?"

"Yeah. Like never."

"After teaching choir for twenty-two years, you don't think I know when someone is trying and when he is not? Wally, I don't care if a boy can sing worth a hoot or not. I don't care if he's a scholar, an athlete, a student body officer, or the class geek. What I do care about is that he comes into my class and tries. You didn't try, Wally. And, unless you try, you will not pass my class."

He was smiling, but I got the message. Actually, I would much rather that he just yelled at me a lot instead of reasoning things out so calmly like an adult.

"I don't sing very well . . . "

"Then I'll teach you. But you have to try. That's your end of the bargain."

I hate it when adults are right. Inside, I knew all along why I got the bad grade. I dropped the rock on myself.

Mr. Ashbury clapped me on the shoulder. "Then tomorrow you'll exercise those vocal cords?"

"Tomorrow. Only you'd better expect some funny looks from the guys closest to me. It'll be the first time they've really heard my voice."

"Glad you came in, Wally. Bad news isn't much fun to hear, but I think you're on the right road now."

"See you, Mr. Ashbury."

I also talked with Mrs. English. She said that maybe I deserved an A but that she thought I was slacking off in class a bit. She said if I got an A the first quarter, she feared I'd try to coast the rest of the year.

"You have as much talent as any student I've taught in the last ten years, Wally. But you are a little lazy."

For the second time today, I had to swallow hard and take a shot to the old ego.

In basketball, I dribbled the ball off my foot twice.

Seven more guys need to be cut before the first game next month, and for the first time, it hit me that I may not make the team. Coach Ackley said we'd start playing against each other tomorrow, and I'm nervous. These are dark days for Wallace Whipple.

In seminary this week, we studied the part where Alma wrote about those who are compelled to be humble. I can relate to that. Boy, can I ever relate!

WEDNESDAY, NOVEMBER 21

I'm in a slump. Nothing is going right.

Julie and Joe came down the hallway at church and walked by me as if I were an inanimate object.

Lumpy has the flu and wasn't at school. Orville tried to cheer me up at lunch by telling me about the time he rode his first bull ("Ride lasted about half a second, and then the bull showed me who was boss of the outfit.") but it didn't do much for me.

"You're lower than a snake's belly in a muddy road rut," he drawled.

And maybe the hardest thing of all to take is basketball practice. There are twenty of us left, now, and I figure Coach Ackley will keep twelve or thirteen players. He divided us up into four teams to scrimmage half-court. He told me to play center.

I am not a center. True, I am tall, the way a center should be. But I am so skinny that I almost have to pin the shoulder straps together on my basketball jersey or else it will fall off. I have biceps the size of a golf ball. I can bench press maybe thirty-four pounds. I have to wear plaid shirts because if I don't, people can't see me when I turn sideways. No one has ever confused me with Hercules.

In basketball, centers should not only be tall, but also broad-shouldered, big-boned, and a little nasty, none of which I am. So in the scrimmage, I got pushed around a lot, never really got my hands on the ball and generally did nothing to distinguish myself. Once I did get a pass about twenty feet away from the basket and Coach Ackley blew his whistle. Play came to a stop as he charged onto the court and sort of hollered, "Whipple, you're the center. What are you doing a mile away from the basket? Let that be a lesson to all you big men. Stay at home around the basket."

Well, that was basketball today. One step closer to hoopster oblivion.

The one bright spot occurred today when I got home and found Mom on the phone, wrapping up talking with Mr. Burrell, inviting him and Orville over for Thanksgiving dinner tomorrow. "If I waited for you and Orville to work it out, we wouldn't have had dinner with them before you leave for college," Mom said. "So I took matters into my own hands."

They'll be here at four, and I'm looking forward to it. Maybe a couple of days away from the pressure of being sixteen years old will help my frame of mind.

THURSDAY, NOVEMBER 22

Thanksgiving. Ahhhh.

Good food. Good football. And more than good company. The Burrells arrived right on time. Mr. Burrell ("Call me Stan, pardner.") looks just like what a cowboy should look like. Wiry. Leathery. Dark hair, just a tad of gray around the temples. Kind of a squinty-eyed gaze. And he talks western better than Orville. I half-expected to see his horse tied up outside.

Anyway, they're both dressed about the same. Corduroy sports jackets, string ties, blue jeans, hats, and cowboy boots. Mr. Burrell (I'll work up to calling him Stan) hands Mom a dozen flowers and she is immediately impressed. He walks up to Dad, extends his hand, and says, "Pleased to meetcha." Dad takes an instant liking to him, and in about three minutes, they're both talking hardware, hay, and horses. Orv is every bit as polite as his dad. He greets both my parents, introduces himself to Chuck, and then takes off his hat and gently takes Natalie's hand as he meets her. Now, Orville is definitely in the "cowboy hunk" category and Natalie almost melts into your basic bucket of goo when he says howdy to her.

Natalie wasn't too wild about having strangers barging in for Thanksgiving dinner (her words, not mine), but suddenly she gets stars in her eyes and starts fussing with her hair and talking in a very syrupy way.

"It is so nice to meet you and your father, Orville. My brother Wallace has said so many nice things about you that we've all been absolutely dying to meet you. I've been so excited about dinner today, ever since mother informed us that you had accepted our invitation," she gushed. And she didn't hardly take her eyes off him the whole evening. Who would've figured? My sister, who will someday have a wing at the mall named after her, falling like a rock for Orville the Cowboy.

The Burrells are a hit the entire time. Orv goes outside with Chuck and me and shoots baskets for a bit. He keeps encouraging Chuck, telling him how close his shots are coming. At dinner, they bow their heads and don't seem a bit embarrassed when Dad offers the Thanksgiving prayer. After we're done, both of them pitch in and help with the dishes, despite the protests of my mother. Somewhere between basketball on the driveway and dinner, Natalie slips away and sheds her baggy sweat pants and sweat shirt and reappears in a dress, complete with make-up. Naturally, she ends up sitting next to Orville.

"I think it's in good taste to dress up a little on Thanksgiving," Natalie flutters to Orville, although to this point the most she'd dressed up for Thanksgiving in recent memory was the year she tied the laces on her aerobic workout shoes. "But I had been so busy helping mother that I just didn't have time." At this point, my mom almost gags on her pumpkin pie because the sum total of Natalie's kitchen duty today was opening a can of olives, and that came only after a prolonged protest.

About eight in the evening, Mr. Burrell stands and reaches for his hat. "Thank ye, Mrs. Whipple, for a mighty fine piece of cookin'. And you, too, Natalie. We appreciate the hospitality of your family. But we best be gettin' along."

Orville thanks my mom, shakes hands with my dad and Chuck, and smiles toward Natalie, who almost passes out on the spot. Then the two men from Heppner head off into the night.

What can I say? A great day. Period. We hated to see them go.

"Nice fellas, both of them," Dad says, looking contented.

"Very much the gentlemen," Mom compliments. "I'd just like to give them both a big hug, those dear men. I think they liked my cooking."

"Orville plays basketball good," Chuck enthuses. "He called me 'Chuckwagon.'"

"Do you know if Orville has a girl friend?" Natalie asks dreamily.

True, I have been in a slump the last few days. What I'm learning about slumps is this:

One, everyone has them. I think.

Two, they never last forever. I hope.

Three, the best way out of a slump is to break it by doing something for someone else. I'm sure.

FRIDAY, NOVEMBER 23

I've been putting off writing my poem for too long. It's due next week and Mrs. English said we'll each read ours in front of the class. She told us to write about an experience that was important to us and not to worry about trying to sound like a poet. Anyway, I got down to it today, worked hard on my poem. I mean, it took me at least thirty minutes to write. For the sake of posterity, here is my first-ever poem:

Fear In Their Eyes
By Wallace F. Whipple, Jr.

When they take the court
I can see it in their eyes

They are afraid and
I think to myself,
"We can take these guys."

The game begins
And there's a cry from the crowd
As I get the ball and jump
Almost touching a cloud.

My release is perfect
There is no trick.
My opponent grunts in anguish
And looks a little sick.

The ball—it rises all
On a perfect arc
And nestles in the net
Like a nest receiving a lark.

On the game goes
We pull away and win.
It comes to us so easily
It is almost a sin.

The buzzer sounds
The other guys are distraught,
But I shake their hands and
Tell them it wasn't for naught.

"You played well," I tell them
"And this is not in jest.
It just so happens that
You were beaten by the best."

So what, if it's not John Donne? I like it. Especially
the way I worked in the word "jest," which is very po-
etic. And best of all, nobody dies, falls in love, or does
anything else disgusting.

SATURDAY, NOVEMBER 24

This day marks one of my worst nightmares come true. Or so I thought. But spending an hour in the mall with my sister turned out to be an amazing experience.

It started out innocently enough. We were going to swing by the mall and pick out a new outfit for Natalie because Tuesday is the cheerleading tryout, and she told Mom it was important for her to look really good all day so that even people in the hallway would notice and vote for her. I'm not sure I follow the logic, but Mom bought into it. So Dad is at work, and Mom and Nat are headed toward the mall, when the phone rings. It's Dad, who was on his way home from work but couldn't get his car started, which happens about every third week. Mom and he do some quick planning and the next thing I know, Natalie and I are being dropped off at the mall, while Mom and Chuck are on their way to pick up Dad at work. Mom says she doesn't want to leave Natalie in the mall alone, so that's why I've been drafted.

Actually, I think the mall is the safest place in the world for Natalie, because that's where she is most comfortable, plus, everyone there knows her. Of course, there is the possibility that she will get a line of credit somewhere and charge $2,000 worth of clothes if left unattended, and my duty was to guard against that. Mom promises she won't be gone long and that I should just tag along with Nat and help her if I can. We agree to meet Mom, Dad, and Chuck at the indoor fountain in thirty minutes.

As soon as the car chugs around the corner, Natalie is off like a bullet for her favorite store: a place called (surprise!) "Lookin' Good." She bolts through the door and I'm already trailing thirty feet behind. She makes a quick move to her left, fakes one way, goes the other, and ends up at a rack with skirts. I am in awe. She is to shopping what Carl Lewis is to sprinting. She elbows her way by another girl and in a positive flurry, goes through about fifteen skirts, evaluating color, length, and style with almost computer-like speed.

"Come here and hold these," she demands, thrusting six skirts in my direction. I hear and obey. I recognize an artist at work, and, in a small way, feel privileged to be a witness. Two minutes later, she comes up for air, a crazed look in her eye, and six tops to match the skirts. "I'm going to try these on. You sit over there and when I come out, you tell me if I look good, even if you don't have much taste."

"You can't try on all those clothes and still be back at the fountain in twenty-five minutes to meet Mom," I protest weakly.

"Oh yeah? Bet me."

She disappears inside the dressing room. In short order she comes out, dressed in combination A.

"Well?"

Being wise in matters of Natalie and dress, I tell her exactly what she wants to hear. "You look really good. Seriously."

"Seriously, do you think so?"

"Yes. Seriously."

She disappears and reappears in two-minute intervals. Her mind is like a computer, compiling facts, assimilating information, drawing conclusions. If she would apply herself in the same way to her schoolwork, she could become an astronaut, a physician, an Egyptologist, whatever. I am truly amazed.

She darts back into the dressing room and returns with the combination she likes best. She waltzes up to the counter, hands the clothes to the salesgirl, and says blithely, "Hold these for me. I'll be back in a few minutes."

"Sure thing, Natalie," the salesperson says.

Nat turns and walks briskly toward me, then right by me.

"Nice work. We still have six minutes before Mom will be back," I say, trotting to catch up with her.

"Good. That's enough time to check out one more store."

"You're kidding!"

She stops dead in her tracks, whirls around, and looks me straight in the eye. "I don't *kid* when it comes to shopping." And off we go, to a place called "Clothes, Clothes, Clothes." Somehow, some way, she hurtles through another dozen outfits in four minutes and thirty-five seconds. "Nothing here I like," she sniffs. "We'll go to the fountain now."

Mom isn't at the fountain, yet. Natalie looks impatiently at her watch. "I hate to waste this time. I'll be back in fifteen minutes."

I am not about to stand in her way. I now have a testimony that she can cover two stores in fifteen minutes, with probably enough time left over to down a yogurt cone. She charges off in a new direction with a singleness of purpose that I have rarely seen in anyone. Like, the only thing that comes to mind is Lumpy when he sits down in front of a pizza.

To wrap it up, Mom and Dad arrive ten minutes

later. Natalie shows up soon after. She and Mom set off for the first store, and in only a few moments, they come back with the outfit Natalie had on hold. "I'll look really good in this," she declares to the passive men of the Whipple family. And you know what? She will.

Now it's evening, and I have been contemplating what I saw today at the mall. I have heard that everybody in the world has a talent, something they do better than anybody else. I'm not sure if I believe that, but I do think that all people have gifts. One of Natalie's gifts, if you can call it that, is shopping.

Sure, that may not seem like much in the way of socially redeeming values, but it does keep a lot of merchants in Portland happy. And I am dumbfounded at how good she is at it. Natalie is world-class. I never realized it until today. A world-class talent right under my roof. She's quick. She's smart. She's aggressive. She's got uncanny instincts.

And one other thing. On the way home, she actually thanked me for helping her in the mall. And she meant it. Natalie is so seldom sincere that it is easy to recognize the rare occasions when she is. And I said she was welcome, and that I hoped everything went well for her on Tuesday.

And I think I meant it. Can it be that Natalie and I are actually starting to get along better?

MONDAY, NOVEMBER 26

It's gut check time. Final cuts for the 10th grade basketball team will be made today. Phone call from Lumpy after dinner:

HIM: "Do you think you'll make it?"

ME: "Me? Of course. I am deeply hurt you would think otherwise. You know my abilities. You've seen me play. You know what I can do."

HIM: "Sounds like you're on the bubble to me."

ME: "You got it. Stress city. I haven't been this nervous since I talked with Julie for the first time."

HIM: "Correction. Since you *tried* to talk with Julie for the first time. Looper voo who'd, Wally."

ME: "Thank you for the pleasant reminder."

So I get through the school day, zombie-like, my stomach making like a yo-yo, my nerves sending tens of millions of electronic blips through my synapses and up into my brain, all with the same message: "You're going to choke, Whipple!" There will be one scrimmage today, and I need to do something to make myself stand out from the crowd of other would-be benchwarmers. I need a gimmick . . . or to hit about a half-dozen, three-point shots.

I was dressing alongside Andy Salisbury, another guy trying out who is roughly in the same boat as I am. We both knew this might be our last practice.

"You ready?" Andy asked, as he pulled up his socks. "Guess it's do or die time for us today."

"Yeah. My basketball career may come to a grinding halt today."

"Mine, too," Andy said glumly.

The practice was just what I expected. The guys who Coach Ackley has all but told they have made the team, started playing first. They looked good, crisp. They were confident, knowing well that they would pull on the white and maroon jerseys for our first game next week and get plenty of playing time.

They made me ill.

Andy and the rest of us who dwelled on the fringe of outer darkness sat and sat. Then, about ten minutes before practice was over, Coach Ackley put all of us scrubs into the game. And it was more of just what I expected. Everybody out for himself. Guys were taking long, impossible shots, trying every fancy move they'd ever seen on TV. One guy tried to dribble behind his back and another threw a no-look pass that ended up about four rows into the bleachers.

And me? I didn't do anything fancy. Just rebounded, passed, and hustled.

Near the end of the practice, when I was already thinking about how I'd tell my family I didn't make the team, I did get the ball on a fast break. Andy was cutting in from the left wing. This was my chance. I could go straight to the basket and over the defender, your basic in-your-face move. But the defender was coming out at me. Andy was wide open for an easy lay-in.

What's the use? Do the right thing, Whipple. You always do. I flipped the ball to Andy who made the basket. He pointed to me on the way back down the court and yelled, "Nice pass, Wally!" but Coach Ackley was oblivious. The scrimmage ended.

To put it bluntly, I don't think I have a prayer of a chance to make the team.

All of this brings up huge problems. First, there is my delicate self-image. Basketball is me. It's what I think about, what I live for. Now, it doesn't look like I can even make a crummy sophomore team. This is hard on the ego.

Then there are the obvious explanations. Mom

and Dad will take the news okay. Natalie? Hard to say. She may gloat. But even she might give me some sympathy because she knows how much it means to me. Chuck will be tough. He thinks I'm the greatest basketball star this side of Michael Jordan. He won't understand.

Lumpy, Orville, the guys at church? I guess they will be okay. Julie, Edwina? Hmmm. They might think it's no big deal. Joe Vermeer. Ouch. He won't say anything, but I know what he'll be thinking. "Whipple must not be that good." Ouch again.

This is difficult. I am not looking forward to tomorrow. It's going to be tough to walk by the gym after school and hear the basketballs pounding on the floor and know I'm not part of the team.

Sometimes I just wish I were an adult and had all the hard stuff out of the way.

TUESDAY, NOVEMBER 27

Totally excellent! Awesome! Victory snatched from the jaws of defeat. Radical to the nth degree. Amazing. More than amazing. It is . . . righteous.

I made the team!

Yeeoowww, Whipple!

I heard from Jerome King in choir that I had survived. I didn't quite believe him, so I ran down to the locker room after class. True, it made me five minutes late to social studies, but it was worth risking the disapproval of Mrs. Aparicio. I looked at the list. Twelve names. Beautiful names. A splendid collection of outstanding athletes. Because there, on the next to the last line, was my name. And there was Andy Salisbury's name, too. I was so happy I wanted to cry. I wanted to do good and noble things. Like, sign autographs on basketballs and give them to poor children and establish scholarship funds throughout the world in my name. I decided that being a hermit in Wyoming was selfish and that I have more to give and that I could make a difference. I wanted to sing patriotic anthems, help little old ladies across the street, throw down my coat over mud puddles when beautiful princesses stepped off the curb. I wanted to write great books and throw out the first pitch at a World Series game. I wanted to vote and get married in the temple and say kind things about Viola Barkle, though taking her out was still too much of a stretch for me.

I wanted to meet Julie Sloan in the hallway, who would immediately notice the new, more confident, Wallace Whipple swaggering down the hall. "Wally, you look different in a very appealing way. Perhaps it is your swagger," she will say.

And I wanted to know why I had made the team after showing hardly anything in practice the last few weeks.

I only had to puzzle about the last question for sixty seconds. Coach Ackley came up behind me as I stood there. "Congrats, Wally. You made the team."

"Uh, yes sir, I did. There's my name right there."

"You want to know why you made the team, Wally?"

"Because I'm a good player with lots of potential?" I offered weakly.

"Not really. You made the team because you are tall. Six-three and still growing. You can't coach someone to be tall."

"Oh." Suddenly, I was feeling like the old Wally Whipple again. Wyoming here I come.

"And one other thing. During the scrimmage yesterday, I knew each boy was going all out to impress me. You all understood what was on the line. So I expected lots of wild shots and fancy dribbling, and just about everybody did their part. Frankly, I wasn't too interested in you, either, until you caught my eye at the end."

"How did I do that?"

"You had a chance to shoot the ball then, but instead you saw Salisbury open and you passed it to him. That impressed me. You see, I'm not looking for stars on third string. I'm looking for guys who are unselfish, willing to play a role, not glory hounds. You and Andy seem to fit that role."

"Uh, yes sir, that's me. No thoughts of glory here, Coach. I know my place," I uttered, quickly scaling back my plans to sponsor scholarships and appear as a guest at the World Series.

"Anyway, see you at practice."

Being tall is not what I wanted to hear as the reason I made the team. Being unselfish is not exactly what I wanted to hear, either. I wanted to hear about unlimited potential and immense talent.

But the important thing is this: I am on the tenth-grade team. And there are only eleven other sophomore guys at Benjamin Franklin High School who can make the same claim.

Go, Whipple!

THURSDAY, NOVEMBER 29

I have had two days to let it all sink in. My dad

was so excited when he heard I'd made the team that he gave me a bear hug. Mom said it was wonderful and she hoped I would make a lot of touchdowns. Chuck gave me a high five and an elbow bash. Natalie didn't say much because the cheerleading try-outs are tomorrow and her mood is alternating between pouting and tenseness. I honestly . . . hope . . . gritted teeth . . . forced smile . . . that she becomes . . . jaw tightens . . . a cheerleader.

There. It was a little easier that time.

FRIDAY, NOVEMBER 30

Natalie won, and her school gym is going to be filled with the sound of her shrieking this entire basketball season. I'm happy for her, although in a way that Bishop Winegar may not understand. Put it this way, if Natalie had lost, she'd have sulked for weeks.

Natalie gets on the phone right after dinner and calls every living soul she knows. No matter who it is, whether she likes the person or not, she manages somehow to work in the fact that she is now a cheerleader, within the first thirty seconds of conversation. She even asked me if Orville would like to know. I told her that I'd break the news to him tomorrow. "Well, only if you're sure he wouldn't rather hear it from me," she said. Natalie continues to amaze me. No lie.

It wasn't until after she was elected that she realized there are five practices a week, most of them in a part of the gym where no one can see her. That was a blow. I really think she figured once she was elected, all she would have to do is show up for the games, look good, bounce around, and shout stupid little rhymes with a central theme of, "go team, go!"

Meanwhile, my own extracurricular activities are not going well. It has been awhile since Julie said good morning or Joe told me, "Hey." And I have yet to touch the basketball in practice, although we've scrimmaged every day.

I need to have my faith in humanity, which includes myself, restored a bit. I wonder if we could invite Orv and his dad over for dinner again?

It worked last time.

CHAPTER 4

DECEMBER

SUNDAY, DECEMBER 2

Yesterday was slow. No plans, other than taking in a basketball game or two on TV. Natalie and Mom went off to the mall. Now that Natalie is a real cheerleader, she has persuaded Mom that she has a certain image to keep up because she is a role model for younger girls at school. Naturally, the way she dresses is important, she told Mom, somehow keeping a straight face. And it would be a good time to add some new items to her wardrobe, given her new status in school. Mom listened to all of this carefully, then said, "I think going to the mall would be a good idea, Natalie. I hadn't realized all of the social obligations that go along with being a cheerleader." Natalie almost fell off her chair. I think Mom had planned to do some Christmas shopping anyway.

MONDAY, DECEMBER 3

Poetry. Blah. Yuck. Grr.

Mrs. English is calling on us to present our immortal poetry in class now.

Today, she sat at her desk and cleared her throat, looking over her roll, and announced her first victim. "Katrina Baker, may we hear your poem?"

Katrina is a nice girl. I felt sorry for her, having to lead off. I also felt sorry for myself, because she sits on the opposite side of the room. I have this theory about calling on people in class. Teachers seldom call kids from the same side of the class twice in a row. Next time, Mrs. English is going to either go to the middle of the room or to my side. True, I have a poem ready, but I am not eager to stand up in front of the class and read it. Reading poetry is not my strong point.

Katrina walked to the front of the class and began reading after taking a deep breath. It was a poem about friendship, and I found myself not only listening but also kind of enjoying it. The last two lines were something like, "You were there, you are a friend. I will be there when you need me." I looked at my basketball poem and worried that it might be trite. "Very good, Katrina. You took something that was important, expressed it in an intense style, and left an indelible imprint on us. Thanks," Mrs. English said. She looked over the list. I knew it was coming my way. The lines about the ball rising in a perfect arc and landing in a nest like a lark started to gnaw at me.

"Orville Burrell."

Close. Really close. There but for the grace of Orville, go I. One seat away. Whew.

"Yes, Ma'am?"

"Are you prepared?"

"Yes, Ma'am, I am."

"Let's hear what you've written, then."

The class buzzes. Let's face it. Orv is still a mystery to most of us. Everyone expects he's written a poem about his dogies going to sleep at night, about eating chili cooked by a guy named Slim, and about falling asleep under a full moon as the coyotes yelp. He's also worked the flag into it and will use the word *buckaroo* at least four times. That's what we expect, and the class is getting ready for some real entertainment, after which they will move in for the kill. I feel sorry for Orville, who is more than a decent guy and deserves better.

We teenagers, I realize, can be cruel.

Clomp, clomp, clomp. Orville seems a little uneasy. He has a paper in his hand but he doesn't even look at it. Then he begins talking. I know what he said because he gave me a copy of his poem later.

> She loved the wildflowers—
> Purple and yellow
> When they broke through
> The spring's new grass.
>
> When the cottonwoods leafed,
> And the air near the stream
> Was tinged with a sweetness—
> That's when she walked,
> For hours and hours.
>
> Everything was new.
> Everything was fresh.
> Wild roses bloomed

On the dark side of the mountain.
A duck in the marsh swam
With her six downy, brown babies.

She told us what she had seen.
And we hoped that the mountains,
And the flowers,
And the baby ducks
Could do what none of us could.

It was her favorite time of the year.
It was her last.
And spring will never again
Be quite so simple or so sweet
As in years gone past.

After he finished, he looked up, and this great big guy, cowboy tough, always in control, hard as a winter prairie wind, just smiled, and said, "I miss you, Mom."

In the class, we are talking about major-league silence and wet eyes. Mrs. English just sat at her desk, dazed. Orville walked back to his desk and sat down quietly. Finally, Mrs. English looked up, and her eyes were red, too. "Thank you, Orville. That was beautiful. I'm sure your mom knows how you feel."

If I was hesitant before about reading my poem, I was now close to frantic. Orville writes something like that, and I may have to follow with "and this is not in jest, you were beaten by the best"? My theory about teachers never consecutively calling people from the same side of the classroom better prove out, or I was going to be in big trouble. I'd be better off reciting "Mary Had a Little Lamb."

I wondered if it was okay to pray at a time like

this. I decided probably not, since I had gotten myself into this jam, and I felt a little guilty about asking to be bailed out, because I didn't deserve it.

Anyway, I got lucky. Mrs. English asked only one more person to recite that day. I think she was so touched by Orville's poem that she just didn't want to get into being the teacher and critiquing poetry right then. Maybe I owe one to Orv.

And how about Orv? The more I get to know him, the better I like him. He's a lot more than rawhide and big belt buckles. There is a real human being there, one who is sensitive, smart, and a good guy. I feel a little ashamed that I joined with so many others who underestimated him. It will not happen again. You can't judge a cowboy by the tooling on his belt. Does that make sense?

One other thing: I think I'd better write a new poem.

WEDNESDAY, DECEMBER 5

This is big-time stuff. We have front-page news for the local gossip columnist. Not that I wish ill upon my fellow man, because that would not be part of the new, more mature, version of Wally Whipple. But it happened. I witnessed history this morning at seminary. Class breaks up, I got out into the hallway to catch my ride to school, and there is Julie . . . now get this . . . WITHOUT Joe!

Whoa! For two months I am witness to a ritual. Julie gets out of class and hangs out in the hallway until Joe gets out. They meet halfway up the hall and then walk slowly to the door. Is that love or what?

Julie and Joe. Everyone knows about them. They are a pair.

Then today, zippo, zero, nada. The romance has gone pfffft.

Yeah, they're both in the hallway, but neither acknowledges the other's existence. Is this a break or what? I can read it in their eyes. Since it's not a case of religious differences, it must be politics. She is a Democrat, he is a Republican. Or vice-versa. It doesn't matter. All I can think is that the Joe/Julie combination is history, right in there with World War II and Elvis Presley. Am I making sense? Am I rambling? Be cool, Whipple. Okay, I'm cool. Now, what next? A plan, that's what I need. He who fails to plan, plans to fail. I desperately need to talk with Amy Hassett. Opportunity is knocking. Joe has broken her heart, and the old swinging door to her aorta is wide open. And Wallace Whipple is right there, poised to walk through it.

THURSDAY, DECEMBER 6

I called the resourceful, Amy, who always knows what is going on.

Joe and Julie decided they were getting too serious.

I don't know what it means, but let's hear it for seriousness.

Amy said Julie, being new to the area and all, wanted the chance to date some other guys. Joe, getting close to graduation and with a mission coming in two years, decided he doesn't really want to get too far into a "relationship," says the marvelously informed Amy. I tell her I agree and that they had made a very mature and wise decision. I, for one, am not serious about anyone, I told Amy.

"Do you like Julie?" she asks.

"Me? Ha! Like Julie? Ha-ha! As a friend. Yeah, as a friend, that's all. But, do I *like* her? No way, not me. We're just friends."

I have this problem when I'm trying to hide something. For some reason, I start to babble. I hope that Amy hasn't noticed this minor character flaw in an otherwise extraordinary human being, but she probably has because it's fairly obvious.

"Well, I think if you asked her out, she'd probably say yes."

Orbit City! A date with Julie! Just for the asking. She might really like me. This could be a clue, Whipple. Maybe she pulled Amy aside and confided, "I know I've been dating Joe a lot, and he's a really nice guy, but the man I really want to go out with is Wally Whipple. Can you maybe let him know that I'm available? In the meantime, I'll dump Joe."

Life is definitely superb. This is sweet. And I'm going to enjoy it because I've been a teenager long enough to realize that the way I feel now may not last beyond tomorrow.

FRIDAY, DECEMBER 7

Life is still excellent, even if I haven't been able to make much of a mark in our basketball scrimmages. I have decided that I will not mention Julie's name once in my journal today. Well, maybe once.

Julie.

There, I have it out of the way.

On to other things. Like Christmas shopping, which I need to start devoting some brain time to.

First, Chuck. A mini-basketball, I think. He would like that very much and it fits into the budget.

For Natalie the clothes hound. I've spotted a blouse in the notions section of the grocery store that I think she will like. The reason is that there is a whole bunch of them and they all have different names stitched on the back. One has "Natalie" on it, so I'm in luck. Surprisingly, it is also in my budget, roughly the same price as the mini-basketball.

For Dad. Tough. Maybe some golf balls. Or, maybe a gift certificate from a store. Could pick one up for five bucks. That might do it.

For Mom. Hmmmm. Another tough call. Maybe a flower vase. Or maybe a tape of Frank Sinatra. She likes him, and so do I, particularly the early years.

I am only in the formulative stages of all this planning, but I'm on the right track. And I've only mentioned Julie's name once. Make that twice. We need to go out on a date.

If I only knew what to do on a date. I've never been on one.

SUNDAY, DECEMBER 9

December is my favorite time of year. The reason is Christmas, of course. When I was a kid, I liked it for the obvious reasons—presents and time off from school. Now, in my more mature years, I like it for the right reasons—presents and time off from school. Just kidding. I understand why it is important, and I enjoy the feeling of Christmas a lot. I'm not a dummy, and I know that about three more Christmases at home and then my life will change radically. I'll be at college and kind of breeze in for the holidays, then two years away on a mission, and after that, who knows?

I could be married and visiting my in-laws for Christmas in some far-away land such as Chicago. Listen to me! In-laws . . . marriage . . . missions . . . college. And it's all right around the bend!

This is also the best time of the year to be around Natalie. She gets almost nice and takes on the trappings of a human being in some ways. Oh, it's for a purpose, all right. She figures the nicer she is, the more presents people will buy her for Christmas. Truth.

Now for more pressing things. Christmas cards. I want to show Julie what a caring, sensitive person I am, and one way of doing so would be to send her a Christmas card. Good idea. But there is a problem. If I send only one Christmas card, then maybe word gets around that Julie got a card from me. It looks too obvious that I'm trying to impress her. So I need to send at least several cards, so that I don't look too much like a put-on, even though that's basically what I am.

Further complications, folks. The Joe Factor. Let's just say that Julie and Joe decide they've made a terrible mistake, and that they need to get back together. That's definitely possible. So they do, and Joe finds out that I sent a card to Julie. Joe gets steamed because he thinks I'm cutting in on his act. Or worse, he just laughs and thinks Whipple is a geekster supreme. The way I have it figured is, that if I send Julie a card, Joe gets one, too. Two cards on order.

Make it three. If I send a card to only one girl, it

will again be obvious that I've got a mad, raving crush on Julie. So I need to send a card to another girl. Who better than Amy Hassett, who might even mention how sweet I am to Julie for sending a card? Then Julie is impressed twice.

Four and five coming up. Lumpy should get one because if I send one to Joe, I need to send one to Lumpy, who is my best friend. And Orville gets one, too.

Five cards. That's my limit. No wait. One more, to Edwina Purvis, whose help has been the difference in math class. Six cards. Limited out. My max. No more.

Seven is a good number. Sister Lawson. I'm sure she'd enjoy a card. But that's it. Seven cards, positively and final. Seven.

I will check with Mom who buys about 2,000 Christmas cards on the 26th of December each year because they all go on sale. Certainly, she can spare seven cards because she has enough stashed away to send one to every man, woman, and child in Multnomah County, three times over.

This is definitely getting me into the spirit of the season. Wallace Whipple, the Christmas card king!

MONDAY, DECEMBER 10

News on the basketball front. Our first game is December 18th. It's funny, but I'm not the least bit nervous. The reason is simple. If you hardly get a chance to play in practice, why worry about playing in a game? I wonder if the coach knows I exist.

I finally read my poem today, the very last person in class to do so. Nobody seemed to listen much be-

cause we're all a little overdosed on poetry. My poem
went like this:

> I know your eyes are on me
> And, somehow, that makes me feel tall.
> I always want to be fair with you
> And never let you down.
>
> I'll teach you what I know,
> I'll show you who I am.
> When you need help,
> I'll lend a helping hand.
>
> Yes, I know you watch
> Everything I do.
> You look up to me, little brother,
> And I look up to you.

Mrs. English said it was a nice poem, and Orville
thumped me on the back after class and told me he
thought Chuck was a lucky hound to have me for a
big brother. That made me feel really good.

It's late, almost 11 P.M., so I need to turn off the
light and let the sandman do his stuff.

Sidenote #1: Strange thing after practice tonight. I
left my math book in my locker, so I went back to get
it, so that I could finish my homework. I walked upstairs to the second floor, turned the corner, and there
in the dim hallway, saw Les Lorris slinking around. He
looked startled, then realized it was only me, a
scrawny, expendable sophomore who was already
afraid of him. He came over really close and snarled
at me, "You didn't see anything here, clown. You got
that?"

I didn't think it was the time to tell him he needed

a mint, so I just nodded. A custodian came out of one of the nearby rooms, and Les sort of shoved me in the chest and took off in a hurry. I don't know what to make of this, other than what I suspect is that Les was not staying after school tonight to clean the chalk-boards.

TUESDAY, DECEMBER 11

The nagging feeling about doing some missionary work with Orville is still around. I got my chance to spring into action and play Ammon today at lunch.

Lumpy was stuffing his mouth with the food of champions, pizza, when he asked me about our sem-inary class Christmas project, which is to help a needy family. Orv picked right up on the word "seminary."

"What's seminary? You two going to wind up priests or something?"

Lumpy and I looked at each other. "We already are."

"You guys? I'm confused as a rabbit with no ears."

"Well, in our church, nobody gets paid. All of us help out with what needs to be done. All the men in good standing, from twelve years and up, hold the priesthood. We're a part of the priesthood called priests," I explained carefully.

"I'll be. Never knew I was associatin' with two real, live priests. But what's this seminary part?"

"Your turn, Lumpy."

He explained seminary pretty well. I was getting excited. I mean, this is the stuff you hear about in church every so often, so you know it goes on, but in the back of your mind you're saying, "Never happen to me." Lump finished off seminary and Orville sat back on his chair.

"You reckon I could go to seminary? I'm used to gettin' up early and I haven't adjusted none too well to sleepin' in until six. Might as well learn something first thing in the mornin'."

We told him it was okay for anyone to attend seminary. He decided it would be best after Christmas, since there were only a few days left before the break. We invited him to the Christmas activity, to help him get acquainted a bit.

I told everyone at dinner about our conversation. Mom and Dad were pleased. "He's such a sweet young man, he'll fit right in," Mom said. Chuck thought it was cool, and Natalie, I'm sure, started to envision a temple marriage.

So let's call this one a good day. Yeah, basketball practice wasn't much, and I got a C on a test in social studies, but it doesn't seem so important when compared to what happened at lunch today.

I think Ammon knew his stuff. I mean, he had some good success in a foreign culture, and maybe I did, too.

If you consider cowboys a foreign culture.

WEDNESDAY, DECEMBER 12

Two more Christmas cards. One to Brother McNair at seminary. Another to Brother Hansen, my quorum adviser. That makes nine. No more. Zeroed out. Nine cards. I don't want to get carried away.

THURSDAY, DECEMBER 13

I remember a poem from Mrs. English's English class, by Emily Dickinson. It started out something like, "My life closed twice before its close . . . "

I can relate to that. I may have come close to dying today, and I'm not sure I'll survive tomorrow. Life has taken an ugly twist.

The characters in this drama are (1) Wallace Whipple, whom we know and love; (2) Les Lorris, whom we already know and don't love; (3) Orville Burrell, ditto for #1; and (4) Mr. Otis McCloud, vice principal for discipline at Benjamin Franklin High School, who is about four inches taller than me and one hundred pounds heavier and a man with little patience with students who fight.

There's that word. Fight. I'll start at the beginning.

At the end of third period, I swung by my locker to grab a health assignment that I'd left there. I got my paper, slammed my locker shut, whirled around, and ran dead into Les Lorris and his girlfriend with no chin. It was dumb, I know. I was in a hurry and wasn't looking where I was going. I knocked Les back a step, and all of his books dropped on the floor. Some sort of animal instinct kicked in, probably similar to what a field mouse feels before being swooped up by a hawk, because I immediately got this sense that I was in deep trouble.

"Sorry, Les. My fault. One-hundred percent. Let me help you with your books. I really am sorry, man."

"Shut your ugly face up. You did that on purpose," he snarled, his teeth clenched. Looking back, it was the clenched teeth that told me I was in for it. The only other time I've seen that look was in some old western movies, just before Black Bart and the handsome drifter in the white hat would shoot it out. I am not making this up. Clenched teeth. That's what went through my mind.

"Uh, it was an accident. Honest," I sputtered, trying to be gracious. And humble, which comes naturally to me at times like these.

There was a small crowd gathering now, like sharks when they smell blood. Les pushed me hard into the lockers, and I went down in a heap. Then he came up and kicked me in the stomach.

I retaliated. I gathered my strength, let out a primal grunt, and swung a mighty blow, hitting his ankle. Ha! Bet he felt that. May never walk again.

Well, not quite. He pulled me up by my collar and cocked his fist. About fifty kids were gathered around, most of them excited and yelling, "Fight! Fight!" although that may have been somewhat of an exaggeration.

I didn't want to die, but realized this might be it. Was my life in order? I needed to repent of some things I'd done to Natalie. But it may be too late. I'd never date Julie, never see Chuck's first basket. I'd never live to shave more than once a week, or outgrow facial blemishes. Too soon, too soon, my life was over, too soon.

Then came the miracle. My guardian angel. I'd like to say that I sprang back to my feet, and through masterful fisticuffs, boxed Les into a helpless heap of blubber. Truth is, I was quivering pulp by this time, just hoping for a speedy and relatively painless journey into unconsciousness. Well, I survived okay, thanks to Orville.

Yup, Orville. Yippie-yo-kai-yay.

I sensed movement in the crowd. Orville breaks through the ring of kids and walks up to Les, milli-seconds before I was about to be put into orbit. Orville was so calm. He had a smile on his face, and he looked at Les and said, "Put him down or you'll be dealing with two of us."

"This ain't your problem, jerk!" Les snapped at him.

"He's my friend, and when you take him on, you get me as part of the deal."

"Yeah, I get it. It takes two of you. Well, I know when to quit." Les loosened his grip on me, started to turn away from both of us, then whirled with his fist coming right toward Orville.

Orville didn't flinch. He caught Les's fist in one of his meaty hands and held it for a second.

"You're a sorry dog," Orville said in a low voice. "A real sorry dog."

He flung Les's fist back, took one step, and landed a shot on Les's chin. Les immediately saw stars and birdies and slumped to the ground. Cheering broke out.

I stood up by Orville, my legs still wobbly. "Guess we showed him, Orville."

"We did, pardner. Glad I was there to help out a touch."

"More than a touch. One punch and he was in la-la land," I said, gazing at Les's prone body while Roni the Chinless cooed and hovered over him. "What do we do with him? I've never won a fight before. Heck, I've never been in a fight before. I don't know what to do."

"We do nuthin'. If he's still here at the end of the day, let the janitor take him out with the trash. If that don't happen, let the coyotes pick at him."

A friend of mine, Rick Magin, came up to us and peered over Les's motionless form. "You guys better get out of here. Maybe nobody will report you."

We hustled out. I was still so woozy, I could hardly walk.

"You okay, Wally?"

"Yeah. Well, not really. But I will be okay. Hey, Orv, thanks. You saved my face from permanent damage which would have been a tragedy felt worldwide."

"No problem, Wallace, my man."

We split up and went to our classes. I was beginning to think I might skate through the whole thing when I got a note from the principal's office in my last class of the day. It said that Mr. Otis B. McCloud wanted to see me tomorrow at 9 A.M. I hoped the B in his name stood for "Benevolent," but I had my doubts. Frankly, I liked my odds with Les Lorris a lot better.

I called Orv tonight, and found out he got summoned for the same time. I can't believe this is happening. Less than five months into my high school career, and I'm looking at being suspended for fighting. Sweet, lovable Wally Whipple, whose biggest problem before today was a Christmas card count that was too high. I hope Mr. McCloud is in the holiday spirit tomorrow.

FRIDAY, DECEMBER 14

I'm not suspended. Let me repeat that—I'm not suspended. Unbelievable!

Neither is Orville. Truly amazing!

This is how it went. Orville and I met outside of Mr. McCloud's office a few minutes before nine. I was so nervous I could hardly talk. Even though Orv looked calm, he was going through toothpicks at the rate of one per minute. (I have learned how to detect if Orv is nervous. One of the best indicators is his rate of toothpick consumption. The faster he chews toothpicks, the more nervous he is.) Ten minutes and ten toothpicks went by. Still, no Mr. McCloud. Was he also calling in our parents?

Finally the door opened. "Gentlemen," said Mr. McCloud, motioning us in.

We came in and meekly sat down. He sat on the corner of his desk and looked at me. "You sure you were the one who was fighting? You don't look the type."

"No, sir. I mean, yes, sir. I'm here because of the fight yesterday."

"With Les Lorris, I understand."

"Yes, sir."

"Well, who won?"

"I guess we did, sir. At least Les didn't look so good when we left."

He turned to Orville. "You're new here, I understand."

"Yes, sir. From Heppner, little town in eastern Oregon."

"Do you think fighting is a way to establish a reputation here?"

"No, sir, I don't. I was trying to help my friend."

"Is that true, Whipple?"

"Yes. Les was about to turn me into a grease spot, but Orville stepped in. It wasn't his fault, he was just helping me. We're friends." I felt an extreme surge of nobleness. "Don't blame Orville. It is I who should be punished."

"I see." Mr. McCloud went behind his desk and sat down. "You know what happens to students who fight in school, don't you?"

"They get suspended, I guess," I squeaked.

"How big are you, Burrell?"

"I'm a tad over 6'2" and weigh purtin' near 190 pounds."

"I'm going to give you a chance, Burrell. You seem like an okay kid. You can be suspended a week from school, or you can turn out for wrestling. The season is well underway, I know, but I think Coach Waymon would like to see a student your size on the team. He's a little weak in the heavier weights."

"I'll wrestle, sir. But it doesn't seem fair."

Mr. McCloud frowned, expecting Orv to complain. "Why?" he demanded.

"Well, I'm used to wrasslin' steers, and taking on little biddy city boys don't seem like much of a challenge."

Mr. McCloud almost smiled. "Give it a try, Orville. So, I understand you took out Lorris with one punch."

"That's true, Mr. McCloud. He went down easy. Like a shot bird."

This time, Mr. McCloud did grin a bit. "Lorris has a bad reputation. This is his third high school and he won't be returning. We suspect he's been stealing some computer equipment. It's a police matter now. I checked with a couple of kids who saw the fight, and they back up your story. Just don't let it happen again, gentlemen. Understand?"

We both nodded.

"You're dismissed."

I felt a vague disappointment. I wanted to be punished, take a bullet for Orv. I cleared my throat. "What about me, Mr. McCloud?"

"Oh, yes. You, Whipple. You ran cross-country, right?"

"Yes."

"And you're playing basketball now?"

I nodded.

"Well, go out for track in the spring. A tired kid usually doesn't get into trouble." (Obviously, he had been recruited into the Parents' Conspiracy by my mother.) "I can't believe someone as scrawny as you got into a fight. Steer clear of troublemakers, Whipple. Lorris would have turned you into oatmeal if it weren't for Burrell here."

"Yes sir, and I will, sir."

Orville and I hustled out of his office before Mr. McCloud had time to change his mind. "Not as bad as I expected, Orv."

"We did right fine. And the thought of wrasslin' don't bend me shapeless. I may even be good at it, and it'll give me something more to do."

That's where it ended. Except for one more thing. The school was buzzing over the fight. Les, it seems, wasn't about to win any popularity contests. As we walked to our next class, I could hear some of the kids whispering, "Those guys punched out Lorris."

So this is fame. Not exactly how I imagined I'd achieve it. But I don't think anyone is going to mess with Wallace F. Whipple for a long time—especially if Orville is right behind me.

SATURDAY, DECEMBER 15

One more hurdle to clear concerning the fight. I knew I needed to tell my parents.

I chose dinner tonight to break the news. Dad had worked all day, and he was tired. Mom had put in a busy day, and Natalie had been to the mall so she was in a good mood. Very casually, I mentioned the subject.

"Mom . . . Dad . . . I had a little problem at school on Thursday."

"Get ripped on a test, Son?"

"No, I sort of got into a . . . fight—"

"A WHAT?" both of my parents shouted.

"A fight. With a guy named Les Lorris. It wasn't my fault, and the police are after him anyway because he stole some computer equipment, and I won the fight because Orville came and knocked Les into la-la land."

"Orville helped you out?" Dad asked.

"Yeah. Orville. I'm not sure I could have taken this guy without Orville."

Big lie, I know. But this is my family, and I don't want to look like I can't take care of myself in front of them. It's a terrible thing for a mother to think of her firstborn son as a wimp.

"Orville is so cool," Natalie gushed.

"Are you hurt?" Mom questioned.

"Well, no. Not that much, anyway. Nothing permanent." I could see that being injured might gain some valuable sympathy for me. So I stretched things a little.

"My stomach isn't doing too well, but it will straighten out in time. He hit me when I wasn't really looking (read that because my eyes were closed and I was praying) but then I got a good shot in at him . . . "

"You *hit* him?" my dad said, a note of awe in his voice. At least I think it was awe.

"Where?" asked Chuck.

"Well, I guess you would call it a shot to the lower body." How could I tell them it was really more like a slap on the ankle? "Anyway, then Orv came and boom, one punch, and it was all over. We went to the vice principal's office and worked things out. He was very understanding and almost thanked us, man-to-man, for doing the school a public service. Les won't be coming back to Franklin."

"I bet Orville really laid one on him," Natalie sighed. "He's so cool."

"Yeah, he did okay for himself."

"Tell me a little bit more about your punch, son."

"Not that big of a deal, Dad. After he hit me first, I just sort of came back at him. It wasn't a knockout punch, but he felt it, I guarantee it."

I hadn't been exactly one hundred percent truthful up to this point. I was so far into it that I couldn't really get out. I felt good about my understanding of repentance.

"But you gave him the old Whipple sluggeroo," said my dad, who was showing more interest in my punch (slap) than in my ailing stomach.

"Yeah. Right. The ol' sluggeroo, Dad."

He sat back and smiled. "Wally, you know that fighting is not the answer, but there comes a time when you have to defend yourself. Sounds like that's what you did."

"Right, Dad. Sort of like when the United States goes to war."

"Orville is so cool," Natalie gushed again.

We got back to our meal and the subject was dropped. But a couple of times during the course of dessert, Dad looked over and winked. Maybe this is what male bonding is all about.

SUNDAY, DECEMBER 16

Christmas is nine days away. I've pretty much finished my shopping, but the cards are heavy on my mind. My problem is that I don't know how to sign them.

Let me back up. Mom gave me some cards with a snowy winter scene in the forest and a horse-drawn sleigh pulling up at night loaded with a Christmas tree. There's this cute cottage with yellow light pouring out of the windows and a woman standing in front of the doorway, waving to the man on the sleigh. A few little kids are peeking out from behind the door and you can see Christmas stockings hanging from the mantel. The guy on the sleigh is waving back with a smile about the size of a quarter moon. Obviously, he's the dad in the family. Inside, the card says, "Peace on Earth."

It was easy to write to Brother McNair, Sister Lawson, and the other adults. You just write, "Merry

Christmas, Wally Whipple." That's it. But with Joe, Lumpy, and most of all, Julie, I am locked in a dilemma.

For Lumpy, you don't want to say anything too syrupy. After all, this is a guy who eats my leftover pizza crusts at school. For Joe, it has to be something cool. For Julie, I need help. What do you say to the girl you're in *like* with?

Maybe I should write, "Merry Christmas, your friend, Wally." Naw. Not enough of a message. Sort of the dead fish approach.

See, what I really want out of the Christmas card is that she'll look at it and be moved to tears. She will go to her parents and tell them that Wallace Whipple is the most wonderful human being she has ever known—sweet, gentle, caring, and yet ruggedly handsome. I want her to say that she hopes they can meet me someday because I am definitely son-in-law material.

Okay, first step. I wrote her name just below "Peace on Earth." Good start. Solid. Personal. "I hope this is the merriest Christmas ever. I have grown to ad"—NUTS!!! I had started to write "admire you," but that would be too personal. I've got to keep some distance, you know. Now, to find a word that begins with "ad" to get back on track. I cannot afford any scribbles on my first Christmas card to her. Advance. Admonish. Ad-lib. Advertise. Admiral. Adding.

Try this. "I have grown to additional spiritual heights in seminary and hope you have, too." Nice work, Wally. Brings in the spiritual side of things, and it also works in a subtle sports motif. Heights=basketball=sports=me. Finish it off with a "Merry Christmas!" and it's done.

I'm exhausted after that one. I just write thanks for being a good friend to Lumpy and Orville, then jot down, "Have a good one," to Joe. I'm not sure what I mean by it, but it does sound cool.

The cards will be in the mail tomorrow. For now, I'm tired, and this is a big week coming at school. I'm going to click off my light now and have a good one, myself.

MONDAY, DECEMBER 17

Everybody needs a break. I got mine today at basketball practice.

End of practice. Coach Ackley gathers us around and tells us that tomorrow is our first game, as if no one knew. I'm standing near the back of the circle of players, only halfway paying attention. He clears his throat and looks at us seriously. "Guys, I think that an athlete should be distinct among the students. You should represent a higher standard, especially on the days we have games. I want you to stand out."

I'm thinking, so what's the point? Do you want us to shave our heads?

"I would like each of you to wear a suit to school tomorrow, or at the very least, a sports coat and tie. I'm serious about this, guys. **If you don't make a special effort to stand out from the student body, then you will not play.**"

Euphoria! The gates to Hoop Heaven are swinging wide open! I have a suit! I will wear it! And the best news is, I know for some, no, make that all of the other guys, Coach Ackley is asking the impossible! They'd rather be caught on national TV playing with dolls than wear a tie to school!

But I can do that! Anything to play. I even have more than one tie!

Is Coach Ackley serious? I studied him as he droned on with his rah-rah talk. He has bad side-burns. He wears plaid shirts with striped ties. He wore a leisure suit to school once this week. Yes, he's serious, and I love it. And the reaction of my teammates, especially those ahead of me in the playing rotation, which is everyone, except perhaps Andy Salisbury— their eyes glaze over. Their mouths form hard, straight lines. Their eyes droop. They are thinking, "No way, man, am I putting on the duds for you just to play some hoops tomorrow."

This is it. I'll not only play, I'll star. Coach Ackley will smile in amazement and delight as the slumber-ing volcano named Whipple finally erupts. I'll score at least eighteen points. Naw, make it twenty-five, with a dozen rebounds. My floor play will be flawless, my defense, superb.

That's only the beginning. I play brilliantly throughout the season. Then the next. I become a high school legend and play in all-star games all over the country. A scholarship to BYU awaits. After my mission, I come back to earn honorable mention All-American. I am drafted by . . . oh, let's say the Chicago Bulls in the first round. Knowing that Michael Jordan, who has come out of retirement, is going to do all the scoring, I concentrate on defense and re-bounding. Slowly I work my way into the starting lineup. Sportswriters around the league begin to talk about me as "Chicago's quiet force, a man who does so many things well that never show up in the box score." I am featured on a halftime show during the "Game of the Week." I come across as poised, humble, a natural role model for youth. My parents are featured. Mom says how grateful they are that with my fat contract, I was able to build them a new home in Lake Oswego and that my father could retire early from the hardware business. My dad says, with a tear in his eye, "True, he's a great athlete, but he's an even better person." Moist-eyed, the host of the show turns to the camera and says to the nation, "This is one reporter who will second that. Whipple is a star of the first magnitude, on the court and off."

The NBA championship series rolls around. It's Chicago against the hated Lakers. Seventh game. Close. The crowd is going berserk. Then it happens. Jordan hurts his knee. We all gather around him and he looks up at me in obvious pain.

"Dubs, (that's what he calls me, a little play on my initials) I can't do it. You've got to be the man. I know you've been sacrificing your scoring for the team, but man, you've got to step up now. For all of us, baby."

The coach nods in solemn agreement.

"Count on me, MJ." (MJ is what I call Michael Jordan, a little play on his initials.) The buzzer sounds. I pull up my socks and trot back on the court, a determined glint in my eye. A man's gotta do what a man's gotta do.

Time in, four minutes left . . . we're down by two. I get the ball. I fake a pass, then dribble to the three-point line and put it up. Nothing but net! We're up by one. I rebound a Laker miss, drive the length of the floor and slam it in over a befuddled defender. Bulls by three. And it's all Bulls after that. We win by a dozen, and when the buzzer sounds, my teammates mob me. MJ, ice pack on knee, hugs me in front of a world-wide television audience. I feel great, but I am still modest and self-effacing in victory. It is at this moment that I announce my plan to fund scholarships for inner-city kids and third-world students. I am a lock for every good-guy award that is given in sports.

Yes, I see it all now. **AND ALL BECAUSE I'M GOING TO WEAR A SUIT TO SCHOOL TOMORROW.**

Coach Ackley, I thought you were kind of a dweeb, but I understand you better now. You are simply a shrewd man with a talent for motivation.

TUESDAY, DECEMBER 18

This is, possibly, the worst day in my life.

I know I've thought that before, but this may be it.

Why didn't my parents just name me "Dork" and let everyone know right off, rather than having to wait about two minutes to find out what I'm really like?

Why can't I read between the lines like every other teenager? All those guys listening to Mr. Ackley knew he was just talking and not really meaning any of that stuff about wearing a suit to school.

Why can't I fit in, go with the flow, be a part of something . . . anything?

Yes, I wore my suit to school.

Natalie got up just as I was leaving and almost disinherited me. The last thing she said to me was that

I'd better get my act together before she shows up at Benjamin Franklin in two years.

At seminary, I got stares. Lots of them. Kept up the brave face. "Game day. Coach says to dress up." I kept thinking of Michael Jordan calling me "Dubs," knowing this was but a fleeting awkward moment.

School. A nightmare. I heard whispers all day. Some kids pointed at me. I was a lock for the Nerd of the Year Award. Only Orville acted as though I was not dressed in the emperor's clothes.

But I put up with it all, waiting for the game. I'd have the last laugh when Coach Ackley named me as one of the starters. I made sure he saw me in my suit. I walked by his classroom a couple of times, then right by the coaches' office just before game time. I know he saw my suit. The only kid on the team to wear one. It felt super to change out of my suit and into a basketball uniform. I ran my fingers across the stitching that spelled "Franklin" across my chest in raised maroon letters against the white top. We charged onto the court and I felt like I could jump ten feet in the air.

Warm-ups were great. My shooting motion was smooth and sure. Maybe I should have invited Julie to the game. Never had I been more ready, and suddenly, the game was ready to start. I kept my head slightly bowed, trying to look humble at being asked to start the first game. I had suited up, and I deserved it.

"Starters . . . Lacey, Griffin, Call, Jones, and Samuelson. Guys, this will set the tone for the entire season . . . "

I looked up in shock. There must be a mistake.

Coach Ackley said yesterday . . . he said, just yesterday, . . . I had worn my suit . . .

I had a small hope that maybe I'd at least get to play part of the game. Coach Ackley had to have seen me. I have to play today . . . it means everything to me. But it didn't happen in the first quarter. Not in the second. I knew I was sunk. The bench was my place.

Our team got beat by about twenty points. But I didn't pay much attention.

After the game, everyone hustled into the locker room. They quietly got into the shower, thinking about the way we got trashed in the game. I waited until they were all in, then jerked my suit from the locker, dressed in a hurry, and left before anyone could see me. Thank heaven it was dark. I walked home in a drizzle, my tie stuffed into my pocket.

"Hey, son! How did the game go?" Dad called out as I walked in.

"You look so nice!" Mom said.

"Did you score lots of points?" Chuck asked.

"I bet the dork didn't even play," Natalie huffed.

I made it to my room just before I started to cry.

WEDNESDAY, DECEMBER 19

I felt a little better today, but not much.

Basketball practice was hard. I didn't want to go, but knew what my dad would say if I even mentioned quitting. So I went, listened to Coach Ackley tell us how disappointed he was in our performance, then sat on the bench during the scrimmage.

Dad came up to my room while I was in the middle of some intense staring at the ceiling.

"Bet you feel pretty down, Wally."

"Oh, not really. Well, a little, maybe."

"I'm sorry that you didn't get to play. I know you're a good player and that you'll do well if you get the chance."

"Yeah."

"And it may be a bit hard for you to understand right now, but you did the right thing by wearing your suit to school. An adult, someone you trusted, someone in a position of authority, asked you to do something special. And you, in good faith, did what you were asked. You can't help it if he doesn't have the integrity to follow through on a promise. Obviously, his word doesn't mean much to him."

"I guess so."

"Wally, this won't be the last time an adult or someone you trusts, lets you down. It's difficult to learn, but it's just the way some people are. Today, it's a basketball game. Tomorrow, it may be a friendship or a business deal. You can never predict. You just have to use your best judgment and be sure you've done what your conscience says is right. I'm only sorry that in this case, you got hurt."

"Thanks, Dad. I'm not hurt that much." But we both knew the truth.

He got up and left. I know my dad isn't the slickest guy in the world. It's a cinch that Natalie didn't inherit her sense of fashion from him. Yeah, his hair is thinning, and he could stand to lose ten pounds. Sometimes, I think it would be fun to have a real young-acting dad, the kind who lets you call him by his first name and goes to the movies with you and who can talk sports with you all night. The kind with

a good haircut and who drives a sports car. I really
know better. It's more important to have a dad who
knows and understands me and can talk with me at
the right time, even though he doesn't know the difference between a compact disc and a slipped disc.
Tonight, I needed him, and tonight he was there.

FRIDAY, DECEMBER 21

I've had this talk with myself and it goes like this:

First Wally: I feel lousy. No one understands me.
My coach gave me the shaft. I want to quit the team,
and I feel sorry for myself.

Second Wally: Chill out, man. Go do something
for someone else, and you'll feel better. No one likes
to be around a whiner.

Although I don't like to admit it, the second Wally
is right. The experience from Tuesday still leaves me
numb and wondering about a lot of things. And it's
difficult to look at Coach Ackley without thinking
here's a guy with either a really short memory or
someone who doesn't give a rip about his word.

But a couple of things happened today that
helped me realize that shoving your own problems
aside and taking on something for someone else is a
good prescription for wiping out the blues.

Witness:

At seminary today, Julie came in a few minutes
after I did. She looked right at me and smiled. Then
she sat down by Amy, a few chairs away, and smiled
at me again. I am not making this up. They were
bona fide, genuine, you-are-someone-out-of-the-ordi-
nary kinds of smiles, directed to my very own person.

After class, she got up and almost ran right toward me.

"Wally, that was so sweet of you to send me a Christmas card!"

"Oh . . . well, it was nothing. I mean, it was something, but not a big deal. It was my way of telling you . . . that I hope . . . "

I was about to start talking in tongues again, fighting the urge to say something like, "Crupom und velt essen dee hoolidays."

Then, in the nick of time, I remembered what one of the other cards said that Mom had offered me. " . . . that you have a joyous and memorable holiday season." Whew. She gave me a look of slight puzzlement. "Well, I'm sure that we will do just that. We'll have a joyous and memorable holiday. Thanks, Wally." Then that smile again.

I decided that since I was on a roll, I might as well shoot for the stars. "Julie, did you by chance show the card to your parents?"

She looked puzzled. "No. Should I have?"

"No. Just thought I'd ask."

But wait folks, there's more.

Joe, without Julie, stopped me near the doorway.

"Got your Christmas card, Wally."

"Oh right. Christmas card." I wondered what he really thought.

"That was cool. Thanks. I'll have a good one, and hope you do, too."

The interesting part was that everyone I sent a card to, thanked me today. Sister Lawson called and thanked me. Brother Hansen did, too.

I may be on to something with the Christmas cards. 'Tis the season.

Tomorrow I get a chance to do something else that fits in with Christmas. There is this family in 11th Ward who has been having a hard time and isn't expecting much of a Christmas. But our seminary class has different ideas. Through careful planning, organization in painstaking detail, and with the able assistance of some crafty adults, we have hatched a plan to get into the Bradshaw's home while they are away and strew their place with gifts for their family. I take only a modest amount of credit for the scheme, although I *was* chairman of the committee that planned it. I am looking forward to our sneak attack on the Bradshaws. It's not often you get to be devious for a good purpose.

SATURDAY, DECEMBER 22

Secret agents of the seminary class: Your assignment, should you choose to accept it, is to sneak a mess of Christmas packages into a home this evening. Should you be apprehended, you will be responsible for your own escape, and the bishop will disavow any knowledge of you.

Just kidding. But we had a blast tonight, sneaking into the Bradshaw's home and playing Santa Claus. Never mind the details of how we got the Bradshaw's out, how we made sure their door would be unlocked, and all of the secret planning that went into it. Let me just say that inside the mild exterior of Brother McNair, beats the heart of one sneaky dude.

So the Bradshaws are gone. We've met at the

church, each of us lugging a bunch of gifts for the kids and a few for the parents. Joe's here, so is Lump. We even got Orville to come. We get into the cars and drive to our meeting point, a block away from the Bradshaw's. Then, under cover of darkness, we make our way to the home and stack the presents under the tree, around the tree, in the kitchen, in the living room, everywhere. The place is looking like a picture out of a Christmas catalog.

I, as one of the project organizers, stand near the door, directing traffic. My commands are swift and decisive. There is a constant hum of giggling and a definite feeling of excitement as the seminary elves do their number. The Christmas sneak-machine is well-oiled and running.

Then, disaster strikes. Headlights swing down the street and it looks very much like the Bradshaw's car. It slows and begins to turn into the driveway. "Kill the lights! Everybody out!" I say, hoarsely. General scurrying occurs. "No! The back door!" I instruct, still calm and authoritative.

The momentum shifts, and there is a thudding of feet to the back door. The door opens, and all the elves escape.

All but me. Being a good leader, I have made sure my troops are safe without regard for my own well-being. Footsteps on the front porch! The doorknob turns, and, in desperation, I dive into a closet near the kitchen.

"Hey! What's gone on here!" I hear Brother Bradshaw shout. "Christmas come early! Who did this? Kids, come here, you've got to see this!"

I hear more footsteps, as the children rush in. I

wonder if I've been reported missing-in-action yet. I decide that I need to make my move soon, or either I'll get caught or I'll have to spend a long time in the Bradshaw's broom closet. My best shot is through the front door. I listen closely. The children are pumped. Brother and Sister Bradshaw's knees thump to the floor to inspect all of the presents near the tree. I open the closet door and tiptoe toward the front door, looking over my shoulder at a scene of holiday happiness. All any of them would have to do now is turn around and I'm a dead elf. I quietly open the door. One of the little kids spots me as I fling it open and make a break for it.

"Look!" she shouts. "It's Santa Claus! I saw him! I really saw him!"

But it's too late. Santa Claus is halfway down the street, his long legs churning. I get around the corner where the cars are parked, safe at last. Someone, Joe I think, yells, "Here he is!"

They *did* miss me. A small mob of seminary classmates surrounds me, pounding me on the back. I get a few hugs. Maybe one was from Julie. I feel like a hero, at this moment of triumph.

And for some crazy reason, I wish Coach Ackley were here. Then he'd know I'm not a nobody.

SUNDAY, DECEMBER 23

Things have been in a whirl this last week. So much, that I've not even taken time out to acknowledge some really important events in my life.

First, I'm out of school for two weeks. Christmas vacation.

Well, I had a list of other important events, but they pale in comparison to item #1. I can use a breather. I have been studying harder, trying to raise the old GPA. Basketball is tiring me emotionally. Even sitting on the bench drains you, I've decided. With two weeks of Christmas vacation dead ahead, I can recharge. Coach Ackley only scheduled two practices during the break.

Today was Christmas sacrament meeting. Lots of music, which I enjoyed, now that I'm learning to sing better. Bishop Winegar spoke about Christmas gifts, those that come from the heart. I couldn't help thinking about the Bradshaws and how good it felt to do something for them. The other speaker today was Brother Miles, our stake patriarch. He is originally from Canada, and he told us about Christmas growing up on a farm in Alberta. His description of a snowy Christmas day sleigh ride, the fragrance of fresh-baked rolls and cookies his mother made, and the tree they cut right off his family's land, helped me catch the mood and the feeling of Christmas. Thank you, Brother Miles.

Back to the updates.

Orville is leaving for Heppner tomorrow. He'll be spending Christmas there, and he seems excited about going home. He'll be able to see his horse, his nephews, and walk around the place. For all of Orville's cowboy toughness, he's a marshmallow underneath, and I know he's been homesick, especially the last few weeks.

Lumpy is headed to California to visit grandparents. He promises to come back with a tan. Julie is staying in town. Big whup for me, I know. As if I'm going to call her and ask her out three times over vacation.

I think it's time to call it a day. I'm feeling a little lazy and a bit drowsy.

Good-night, Planet Earth. This is Wallace F. Whipple, going off the air.

TUESDAY, DECEMBER 25

My favorite day of the year.

With a five-year-old in the house, you'd expect Chuck to be the first one up. Not here, though. Remember, this is the domicile of Natalie Elaine Whipple, who began her stirrings at 5 A.M. Yes, that's five in the morning, when everything was still dark. The hour when Santa was still in town, and all normal human beings, even on Christmas Day, were wanting to catch a few more winks.

Natalie starts by coughing. Big, deep, phony coughs. Her reasoning must have gone like this: "Okay, like, if I start coughing, really serious coughing, coughing to the max, it will wake everyone up. Since everyone knows it's Christmas, they'll all get up because of my serious coughing, and, like, Mom will ask if I'm okay. I'll go, sure. I'm okay, but I can't get back to sleep. Then she'll go, wow, I can't either. Then I'll go, well, since we're all up except for Dad, Wally, and Chuck, let's just start **OPENING OUR PRESENTS NOW!** Mom will agree, then we'll get down to some serious gift-opening."

I know that's what she thought. And that's the way it happened. After about her ninth cough—one that must have registered on the Richter Scale—I hear some stirring and then my Mom's soft voice. "Natalie, honey, are you okay?" Natalie mumbles something back, and the next thing I hear is the sound of footsteps down the hallway into the front room where the Christmas tree is.

"Oh, it's so beautiful! Let's get Wally and Chuck up and show it to them," Natalie says, breathlessly. Now this is a twist I hadn't anticipated, and I must admit that it's a slick move on my sister's part. She wants to share the beauty and joy of Christmas morning with her beloved siblings. Right, Nat. I hear Dad stirring and then thumping his feet on the floor. Then Mom is next to me, gently rubbing my shoulder. "Wally, it's Christmas. Let's go gather by the tree." Chuck is soon up, groggy, but he heads out of the room, too. "Let's go, Wally," he says, rubbing his little fists in his eyes. "Natalie wants to open her presents."

So there we are at 5:30 A.M., sitting around the tree. Only Natalie is alert, and she is positively shining. Dad opens his Bible and turns to the second chapter of Luke. He begins the family Christmas tradition, reading about the birth of the Savior, before we open presents. Dad gets through verse five, about Mary being great with child, when Natalie stands up and says, "Oh, that was great, Dad. It made me feel spiritual, seriously. Now let's open some presents!" Dad points out that we still have about twenty more verses to read before we get through. Natalie's smile flickers, and she says something like, "Oh. I thought we were through."

We finish the Christmas story, and Natalie pops up again. "Let me play Santa! I'll hand out the presents!" Before either Mom or Dad can answer, she has the most elaborately wrapped gift of all from under the tree in her hands. "What a surprise! This one is for me!"

And so it went. Natalie plows through all of her gifts at a speed roughly equivalent to that of a rocket launch. She makes two neat piles of her gifts, one the keeper pile, the other the take-back pile. I am slightly troubled when the blouse with her name on the back goes into the take-back pile, though I see Mom quietly nudge it back into the keeper pile when Natalie is not looking.

The rest of us do fine, just enjoying the morning. Chuck gets a football helmet and some books, plus a bunch of clothes. My Dad hands me a big square box and inside of it is a really nice leather basketball, better than any I've ever had.

"You know what to do with that, Wally," he tells me, winking.

Give Natalie this much. She is entertaining, and our family wouldn't be the same without her. Not necessarily worse off, but not the same. After all the gifts were opened, Mom asked about her cough.

"What cou—oh yes, my cough. Well (cough) I think it is (cough) getting better (cough). But some rest will do me good (cough). I think I'll go (cough) back to bed now." And off she goes, leaving the rest of us to enjoy Christmas morning: bleary-eyed, fuzzy-brained, peaceful, and with the good feeling inside that Christmas morning may be the best few hours our family has together each year.

FRIDAY, DECEMBER 28

Okay, so I took a few days off from my journal.

It's Christmas vacation. I've got the right, right? The blush of Christmas is over, so I now only have New Years to anticipate. And with the new year comes—ta-dah—drum roll please—hand me the envelope, Vanna—RESOLUTIONS!

1. Eat more Mexican food.

I like this goal because it is attainable. (I feel, when setting goals, that at least one should be a pushover, sort of a confidence builder.) It is also a goal that will be pleasurable to work on.

2. Make my move with Julie Sloan.

Tougher resolution. I'm not even sure what I mean by it. Redefine, Whipple. Go out on a date with Julie. Once. There. That's more like it.

3. Play in one school basketball game.

This needs no explanation.

4. Get my driver's license.

See goal #2, above. If, no, make that "when," I go out with Julie, I must drive. Can you see it? Me at the door, picking her up. "And I'm sure, Julie, you know my father, Mr. Whipple, who will be our driver and chaperon for this evening. You may call him Wallace." No way! Getting my license is, as I see it, the key to opening my social life, the transformation from ugly duckling to studly swan. It will be an emergence, a new social force. My learner's permit up to this point has been enough to avoid ridicule from my friends, but I need my license!

5. Get my Eagle Scout award.

It will take some doing, but I can nail this one. I want to have it before basketball, dating, and eating more Mexican food consumes an even greater portion of my life than now.

MONDAY, DECEMBER 31

The big New Year's Eve Dance tonight at the stake center, and my confidence is soaring.

Had a great omen. I cut myself shaving!

I haven't shaved in . . . let's just say it's been a while. So I had a face full of iron filings, sandpaper tough. I ask Dad if I can borrow his razor and shaving cream. He looks at my beard for a second and says, yeah, he's noticed that I was looking pretty scruffy. So I wet down my face, and on the first swoop under my chin, I catch a nick, and it starts to bleed! This is totally excellent!

At the dance, girls will see the cut and ask what it is. Then I will tell them, very casually, that I cut myself while shaving. They'll go nuts. It's like being injured in a football game. Something very male.

I studied my cut in the mirror tonight, and I think I look even better with it. What a break! I have this feeling that everything is going to go more than okay for me tonight. My first shaving cut, and it happens the night of a big dance.

Is this great, or what!

CHAPTER 5

JAnUaRy

TUESDAY, JANUARY 1

There's this thing about stake dances and me. We don't seem to get along very well.

I haven't been to many, but they have begun to take on a monotonous pattern.

Step 1: My dad drives us to the dance. Lumpy is along. About a block away from the stake center, I tell Dad we're close enough and that we don't mind walking the rest of the way. Dad, being cool, says okay, and pulls over. It's a matter of Lumpy and me being males old enough to drive but not having our licenses. It's not cool to be seen being dropped off at a stake dance by a parent.

Step 2: Lumpy and I walk to the church. We talk about checking out the girls and who we hope will be there. We talk about how we are going to make such a great impression that every girl at the dance will be brokenhearted unless we pay attention to her.

147

We speak of the heavy burden of social responsibility we bear, and how we must be certain to dance with a few of the socially impaired girls there because it is the right thing to do. Besides, it will demonstrate how sensitive we are.

Step 3: We arrive at the cultural hall. Lumpy immediately heads for the kitchen to find out what the refreshments are. I walk into the dance and try my hardest to look very casual.

Step 4: Lumpy reports on the refreshments.

Step 5: We think about asking some girls to dance.

Step 6: We decide it is too early to dance because not everyone is there yet.

Step 7: We think about dancing, but decide it is not the right song.

Step 8: We think about dancing, but decide the girls we wanted to ask are already dancing with some other guys.

Step 9: We think about dancing, but it is time for refreshments and decide to wait until after we eat.

Step 10: Refreshments.

Step 11: We think about dancing, but decide we are too full from refreshments and we don't want to get a sideache.

Step 12: We think about dancing, but figure it is too stuffy, so we walk outside to get some fresh air.

Step 13: We think about dancing, but decide there aren't any good songs being played that night.

Step 14: It is the last song of the night, most of the girls are already on the floor, and we think about going home so nobody will see that we didn't drive.

Step 15: The closing prayer is said, and we hustle out to the parking lot, where my dad, being cool, has parked as far away as possible from the door to the stake center. "How did it go, guys?" he asks. "Great," we reply in unison. Later, Lumpy and I will talk about how we really dazzled the girls and how we can hardly wait for the next stake dance.

Right.

The New Year's Eve dance followed the pattern. The only variation came when Amy Hassett walked over my way (actually she trapped me in the corner as I cowered) and said, "Wally, you're such a wall-flower. Let's dance."

"Who me? Dance? Ha! Dance? Ha!"

With that, Amy grabbed my hand, and we headed to the floor, and I sort of thrashed around while try-ing to look cool. That was it. Nobody noticed the cut on my chin except Lumpy, who asked me if I had a new zit. All that blood in vain.

So here it is, January 1, and Dad and Chuck are doing what all fathers and sons should be doing this day, watching football. But, I'm up in my room, scrib-bling in my journal, brooding. In the great transmis-sion of life, I am continually stuck in neutral.

Am I weird?

Take a look at the evidence.

Frank Sinatra and Perry Como are two of my fa-vorite singers. Most guys my age don't even know who they are. I tried to lip-synch my way through boys choir. Deep in my soul, I think I can be a bas-ketball star, but I'm hanging by a thread to my third-string position on the sophomore team. I'm absolutely head over heels in *like* with a girl to whom I have spoken a grand total of six sentences, and only two of them in understandable English. I send Christmas cards to my friends. I practice looking ruggedly hand-some in the mirror. I have these huge impulses to do great things, like solve the economic problems of Central America or invent a cure for acne, but I can't solve the problem of asking a girl to dance. And this is just the short list.

Is this normal? Is all of this really happening to me?

Being a teenager isn't always a lot of fun. Oh, yeah, I know what the TV commercials make it out to be. Volleyball on the beach with all these fantastic-looking girls; drink the right soda pop and you'll be elected student body president; use the socially cor-rect toothpaste, and you'll kiss the girl good night on the doorstep on your first date. But is that real life? It isn't the life that Wallace F. Whipple is experiencing.

I look at Natalie, and she is so comfortable around kids her age. She would have known not to wear a suit to school if she were in my place. She would have blown off the coach's rah-rah talk and known she would have played anyway. She would have laughed about it with her friends and made fun of anybody who did wear a suit. But me? I was born to wear a suit to school on the day of my first basketball game.

Maybe it's genetics. Maybe some people have a DNA molecule with the word *cool* printed on it in very tiny letters. You've got the word, you're okay, you're cool. You don't have it, you're out of luck, doomed to eternal nerdiness, a dork of the highest order.

Is that me?

I don't know. Maybe it is. I think it is. But I cling

to this thin hope that I will be okay someday, that it will all come to me and make sense, that I will know my place in the universe.

A place in the universe. Is it too much to ask?

WEDNESDAY, JANUARY 2

No time to recover from the holidays. Back to school today.

I was in a deep sleep when Dad came up to get me started. You know the feeling, stones tied to arms and legs, nothing but peaceful blackness all around, complete oblivion.

Then, there is Dad. "Time to get rolling, Wally."

"Grustime ta et brekfust?"

"Yes, Wally. I have some breakfast downstairs."

"Thans, Dath. Boy, ammi ever tire."

The highlight of my day was seeing Orville at seminary. He called me yesterday to ask if seminary was still on, and I told him I was unaware of any major changes in church policy over the holidays, so I'd see him there.

Orville was waiting for us as Lumpy and I straggled in from the car.

"You boys look like you could use some toughening up."

"Yeah, Orv. We're not that tough, especially at this hour," I mumbled.

I had told Brother McNair that a visitor might be coming, and he was really pumped about it. Everybody remembered Orv from our service project at the Bradshaw's, but Brother McNair asked him to tell the class a little about himself, which he did, ending up with, "So here I am, and I'll be pleased to meetcha as time slides by."

He smiled, then clomped over and sat down by me. It was kind of like having a celebrity in class. Orville had acquired a certain amount of instant fame when he flattened Les Lorris. Most of the class took the time to say hello, which made me—and Orv—feel pretty good about his first morning.

I've had these secret plans about Orv, getting him to seminary first, having him get to know some of the kids, then getting the missionaries to teach him. This is another of those rare cases where sneakiness is probably okay. Orv is a great guy. All along, I have thought I've been doing him a favor and that he was learning a lot by hanging out with Lumpy and me.

Now, I'm thinking it works both ways. We're learning a lot from him.

THURSDAY, JANUARY 3

Mr. Ashbury called me up to the piano today. I swallowed, imagining he was going to say something like, "Wally, I've made a terrible mistake. You were right to lip-synch the first term. You have a terrible voice, and the choir was better off without you singing. I would like to request you resume only mouthing the words."

But no. He told me that he appreciated me trying and that I was bound to raise my grade up to a C.

I could barely contain my excitement.

FRIDAY, JANUARY 4

Orville says it's no big deal but that he is going to

be wrestling on Friday. Apparently, he has worked himself up to the first team. Lumpy and I decided we'd go and watch him after school.

"Shucks, it ain't no big whup," he protested when I told him we'd be there to cheer him on. "It's still just throwing little biddy city boys around." Still, I think he was glad he'd have someone there pulling for him.

Orville's match was near the end, and nobody there will ever forget it. First, he walks out to the ref's circle, a big grin on his face. He listens to the ref while the guy he's going to wrestle does the head game on him—glaring at him and trying to look tough. Orville either doesn't notice or isn't fazed by it because he continues smiling and acting more like he was on a summer picnic. This seems to infuriate his opponent all the more, who starts pawing at the mat, putting on a tremendously ugly face, and kind of snorting. Just before they begin, the ref tells them to shake hands.

"Howdy, pardner, I'm Orville Burrell from Heppner, Oregon. Pleased to meetcha and I hope to give you a good workout. I ain't been wrasslin' long, but I'm used to doggin' steers, so no offense, but I don't think you'll be as tough."

The other guy just stares with his mouth open, psyched out of his head.

The whistle blows, and the other guy makes some moves. Orville just sort of spins away from him, still grinning and looking like he's having a great time.

The other guy gets into some serious grunting and grabbing. He pulls Orv onto the mat and gets a point out of it. Orv gives us a look as if to say, "Okay, he's had his fun, but it's time to get this over and go fetch supper." He wraps his opponent in his thick arms and flips him over on his back. Orville then pounces on him and twists the guy's arms back. He has no more chance than an insect pinned to a mounting board. The ref gets on his knees, counts three, and Orville has won his first match by a pin, less than a minute into it. Orville then extends his hand to his vanquished opponent, helps him up, and, in the most sincere voice imaginable, says, "Hope I didn't hurt you none, pardner. You're a mighty feisty little guy." This to a guy who is in the same weight class as Orv, about 190 pounds.

He walks off the mat, mouths the words, "Piece of cake" to Lumpy and me, then sits down calmly on the bench while his teammates pound him, and the coach is left scratching his head, trying to sort out what he has just seen.

Orville will go a long way in wrestling this year. Like he says, it ain't nothin' like wrasslin' a steer.

SUNDAY, JANUARY 6

Natalie has been assigned a talk in church in three weeks. For most people, this is not a big deal. But my dear sister is not most people.

Natalie, you see, has decided that she should give a talk on cheerleading.

"You can't do that!" I protest. "You're just using your talk to show off and let everyone in the ward know that you're a cheerleader. That's not right. It's immature." I thought the word *immature* might get to her. It didn't.

"You're just jealous because you're not a cheerleader," she fired back.

"Jealous! I don't want to be a cheerleader. I think cheerleading is stupid. I have no desire to jump around and yell silly things while dressed in clothes that would otherwise mortify me. You're trying to change the subject."

"I am not," she huffed.

"You are, too."

"Am not."

After about sixteen more exchanges, exactly like the above, I changed tactics. "Cheerleading is not a gospel topic. You can't talk about it in church. It would be like me talking about jump shots or how to fix a flat tire. They are temporal topics."

"I can talk about anything I want. I have my free agency, or have you forgotten? And it's a free country, too."

"Natalie!"

"Wally!"

With that, she stomped off and went to her room. Mom came in and asked what was going on. "She wants to give a talk in church on cheerleading."

"That might be cute," Mom said. "And she does have her free agency."

I gave up. I went outside for a walk. Sometimes you've got to face the fact that you're going to lose a few.

Especially when you tangle with Natalie.

THURSDAY, JANUARY 10

More basketball blues.

Oh, yeah, I did get into a game. I'm official now.

We dropped our third straight, this one by thirty-four points. Massacre City.

Anyway, the other team is using us to mop the floor, we're behind by a zillion points, and everyone on our team has played, except for Andy Salisbury and me. There are forty-four seconds left, and Coach Ackley barks out, "Whipple! Salisbury!"

We rip off our sweats, which are at least thirty years old and smell worse than the locker room. Andy and I obediently trot up to the coach, trying to look as though this is not a big deal. "You guys go in for Stratton and Samuelson. Get us back into this thing!"

Okay, Coach. Let's see. We are down by three dozen points, and there is less than a minute to play. Perhaps if Andy and I come up with a thirty-point play, the score will at least be respectable. I file through my mental list of thirty-point plays and find nothing. Not to worry, Coach Ackley, we'll take care of it.

The ball rolls out of bounds, the ref waves us in, and we hustle onto the court, much to the chagrin of Stratton and Samuelson, who figure that being replaced by us is the ultimate insult.

Anyway, I did get my hands on the ball once, threw a pass to Andy, who threw a pass to another teammate, who threw a pass out of bounds. The other team gets the ball, comes down, shoots, and misses. One of our guys gets the ball, throws a long pass to Andy, who nails a jump shot just before the buzzer, to pull us within thirty-four. The crowd, all twenty or so of them, goes nuts because everyone loves to see a third-string player score. Actually, it was the highlight of the game for us, and it may be the highlight of the entire season. That's how bad we are. While I was truly happy to see my bench soul mate make a basket, I also think I'd rather sit on the bench than be put into a game with forty-four seconds left and down by thirty-six points.

Oh, well. Look at it this way. While I was on the court, we outscored the other team 2–0. Can't blame the loss on Andy and me.

FRIDAY, JANUARY 11

At lunch today:

Lumpy: "Why don't you ask her out? That's the only way you'll know if she really likes you."

Me: "Well, I don't know. I mean, I think she likes me, but I don't know if she *likes* me."

Lumpy: "You can't wait the whole year and never find out. Get it over with. If she says something like, no, she's busy for the next sixteen weeks of her life, or that she can't go out with you because her Aunt Matilda is in town for the evening, then you take it as a bad sign and figure she doesn't like you."

Me: "I suppose . . . but what if she doesn't *like* me?"

Orville: "Whaddya mean, if she doesn't like you?"

Lumpy: "It's not just liking someone, it's *liking* someone. There's a difference."

Me: "Yeah. Big difference between the two."

Orville: "I think I got it. Someone can like someone but not *like* someone, and someone can like someone but really *like* someone."

Me: "Sort of."

Orville: "I'm as confused as a snake that grows feet."

Lumpy: "Well, are you going to show some guts, or are you going to be a wimp and just wander around staring at her in seminary and walking by her locker three times a day, just to see if you can bump into her?"

Me: "Ha! That's ridiculous. Me, hanging around her locker? Ha! I have some pride, you know."

This is, however, a complete lie, and I will need to repent soon. Not only do I change my route at least three times a day at school just to walk by Julie's locker on the slim chance that I will catch a glimpse of her, I also occasionally walk six blocks out of my way on the trip home so that I can stroll by her house. I have high hopes that someday she will come out and say, "Wally, I've noticed you look a little tired. Being a basketball star probably takes a lot out of you. Would you like to come into my house for dinner and meet my parents?"

That's not all of it. I know who her younger brother and sister are, where her dad's office is, and that her mother's first name is Carolyn. I know that Julie's birthday is June 14th. Strange, I know, but being in *like* does crazy things to you, including practically forcing you to tell white lies to friends at lunch.

Lumpy: "So you gonna do it?"

Me: "Well . . . "

Orville: "Doesn't 'pear to be too tough. Jus' sashay on up to her and say, 'Missy, I was wonderin' if you'd do me the honor of goin' out come Saturday.'"

Me: "Okay, okay. I'll do it. I'll ask her out."

Lumpy: "Knew you had it in you."

Orville: "You're riding high in the saddle, pardner."

All right. I'll ask Julie out. I made a promise to my
friends, even if it was under some duress. There is but
one choice. I am a man of honor, except for the occasional untruth that tumbles out of my mouth, the
most recent of which tumbled out about forty-five seconds ago.

Of course, I didn't say *when* I'd ask her out. Is a
year after my mission too soon?

SUNDAY, JANUARY 13

The great debate between Natalie and me about
her talk rages on. I have heard her through the bathroom door, practicing in front of the mirror. She can't
decide how to begin. Some of her choices:

"As many of you know, I am privileged to be a
cheerleader . . . "

"As I was at cheerleading practice Wednesday
night, the thought occurred to me . . . "

"Cheerleading requires hard work, dedication, enthusiasm, unselfishness, and commitment. It is like the
church in many ways."

"For those of you who do not know, I have been
blessed with the opportunity to be a cheerleader."

"When I was elected to be a cheerleader, I was
really humbled."

And then there is my favorite, "Cheerleading is a
lot like life."

TUESDAY, JANUARY 15

In the hall, after seminary today, Joe stopped me. "How are the hoops going, Wally?"

For a brief second, I have an impulse to stretch things a bit, like saying I had an off game and only scored twenty-one points last week. But why fib? All Joe has to do is look at the season scoring summary on the locker room door, and he'll see that my name is followed by a long string of zeroes. But Joe is so cool that maybe he'll understand. So I fess up.

"Not so good, Joe. I haven't played much. Like one minute this season."

Joe nods slowly. "Ackley?"

"Yeah."

"You have my sympathy."

"I don't think he's too swift of a coach."

"He wouldn't know a good player if he saw one. When he was my coach, he hardly played me, either, and I've done okay since. Hang in there, dude."

"Yeah. I'll hang in there."

Suddenly, I have hope. Maybe it *is* the coach and not me. I can only hope. In the meantime, I'll hang in there, though it is getting tougher every day.

FRIDAY, JANUARY 18

Another moment of truth is near. Grades are being sent home today.

Having been humbled once, I am not eager to predict how I will do. Nevertheless, Wallace Whipple can take whatever life dishes out, with only minimal whimpering. Most of the time.

My grades should go something like this.

Boys Choir. No surprise. Mr. Ashbury has all but guaranteed me a C.

Still, this bothers me somewhat. What happens if I die tomorrow? I've read that music is a big part on the other side. A C in choir may not look good.

Pearly Gates Guy: "I see that you lived a good life. You were kind to most people, with the exception of your sister, Natalie, but we can overlook that. We have quite a file on her, you know. You helped the poor, supported your parents, and didn't give them too many gray hairs. You ran cross-country, even though you weren't very good. That shows perseverance. You had a genuine impulse to try to help Third World nations, and you were an exceptional big brother to Chuck. Not a bad life, Wallace."

Me: "Thank you, sir."

Pearly Gates Guy: "Hmmmm. I see you only managed a C in choir, however. We're big on music up here. Good music, that is. Like the Tabernacle Choir, Mozart, Bach, Mahler, and Tony Bennett. A C in choir. Mmmmm. I think for starters, Wallace, we're going to have to knock you down a few places until you can show us that you are ready for our style of music here."

Me: "Thank you, sir."

Pearly Gates Guy: "The elevator is over there. Press the down arrow, please."

Me: "Thank you, sir."

Pearly Gates Guy: "And knock off the 'sir' stuff."

This brings me to Social Studies. I think this may be an A. Mrs. Aparicio and I have connected since day one. No worse than a B here, anyway.

P.E. Another A. Take it to the bank.

Health. Probably a B. Mr. Catton is a plain, old, tough grader. The only guy who got an A last quarter was Alvin Hashburn. Alvin is the kind who always stays late to chat with the teacher and cleans the erasers at the end of the day. There are limits to what I'll do for a grade, understand?

English. My favorite class and my favorite teacher. Still, I think I'll only get a B. I need to put a little bit more of my heart and soul into it for an A.

Math will be a B. Thank you, Edwina Purvis. I've started calling her on the phone when I'm stuck on a problem, and she talks me through it. I'm learning as much from her as from the teacher. And Ed is so nice about it. Never a hint of an attitude. "Wally, don't you have it down, yet? Run out of fingers and toes?" It's always, "Hi, Wally! Oh sure, I can help you on that one."

Let's see. Two A's, three B's, and a C. Quick—call Ed and find out what my GPA is. Naw, let's see. Divide by 23, add a second integer, take the square root and dip it in root beer, throw a side of beef into it for good measure, and it comes out to a 3.2. Still not enough to get into Harvard, but up considerably from last quarter. We'll check the mailbox on Monday and see how close I came.

SUNDAY, JANUARY 20

I met with Brother Hansen today, and we came up with a few more details on my Eagle Scout project. There is a rock shelter on the slopes of Mt. Hood that needs some restoration. It's a safe spot for climbers who get trapped by sudden storms. Mt.

Hood is really a deceiving spot. You can start to climb it in the morning, and the weather will be clear and warm. Then a storm comes busting in from the Pacific, and people are suddenly in trouble, big time. The little stone house has fallen into disrepair, and my project is to raise some money through a cookie sale, then get the troop to head up there in the summer and make the repairs. Good project, huh?

One of the keys to this is my mother, who happens to be the world's best (and this is not an exaggeration) chocolate chip cookie baker. I figure that if I hand out a few samples, we'll have people lined up outside of our house asking for a dozen. They're so good that Brother Hansen (who has been to our house and sampled Mom's cookies—says it's part of his calling) thinks we can charge $5 a dozen.

I'm glad to get this plan down cold. I want to get my Eagle before much longer because I know other things will soon interfere and make it difficult to wrap it up. Things such as starring on the basketball team (Ha!), more homework, maybe a job, and lots of time spent with Julie.

Lots of time with Julie Sloan? Did I write that?

MONDAY, JANUARY 21

Came home from basketball practice. I walked in through the back door. Mom and Natalie were talking, and I could tell that it wasn't the most pleasant conversation in history. I came through the door and the talk stopped.

"Oh, hello, Wally. How was your day? Your report card came, but we didn't open it."

"Day was fine, Mom. I'm kind of tired, so I think I'll go to my room and crash for a minute."

I left, then heard Mom say to Natalie, "That's it. No more conversation. Wally is very sweet, and I want you to show some kindness to him for a change."

I'm not sure exactly what the conversation was all about, but I noticed that Natalie came to dinner a few minutes later, wearing the blouse I bought her for Christmas, the one with her name stitched across the back.

Funny thing, Natalie didn't talk much at dinner.

TUESDAY, JANUARY 22

Yes, we are feeling a little pressure. I spent a good share of Monday evening in my room looking at the envelope with my report card in it. Mom and Dad are cool. Sure, they want to know how I did, but they also respect me as a semi-adult who shaves and is almost ready to date and who wants all people everywhere, with the exception of Les Lorris, to be successful. So they never look at the report card first, and it gives me a chance to think up excuses.

Me: "The reason I got a D in choir is that the teacher is a very hard grader and the class comes early in the morning. My vocal cords are not warmed up. I tend to croak. The other guys look at me funny, and so I decided to not sing loud. Like, not sing at all. Which the teacher, Mr. Ashbury, noticed, because he is paid to notice things like that. So I look at my poor grade in the class as a sacrifice for the rest of the choir. I take the bad grade in order for the choir to sound better. That's the kind of son you have. Always putting others first. Do you understand what I mean?"

Mom and Dad in unison: "No!"

Anyway, I waited until this morning to open it. My rationale was simple. If I get worse grades than I thought, I will brood all night and not get much sleep. I will be tired and fall asleep in class, thus contributing to my downward spiral. Case #2. If my grades are better than I thought, I will be too excited and not sleep well. I will be tired and fall asleep in class, thus contributing to my downward spiral. In either instance, I lose. Therefore, the prudent man only has one logical choice, wait until morning.

I did. Now . . . drum roll . . . shine the light . . . ladies and gentlemen, we have an important announcement to make. We'll save the news from the Middle East and get back to the Super Bowl game in a few minutes. Listen up, Wallace Whipple **DID BETTER THAN HE THOUGHT HE WOULD ON HIS REPORT CARD!**

Yes! The sweet feeling of triumph. I want to break into a chorus (however off-key) of "We Shall Overcome." There *is* joy in life. I can look Julie square in the eye, and say, "You are not going to marry a dummy, whether it is Joe Vermeer, or me."

Mr. Ashbury—sweet, sainted man that he is, gave me a B.

That brings the old GPA to a respectable and shining 3.33.

My next move was to leave the report card in a fairly conspicuous place. How about taped to my parent's bedroom door? No, how about the bathroom door, which surely receives more traffic? Be subtle,

Whipple. Be reserved in victory. The refrigerator door. The perfect place, where everyone will see it.

So that's where I taped it, just before leaving this morning. Mom noticed it. Dad noticed it. Chuck saw it. Even Natalie said, "Wow!" You did audaciously better on your report card, Wally."

I feel good. But I need to get some rest. If I don't, I'll fall asleep and begin the downward spiral.

Whipple, don't fall off the mountain before you even get to the top!

WEDNESDAY, JANUARY 23

So I just happened to be wandering around by Julie's locker after lunch, and she just sort of happened to be there. Lumpy and Orville had already peeled off for class, and the hallway was almost vacant, except for Sister Sloan and me.

Seize the moment, Whipple.

Okay, be cool, I tell myself. Do not start speaking in Swedish. Go up to her and say something very clever, something that will immediately draw her into a witty conversation, which will naturally lend itself into asking her out for a date. Yes, this is my game plan.

"Julie, so is this your locker?"

Dismal, really dismal, Whipple. What do you think? She's twirling the combination of a locker that isn't her own?

"Hi, Wally. Yes, this is my locker. I thought you knew that because it seems like I've seen you around here before."

"Uh, not exactly. I mean not right here, standing

with you and talking about your locker. It's a nice locker, though."

My confidence is failing.

Every locker is exactly the same at Benjamin Franklin, all painted the dullest gray imaginable. There is no such thing as a nice locker anywhere in the entire building. In the great conversation of life, I am afflicted with chronic laryngitis.

"I guess it is a nice locker. I haven't really thought about it much."

I need to make a comeback and make it fast. What would Joe Vermeer say? I seize the thought as a drowning man clutches a life preserver.

"Yo, Julie," I blurt out.

She stares at me. "Did you say yo?"

"Yeah, I said yo."

"Oh. Yo. Joe says that a lot."

"Right. Joe Yo. Joe knows yo."

"Yeah, Joe knows yo."

She giggles. A breakthrough. For a moment, my confidence slows its rapid descent. How lucky do I feel? Should I ask her out? Think of what Lumpy and Orville would say at lunch tomorrow if I very casually said, "By the way, Julie and I are going out this weekend."

They'd gag on their corn dogs. They'd fall off their chairs.

"Hey, I told you I'd ask her out. You doubted the Whipple man?" I'd say, with just a touch of in-your-face in my voice.

Go for it, Whipple. She's here. You're here. Two people, traveling through time and space, meeting at this precise moment at this exact spot. Fate has it that you will ask her out NOW.

"Julie . . . I was wondering if . . . " my voice falters as my heart races toward the two hundred beats per minute range. Think of Nephi. He really didn't want to go back for the plates of Laban, but he knew it had to be done. This is the same situation. Well, sort of. This has to be done.

"If what, Wally?" She looks at me with the most beautiful brown eyes I've ever seen. Is that perfume I smell, or am I imagining things?

"If you . . . saw the movie that was on channel 10 last night."

She looks disappointed. "No. I studied right up to Young Womens last night and didn't have time for much television."

"Well, that's okay because I didn't see it either."

The bell rang. She told me she had to scoot to her next class. I told her it was a coincidence because I also had to scoot to my next class. "Just a couple of scooters, I guess," I rambled, forcing a small laugh.

"Right, Wally."

I made some geeky scooting motion down the hallway while every sweat gland in my body went on red alert.

Once again, I have shown the uncanny ability to freeze at the critical moment, to moisten my foot with my mouth, to say things that make no sense whatsoever at a crucial point.

I'm beginning to think it's a curse. There are certain brain cells that function normally, just sort of buzz around in the gray matter, until I am ready to make an impression on Julie. Then they all stop dead in their tracks, and say, "Let's get the kid again. This is so fun! Can you believe what a dork he is without us?" They halt the billions of tiny electrical charges that link my brain and tongue and I'm left on my own—a babbling idiot.

Just once, I'd like to get my brain and body in synch when I talk with Julie.

THURSDAY, JANUARY 24

My relationship with Natalie at the moment is somewhat strained. For awhile, things were getting better between us, but her ego, which was already world-class before being selected a cheerleader, has grown to the dimension of a mid-sized military installation. Part of the problem, I admit, is that I'm not exactly looking for the best in her. Tonight was an example of how we are bringing out the worst in each other. It started after dinner.

"Do you think Orville would like to come to church on Sunday?"

"Why? Just to hear you talk?"

"No. I thought he'd like to come to church since he's been going to seminary in the morning. It seems like the next step for him."

"You just want to show off for him."

"That's not true. Even if I weren't speaking, I'd . . . well, I'd like to see him come anyway. He'd be a good Mormon."

"I have an idea. Let's go down to the newspaper tomorrow and place an ad in the religion section for Saturday. It will say, 'Come and hear the thrilling story of how cheerleading saved a soul. Listen to Natalie

Whipple explain how she became a better person by jumping around and waving her pom-poms.'"

"You're not sensitive. All you can think about is pizza and basketball."

"Ha! That's a revelation coming from you. You only care about mirrors, clothes, and guys."

And on we went, generally behaving like children. Maybe that's an insult to Chuck, though. He doesn't act like that.

I spoke with Dad about Natalie's talk. He agrees that she might be doing the right thing for the wrong reason. "But your mom and I have decided just to let her do what she thinks is best. Natalie is old enough to know what is right and old enough to recognize her motives," Dad said.

I need to ease up on Natalie a bit. Maybe it was my own ego that got in the way. I saw something that I thought was wrong and kind of got steamed over it, not really thinking about her feelings.

Who needs to change here? Both of us?

FRIDAY, JANUARY 25

Orville is becoming "big-time" at Benjamin Franklin High School.

He wrestled again last night and went through the same routine, right down to shaking hands and booming out a, "Pleased to meetcha," before apologizing to his opponent for what he was about to do to him. It's not a show with Orville, either. He's not trying to get the mental edge. It's just the way he is. And the kids at school are catching on to it.

Wrestling attendance has doubled. Granted, forty

people isn't exactly a mob, but it's better than the pre-Orville days. And whenever he's about to wrestle, you can hear the chant, "Orville! ORVILLE! ORVILLE!!!" When he wins, the crowd goes nuts.

Orv just smiles and gives his big old cowboy wave to the stands. The coach used to try to give him all these tips on techniques, but now he just sits back and watches. Orville is a natural and almost playful on the mat, letting the guy he's wrestling try a few moves, before he puts him away. "Don't want to hurt them fellers' feelings," he explains. Orv hasn't lost yet. In fact, he's won all his matches by pins. He may make the varsity before the season is over.

I see some of the really popular kids at school starting to pay a lot of attention to him, and while he's polite to everyone, he still hangs out mostly with Lumpy and me. Add "loyalty" to his list of good characteristics.

Natalie is right about one thing: Orville *would* make a darn good Mormon.

SUNDAY, JANUARY 27

Okay. Wallace Whipple is a big man. He knows and can admit when he's wrong. So I will say this for the record.

Natalie gave a good talk.

My sister, the mall princess who loves clothes and being seen with the right people above all, gave a good talk on the theme of cheerleading.

She started off by saying, "As some of you know, I am a cheerleader at school." I nudged my dad and rolled my eyes. This was a train wreck coming, I could feel it. Then she went on. "Our basketball team isn't very good. In fact, we've won only one game. Sometimes it gets hard to cheer and put a lot of energy into it when your team is getting beat, but that's really the time they need to be cheered up. Anyone can cheer for a winner."

Then she went on and told about one of her friends whose parents are going through a divorce. She said that she made it a point to sit by her friend every day at lunch and mostly just listen to her.

I didn't know my sister had that in her.

Then Natalie related how the Savior went to people who were the sinners and outcasts, the people who were down, and gave them a message of hope.

I was impressed by this time. Mom and Dad were grinning. I wished Orville *had* come. I knew I would have to begin repenting.

She concluded by saying that the most important kind of cheerleader isn't the person who shouts encouragement to a team but is the one who is sensitive and will help people to feel better about themselves when they are discouraged.

I said, "Amen."

On the way home, I sort of apologized to her. "That was a good talk, Nat. I didn't think you were going to work a church theme into cheerleading so well, but you did a great job. Sorry about the hard time I gave you. Even a guy who is almost perfect can have an off day."

She looked at me with supreme indifference, then fluffed her hair and inspected her fingernails. "Never doubt Natalie Whipple. Never."

After today, I don't think I'll dare.

MONDAY, JANUARY 28

The key word here is *if*.

If I read Julie's face correctly last week in the hall-way, she was disappointed that I didn't ask her out. Is this my imagination? I don't think so.

Why is this important in my life right now? Because the "Anything Goes Dance" is coming up in two weeks. About ten years ago, the student body of Benjamin Franklin High School, in a rare display of unity, decided to put an end to the funny little Valentine cupids with hardly any clothes on who shoot arrows of love. Enough of the mushy love junk, let's do something fun, was the general idea. That was the beginning of the "Anything Goes Dance." Girls ask boys. Dress in a tux or your P.E. uniform. Bring a bag of hamburgers to the gym for refreshments. Get it? Anything goes, as long as it is not illegal or danger-ous.

So I harbor this hope that IF I read things right in the hallway, and IF Julie sort of wants to go out with me, and IF she thinks about the "Anything Goes Dance," THEN she has but one choice. Ask Wallace Fremont Whipple, Jr. Fate has brought us together. Our *like* is greater than my irrational fears of talking to her.

This is going to be a nerve-wracking week. I have to act cool and not blow my chance. This brings me to the next topic on my mind, How to Act Cool Instantly.

1. I will act more mature. This means no bubble gum in class, wishing success for everyone, and not putting my mouth down to plate level in the cafeteria.

2. I will shave more often. This needs no explanation.

3. I will speak in fragments and short sentences. Yo, woman. Hey. Comin' your way. Dude. Totally righteous. Et cetera.

4. Dress better. No shirts with pockets at school. Nothing green. Nothing pressed. Nothing that looks new.

5. Answer more questions in seminary. To show that, even though I am getting cooler by the minute, I am still a spiritual guy underneath and have my priorities straight.

The dance is Friday, February 15. Yo. I'll be there. And it will be totally righteous, dude.

TUESDAY, JANUARY 29

I got a pep talk today about basketball, and my life will never be the same.

No, it didn't come from Coach Ackley, my teammates, or even Lumpy.

It came from my mom.

"I've seen you at a couple of games now, Wally, and you don't have any enthusiasm," she told me tonight while I was doing the dishes. "You've always been so excited about basketball and enjoyed playing. Now, even in warm-ups, you just look like you're going through the motions."

"Hey. That's because I know I won't play, Mom. No use in breaking my back in warm-ups and then sitting on the bench the whole game. Yo."

"Wallace. With that attitude, I wouldn't play you, either."

Ouch. That hurt. Benched by my own mother.

"If I can see you've got a bad attitude, then your coach surely can. You've been feeling sorry for yourself ever since you wore your suit to school. You've got to put that behind you and try harder."

This is what I call an FBL—a full-blown lecture. That's when a parent sees something in your life that they determine is very, very wrong, and they want to call your attention to it, now! Every parent gives an FBL, occasionally. I think it is part of being a parent, although when I am one, it will be different.

I hate FBLs.

"Yo, Mom. He has me playing the wrong position. I'm a natural guard, but he plays me at center where everyone is about five inches taller than me and sixty pounds heavier. I can't do anything against the bigger guys."

"YES YOU CAN! Where's the fire, Wally? Since when do you back off from a challenge? Maybe you can't score a touchdown, but you can at least let them know you're out there. Why don't you push someone? At least then, the ref will blow his whistle, and you'll get something beside your name in the scorebook."

She's right on this count. I have been bothered by the string of zeroes next to my name in the team scoring summary. A foul, though not as glamorous as a basket or a rebound, would at least break up the long string of ciphers. Okay, Mom. I will foul someone next time I get the chance, though it is a little weird to think that your mom is suggesting that you throw an elbow or shove someone.

"I want you to try harder on Thursday. I know

you're a good player and that your coach hasn't given you much of a chance, but you need to create an opportunity for yourself."

"Okay, Mom. Yo. I will try."

"And stop saying yo. It's a silly word."

"Totally righteous, Mom."

End of FBL. Phew!

By the way, no phone calls from Julie asking me to the dance. Not yet, anyway.

WEDNESDAY, JANUARY 30

The FBL worked. Yeah, I'm not crazy about writing this, but Mom was right.

I made it a point to be a lot more active in warm-ups today. I cheered and clapped for my teammates. When the game started, instead of taking my usual spot next to Andy at the end of the bench, I plopped down right next to Coach Ackley.

And I got to play.

Three glorious minutes! We were behind by seventeen, and the coach, in a fit of disgust, cleared the bench. "Whipple, go in at center. You're quicker than that guy. Get us a couple of buckets."

So I went in. Now, the big guy playing center for Jefferson High almost started to laugh when I trotted onto the floor. Thoughts of breaking my noodle-like body in half obviously flashed through his mind. First time down the court, he posted me up, got the ball down low, and started to back in. I remembered Mom's talk. I held my turf. When he pushed, I pushed back.

And I got a foul! A sweet, delicious foul. No longer

was I Whipple, 0–0–0–0–0–0. I was Whipple, 0–0–0–0–0–1. It felt great. Coach Ackley clapped his hands. "Way to let him know you're there, Whipple!"

Later, I got my first rebound of the season. With twenty seconds left, I got the ball on the left wing and outquicked the guy to the basket. Trouble is, it had been so long since I had shot in a game that I blew the lay-up.

At the end of the game, Coach Ackley slapped me on the rear end and said, "Nice hustle, Whipple. Wish it would rub off on the rest of the team."

A faint hope glimmers that I might still play in the NBA. My once-promising career could yet be salvaged.

Give an assist to my mother. Yo!

CHAPTER 6
FebruarY

FRIDAY, FEBRUARY 1

This is one of those times when you feel the whole course of your life changing. It's kind of like the time I looked in the mirror and realized that I needed to shave. Or the time when my parents told me I was going to have a new baby brother or sister. Or when my ophthalmologist cleared his throat, and said, "You'll need to wear glasses in a year or two, Son." All of a sudden, I have seen myself in a different way, and I realize that somehow I'll never be able to return to what I have been. This kind of news will never be recorded in the *New York Times* or even in the *Mosquito Valley Gazette.* Still, my life's star has veered into a slightly different orbit.

I got asked to the "Anything Goes Dance."

But not by Julie Sloan.

By Ed Purvis, girl math genius.

I was at home, minding my own business, plumb

tuckered out, all done in for the week. (Am I beginning to sound like Orville, or what?)

The phone rings. Natalie, who gets about ninety-seven percent of our phone calls, anyway, answers it.

Someone on the phone asks for Wallace. I know, because Natalie asks, "Senior or Junior?" to differentiate between Dad and me. Nat starts giggling. "Oh, you mean sophomore." She puts down the phone. "Oh Wallace, lover boy, . . . you have a phone call. It's a G-I-R-L."

The whole family stops dead in their tracks. Dad puts down his paper. Mom looks up from her book. Chuck pulls his headphones off. They stare at me.

Shakily, I rise to my feet and begin the longest walk of my life . . . each . . . step . . . coming . . . so . . . slowly. My arms and legs feel heavy. My brain feels fuzzy. Is it Julie? Is this the big moment? Is the light of my life going to—No! Perish the thought. You are Wallace Whipple. Stuff like this just doesn't happen to you. It's probably Viola Barkle, and she wants to arm wrestle.

My throat is dry. I pick up the receiver. My dad pretends to read the paper again, and my mom blinks and turns away. Natalie is looking at me from across the room, arms folded, a slight smirk on her face. Chuck gapes open-mouthed at me, as though he has just been told his big brother is wanted for armed robbery in fourteen western states.

"Hello . . . " I croak into the phone.

"Wally? This is Edwina Purvis from math class."

A flicker of hope flashes. Maybe Ed is doing her homework and needs some help. Then reality slaps me like a two-by-four across the forehead. The world has yet to see the day when Ed Purvis will need math help from Wally Whipple. My instincts, though barely functioning, tell me what is coming next.

"You know that the 'Anything Goes Dance' is coming up in a couple of weeks, and I was wondering if you'd like to go with me?" She says it so gracefully, so effortlessly, she might have been offering me chewing gum before math class. "We could have dinner at my house, and then go to the dance. I think we'll have fun."

I've heard that powerful survival instincts can be summoned in moments of crisis. Mothers who cannot swim a stroke, plunge into raging rivers to save their children. One-hundred-pound weaklings lift the end of a car to free someone who is trapped. Maybe that happened to me. The will to keep my life intact mounded up like a huge ocean wave.

"I . . . don't . . . know," I rasp into the phone. "I think . . . my . . . Aunt . . . Matilda . . . is coming that . . . night . . . and we may . . . have . . . family plans . . . "

Family plans. A stroke of genius. No one can argue with family plans. Almost as safe as being out-of-town and better than being sick.

She sounds disappointed. "Does that mean you can't go?"

Trouble. Mom is looking at me in a way that could make a rock crumble. I realize that if I say no, I may have only seconds to live. "Mother's Stare Turns Son to Dust," the headline will read. In desperation, I grasp for the only straw that might save Ed's feelings and also save my life. "No . . . it means that I, uh, I'll tell you on Monday. I need to check with my parents."

Whew. I have at least another weekend to live, although Mom is not looking exactly loving at this moment.

"Oh. Well, that's okay. I wanted to ask you early, so that no one else would get to you first, Wally."

"Uh, thanks Ed. I hope we can work it out. Really." This is one of the bigger fabrications of my young life, a life which may rapidly be nearing its end.

We said good-bye and I hung up. I turned and faced the jury.

"What was that all about?" Mom demanded. "And exactly which side of the family is your Aunt Matilda on?"

What happened next sort of tore apart, at least temporarily, the fabric of our family. Rather than recite the painful details of the following forty-five minutes, I will only summarize the positions taken by the various participants in the "Wally-this-is-not-a-proud-moment" episode. Remember, these are only a few of the highlights, and they do not include the grimaces, hand-wringing, sneering, and looks of disdain and disappointment that were directed toward me.

MOM: "You should remember her feelings. It is most important that you do not hurt that girl's feelings in a situation like this."

DAD: "I think there is an obvious right-and-wrong choice here, Wally, and I hope you'll remember the way we've tried to rear you all these years."

NATALIE: "Is she cute? Do you know where she buys her clothes? Why does she want to go out with you, anyway? She must be weird."

CHUCK: "Why is everyone so mad at Wally?"

I have a big decision to make. This may not be the most pleasant weekend of my life.

Is all of this normal? What *is* normal?

SUNDAY, FEBRUARY 3

The subject of my possible first date never really surfaced yesterday. I think Mom and Dad had a secret talk after I went to bed on Friday and decided it was best not to mention the matter. Heck, they already got their licks in.

Even though nothing was said out loud, the tension was thick between us. I went to church today sort of hoping for inspiration. I was really hoping for someone to give a lesson or bear their testimony about free agency. Maybe an older parent, who would tell about how he once forced his teenaged son to do something that the son really didn't want to. And how he is now able to look back with the wisdom that the years have brought, and understand he should have allowed his son to use his free agency and choose for himself. And that if he had done so, great blessings would have been received by their family, and life would have been just a whole bunch better, and his son wouldn't be doing five to ten years for some horrible crime. Then my mom and dad would look at each other and nod their heads sadly. "Maybe we were too tough on him, Pamela. I think we need to apologize."

And later, when they apologized to me, I would, of course, graciously forgive them, but with a stern warning that it had better not happen again.

But no one rose to the occasion. My priesthood lesson was on tithing.

Let's go through this logically.

1. It's not that I don't like Ed. It's just that I don't *like* Ed.

2. Then there is the IF factor. What if Julie calls, sends me a telegram, or hires a skywriter to ask me out? Then I'd have to tell her no and possibly break her heart and stop a potential temple marriage dead in its tracks.

3. I like Ed, but I don't *like* Ed. Did I say that before?

4. And how about *my* feelings? Mom keeps looking at me, and I know what she is just ready to burst out with. "DON'T HURT HER FEELINGS, WALLY." Well, I've got feelings, too.

5. Then there is the first date factor. Dad told me not to worry, to go out with Ed, and that nobody will remember a few months later. Bet me. I'll remember my first date throughout the eternities, no matter who it is I go out with. I'd like it to be a nice memory.

Less than twenty-four hours to go before I give her an answer.

Maybe I'll get lucky and break a leg, catch the flu, or we will move to Wyoming before tomorrow morning. Is it okay to pray for the flu?

MONDAY, FEBRUARY 4

Early morning check-up time came when my alarm went off.

A quick pull at my bedroom curtain revealed that it did not snow last night, and I will have to go to school. For a moment, I thought maybe I was sort of a little feverish. But Mom would see right through that. And my leg felt fine, no compound fractures having occurred while I slept. Time to get up and face the music.

I told Lumpy and Orville about my dilemma on the way to school after seminary. I needed some sympathy, since my family was giving me absolutely none. As it turned out, Orv and Lumpy didn't exactly open the floodgates of compassion.

"You don't go out with Ed, then I think you're yanking off your boot socks and puttin' them on the supper table," Orville snorted.

"What?"

"He means that telling Ed no would really stink," translated Lumpy, who is becoming fluent in cowboy talk.

"How so, Orv?"

"It ain't that complicated. A nice girl asks you to dinner and a dance. You just tell her okay, then go and have a good time. You ain't acceptin' a proposal for marriage, you don't even have to like the girl all that much. Spend a nice evenin' and have a good time. It ain't that big of a whup. Jus' grab the bit in your teeth, and run with it."

"What about you, Lump?" I asked, hoping for a different opinion.

"Same thing as Orv. We know it's your first date, and you'll be flustered and incoherent for much of the night, but dating is natural for teenagers, just like eating food that isn't good for you and sleeping in on the weekends."

It seemed obvious now. There's something about hearing it from friends instead of parents.

Along comes math class, and I take my place as usual. Ed smiles and says hello. Then Mr. Herk gets right into it, and I don't have a chance to say anything to her. The class drones on, then the bell rings. Very casually, I look over at Ed, who knows that an answer is at hand.

"I checked with my parents, and I guess my aunt isn't coming. So yeah, I can go to the dance, and I think we'll have a nice time, although I don't dance very well."

She looks satisfied, and says, "Great. Glad I got you before some other girl did."

Nothing to it, I decide. Boy and girl get together. Happens millions of times all over the world every day. It's simply a case of percentages, my number coming up and joining the throngs. Piece of cake, Whipple.

Like Orville said (although I think he was simplifying it for my benefit), it ain't no big whup. On the other hand, why does my mouth feel like cotton and my heart race like a rabbit's when I think of what will happen on February 15th?

WEDNESDAY, FEBRUARY 6

I'm being calm about all of this. Mature. I am not lying awake at night and wondering what will happen in nine more days. NINE MORE DAYS! THAT'S ALL I HAVE LEFT!

I'd like to talk this over with someone, but I don't know who. Can't really do it with my parents. See, for about the last three years, I really have been kind of watching girls, and at some point decided that maybe I'd underrated them in my life. It's not the kind of thing that you can sit down and talk over with your parents, no matter if your relationship is okay or not.

ME: "Mom, Dad. Come into the living room and please be seated. Comfortable? Good. As you both know, I'm changing in many ways. I am becoming a young man. Part of my maturing process is that I have decided that females will someday be an important part of my social, cultural, and spiritual life. Wanting to be well-rounded, I just thought I should bring you into my thinking on this topic. You'll notice some changes in the next few months, as I begin to date and acquire the social polish and skills that will be integral to my future success in life. So don't be alarmed, it's a very natural thing, and I'll continue to be the same respectful, loving, and athletic son that you've come to know and grown to love over, lo, these many years."

DAD: "Thank you, son, for the update. We are vitally concerned about your life and are pleased that you are keeping us informed."

MOM: "And you've handled this so maturely, Wallace, although we're not surprised."

ME: "I appreciate that, Mother. As you know, I always attempt to be mature. I also want both of you to know that you can always talk to me, no matter what the subject. Our relationship is based on open communication. And now, shall we listen to some music? I think Tony Bennett would be appropriate."

DAD: "Splendid choice. And you may call me Wallace from now on."

Ha! We know it doesn't work that way. Just the opposite. I've been trying hard to keep my interests a secret from Mom and Dad. They don't know who Julie Sloan is, for example. I'm leading sort of a double life. Maybe it's because, although I'm sixteen, I still don't feel old enough to do things like date, show an interest in the opposite sex, or use hairspray. I mean, I feel like I'm imitating the things that I see older people doing.

And here's the part that gets me. I know that as soon as I start doing these things, I'm going to be on the path that leads to adulthood. Really. I have a hunch that when all of this teenager stuff is over, I am going to be an adult. And I'm not exactly crazy about the idea. I see what my dad goes through to provide for our family. House payments. Job. Responsibility. Insurance. Taxes. Voting. Knowing how much ice cream to buy at the store. Paying Natalie's clothing bill each month. Worry about your kids, even though they may be nearly perfect. I mean, I CAN SEE ALL THAT STUFF AND MORE AND IT NEVER LETS UP. And my thinking is, I'm not sure I want that feeling of perpetual responsibility. And I know it's going to start next week when I go on my first date. Is there no escape?

THURSDAY, FEBRUARY 7

The real sports news today belongs to Orville. The head wrestling coach said Orv was ready for the varsity. Next week, the coach promised, Orville would make his varsity debut. He'll be the only sophomore on the team. I could tell Orville was jazzed. It's not his way to show a lot of emotion, but I could tell he was pleased. "Maybe them varsity boys will give me more of a tussle," he said.

Just goes to show you can be a nice guy and still not finish last.

FRIDAY, FEBRUARY 8

Ah, Friday night, the natural habitat of the teenager.

I went to the varsity basketball game tonight. We won. Good. After sitting through loss after loss on the sophomore team, it was nice to see a Franklin team win at some level. After the game, Lumpy, Orville, and I went to Hamburger Bob's. We tried Bob's new creation, the combination burrito pizza with double onions. Not bad, though I made a mental note not to eat it within twenty-four hours of going out with Ed next Friday.

NEXT FRIDAY!

This is getting close. Why is time passing so quickly? I still keep hoping that I can find a legitimate and graceful way out of this. Faith, Whipple. You gotta believe.

After Bob's, we went to Lumpy's house and watched the late horror movie. We're sitting there watching the show, and we get onto the subject of dating. Lumpy isn't much help on the topic because he's never been on a date, so his views are purely theoretical. Orv isn't much more help, because back in Heppner, he says, "you just sort of hang out, 'cause you got to go all the way to Pendleton if you want a nice place to eat or to take in a movie that wasn't made when Moby Dick was still a minnow."

So what we came up with is this: The Beginner's Guide to Dating. And we should know, since we are all basically, beginners. We wrote the guidelines down on the back of an empty pizza box. Truthfully, the three of us combined didn't know enough about the subject to come up with anything that would be useful. We ended up throwing away our ideas along with the pizza box. We've got a lot to learn.

SUNDAY, FEBRUARY 10

Here it is Sunday, and I'm doing one of the things that doesn't break any of the major Sabbath commandments: thinking of others. I know, Whipple, what a guy.

One person in my thoughts is Chuck. He's zipping through kindergarten pretty well. Chuck is very bright. While the rest of the class is learning to count blocks, Chuck is into square roots. He got into a discussion with his teacher the other day about square roots. He told her the square root of 8 is 2.8, not 3, as she tried to tell him. Chuck's birthday is next month, and I'm wondering what I can get him. Maybe a personal computer.

Next up is Julie. I hope she isn't disappointed that she won't be going to the dance with me. Being in social demand is tough, if you're sensitive the way I am.

Natalie. She's been pretty quiet about this Friday. My hunch is that Mom pulled her aside and said something about if she teased me at all about going on a date, then she would be grounded until roughly her third year of college. The silence is eerie. I know Natalie. It is against her nature to have a once-in-a-lifetime chance to humiliate me, and not be able to take advantage of it. She must be a crazy woman inside. I love it.

Orville. He keeps coming to seminary, though he doesn't say much about it. I wonder if he's really a religious guy. He could still have his pick of friends to run around with, but he stays loyal to Lumpy and me. He's true blue.

Edwina. Five more days. My first date: an event that will be recorded and remembered forever. Mom keeps looking at me and smiling and saying things like, "Gosh, you sure are going to have a good time on Friday. I almost wish I could come along, too."

This is it. Come Friday, I will take my first shaky step into adulthood. I'm nervous. I mean, there is a lot to consider. Like, how much aftershave should I put on? And should I chew gum or risk having bad breath? In the great golf game of life, am I about to hit a hole-in-one or make a quadruple bogey?

MONDAY, FEBRUARY 11

Today, in seminary, I kept sneaking glances at Julie, wondering if there might be any telltale signs of a broken heart. She's holding up well. Once, she caught me looking at her, and she smiled. Stupid me, I quickly looked away and pretended to have something in my eye. I mean, I'm not only tongue-tied, but I can't even smile at her. Dumb.

I was dying to know if she has a date to the dance. So I figured it was to time to contact superspy,

Amy Hassett. At school, I casually asked her if Julie was going to the "Anything Goes Dance." Amy said she didn't know but would find out. Smooth, Whipple.

Oh yes. Seminary lesson had to do with Helaman and his two thousand stripling warriors. Just a theory, but I bet Helaman could have put together a heckuva basketball team from those two thousand warriors.

Maybe I missed the point of the lesson today.

TUESDAY, FEBRUARY 12

Coach Ackley is winding down. We haven't won a basketball game all year, and I think he's sort of written the season off. Let's face it, as a basketball team, we are a natural disaster. This afternoon, he let us off after only thirty minutes of practice. I was stunned. He just blew the whistle, and said, "That's it for today, guys. Hit the showers." We all looked at each other in disbelief.

So I had some free time. I decided to walk over to Natalie's junior high. The basketball team had a game, and I wanted to see Natalie the Cheerleader, in action.

I slipped into the gym without her noticing. Now, I figured that because she was in front of a group of people, Natalie would really be into it. I mean pompoms waving, yelling emotionally at the crowd, tears welling in her eyes if her team was behind, splits, cartwheels, and total cuteness. Natalie does cute very well, especially in front of a crowd of people.

Was I ever surprised! It was a close game, but Natalie was almost listless. Just a few token cheers. A little bit of "Jimmy, Jimmy, he's our man . . . ", and that was it. I couldn't figure it out. This is not the Nat I know. There was a time-out, so I crept down the aisle and sidled up to her.

"Natalie, do you feel okay?"

"Huh? Oh. It's you." She looked around the gym, uneasy to be seen talking with her brother, the Prince of Nerds. "No. I feel fine. Why don't you go home now?"

"You're not bouncing around the way I expected. Is something wrong?"

She looked away as the game started again. One of the other cheerleaders came up to her. "They're putting number 24 in the game. He is so gorgeous."

Suddenly, Natalie looked excited. "He is. Seriously. These guys are all hunks. I can't believe it. They're the best team yet, by far."

I couldn't believe my ears. Even for Natalie this taxed my imagination. "Natalie! Are you rooting for the other team because they have cuter players?"

She looked wounded. "Well, not really. But I wish I knew number 24's name," she said dreamily, gazing on the court as he dribbled by.

"You can't do that! It's not right. It's un-American!"

"Number 14 isn't bad, either," her friend said.

"Not bad at all."

"Natalie, do you even know who is ahead?"

She turned and glared at me. "Of course. Someone's ahead, that's the score."

"Natalie!"

"Wally, I have to start cheering now. You know, it's like my job." She turned to her friend. "I think we should start a sort of 'nice try' cheer for the other team if they miss a shot. I think that's being really good sports."

"Seriously," her friend chattered. "Really good sports, for sure. I hope number 24 misses a shot."

With that, she and Natalie bounded off and joined a huddle of other cheerleaders.

I decided I'd seen enough. I walked out of the gym. Just as I got to the door, I heard a cheer, "Nice try, nice guy, go number 24!"

Natalie never ceases to amaze.

WEDNESDAY, FEBRUARY 13

Eight Things to Prepare for the Date with Edwina:

1. Start acting cooler. Now.

2. Although I have to start acting cool, I still have to be nice. Nice and cool is a tough combination, unless you are a Joe Vermeer and have the genetic base for it. I am not Joe, however, so I must think up some cool things to do on my own, which is a stretch for me. Maybe this: "Hey, Ed. Yo. You smell good."

3. Do not ask anyone about how I look before going out. Reasons:

a. Natalie will make fun of me, no matter what I wear.

b. Mom will want me to wear a sport coat.

c. Dad will tell me I look too formal if I wear anything more than a pair of sweat pants and a Portland Trailblazer T-shirt.

d. Chuck will tell me I look fine.

Amendment to #3. Ask only Chuck how I look.

4. Bring Ed some flowers. This is something Joe Vermeer would do, I think.

5. Even though I am bringing flowers to Ed and want her to have a good time, I don't want to, well, encourage her. This sounds funny but makes perfect sense to me.

6. When giving reviews of the date to parents, Lumpy, Orville, Natalie (maybe), and anyone else, I have to say good things about Ed, no matter how miserable the date might be. This is to save face.

7. If sitting in the front seat of the car (Edwina has her license, so humbling as it is, she'll drive, and I'll be the passenger), sit about midpoint between her right hip and the door. The same is true for girls if the boy is doing the driving. Midpoint. Edwina taught me that in math, which goes to show you even geometry has some practical application.

8. At the dance, go up to someone who is popular and say, "Hey." Someone like Joe, who will say hey right back, thus proving to your date that you are someone of at least marginal importance.

I think that's it. Less than forty-eight hours, and I will be knocking on her door, ready for my first big plunge into the netherworld of dating, girls, romance, and adulthood.

Unless I chicken out and move to the Yukon tomorrow.

THURSDAY, FEBRUARY 14

Tonight, as I sit on the edge of my bed writing in my journal, Chuck lies sleeping across the room, unaware of the torment that I am going through. I would gladly trade places with a bug under a rock in Siberia. Because, in the sad and pathetic life of Wallace F. Whipple, this is the darkest of the many dark days he has endured. I am seriously thinking of packing up my belongings, shaking hands with Dad, kissing Mom good-bye, telling Chuck to be tough, sticking my tongue out at Natalie, and leaving, just leaving, to begin a new, less-complicated life.

No. This has not been a good day.

Basketball. After playing in two consecutive games and doing pretty well, I thought I'd earned more playing time. Not so. Close game. We lost 56–55, and Coach Ackley stayed with the starters most of the game. I got only permanent "pine time" on the bench.

But that wasn't the worst part of the day. Not by a long shot. Seminary did me in. Not the class, but what happened on the way in. Lumpy is sick, so Orville and I drove in his pickup. We got out of the truck, walked through the door at church and into the foyer. Orville stopped to get a drink, and I waited for him. Around the corner I hear two female voices which I instantly recognize as belonging to Julie and Amy. We hadn't quite reached the hallway where they're standing, so they can't see us. I hear something that catches my attention: my name.

"Are you going tomorrow night?" Amy asks.

"Yes, with Joe."

"Wally Whipple was trying to find out. I think he was hoping you'd ask him . . . "

"Wally?" Julie sounds amused. "Are you kidding?" They giggle.

"I never would have thought of asking . . . "

I did not want to hear what was coming next. I

have two choices. I can either go back outside and sit in Orville's truck and wait out seminary, or I can decide not to be a wimp and walk around the corner and confront the two girls who obviously think it's a big joke to go out with Wallace F. Whipple, Jr. I knew what I should do. I marched around the corner, and, for once, I had no trouble at all talking with Julie.

"Good morning, Julie. Good morning, Amy. Glad both of you are so cheerful."

They sputter something back and look very uncomfortable. I march straight into class with Orville a step behind. During class, I know Julie is looking at me, probably wondering how much I had heard. At the end of class, I'm the first one out the door. Julie and Amy are both hustling after me, but this is one case where having long legs is an advantage. I'm in the truck, and we're out of the parking lot before they get out of the building. The rain splashes against the windshield, and it's quiet for the first few blocks.

"I think I know what's happenin' here, Wally," Orv sympathizes as we cross 39th Avenue. "You broke some rough trail this morning, but you handled it fine."

"Yeah, I guess so. But I feel so stupid. How could I have ever thought that someone like Julie would pay attention to me?"

"Don't go jumpin' to conclusions. You ain't bucked off yet. Maybe Julie's never paid you any heed because she thinks you are out of her class, too. What you're doin' is saying that you're below her somehow, and that ain't necessarily true."

"Yeah. Maybe." But I knew better. In high school, it's pretty easy to know right where you stack up.

You're reminded where you fit in—dozens of times each day.

The rest of the day was uneventful, including the basketball game. Tomorrow's the big day for Edwina and me, and I'm having a hard time concentrating on things. I'm going to be lots of fun.

And I know that Edwina deserves better. Brother, do I ever know.

So here I sit. Valentine's Day, when the whole world is out being romantic. And me? I'm sitting up here in my room while my younger brother sleeps and feeling like the world's biggest jerk for thinking that Julie Sloan might like me in something more than a brotherly way. This is not a good feeling.

But I sort of deserve it. After all, I am Wally Whipple. No more. No less.

FRIDAY, FEBRUARY 15

I woke up about ten minutes earlier than usual. I started thinking about how nice it would be to feel deathly ill. I ran through the list of things that might hurt—arms, legs, throat, head, feet, teeth—and everything was fine. I ran my hand across my stomach, which is where chicken pox first show. Smooth.

I sat up in bed, remembering what a dweeb I felt like overhearing Julie and Amy. I flopped back on my bed. This teenager stuff is not all it's made out to be. I mean, it's not being a star athlete and going to the prom with the prettiest girl in school. It's not being surrounded by hordes of adoring friends and hitting a party twice a weekend. It's not driving an awesome sports car, breezing through school with straight A's, looking good all the time, and being a lot smarter than any teacher or parent that you encounter.

Being a teenager is work. Like Coach Leonard used to tell us when we felt like throwing up while running in cross-country, you've gotta gut it out at times. That's what a teenager has to do. Gut it out and hope for as few mistakes as possible.

My alarm went off, and I decided to get this day started. Thank heaven days are only twenty-four hours long, and if I'm lucky, I get to spend about half of them asleep.

I skipped Seminary. I couldn't face Julie, so Orv just drove us to school. The first time I'd been early all year. School was fine. Edwina didn't say much except that she'd see me at 7:30. I spent the greater portion of basketball practice watching the first and second teams go through the motions of a scrimmage. Then . . . boom. It was 6:30 and time to get ready for my date.

I shaved, although I didn't really need to. I splashed on an average amount of aftershave, only about two handfuls. I put on my best blue shirt with gray stripes, my favorite old blue slacks, threw on a sweater, and was set. I looked in the mirror for a solid five minutes, trying to look ruggedly handsome and telling myself over and over to stop being nervous.

Confidence. Be confident. You are Whipple the Man, Whipple the Conqueror, Whipple the Fearless, Whipple . . . who can't dance worth beans. That's okay, maybe Ed can't dance either, and we'll be on the sidelines all night talking about what it will take to get the national economy moving again. An evening of intellectual conversation with Edwina, the mathematical wizard. Ugh!

Natalie looks into the bathroom. "You're going dressed like that?"

"Yeah. I think I'm kind of ruggedly handsome in these duds."

"No, just rugged. Your slacks. They're an inch above your ankles, and they've got those little cloth pills all over them. You'll embarrass the family. You need help."

"But they're my favorite pants—"

She's down the hall and returns with some other pants and a different shirt. "Try these," she orders.

I do. Meekly, I call Nat back. "Well?"

"Better. Now let me get some hairspray and see what I can do up top for you."

This is mortifying. First she picks out my clothes, then she wants to do my hair. What's next? I refuse to wear hairspray. A guy has to draw the line somewhere. You can only push him so far before he boils over. A man's gotta do what a man's gotta do.

I was ready to give Nat this line of male logic, but before I could, she was back with brush in one hand, hairspray in the other, and a comb clenched between her teeth. "Hold still!" she ordered, and I did. A few minutes later, my hair was all lacquered in place. "There. You look decent. It wasn't easy, but no one will confuse you with an ape, anyway."

Natalie fluttered away, basking in her triumph. I had ten minutes left before my death march to the car, after which Dad would drive me to Edwina's house. I stole into my room and grabbed an ink pen and pulled back my shirt sleeve. On my wrist, I scribbled a few reminders of things to talk about.

School. How nice her parents are. Brothers/sisters. The weather. Math class.

I looked at my watch, and it was 7:24. I had to go . . . I could not delay the inevitable any longer. Slowly, I walked to the family room where my dad and Chuck were watching television. "I think it's time to go, Dad," I croaked.

"So it is." He got his coat on and headed out to the car. Mom came out of the kitchen and told me how nice I looked, although she did suggest that it would have been nice to wear a sport coat and a tie. Chuck told me good-luck. Natalie stood by the doorway, no longer able to contain herself. "No kissing on the first date, Wally, and remember not to lick your paws before eating." Mom gave her a look that is seldom seen in our household and handed me a bouquet of flowers she had bought and insisted I take to Ed.

Then I was in the car. Dad whistled and acted like it was no big deal to be driving his firstborn to his first date. Yeah. Sure. I know a little of what Isaac must have felt when his dad invited him to go for a hike into the mountains. We pulled up to the Purvis place, a really nice home near the top of Mt. Tabor. "Have fun, Wally. This will be a good experience for you."

Good experience. Everytime you are about to do something painful, embarrassing, or just plain hard, your parents always say, "It will be a good experience for you."

"Thanks Dad. For everything. Take care of Mom while I'm gone."

"Wally, you are going out on your first date, not

off to war. You'd better lighten up or neither you nor
the girl are going to have much fun tonight."

"Whatever you say, Dad." Then, I was out of the
car and on my way to the porch. Almost as if it were
a dream, or I were someone else trapped inside the
body of Wallace Whipple. I reached for the doorbell
and pushed. I said a prayer, something to the effect
of, Please, just help me to survive tonight.

The door opened. A tall man with a mustache and
thinning gray hair opened the door and smiled. "You
must be Wally. I'm Will Purvis, Edwina's father.
Please, come in."

I stepped in. "Pleased to meetcha, Mr. Purvis."
Their house was huge and had paintings and statues
all over it. The carpet was thick, softer than my mattress at home. There was a grand piano in the corner
of the living room. The Purvises had big bucks and
were into classy things, I could tell. Art, music, and
white furniture.

"You have a great place here, Mr. Purvis."

He took me into a little room off the entry, and I
sat down in a chair that was so plush that I must have
sunk about six inches. Mr. Purvis sat down opposite
me. This was really awkward. He smiled, then I
smiled, then he smiled, then I smiled. I felt a desperate need to say something—something that would
show him my wit, charm, and intelligence. "Are you
a Democrat or a Republican?" I blurted out.

He looked startled. "Well, I'm a Republican,
Wally."

"Oh, so am I! I mean, I will be when I get old
enough to vote. I am very much in tune with politics.
Like, I've always wondered if the nation went too

hard on Richard Nixon. But I enjoy being a future Republican because I've long felt that girls should date Republicans although there are some very fine Democrats around, too."

This did not come out like I wanted it to. Mr. Purvis had a puzzled expression on his face. I thought I should change the subject in a hurry. "So, what is your professional profession, Mr. Purvis?"

"I'm a physician. An internal medicine man."

"Oh. Internal. Like inside people's bodies? I bet you see a lot of stuff."

"More or less, Wally."

"I've always been interested in medicine, too," I babbled on. "I mean, that gives us something in common. That and being Republicans." The truth is that I've never considered medicine for the simple reason that I tend to pass out at the sight of blood.

But I was under pressure, and my brain and mouth were out of synch. Mr. Purvis cleared his throat and decided to try again to see if there was any sign of intelligent life in the room other than himself.

"What branch of medicine are you interested in, Wally?"

"Well, Will, I like feet, so I was thinking about becoming a foot doctor."

NOTE: I can't believe it! I called Ed's dad by his first name. Rats! I was going down faster than the *Titanic*.

"A podiatrist?"

"No, a foot doctor, not someone who raises poultry and other things such as chickens."

That probably did it for Dr. Purvis. No doubt he had serious questions about his daughter's taste in males. But for some reason, I got podiatry and poultry mixed up. I tried to save the situation with one last desperate attempt at adult-like conversation.

"So, do you like sports?"

"No, my practice keeps me busy, and I have little free time."

He swallowed hard. I was getting this sense that he was starting to shake a little. He said something about going to check on Edwina. He left slowly, looking over his shoulder at me one more time before he left the room. I imagined that he might be going to see if he could talk Ed out of the whole date. I could almost hear him saying, "Dear, the young man you've asked over tonight is a complete, slavering idiot, and I forbid you to ever see him again. I shall tell him you are not well, and have Jeeves drive him home."

A few minutes went by. I was jumpy as a cat in the dog pound. Where was Ed?

I heard footsteps coming down the spiral staircase.

It was Edwina, at least I thought it was Edwina. She looked gorgeous! I stood up. At school she never wore anything other than jeans and a top. But now, she looked like she had stepped out of the pages of a fashion magazine. She was wearing a long, black skirt and a white blouse, and her dark hair was swept up into a fancy style. Even Natalie would be impressed.

"Hi, Ed. Am I ever glad to see you! I don't think I bowled your dad over. I can't believe some of the things I said to him."

She laughed. "He told me about the Republican or Democrat question. I said, 'Yep, that's Wally.' Don't worry, I think he enjoyed your strange conversation. Daddy has a great sense of humor."

"That's good, because I put it to the test, for sure," I said, feeling a little more relaxed. "These are for you," I said suddenly, handing her the flowers.

"Daisies! My favorite. Thank you, Wally. That was so sweet. I think dinner is ready. Should we eat?"

It occurred to me that I hadn't put anything in my mouth—with the exception of my foot with Dr. Purvis—since noon. I was hungry, big-time. I hoped she had ordered two pizzas with everything and some root beer. "Dinner sounds great, Ed."

She led me into a dining room. It was dark, except for two candles flickering on a formally set table. A green salad was on our plates and there was soup and bread.

Ed stood, as if waiting for something. I finally caught on and helped her into her chair. Then remembering my best manners, I carefully unfolded my napkin and placed it on my lap, which is something I usually forget to do at home. Mom would have been proud. The meal turned out to be a feast. Not pizza or Mexican food, but really good anyway. Baked salmon, wild rice, vegetables that actually tasted good, and a nice cake with some kind of creamy filling. Old Ed really put on the dog.

I finished off the remains of my cake and patted my stomach. "Great meal, Ed."

"Thanks, Wally. I did most of it myself, although Mom helped a bit. We better get to the dance now. It's almost nine."

"What about the dishes?" After a meal like that, I figured that offering to scrub a few pots and pans was the least I could do.

"Wally, that's just like you. Don't worry, they'll be taken care of."

We walked through her house, which was about the size of a football field, and went out a side door. Parked on her driveway was a little red sports car, the kind I had only seen in my dreams or in commercials. "Wow! Is your dad going to let us borrow this?"

Ed scrunched up her face. "Well, really, it's my car."

I couldn't believe it. I was going to pull up in front of school in a car like that. This night was looking up. Vegetables that I liked, and now a hot car to drive in. Dating has its up-side, I decided, especially when you are with someone rich. I went around to the driver's side and opened the door for her. Nice move, Whipple. Then I hustled back and got in. Full stomach, nice car, and I hadn't even spilled any food on my sweater. So far, so good, except now I had to make conversation. "Gee . . . here we are," I said. Not exactly a line from Romeo and Juliet.

"Right. Here we are," Ed said, waiting for a traffic light to change.

It didn't take a giant intellect to realize that things were flattening out some. Time to kick in my plan. I very coolly stretched my arm out and sort of pulled back on my sweater. The first topic on my wrist was school.

"So, how is school going, Ed?"

"Fine, Wally."

Okay, so much for school. I stole a glance at my wrist. Next was, how nice her parents are. "You sure have nice parents."

"I think so. But did you get to meet my mom? I thought she left before you arrived."

She had me. No, I hadn't met her mom. Time for quick thinking. "Ah . . . no, I didn't meet your mother, but I saw a picture of her. And she looked like a really nice lady in the picture. I think you can tell a lot about people from their pictures, especially their eyes. I think eyes are the window to the soul." Nice save, Wally.

"That's a good thought."

"Yeah, it is. It's one of my favorite thoughts, although I don't have many." We had been in the car three minutes, and I was already on topic #3, brothers and sisters.

"Do you have brothers and sisters?"

"No. I'm an only child, although I hope it doesn't show too much."

"Oh no, not at all, except maybe for your car."

At this point, I decided to bag the notes written on my wrists. I would have to rely on my own wits, not exactly a comforting thought. We drove on in silence for about two minutes that seemed like two hours. Then Ed finally said, "Tell me about the basketball team. I went to one of the sophomore games, and I don't think you played. That must be discouraging. Isn't the coach very good?"

"Not very good? Let me tell you, he would have cut Michael Jordan. He doesn't hardly know a zone defense from a no passing zone."

"You really think he would have cut Jordan?"

"Yeah. I really do. Heck, he would've played Shawn Bradley at guard."

Without the benefit of notes on her wrist, Ed unlocked the key to conversation with me. We talked about sports, my jump shot, Coach Ackley, who would win the college championship, and so on, for the next forty-five minutes. Right through our entrance to the dance, right through the first eight dances. She kept asking me more questions, and I kept answering them. She's a girl you can really talk to.

It dawned on me that so far our date had consisted of one great meal and me talking about myself. I remembered the purpose of attending a dance, namely, to dance. I didn't want to dance but decided I should extend myself and ask her. Maybe she would say no. My conscience would have been satisfied, and I could go home without humiliating myself. A slow number came on, and I decided to pop the question. "Like to dance, Ed?" I asked very casually, masking my deep inner fear.

"Sure."

It wasn't the answer I wanted, but nonetheless, I took her hand, and we headed for a remote corner of the gym where I was hoping no one would see my lurpy attempt to dance. I took her hand in mine, put my other hand on her back very gingerly and began to shuffle my feet. Not ten seconds into the dance, I slid my foot right onto hers, and she winced. "Sorry, Ed." Then it happened again. "Sorry, Ed." The third time it happened, I blurted, "I'm not much of a dancer. All I want to do tonight is survive and hope that your feet work when it's all over." Ed nodded, sighed, and said, "Me, too."

During the course of the evening, we danced a couple of more times, though never to any slow numbers again. The big advantage to fast numbers is that you aren't close enough to do bodily harm.

After the first of our fast dances, I got a huge shock. I happened to look over at the doorway, and there, dressed in a cowboy hat, boots, and western tie, was Orville Burrell. And on his arm, looking very happy, was Viola Barkle, she of the bulging muscles and hulking frame, also dressed in western clothes. I had to talk with Orv immediately. I took Ed by the hand and we headed over to where he and Viola were standing. "Orv, my man, I didn't know you were coming tonight."

"I hardly did either, pard. Viola jes' called me up last night and asked me if I was hankerin' to go dancin'. I told her, why sure, except I got to wrassle first, so we'd be a touch late. She said that was okay with her, and she fixed up a great mess of food for dinner tonight, and here we are."

No digs, no signs of mortification, other than he seemed to be chomping hard on his toothpicks. No rolling of the eyes at being caught in public with the best female shot putter in Oregon high school athletics. In fact, Orv was treating Viola as though she were Cinderella, and I'd never seen Viola look so happy. Maybe she was Cinderella for tonight.

There is a message here, Whipple. Get it?

Anyway, Ed and I hung around the dance for another hour. Orv and Viola discovered a mutual interest in country music, and we decided to all go to his apartment to sing a few songs. I was very ready to leave by that time, and Edwina said getting away sounded like fun. That's how we finished the evening; the sports car following Orv's pickup to the Burrells' where we sang a few songs (most of which I was able to sing close to key, thanks to Mr. Ashbury). We ended up laughing at stories that Mr. Burrell told us about his days sheep ranching in Montana.

About midnight, Ed drove me home. "I had a really good time tonight, Wally," she said as we sat in the car at the curb in front of my house. "I never dreamed we'd end up singing country songs at the Burrells', but it was a real kick. And my feet feel better. I'm sure most of the bruises will be gone by next week. I can always have Daddy look at them. That's the advantage to having a doctor in the family."

"I had a nice time, too. And I really wasn't expecting it—not because of you, but because this is sort of like my first real date, and all I really wanted to do was just get through it and not do anything that my sister will hear about and use to torment me the rest of my life. I hope your dad and my sister never meet and start telling stories about me. Tell your dad I really am okay, underneath."

"I will. This is my first date, too. I like you in a lot of ways, Wally. You treat me differently. To you, I'm not just Edwina Purvis, the girl who gets good grades and has her own car and lives in a big house. You seem to like me for who I am. And I like the way you call me Ed, not Edwina. Nobody else does that."

"It's okay, Ed. And I didn't even know you had your own car and lived on Mt. Tabor, until tonight. Heck, it doesn't make any difference to me." This is only a small lie, because, as the night unfolded, I thought less and less about the sports car and the fact that Ed's allowance was probably more than half of the income of many blue-collar workers in my neighborhood.

"Just one question, Wally. I noticed you kept looking at your wrist a lot early this evening. Do you have a rash or something?"

"Here," I said, holding my wrist up to the glow from a streetlight overhead. "In case I got stuck for something to say, this is my list of topics. It bombed."

She laughed, and so did I. I told her good-night and then bounded up to the door. Everyone was asleep, so I walked quietly to my room. It's now two A.M., and I'm still wired even after all this writing, but I want to record one more thought for posterity.

WALLACE WHIPPLE DID OKAY ON HIS FIRST DATE. IN FACT, HE DID MORE THAN OKAY. HE TRIUMPHED!

And I bet Joe and Julie didn't have as nice a time as we did.

I may have to try this dating stuff again. Maybe, even before my mission.

SATURDAY, FEBRUARY 16

Natalie asked me how my date went when she got up about ten o'clock this morning.

"Fine," I said nonchalantly. "We ate, went to the dance, sang some cowboy songs at Orville's, and came home. Nothing to this dating stuff."

"You did what?" she panicked. "You sang cowboy songs? How embarrassing!"

I just smiled and thought that Natalie has a few things to learn about dating.

TUESDAY, FEBRUARY 19

Joe came out of seminary today and spotted me. "Yo, Wally."

"Hey, Joe."

"Saw you at the dance with Edwina Purvis."

I didn't know where this was leading. "Yeah. We went together."

Joe nodded approvingly. "Nice girl. Good move. Edwina's cool."

"Yeah," I said. "Edwina's cool."

WEDNESDAY, FEBRUARY 20

The "Q" word has been haunting me again. Yeah, I've had a few thoughts about quitting basketball, but I've decided to hang tough. We had a break in the weather today, and Chuck was out there pumping up the shots, never making one, but never thinking of quitting.

If Chuck can go a couple of years without making a basket, I think sticking out the season shouldn't send me to Stress City for an extended stay. We have two games left, and if I get the chance to play, I'm going to pretend I'm in the final game of the NBA championship, and the coach has just told me to go in and win it. The game will be televised in foreign countries, all over the world. People in a ski chalet somewhere in the French Alps are going to pause and watch the game. "Zeez Whippoole, he can play ze basketboll, eh?"

I can give my best effort for the rest of the season, even if I'm glued to the bench. It's sort of an honor thing, I've decided. Zeez es ze right zing to do.

THURSDAY, FEBRUARY 21

Wallace Whipple is on the scoreboard. Not once, not twice, but eight times!

We were behind today, 21–6 after the first quarter. Coach Ackley looked like a man on his way to the mental hospital for a long stay. I mean, you could almost see the man breaking down in front of us. Finally, he turned away and cupped his hands around his head. He couldn't bear to watch anymore.

At the start of the second quarter, he said calmly, "Okay guys, it's time for some changes. Starters out. Salisbury, Prescott, Nickleby, Forbes, and Whipple, you guys check in. Make something happen. And you'll be in the whole quarter, maybe longer."

I was going in, and it was only the second quarter!

Now, remember, this is your chance to show your stuff. The eyes of the world are on you. Am I ready? YES! Will I succeed? YES! Can I do the job? YES!

"Whipple, better take off your sweats before you get in there," Coach Ackley reminded.

"Right, Coach. Just getting set to do that."

Into the game we went. There was no pressure, since we'd pretty much already been whipped. The first time down, I moved to the top of the key, and Curtis passed the ball to me. I turned toward the basket, dribbled a couple of steps to my left and let the jumper fly. Boom! Two points! My first basket in high school. It was so easy, just like I had imagined it a hundred times in my mind.

The guys on the bench went crackers. They were surprised. I felt so relieved, knowing that I wasn't going to go scoreless for the whole season.

The game got better. The longer we were out there, the more confident we became. All the stored-up frustration of riding the pines the entire season was unleashed in one wonderful burst. Just before half-time, I took a pass deep in the corner and decided, what the heck, and let it go. The ref raised his hand to indicate a three pointer, and it ripped through the twine. Five points, and it was only halftime. I calculated my season average was now a solid one point per game.

I played all of the third quarter and about half of the fourth. I hit a short jump shot and made one of two free throws. Eight points! Our team came back. We ended up losing by ten, but I figure from the time all of the benchwarmers got in the game, we outscored the other team by five points.

"Nice going, guys. You showed me some heart," Coach Ackley congratulated. "Big changes for next week. That's a promise."

I tried not to think about the last promise he made me, the one about wearing a suit to school.

But . . . one more game next Thursday. Do I dare think it? Will I start?

SUNDAY, FEBRUARY 24

Julie's giggle. How do I deal with it?

Maybe like this. Okay, she isn't perfect. I put her on a pedestal and found out she's human. So forget it. Maybe part of this is my fault. I mean, my imagination was a little out of whack. She'd say hello to me, and I'd assume that meant she would write me for two years while I was on my mission and never date another guy again. She'd ignore me three days later, and I'd want to become a hermit and live my life far from civilization. All of this over a girl who had never spoken more than three consecutive sentences to me in her life.

Being in *like*, I've decided, can make you bonkers.

The mature thing to do is blow it off, chill out, forget it. So I've got it resolved. I wish her and Joe a happy lifetime together. I'll even come to their wedding reception with an expensive gift. If, by chance, Julie begins to say something about how very sorry she feels about the misunderstanding in the hallway so many years before, I will simply dismiss it with a generous wave of my hand. She will tell me that I'm wonderful, and that, at last, her conscience is clear, and she can get on with life. I'd even let their children call me "Uncle Wally."

Very mature, don't you think?

Still, I wish the whole thing had never happened. I still wish she *liked* me, dumb as that sounds.

WEDNESDAY, FEBRUARY 27

The missionaries came over for dinner tonight. At the end of the meal, they gave us a message about finding people to share the gospel with. We all kind of looked at each other and said we couldn't think of anyone offhand, but we'd sure give it a try. I'd been thinking about mentioning Orv's name, but for whatever reason (primarily because I was chicken), I didn't. Leave it to Chuck, the pure-hearted one, to pipe up.

"What about Orville?"

"Who's Orville?" Elder Todd asked.

"He's a guy who moved here a few months ago, and I go to school with. And he comes to seminary, too," I answered. "And he reads the Book of Mormon."

"He's really cool," Natalie chimed in. "Plus, he's a hunk."

"Let me get this straight. He's not a member of the Church, but he attends early morning seminary and is reading the Book of Mormon?"

The elders looked at each other with funny expressions. "I think your friend might be ready for the missionary lessons," Elder McHood said. "Find out, and let us know if we can meet with him. I'd say he's a prime candidate. I'd sure like to teach him before I go home to Arizona this spring. You'll know how to approach him at the right time."

I know he needs the Church, and not a week goes by that I don't think about talking with him. Orv has been progressing. Yesterday he told me how much he likes Mormon "because he was a big feller and didn't mind thumpin' the bad guys."

Is that the start of a testimony? Orville a Mormon? I figured that it took months for someone to get ready. If the elders are right, it could happen a lot sooner.

THURSDAY, FEBRUARY 28

"Dateline: Portland, Ore. The Benjamin Franklin High School 10th grade team ended a season of frustration by winning its final game of the year, a resounding 74–61 drubbing of Cleveland High.

"Leading the way for the fighting Quakers, were

Andy Salisbury with a season-high nineteen points, Curtis Nickleby, who chipped in fifteen points and seven assists, and Wallace Whipple, who added twelve points and nine rebounds.

"'This is a great moment in sports,' the teary-eyed Franklin coach Al Ackley said, as his team poured soda pop over his head. 'It should give hope to the oppressed, the little guys, the nerds of the world.'"

Do you believe how sweet this moment is? The good guys win in the end. This is the way life should be—work hard, be patient, endure, and it will all work out. Sweet indeed.

No more suits and ties to school for this kid. My basketball future is rosy again. I think this calls for a fine celebration with Lumpy and Orville.

The Burrito Bombshell at Hamburger Bob's sounds perfect for the occasion.

CHAPTER 7

March

SATURDAY, MARCH 2

My sister is depressed.

It's not hard to tell. Natalie doesn't hide her emotions very well. If she's happy, the whole world knows about it. If she's unhappy, same thing.

I noticed it first, this afternoon. She was sitting on her bed with the door open, staring at the floor and listening to the kind of music you'd hear in a supermarket. This is not Natalie. Every few seconds, she made a groaning sound.

"Are we having a bad-hair day, Nat? You okay?"

"No. I'm not okay. In fact, I'm feeling crummy."

"Are you sick?" I asked.

"No. I feel perfectly fine."

"But you just said you were feeling crummy."

She glared at me. "It's the other kind of crummy. Crummy inside, you know, like emotional crummy. If

217

you were more sensitive, you'd notice things like that."

"Are you depressed?"

"Well, shouldn't I be? I mean, basketball season is over, and, now, I'm not a cheerleader. I feel like something super important is gone. I felt really good about myself when I was yelling things and doing routines in front of people and watching cute guys. I felt like I was someone important, like I was making a contribution. Now I don't have much to look forward to, seriously. I think a really good part of my life is over, and other than dating and shopping, there isn't much left to look forward to."

She *was* serious. Those were the most heartfelt words I'd heard her utter.

"Nat, you can be a cheerleader again next year. Once you're elected, it's a sure thing you'll get elected again. Go to the mall, and you'll feel better."

"Going to the mall won't help."

Natalie saying that going to the mall won't help is like someone who is lost and crawling across the desert on all fours saying he isn't thirsty. I mean, this is a girl who was born to shop. Now I was feeling genuine concern about her. I needed to pull her out of the dumps. I decided to try a spiritual approach, not that Natalie is exactly a spiritual giant. But since the mall didn't work, maybe a completely opposite tactic would.

"Something that works for me when I'm down is to do something for someone else. That always makes me feel better," I said, thinking of Sister Lawson.

"Are you serious? How could that work? People

should be doing things for me because I'm the one who is depressed."

I could see that the concept of putting others ahead of herself was a little foreign to my sister. "Just try it. Go out and do something nice for someone, and you'll probably feel better. Maybe it doesn't make sense to you, but it works. Haven't you ever had that lesson in church?"

She thought for a moment. "I guess. But it never made any sense to me so I didn't pay much attention." At least she was honest about it.

"Just try it and see if you don't feel better."

She was still suspicious. "Maybe. But if it doesn't work, I'm going to tell you."

"Okay, that's fair. But I think it will work."

"Seriously?"

"Yeah. Seriously."

We'll see how Natalie's great experiment in charity works out. For my sake, I hope it does. Otherwise, she's going to be on my case for a long time, and I'll be the depressed one.

TUESDAY, MARCH 5

I got the report back from Natalie today. Let's just say she has a way to go before she is translated.

"I tried what you told me to do," she said, as I came home from school and dropped my books on the kitchen table. She was sitting at the table, working on her fingernails, her head bent over, her brown hair dangling.

I took the bait. "So how did it work out?"

"It wasn't, like, radical, but I did feel better when I did something nice for someone else."

I was encouraged. Could this be a spiritual breakthrough? The maturing of Natalie? A newer, humbler sister who thinks of others at least once a decade? "What did you do?"

She looked at me serenely and set aside her nail file. "Well, there's this girl at school, and her name is Lindy Hightower, and she thinks she's really cool, but I think she's really conceited. We never hardly talk, like only when we have to. But today, I saw her in the hallway, in the same place that I do most days right after lunch. Usually we just ignore each other, like we look the other way or something, or we make it a point to talk with someone else. Well, when I saw her today, instead of looking away, I go, 'Hi.' And she looks super surprised, and she goes, 'Hi' back to me."

Natalie looked very satisfied and started working over her fingernails again. Obviously, she was expecting me to break into applause for her telling one of her rivals hello in the hallway. True sacrifice. This was her idea of service to others.

"That's it? You said 'hi' to this girl?"

"Yeah. I thought it was pretty cool of me to do that, since it's like we don't really get along. I felt better about myself. You were right—if you're nice to someone when you don't have to be, it makes you feel better about yourself because you're thinking of others. In fact, I've already decided to go 'Hi' again tomorrow if I see her. I'm still depressed but not as bad as during the weekend."

"Well . . . um, I'm glad that it worked out for you okay."

"Yeah, it did. I thought I handled it really well."

"I can see why, Nat."

It's a start, I keep repeating to myself. Natalie may not be ready to be the Relief Society compassionate service leader, but it's a start. What is it that Nephi said? Out of small means, the Lord can do great things?

It's a start, it's a start. Let me repeat that about twenty more times.

WEDNESDAY, MARCH 6

Lumpy and I have been talking about the important things in life, for example, whether we really like Hamburger Bob's new Mexican menu additions (we do); if either of us will go out on another date before high school is over (I'm thinking yes, but Lumpy isn't sure); and if I peaked too early in life by going out with Edwina and having a good time and scoring twelve points in a basketball game—all within two weeks of each other. (Lumpy tells me the best part of life is still to come, but he's never hit a three-pointer from deep in the corner.)

We also agree that one of us needs to get a driver's license soon. The way we see it, getting a license is about the same thing as when the children of Israel got out of bondage. I want to drive the concept home in one word: FREEDOM. This is how our conversation goes on a typical Saturday night:

ME: "You want to go somewhere?"

LUMPY: "No."

But if one of us had our license, the talk would be different.

ME: "You want to go somewhere?"

LUMPY: "Yeah! You name it."

ME: "We could go to the Blazer game, we could go downtown, we could go to the zoo, we could go to the coast, we could go to the mall to check out girls, we could go to Mt. Hood, we could go to a dance, we could go get something to eat, we could even go to the library and study."

See the difference? "Emancipation through vehicular access," as Lumpy says.

"So who goes first?"

"Not me," says Lumpy the Courageous. "My parents will say no. They'll tell me how much it will cost for insurance, how my older brother, Brett, already has his license, and how we don't need four drivers in a family that only owns two cars and, that when I go out and get a job and start contributing more to the family, then maybe I'll get a few more privileges."

"Guess I'll go first," I offer, not wanting Lumpy to endure an FBL.

"Go for it."

Now, I know I'm going to be taking on the Parents' Conspiracy by attempting to get my license.

Parent #1: "Billy got his license last week, and we can no longer control him. He is always gone, and our years of keeping him too exhausted to get into trouble are over."

Parent #2: "Didn't you tell him about how expensive insurance is? That is usually your best defense."

Parent #3: "We did just that, and the little ingrate went out and got a job selling magazine subscriptions. We were thrilled, until in his first year he made more money than his father did. He not only could afford his insurance, but he also paid cash for a late model BMW. Our defense was gone. Be careful, or your teens might actually listen to you and do what you suggest. Congress needs to raise the driving age to twenty-one."

ALL PARENTS: (bursting into applause) "Hear! Hear!"

Nevertheless, I've got to pursue it. My whole well-being—social, emotional, and mental—is hanging in the balance. The only thing I can't pin on driving is my spiritual welfare, but I could probably even make a case for that. ("Dad, if I never drive, I'll never date, I'll never marry, I'll never have children, I'll never progress, and I'll be lucky to duck into the telestial kingdom.")

I must drive. I have to drive. Not since Ed first asked me out have I faced such a challenge. But as with my date with Ed, WHIPPLE WILL CONQUER! WHIPPLE WILL DRIVE!

THURSDAY, MARCH 7

I went to a wiser, more mature person to seek counsel about how to approach my parents regarding the license. Orville, as usual, gave good advice.

"The way I size it up is like this. You gotta make your parents see that there's something in it for them. They're both steady folks, and if you point out the advantages of you drivin', then my guess is they'd be all over that idea, like a dog on a stew bone."

"Like, what do I tell them, Orv?"

"Why don't you mention how you'd be doin' them

a service by taking you and Nat to that young folks meetin' every week."

"Mutual?"

"Yup."

I need to plan, really point out all of the good things that will happen to my parents once I get my license. I can see it now. Dad is resting in his recliner with his feet up, reading the newspaper in the early evening after work. Mom is listening to classical music and reading *Twelfth Night*. I trudge in, car keys dangling, arms loaded with groceries.

"Isn't it nice that Wally has taken over the shopping for us," Mom sighs, contentedly.

"It sure is, Pamela. We should have let Wally get his license the day he turned sixteen."

"Mom, Dad. Off to Young Men's now. On the way over, I'll drop off the dry cleaning and return the rental videos. Anything else I can do?"

"No dear, just drive safely," Mom says. "We do appreciate you so much more now that you drive. It's been a wonderful blessing in our home."

My plan will go something like this: I'll talk with both parents, calmly, maturely, and point out the obvious benefits of having another driver in the family. I will not mention anything about my social life or messing around on Friday nights with my friends. It will be straightforward, no tricks, an open, honest dialogue between parents and their near-adult son. I will work in several points, among them:

1. Driving will make life easier for our entire family. (See above statement regarding groceries, dry cleaning, Young Men, etc.)

2. My grades will improve because I will not have

to walk home from school, thereby wasting valuable time that could be used studying. Also, I will be able to go to the library more often.

3. Driving will improve my sense of responsibility. I will assure them of my awareness of the care that must be taken to safely manage two tons of metal and plastic. That will score big points with my parents.

4. And finally, I will tell them driving is good preparation for my mission because I will learn more about self-control, self-discipline, self-reliance, and whatever other self-s pop into my head.

There. The plan is set. Now, timing is everything.

FRIDAY, MARCH 8

I was cleaning out my basketball locker today after school, basking in the aroma of sweaty warm-ups and foot powder, when Coach Leonard came in. Beside cross-country, he is also the track coach, and I think he was scouting out the locker room in preparation for the upcoming season. A quiver shot down my spine. I knew what he was going to say.

"Wally, I hear you ended your basketball season on a fine note. Congratulations. You have a lot of heart. (If he only knew how much I wanted to quit cross-country!) That's a quality I admire."

"Thanks, Coach." Had he talked with Mr. McCloud? Did he know that I was sort of committed to run track as part of my penance for beating up Les Lorris? Apparently not.

"Wally, how about track? You know, I think you'd be a fine middle-distance runner. Maybe the cross-country courses are not your bread and butter, but something shorter, say the mile or 800–meters, would be more to your liking. With your long legs and natural athletic ability, you could be something special. You have a shot at greatness, and I don't say that to many young men. In your case, I can feel it."

I suppose that dealing with Coach Leonard will prepare me for other unpleasant tasks in life, such as listening to life insurance salespersons or magazine subscription solicitors who work door-to-door.

"How about it, Wally? Will you give it a shot?"

"I'll think about it, Mr. Leonard."

He looked a bit disappointed, then smiled. "That's fair enough. Remember what I said about greatness. There's no feeling in the world like holding your arms wide and breaking the tape with your chest." He patted me on the shoulder, and then I left.

I like Coach Leonard, and I kept my word. I thought about track for, oh, about two seconds, as I walked out of the gym and into the street. And my answer is, "No way, Coach."

SATURDAY, MARCH 9

I'm zeroing in on Chuck's birthday present. I have it narrowed down to a trip to Disneyland ($2,000), tickets to a Blazer's game ($60), his own personal computer ($2,000), or a sweatshirt that says "BYU" on it (about $12). Given my dwindling finances, the sweatshirt is the best bet. Heck, he'll be thrilled with it, anyway.

Orv finished up wrestling this week. He went to the city meet and won his first two matches. Then he got unlucky and drew a guy named Harvey

Grebonsky, who is the returning state champion in Orville's weight class. It was a good match, probably the toughest Harvey's had all year, but Orville lost 8–5. He finished with a 7–1 record, which is great for a tenth-grader. After the match, Orville was only a little disappointed. "That feller was tough as beef jerky rolled in fish hooks. Nice guy, too. We had a talk after it was over, and he says that I wrassled him tough and that he felt lucky to win. I hope he tosses all them other fellers around the mat at the state meet."

I'm a little worried about Orv. He's been talking a little more often about "home," and I know he isn't referring to Portland. For all of his smarts and popularity, and for as nice a guy as he is (remember, he went out with Viola Barkle, who can probably bench press a small truck) he is homesick. I think he'd rather be somewhere else, like where there are wide-open spaces and the scent of cottonwoods and sagebrush. That is to say, at home, where the buffalo roam.

It's selfish of me to think this way, but I hope he stays here for another year. You don't come across a friend like Orville often, and I don't want to see him bop out of my life after only eight months. On the other hand, if he will be happier in eastern Oregon, I guess I know the answer.

I don't dare tell Natalie about this. Although she'd never admit it, she still has a mad crush on Orv. Of course, if I ever feel like ending the whole thing, all I'd have to do is tell her that Orv wants to live on a ranch near Heppner and that Heppner doesn't even have a real department store, much less a mall.

Romance in ruins, instantly.

SUNDAY, MARCH 10

I had my six-month interview today with Bishop Winegar.

He asked me how things were going, and I told him okay for the most part. I told him I tried out wishing for success for others a few times and that it seemed to work. We talked about a lot of choices I'd be making in the next few years, such as college and a career, and he asked me about mission preparation. I also told him that I really like seminary and am learning a lot. I decided this was not the time to mention that the reason I took such an interest in seminary originally, was because I wanted to impress a girl with my knowledge of the scriptures and my overall excellent spirituality.

We talked about some other things—the Word of Wisdom, drugs, being honest, staying morally clean, and so on. Bishop Winegar told me he appreciated what I was doing for Sister Lawson. "She's talked with me several times and said how much she enjoys visiting with you. Your friendship is important to her, Wally. You have a good heart, and that's going to carry you a long way in life. At a young age, you understand the joy of serving others."

That made me feel good. A guy like me, he needs something to hold on to. I mean, looking back at this year, I've had my share of disasters. Getting my first real crush on a girl who thought as often about me as she did her library card. My near-failure in choir. Wearing the suit, then sitting on the bench for most of the basketball season. And the list could go on and on.

Plus, high school in general has a way of making

you think less of yourself. There are so many kids who are eager to put you down. It gets easy to start wondering who you are and what you really stand for. Look at me. I'm tall, I'm skinny, I've occasionally become intimately familiar with facial blemishes, I have to squint to see the backboard (glasses in my future, no doubt), and I'm only sort of ruggedly handsome when I hold my head at the right angle. I want to be someone, but keep getting in my own way. My guess is that I never will be on the front cover of a magazine for something famous I've done or said. So during the times I feel like, Whipple, you are a zero, worthless except for the basic value of the chemicals in your body and your decent jumpshot, I will try to remember what Bishop Winegar told me. "Wally, you have a good heart. And that's going to carry you a long way in this life." That's the kind of spin I need to put on my life.

I told Mom about what Bishop Winegar said, and she seemed really pleased. She told me that having a good heart is something you have for life and beyond. I guess she's right—and in the long run, maybe that is a lot more important than being on a magazine cover.

TUESDAY, MARCH 12

Natalie's depression is winding down fast. We went to a year-end banquet for cheerleaders where she was voted "most sincere cheerleader" and received a little plaque.

Having the plaque has really helped to restore her outlook on life. Plus, she got to show how cute she is in front of all the players, coaches, and parents at the banquet. When Mrs. Cofferd, the advisor to the cheerleaders, gave her the plaque, Natalie got all choked up and gave a little speech that went something like this: "Thanks to all of you people who have made me what I am today, and no matter how far I go, or how much money I earn, or how important I become, I will always be glad to meet you in a restaurant for lunch."

I just about strangled on my strawberry gelatin with the dab of fake whipped cream on it. Mom gave me The Look, which I translated as, "Wallace, don't even *think* about saying anything mean to her or else you will be on bread and water for the next six weeks and grounded until your mission."

Natalie is also continuing her experiment with sisterly love. She told me that she not only regularly says "hi" to Lindy Hightower, but that they actually sit by each other at lunch. Maybe Nat *is* sincere about becoming better friends with Lindy, but I won't believe it unless Natalie invites Lindy to share the ultimate experience with her—going to the mall.

"I think you were right about that stuff, like doing something for someone else," she told me. "Seriously. Like, Lindy and me are becoming friends, and I think we both recognize now that neither of us are conceited, and that we have a lot in common. Like, we dress really good, and we're both cute."

That's my sister. Seriously.

FRIDAY, MARCH 15

I am nervous. More stress is not what I need, but more stress is what I have.

Mr. Ashbury told us today we'll all be singing solos in the next two weeks.

True, my voice is getting better. But I'm not ready to be a soloist at this point in my singing career. Hey, only six months ago, I was still lip-synching. I rate singing a solo right up there with say, walking barefoot across a Slavic nation in mid-winter, in the list of things I'm looking forward to.

I suppose I have no choice. This is one thing I'm learning about life. Getting to be an adult means you don't always get to do exactly what you want to do, and you often have to do things that you really don't want to do. Does that make sense? Perfect sense to me.

Food for thought. I was walking home with Lumpy today, after school. It was a nice March day, which in Portland means that it wasn't raining, and the wind was blowing slightly less than gale force. I was telling Lumpy about the banquet on Monday, trying to coax a laugh at Natalie's expense. Usually, when I tell him about Nat, he's all ears since he has a sister in the fifth grade, and he's trying to prepare for the time when she becomes a teenager. In this regard, I'm kind of like his mentor.

Lumpy didn't give me much of a reaction.

"What's wrong, Lump? Doesn't that seem funny? An award for sincere cheerleading and a really terrible speech."

"Yeah. A little. But you can look at it in another way."

"What other way? Natalie was being herself, which is to say, immature, self-centered, and shallow."

"That's true. I also think that Natalie isn't that much different from us."

I stopped walking. Natalie not different? Sometimes I think we're not even members of the same species, much less members of the same family.

He looked up into the air for a second and seemed to be searching for the right words.

"Not to get too heavy, but it seems like she's trying to find herself. For now, she's Natalie the Cheerleader, Natalie the Cute, Natalie the one who always has to Look Good. Maybe, when she grows up a little more, she'll be Natalie the Friend, Natalie the Mother, Natalie the Okay Person. You know what I'm saying?"

Don't muff the message here, Whipple. I have to look back only a few pages to read about how important it is to have something to hang my own fragile self-image on. Natalie wouldn't understand it in those terms and wouldn't accept my explanation for it, but it is true for her, too, I guess. Lumpy's probably right. In her own way, she's looking, too. The Search for Natalie Whipple.

TUESDAY, MARCH 19

Update on Chuck's birthday: the BYU shirt is purchased and wrapped, hidden in Natalie's closet.

Update on choir: more than half of the guys have sung. My number is coming up soon. Maybe I can cut a deal with Mr. Ashbury, no solo, and I'll clean his chalkboards for the rest of the year. Whipple Caves In!

Update on track: I have successfully avoided Mr. Leonard in the hallways for almost a week now, although once it meant a hasty left-hand turn down into the wood shop wing and a bee-line right through one of the more obscure exits at school, where all the smokers hang out, comparing their tattoos.

Update on driving: I am going to get my nerve up and no matter what, bring up the subject to Mom and Dad this week. Driving has become more than simply an act of getting the car keys and sitting behind the wheel. It has become more than a symbol of my growing maturity. It has become a biological need, like salmon returning to their home streams to spawn and die, although the stakes are a little higher for salmon. Teenagers must drive. This week—honest— no later. It's now in writing, and if I do not follow through, this page will always bring shame to me.

WEDNESDAY, MARCH 20

This has been one of the best days of my semi-adult life. I mean, I couldn't have dreamed of a better day, given the limited parameters of my life, which are basically school, home, church, and sports. This day gives me hope for my future, that I will amount to something, that Wallace Whipple has what it takes in life to succeed. I understand better, now, all of those talks in church about how we weren't sent to earth to fail. I am riding the top of a wave, reaching the peak of a mountain, having front row seats at a Tony Bennett concert. Life is good at this moment, sweet indeed.

My climb to new and higher rungs on the ladder of life started in . . . are you ready for this . . . CHOIR!

Yes, choir. The place where, for most of the year, I've felt as out of place as earmuffs in Miami.

Unwelcome. Misfit. Nerd City. Today, Mr. Ashbury scanned the list of those who had not soloed. A prickly sensation ran down my spine, and my mouth started to feel like I'd been chewing a wad of paper napkins.

"Wally, let's hear from you!" Mr. Ashbury boomed. He always booms, I thought. He's always cheerful. He's getting on my nerves. Lumpy gave me a long, pitying look.

I could do nothing but shuffle to the piano, where Mr. Ashbury sat grinning the way a vulture must over some hapless, dying animal. It was then inspiration struck, and I do mean inspiration. I mean, I credit being in tune for what happened next. I figured, why not, if you're going to make a fool of yourself, you may as well enjoy doing so and sing a solo that you at least like.

"Uh, Mr. Ashbury, can I sing any song I want to?"

"As long as I can play it on the piano."

"How about 'Catch a Falling Star'? The old Perry Como song."

Mr. Ashbury looked stunned. The expression on his face was serious, and, for an instant, I thought I'd made a major mistake, like he figured I was trying to show off or something.

"You know Como?" he asked incredulously.

I laughed sardonically. (*Sardonically* is a word I learned in Mrs. English's English class today. I don't normally write this way.)

"Yeah. I know Como. Real well."

I could see respect in his eyes.

"Como is a master. Wally, you surprise me. I didn't think anyone your age . . . " He shook his head in amazement. He was briefly overcome with emotion. Then he broke into the melody. Now, I've been singing that song since I was a little kid. In fact, one of my earliest memories is of my mom singing it to me. I must have picked it up from her, and maybe that accounts for my weird taste in music. Anyway, it's a song that I've sung at least 47,000 times, and I can get through it decently. I started. My voice sounded pretty good. I got a little confidence going. By the end, I knew I was on key—not only with the song, but also with Mr. Ashbury. We finished up, and he positively beamed at me and gave a one-man ovation. "Very nice, Wally. Very nice. Your improvement is remarkable. We'll have to talk about Como and the other greats. By the way . . . what about Torme?"

"Torme? The 'Velvet Fog'? Only the greatest, in my opinion. We can talk, sure. I'll even let you borrow some of my tapes."

For a second, I thought he would weep. But he recovered his composure and said sort of quietly, "That would be a wonderful gesture, Wally."

I took my seat next to Lumpy, while the next victim marched to the piano.

"You're so lucky, Whipple," Lumpy whispered. "One in a million shot and you pounced on it. Perry Como. Who is he, anyway?"

I am on a winning streak, and even if it is only one day long, I think I'll pop the question to my parents tonight about getting my license.

In a matter of a few minutes, I'll find out how lucky I really am.

THURSDAY, MARCH 21

Yes! The phenomenal roll of Whipple continues, unchecked, gaining momentum, becoming stronger, and taking on a life of its own. Life is good. I haven't felt this way since I won the 7th grade spelling bee, when the class genius/nerd and odds-on-favorite, Milton Glenn, misspelled *deleterious*.

The reason for this state of . . . joy—yes, joy—is that my parents said okay to the license. And the ease with which it all happened leaves me in a daze.

We're at the dinner table, and I feel this urge building within me. (Remember my theory about driving being a biological need? I think I'm on to something.) I can feel this pressure, growing and growing, like I was being squeezed from outside. My food didn't taste good. I couldn't keep up with the usual mealtime conversation. I felt feverish. I knew that the time had come. All the little hormones in my body that say "license" on them were churning through my system. I could feel this incredible surge of energy building, growing, getting larger and larger . . . until I knew I was going to burst! The floodgates ripped away, and I fairly shouted, "Mom, Dad! I need my license!"

Smooth Whipple, really smooth.

As it so happened, Dad was just ready to put a fork filled with creamed broccoli into his mouth. He looked at me thoughtfully for a couple of seconds and then put his fork down.

I'd blown it in a royal way. All of my plans to have an adult conversation with my parents about the advantages of me driving were shredded in one jolt of raw emotion. I would forever be Wally Whipple, the license-less, the guy who stayed at home and who even had to have his parents drive him to Wyoming where he became a hermit. I was defeated, doomed, and my parents didn't even have to roll out the heavy artillery on me, i.e., the cost-of-insurance argument. I was ready to surrender without another word, ready to say, "Uh, forget it, I don't know what came over me. Let's pretend the last sixty seconds never happened and just finish dinner," when Dad surprised me, totally.

"I think we could make that work, Wally."

I almost went into shock. My brain refused to accept the answer because it was so unexpected. Billions of cells all over my body who were working away at keeping things going, suddenly stopped what they were doing, looked at each other, and said, "Did you hear that? Can you believe it? Awesome dude!" And they began to give each other their little cell high-fives.

"You mean . . . I can get my license?" I asked hoarsely, every fiber of my being trembling as the brain cells staggered back to work.

"Yes. Your mother and I could use a little relief from being taxi drivers."

In the corner, Natalie is almost gagging on her meal. I know that she is taking mental notes so that when she turns sixteen, she'll be able to whine, "You let Wally drive when he was my age!"

This is too easy. There must be a catch.

"What about insurance?" I ask.

NOTE: I can't believe I said the I-word. Temporary insanity. I have my parents right where I want them, they say okay, everything is totally awesome, and I bring up insurance.

Monstrously dumb, Whipple. No doubt Dad will smack his forehead, and say, "Gosh! We forgot about insurance. It's so expensive, Wally. We're sorry, but you'll just have to wait until you can pay for your own or until you are twenty-seven years old, whichever comes first." That's what I deserved. But he stunned me again.

"Insurance is spendy, but we can handle it. We do expect you to be responsible, though. Driving is a privilege, and we'll have to make sure that you earn it," Dad said.

"No problem, Dad." I was beginning to regain my composure, and thought at least I should use a little of my strategy so that I could report to Orville with a shred of pride intact. "I think having my license will help improve my grades, Dad."

He looked at me as though my mind had slipped a gear. "No it won't, Wally."

"Yes sir, you're right. A license won't. You're right, as always, Dad."

"Wally, cut it out. And eat your vegetables."

"Sure thing, Dad. Whatever you say."

Broccoli never tasted so good.

SATURDAY, MARCH 23

Yes, this is joy. I know what it feels like, now. Joy is almost having your license.

1. Soon, Lumpy and I will be driving to Hamburger Bob's.

2. Soon, I will be able to walk up to any girl in

school or church and ask her out with confidence, se-
cure in the knowledge that I have WHEELS!

3. Soon, I will be able to drive to church dances.

4. Soon, I will be able to jangle the car keys at just
the right moment in my life, such as when I want to
impress girls.

5. Soon, I will be able to look at Lumpy and say,
"If you wanna go, you gotta pay for half the gas."

6. Soon, I must purchase my driving sunglasses so
that I will look good behind the wheel, even if it is
our twelve-year-old family station wagon.

I could go on, but won't. Let us just say that I am
basking in the glow of this moment, and I hope the
feeling will never go away.

SUNDAY, MARCH 24

We're headed to church, all hustling out the door,
about six minutes before Sacrament meeting begins
and facing a fourteen-minute drive to the chapel.
Everyone is hopping into the car, creating a scene of
all elbows, legs, feet, and Sunday-best clothing. Dad
opens his door, starts to sit down in the seat, then gets
out of the car and stands up.

"Wally," he says, "your turn." Then he tosses the
keys to me and climbs into the backseat. "Keep the
speed down, kiddo, like no faster than the speed of
sound."

Casually, I slip behind the wheel, adjust the mirror, and turn on the ignition.

"WE'RE ALL GOING TO DIE!" shrieks Natalie.

"No problem," I say, and we get to church just as
Sister Hilton starts the last verse of the opening song.

MONDAY, MARCH 25

The first day of spring break, and I had nothing to do . . . nada, zero, zip. It is, however, Chuck's birthday, so I decided to spend a lot of time with him.

We shot baskets (Chuck went approximately 0 for 500), then headed to Hamburger Bob's, for a nice, thick, chocolate milkshake. We just sat there, sipping shakes and talking about all of the major changes in his life now that he is six. Stuff like, writing in cursive, expanding his baseball card collection for investment purposes, and going to school full-time next year.

Chuck liked the sweatshirt I gave him, and Mom and Dad came through with a nice two-wheeler for him. Natalie did okay, too, buying him a portable radio, complete with earphones. Chuck loves radios. After the party at dinner, Chuck sat entranced in the middle of the living room floor with his new shirt on and listening to his new radio.

I like being a big brother to Chuck. What I like best about him is this: he likes me. It's that simple. No matter what kind of day I've had, what kind of mood I'm in, whether I just scored forty-six points in a basketball game or even wore my suit to school and sat on the bench, Chuck doesn't care. I'm still the same person in his eyes.

I guess that means we're friends as well as brothers. Good times, bad times, and everything in between. Maybe that's how you define friendship.

One more thing. I called Lumpy today and asked him if he wanted to goof around this afternoon. He went into an immediate stall and then finally admitted in a small voice, "I've got practice this afternoon."

"Practice for what?"

"Ah, I'm on the track team."

"What? Are you lost in space?"

"No. Coach Leonard just kept talking to me and kept telling me that I have the chance to be great."

"Lumpy, I think he says that to everyone."

"I know . . . but I think he meant it in my case. 'The champion inside,' he was telling me. You know how he is. He should sell insurance, he'd be a millionaire. Anyway, I started to believe him about all this raw potential stored up in me, so I sort of showed up in the locker room one day after school, and the next thing I knew, I was in sweats, running laps. I'm thinking about the 400-meters. But I like the idea of the javelin because I would just have to run a little bit and then heave something. Sort of like what I did all during cross-country, but not really the same."

I didn't try to talk him out of it, and I didn't make fun of him. What can I say? While I was reading a book on my bed late this afternoon and trying only a little to resist the sensation of pleasant drowsiness that was overwhelming me, Lumpy was running in circles around the track and probably trying to hold down his lunch.

Now, I ask, who is in the best position?

WEDNESDAY, MARCH 27

Trouble on the horizon.

It began when I got up for breakfast this morning. Dad had already taken off for work. Chuck was up and watching "Mr. Rogers." Natalie was still asleep, which is not surprising because she's been known to go until noon when there is no school. Mom said hello, then something about needing to go to the grocery store, and I pounced on the chance to show her how helpful I will be when I get my license.

"Want me to drive you, Mom? I could use the practice."

That's where I went wrong. It was the opening she was waiting for. My stomach knotted up, and I found it difficult to breathe for a few seconds when I heard the reply.

"Well, your father and I have been talking . . . "

If ever there were words to strike terror into the hearts of teenagers anywhere, they are these: "Your father and I have been talking." I'm sure it is the same worldwide. On the savannahs of Africa, a parent will say, "Your father and I have been talking . . . " and, instantly, the kid knows trouble is coming. Ditto for a chalet in Switzerland, a thatched hut in Tonga, a crowded government-owned apartment in Russia. "Your father and I have been talking." Curse those words! They are a universal sign that something is about to go wrong, big time, but we are helpless. We are victims of a huge plot that has been passed from generation to generation, something like a genetic disorder.

"Your father and I have been talking, and we have decided that before you get your license . . . "

Here comes the punch line. Before what? Much of my life depends on this. Get straight A's? Go on a mission? Be kind to Natalie?

"... that you need to finish your Eagle Scout project. You have been putting it off, and we think that you'll be even more distracted after you get your license."

THE EAGLE SCOUT PROJECT! Ha! Is that all they could come up with? Piece of cake, no challenge, whatsoever. And yes, she's right, I do intend to be much more distracted after I get my license.

"Okay, Mom, no problem."

"Fine, Wally. We feel strongly about all the work you've put into Scouting, and we don't want you to stop ten yards from the finish line. You can still practice driving, and we hope you have the Eagle wrapped up before school is out."

I decide to display the new, more mature version of Wally Whipple.

"Mom, I'm glad that you and Dad have reminded me of my Eagle Scout opportunity. What you are saying is only fair, and I can live with it. I appreciate parents who want their children to succeed at the truly important things in life."

My mom looks at me as though my cerebral cortex is made of lawn clippings, which tells me I don't quite have the language of maturity down yet. Nevertheless, she says, "That's fine, dear."

I will organize my Eagle Scout project this week. I need to raise that money to rebuild the hiker's shelter on Mt. Hood. The Whipple Express is back on track.

SATURDAY, MARCH 30

Spring break is almost over. Typical of our wonderful Oregon climate, it rained at least part of every day and all of several days. I vegged out a lot. Watched old movies on TV and ate enough potato chips to keep the state of Idaho profitable for the next decade. Did a little homework and actually stooped so low as to watch reruns of "Gilligan's Island" four days in a row. I feel strong, rested, and ready for the world.

Lumpy called to see if I wanted to go to the stake dance tonight. I said, "Okay, let's make a few wall-flowers happy." It will be my last blaze of glory—a fitting end to spring break.

Heck, I'm feeling so good that I may even dance tonight.

SUNDAY, MARCH 31

This is unbelievable. This is how it must feel if someone knocks on your door and hands you a bag filled with a million dollars and says, "Keep it. We've secretly watched you for years and you are a good person who deserves to be wealthy beyond your wildest dreams. Take this, enjoy it, and have a happy rest of your life."

It feels almost that good. Let me relive every glorious moment.

Lumpy's dad drove us to the stake center and let us off a block away in case anyone was looking. We walked from the parking lot as though we had just hopped out of our car after driving ourselves to the dance. I even jangled a few keys in my pocket, although they were only the key to our garage and to my bicycle lock.

We get inside and the dance has already started. Lumpy and I do our usual thing, which is to say that we scope out the refreshments and then walk around trying to look like we're cool while checking out the girls who are there. We're sort of running out of things to do about a half-hour later. We're approaching the critical time of the dance, that is, when it's too early for refreshments and when we have to decide if we want to dance. (Read that, if we have the courage to ask a girl to dance.)

At this point, I get a good idea, which is to look at my hair, so I head for the restroom. If I'm really lucky, I figure that by the time I get back, the refreshments will be ready, and then I will have a good reason not to dance because the eats are on.

Well, I go down the hallway, and I'm the only person there. At least for a moment. Someone turns the corner at the opposite end of the hall and is walking right toward me.

It is Julie Sloan.

My stomach jumps into my throat. What should I do? Turn and walk the other way? Turn and *run* the other way? No, Wally, I tell myself. For once, be cool. Just glide down the hallway, nod, and say, "Yo." Then keep walking. As fast as you can. Remember, she can't follow you into the restroom. Okay, I'm set, got my plan. My feet are still shuffling. My body seems to be in synch with my brain, for a change. Ha! Who is Julie, anyway? Just another pretty face. It's not like I had anything more than a crush on her. No big deal. Fifteen feet apart, ten . . . five . . .

Julie looks at me. I am about to say yo, but she speaks first.

"Wally, do you have a minute? I really want to talk with you."

My attempt to say "yo" sort of dribbles down my chin. I know what is happening here. All the brain cells have gotten together for an emergency meeting and have voted to go on strike. "That's it, we quit. You're on your own, peanut brain. See if you can make an impression on her without us!"

Julie takes my mangled "yo" for a "yes" because she starts talking to me.

"Wally, I've felt terrible for the past six weeks. I know that day in seminary when you overheard Amy and me talking probably gave you the wrong impression. It sounded unkind, and I didn't mean for it to come out that way. I'm sorry, Wally."

Whoa! An apology! I have dreamed of this moment. I have imagined at least one hundred times what I would say, the speech I would give, should this ever happen. I had it down cold.

"Julie, Julie, Julie," I would say, "Don't give it another thought, because I certainly haven't. I was sure that you weren't yourself that morning, and I thought nothing of it, because, frankly, that's just the way I am. We'll remain friends, and I will always think well of you, wherever our paths take us, no matter how far apart we may drift." That was the basic speech. Now, it was all really happening.

"Das okay, Julie."

Das okay, Julie? Oh, crud. Why can't I come up with something that shows my IQ is equal to the temperature of a July day? Why do I choose these critical moments to revert back to the way I talked when I was three years old? Come back, brain cells, come back, quickly!

"I think you're a really nice person. It's just that the thought of going out with you hadn't occurred to me, and I guess I was surprised when Amy mentioned it. I didn't mean to hurt your feelings."

"My feelings weren't hurt," I lied. The brain cells were starting to file back in, punching the time clock. I actually muttered a coherent, albeit untruthful, sentence.

"In fact," Julie said, "I *would* like to go out with you sometime. If you want to, that is."

Want to? I'd almost kill for the opportunity. But I came across somewhat more restrained. "Yeah. Maybe, sometime. But you don't have to."

"It's that I *want* to, not have to."

"Wouldn't Joe be ticked off? Joe and I are friends, and I wouldn't want to, uh, barge in. I mean the problems of two people like us don't amount to a hill of beans in this world." Fortunately, I had just watched Humphrey Bogart in *Casablanca* during one of my extended veg-out periods this week, and I stole the line from the movie. It seemed to fit. It seemed classy.

"You're so funny!" she laughed. "Don't worry about Joe. It's nice of you to be concerned, but he and I are just good friends, and we both know we'll date other people."

"Oh."

"Are *we* friends?"

"Yeah. I think so."

"Good. I feel better. I worried a lot. You've always been so nice to me. Even when you had that frigid voice attack back in September, you still tried to talk with me and make me feel welcome. I'll always remember that."

"So will I," I said. "Believe me, so will I. Uh, I've got to comb my hair now."

"Okay. Maybe we can dance later tonight."

"Yeah. Maybe." Then we split up.

I went to the restroom and just stared in the mirror for five minutes. Then I hissed one well-deserved "Yes!" and went back into the dance and pulled Lumpy away from the refreshments (a task not easily nor often done) and told him everything. He went bananas.

"You know what this means? It means she really likes you. A lot. Cool, Wally. You played it like a pro. Here we all thought you were a dork, not even making sense when you talked with her, and it turns out she really goes for the shy and bumbling type. You going to dance with her tonight?"

"I don't know. My knees feel weak. Actually, I feel a little nauseous."

"Smooth, Wally. Deprive her of your presence a while longer. Stay away, and it will drive her wild. You've got to keep her guessing now. You are in control and need to keep it that way."

I decided to let Lumpy labor under the illusion a while longer that I had a great master scheme for getting Julie to like me. Nothing could be further from the truth, in reality. I just fumbled my way into all this, and my stomach was really flip-flopping the whole time. But, if Lumpy wants to think of me as the Genius of Love, then so be it.

Now, I have tough decisions to make.

Do I ask Julie out?

If so, where do we go?

What about Edwina? I need to do something with her, too.

How do I act around Julie?

Is all this happening to me?

Is it okay to feel flattered that at least two girls in the universe seem to want to go out with me?

Does Julie like me?

I have learned one truth this night: Love can make you feel excellent and nauseous, at the same time.

CHAPTER 8
ApriL

MONDAY, APRIL 1

Almost forty-eight hours have passed since The Amazing Conversation with Julie, and I have but one question. Was it an early April Fool's joke?

Naw. Don't think so. Nobody can fake sincerity like that.

When do I ask Julie out?

If I ask her out too soon, like the next couple of weeks, it will look like I'm too eager, and she will have the upper hand. The cool thing to do is stay remotely friendly and then spring the question on her in about a month. This has an added advantage. If I wait a month, I should have my license, and I'll be able to drive on our date. This will do wonders for the self-confidence. You don't want to show up on the doorstep of a girl like Julie, with your dad in the car parked at the curb.

ME: "Dad, I'd like you to meet my friend, Julie."

DAD: "Well, well. It sure is nice to meet you, Julie. We've heard a lot about you."

JULIE: "Thank you, Mr. Whipple. I really enjoy having your son in our seminary class."

DAD: "Call me Wally, if you don't mind. And yes, Wally is a good boy, although he could get along better with his sister."

And so it goes the whole night. Dad and Julie hit it off great, while I sit there like a jerk. And every time Julie says, "Wally," two of us answer. This is definitely not the way to go.

Orv is home from Heppner. He had a great time, sheared some sheep, got his horse ready for spring. Guess that's what you do in Heppner during spring break.

Natalie and Lindy had a spat. It seems that their taste is too much alike, and they wore identical tops to school. "She was so rude. I go, 'That's my top, Lindy,' trying to be nice to her, but she goes, 'I had mine first.' Like, before I even told her when I bought mine. So, I don't eat lunch with her anymore. And when I told our friends about it, they were on my side so, like, I won, and she lost."

Dad got called into the stake president's office yesterday. The stake president asked him to serve a stake mission. It would be his fourth. Dad said yes.

Chuck is shooting on the driveway every day. Still hasn't hit his first real basket, but he's getting closer. It's only a matter of time.

Lots of homework left for tonight. The teachers are really putting it to us, trying to make sure we don't get out of their classes without learning something. It's

April, and all of us are getting the faint, sweet sense that the school year is almost over.

With any luck, I might survive it.

TUESDAY, APRIL 2

I'm on a roll. Nothing can go wrong for me. School is great, the grades are up. I'm within a few weeks of getting my license, which will mean freedom and independence. And Julie Sloan, the girl I will remember throughout eternity as the first girl I ever really liked, with the exception of my mother and, perhaps, Natalie, the same one who reduced me to dust with a simple giggle in the hallway before seminary, less than two months ago, now wants to go out with me. I am the brother of Chuck, who will undoubtedly be famous and wealthy someday; the friend of Orville, the truest cowboy who ever trod the asphalt of Portland; and the buddy of Lumpy Felton, who . . . who . . . is Lumpy, and therefore unique. All of these things, plus more, I have going for me and, then, I take one huge step backward in the course of ninety seconds, after school today.

What did I do? For one thing, I've made members of the Parents' Conspiracy deliriously happy. I did so by going out for track.

It was so innocent. Orv was walking down the hall toward the gym after school. Being the clever fellow that I am, I think, "Orville + Truck = Ride home for Wally."

"Orv, you got room for me in the truck?"

"Always, bud. But I got track practice, so you'll have to wait a spell."

"Track?"

"Yep. I figured since wrasslin' was so easy, maybe I ought to try something a little more challenging. So I turned out for track yesterday. But I'm going to be one sorry fella, I think. Coach Leonard looks at me and says, 'You look like a shotputter. Go over to the ring there and Coach Hill will help you out.' So I wander on over, and they give me this iron ball to flang around. It ain't no big whup, you just tuck it under your chin, twirl around a little and grunt, then toss the thing. Coach Hill got all excited when he seen how far I can flang it. But shucks, I don't see nothing special about it. Anyone with sense enough to pour water out of a boot can throw the shot."

"But Orv, you went out for track."

"Yep. Why don't you? You sort of promised McCloud you would, and you don't seem the kind to back out of your word. Put them long legs to work. You're getting a little soft, it seems. You puttin' on a few extra pounds?"

"Orv, running was okay hundreds of years ago, when you had to stay in front of the wolf pack. But I'm a slow runner. I could get lapped in the 100 meters. And I think I'm allergic to pain. It makes me feel bad. And I've got important things to do, like go home and do nothing, which is important because it relieves stress."

"So you turnin' out or not? You did allow to McCloud that you would."

My resolve melted. Couldn't let Orv think that my promises meant nothing.

And he thinks I'm getting soft. Soft. Harrumpphh. "Yeah, Orv. I'll try it."

I went with him to the locker room where Coach Leonard immediately went into a low orbit over the earth. "I knew you'd join us, Wally. You're a champion, and you can't keep a champion down." After a quick call to my mother to explain why I'd be late, I found myself running laps in my P.E. shoes and trying to figure out where I had gone wrong in life. First meet in two weeks. At least Orville can drive me home every night.

I wonder if Julie likes track?

THURSDAY, APRIL 4

I'm in the cafeteria today, with the other members of The Posse, as Orville has taken to calling our lunch group. Between double-cheese-and-chili-onion dogs, the conversation turns to me and Julie. Lumpy is still truly amazed that Julie wants to go out with me, to the point where he says it has strengthened his testimony. "Shows that miracles still happen," he says. Anyway, Lumpy starts pumping me about when I'm going to take her out and where we will go. I say something about not wanting to rush things (translation: I'm not going out with her until after I get my license), and that I'm not sure where we should go, but I really didn't think it necessary to worry about it now. The Posse goes nuts.

"You need to go out with her before some other guy comes in and pushes you out the door," Mickey says. "That happened to my brother in college. He waited a couple of weeks to ask a girl out that he knew liked him and he liked her, but in the meantime, another guy asked her out and proposed to her on the second date. Man, she was ready. So when my brother called her up, she said, 'I can't go out with you, Ben, because I'm getting married. Nice knowing you. Good-bye.'"

"You've only got so long," Lumpy agreed. "Like, if you don't ask her out in the next few days, she's going to lose interest in you. It's sweet today, but everything could change tomorrow, especially with a guy like Joe around. Nothing personal, Wally, but you aren't in Joe's league."

Orville grunted. "Why you all making this so danged difficult? It ain't no big whup. You just set it in your mind that you're going out, ask her, then go out. Sounds like she's already done most of the trail work on this one."

I'm not quite sure what he meant, but I nodded as though in deep thought. I wanted to change the subject, so I asked, "Where do you take someone like Julie, though?"

The Posse was silent for a few seconds.

"There's a new truck show up at the Coliseum," Orv suggested.

"Take her to a movie or a play," Rob said. "If you go to a movie, you don't have to work so hard at it. You let whatever's going on do all the entertaining. You don't even have to talk with her except if you ask her about refreshments."

Lumpy had a third idea. "Go to a concert where they play classical music. You know, where they have an orchestra and some guy with long hair who wears a tux who directs it, and they play really old music, like before the 1950s. Julie will think you have really good taste and a brain."

"I like that, Lump. I like those big guitars they play there, too."

"You mean cellos," Orville said.

"Yeah. Cellos. I knew that," I said.

"So a concert it is?"

"Yeah. I can handle a concert."

"When are you going to ask her?" Lumpy pressed.

"Soon. Really soon," I promised, and before they could pin me down, the bell rang, and it was time for English class.

Having your love life, scanty as it is, discussed by your friends at lunch is not exactly a great feeling. I'd rather be doing something much more constructive with my time, such as eating a second chili-and-onion hot dog.

FRIDAY, APRIL 5

I've been doing track for a couple of days now, and I forgot that running long distances leaves you exhausted. Let us now cut to the Parents' Conspiracy Meeting, Portland chapter.

MOM: "Sometimes your children do it to themselves."

ANOTHER PARENT: "How so, Pam?"

MOM: "Right out of the blue, our 16–year-old son goes out for the track team, with no prompting from us whatsoever. His father and I couldn't be more pleased. It's wonderful. There aren't many kids around who would voluntarily go through so much pain with so little to show for it."

It's true. Orville will do well in the shot, and Lumpy shows promise in the javelin. I will probably not come close to winning a race all season. Even Coach Leonard, after praising my heart and my champion will, was stumped about which event I should participate in.

"Wally, speed isn't your forte, so I don't think we'll have you in the sprints or hurdles. Endurance isn't your strong point, either, so that lets out the distances. I guess that makes you a middle distance runner."

That's how I became an 800–meter man. Twice around the track, going as fast as you can. All the other guys who run the 800 talk about strategy— sprinting at the start, gliding in the middle, hanging back until the last turn and then pouring it on. My strategy is just to finish. I ran my first 800 in practice today. The distance coach, Mr. Werner, started to holler at us to "Kick it in, guys, move . . . move!" as we turned the corner and headed into the stretch. I was a good twenty-five meters behind everyone at that point, anyway, and wondered if crawling the rest of the way would be acceptable. Six runners practiced the 800 today, and do I need to record where I finished? Let's just say it wasn't in the top five.

The only time I even halfway look like a runner is when we run our warm-up route behind the tennis courts. On the slim chance that Julie is looking at me, I run as hard as I can. All of a sudden, Wally the Slug flashes a burst of speed, effectively wiping out my energy reserves for the rest of practice. Today, someone mumbled that Whipple must have a honey playing tennis because it was the only time anyone ever sees me sprint.

If this is my only joy to be had from track, so be it.

Why do I do this to myself? Should I talk to my dad about quitting?

SATURDAY, APRIL 6

I'm getting a little weird about asking out Julie. I mean, if I put as much effort into, say track, as I do worrying and wondering about Julie, I would be a lock for the next Olympics.

How desperate am I getting? This desperate—I went to Natalie for advice. Natalie doesn't date, but she knows the rules. I thought that maybe getting a feminine viewpoint might not hurt. The guys in The Posse can only give me advice from a limited perspective. And although Nat doesn't go out yet, it doesn't stop her from thinking about dating, talking about dating, and fantasizing about dating.

ME: "Natalie, for argument's sake, let's just say that I wanted to ask a girl out."

HER: "You thinking about unleashing all your charm again on the poor helpless females of the world? Spare us! Spare us, Wally! Take pity on us. Seriously."

ME: (Ignoring her sarcasm) "Yes, as a matter of fact, I am. And I want it to be a nice date, sort of classy."

HER: "You? Sort of classy? What are you going to do? Take her out for chili dogs?"

ME: "No. But I wanted to ask you what you thought a really classy date would be."

HER: "Seriously?"

ME: "Yeah, seriously."

HER: "Well, I'd like to go somewhere really nice to eat—"

ME: (With great hope in my voice) "Like Hamburger Bob's?"

HER: (With great disgust in her voice) "No. Not anything *like* Hamburger Bob's."

ME: "Oh. Just kidding."

HER: "No, you weren't. Anyway, a really nice place, with a view of the city, and a waiter who speaks French. Then you go to a concert . . . "

ME: (Again with great hope) "Like classical music?"

HER: "No. Like the Savage Squids or the Hurt and Broke Egos. They're coming to Portland. Anyway, then you go to the concert, then you go out for dessert. And dessert has to be at a nice place, too, like somewhere they have a dessert plate, and you don't order it off the menu. And the dessert should be expensive, too. Then you come home and kiss her goodnight."

ME: (Trying to ignore the last statement, although it is not easy to do so): "Uh . . . all this sounds expensive."

HER: "If you like someone, what's money? You said you wanted it to be classy."

Well, that's how the talk went with Natalie. Despite all the air contained in her cranium, I guess I did glean a pointer or two. Still, I'm confused. This has to be a flawless date. Everything has to be perfect, come off like clockwork. The facts are these: Lumpy is right, Julie and I aren't in the same league and I have only one chance to really impress her. If I can fake it for just one night, that Wallace Whipple is indeed cool, then maybe I have a chance with Julie. And if I can fake it long enough, then maybe I will start to actually be cool, and the search for Wallace Whipple will be over. I will have become what I want to be: one cool dude, and recognized as such by everyone I know.

Don't muff it, Whipple!

P.S. This is general conference weekend. Dad and I went to general priesthood meeting tonight and one of the speakers told a story about how his football team got beat something like 106–6.

I can relate to a message like that, I really can. There are days when I feel like I'm down by one hundred points, and I don't quite know which way to run.

SUNDAY, APRIL 7

I watched more of general conference today. Is this a sign of maturity? I actually listened to the talks and enjoyed them. This may scoop me big points with Julie.

JULIE: "Good morning, Wally."

ME: "Yes, it is a good morning. It reminds me of something I heard in conference yesterday . . . "

Well, maybe I need to smooth that one out a bit.

Time to play that fun new game sweeping across the nation, "Guess Your Grades!"

I feel pretty good about school, despite athletics, despite having to get up in the wee hours of the morning when all my cells are saying, "PLEEAASSSSE Wally! Just a few more winks. We'll be good to you today, honest we will!"

If my grades work out, I can already sense more leverage in my bid for a license.

DAD: "Well, Wally, we sure are proud of your performance in school. This is an excellent report card."

ME: (Doing humble) "Golly, Dad, gee, wow. I mean, I'm just a lot like you I guess, other than I don't have my license."

DAD: "We'll take care of that soon, Son. How about this Friday? Then you can ask out the Sloan girl, and your whole life will come together."

ME: "Wow, Dad, that would be swell! You're really special."

DAD: "And so are you, Son."

Right.

Okay, fasten your seat belts.

Choir. Did Perry Como and Mel Torme put me over the top? Despite a singing voice reminiscent of squeaky car breaks, I think a big A is on the way.

Social Studies. An A. I'm clicking in this class.

Physical Ed. My sure thing. Another A.

Health. This is where the string will stop. Mr. Catton is a tough grader, and I haven't done the things necessary to bring my grade up, like studying more, buttering up the teacher, answering questions in class, buttering up the teacher, doing extra credit work, and, if I haven't mentioned it before, buttering up the teacher. Okay world, sigh on the same cue: a B. Curse you, Alvin Hashburn, and all the time you spend after class telling Mr. Catton how well he explains the functions of the endocrine system and how, at last, you finally understand where pimples come from.

English. I don't know, but gut instinct tells me yet another B. Mrs. English still feels I'm coasting a bit, and that makes a lot of sense because I am coasting a bit. I will, however, hope for mercy.

Math. A B. No doubt. I am seriously considering naming my firstborn after Edwina (Ed if it's a boy, Ed if it's a girl), because of the kindness she has shown.

Plug in the calculator. Compute . . . and on the low end, we have a 3.33 and on the high end . . . do I dare say it . . . a 3.83!

Unbelievable! Maybe there is a functioning brain in my head after all!

MONDAY, APRIL 8

Sometimes I don't understand the things I do. It's like my mind becomes disengaged from the rest of my body, particularly my mouth. Words tumble out before I know what I'm saying, and always, it seems, I later feel like crawling into a deep, dark cave and assuming the fetal position.

Maybe I need a computer chip implant that will prevent me from committing social suicide. Everytime I'm about to say something dumb, then it would make a tiny little click, and all of a sudden my vocal cords would jam up so I can't get a word out. "Okay, boys, he's about to do it again. Let's shut the kid down," is what the little computer chip operators will say. "Does he ever need us!"

Unfortunately, I don't have such an implant. Ask Joe Vermeer if I need one.

You see, I've been worried about asking Julie out. It's like, here's Joe, the number one guy at school. The best athlete, the top male student, on the minds and in the hearts of practically every female who makes breathing at least an occasional habit. A guy who, for all I know, may someday be president of the United States, and at the very worst, a heart surgeon. And who, with all of that going for him, has been really nice to me.

And even though I'm something akin to an empty box of cold cereal in the order of his universe, I'm about to ask out his girlfriend.

Yeah, his girlfriend. Even though Julie said she and Joe are just good friends, I still sense a little electricity crackling between them. As sort of a guy thing, I want to make sure all of this is okay with Joe. This has been spinning around my brain for a long time, and it's something I know I need to do.

So Joe is sitting in the library by himself when I wander in during study hall. He's got a thick book open, boning up on physics and scribbling notes. This is where my good sense takes a sudden vacation, and I decide I need to talk with Joe about Julie, now.

"Hey, Joe."

He looks up. "Hey, Wally. Pull up a chair."

I do. This is not easy. Approach #1 flashes into my mind, the macho attempt. Something like, "Joe, I know you've been dating Julie a lot, but it's time for me to move in. I'm taking Julie out, and I don't care what you think or say. Got that?"

No. Never do. How about, "Joe, I'm asking your permission to go out with Julie."

Not good. Orville would go nuts. "Sounds like a wiener approach to me, Wally."

Joe is looking at me, expecting me to talk. Too late to think this one out.

"Joe. I'd like to go out with Julie."

BOOM! There it is. The simple approach. He looks down at his physics book for a second. Maybe he decides that if he ignores me, I'll simply go away. No, Joe! Laugh at me, make fun of me, but don't ignore me. I want to be taken seriously.

Watch closely . . . his head is up . . . what remains of our friendship is now on the line . . .

"Neat, Wally. She's a nice girl. You'll have a good time together."

That's it? No fireworks? No temper tantrums? Is Joe cool or what!

Then the crash comes. Big-time thud. He wasn't putting me down, it was just an honest question that reduced me to potato peelings.

"Why are you telling me? Julie's the one you have to talk to."

Time to mumble strange and foreign tongues again.

"Uh, under blood and start core you and Julie like, ah, go out and didn't want to mess, naw, forget I brought up the wholish idea."

"Okay, Wally."

I regain my composure and decide to try for the home run with Joe.

"Thanks, Joe."

He looks up again. "For what?"

"I don't know. For being you, I guess."

"Can't be anyone else, Wally."

"Right. If you weren't you, then you'd be someone else. I gotta go. See ya."

Heaven forbid that Joe and Julie ever start talking about my vocabulary and speech patterns.

"Yo. See you around, Wally," he yawned.

I scuttled out of the library like a crustacean scuttling across the ocean floor. Then I sort of slumped on some stairs and wondered for the next fifteen minutes why I do such things. I could come to no firm conclusions. For once, I was really glad when track practice came around. Maybe if I ran really hard and got extremely tired, I wouldn't have the energy left to feel like such a nerd.

So I ran hard. I got tired. I don't have any energy left. And I still feel like a nerd.

Arrrgh!

WEDNESDAY, APRIL 10

Natalie is troubled. Not depressed, but uneasy with her life. It has to do with Lindy. They still haven't patched up things since both of them wore the same outfit to school, and it is bothering Natalie because she was really viewing Lindy as someone who is almost as cute as herself, with many of the same tastes and ambitions. (The thought that Natalie might have a clone is scary.) "We even talked about opening our own clothes store someday," Natalie sniffed. "And our plans to do major tannage this summer are over."

"Natalie, have you ever thought about just being friendly to her again? Like your little fight never happened?"

"That would show that I was wrong, and she was right."

"Some people might look at it that way, but some

people would think you were cool if you took the first step toward patching things up."

"I don't get it."

"Sometimes you show that you're strong by appearing to be weaker, or saying you made a mistake, even if you didn't. If your friendship is worth anything, you should take the first step and try to patch things up."

"I get it. Like, if I tell her I'm sorry even if I don't mean it, then she might go, 'Oh. Okay.' Then we'd be friends again. You want me to fake it."

"More or less, although faking it isn't the way I'd say it."

"It doesn't make sense."

"Neither does the fight you had with her. You should be friends. Look, she's almost as cute as you are."

"Well, you told me to be nice to her once before, and I was, and it was okay because she didn't turn out to be as conceited as I thought. So I'll be nice again. But I want to tell you one thing."

"What's that?"

"That even though I act like I did something wrong, you know that I didn't, and I'm just doing this because I'm more mature than Lindy."

"Got it, Nat. This is really big of you."

"Seriously?"

"Yeah."

"Is Orville coming over tonight?"

"Maybe."

"Oh. I've got to go somewhere." And she left, no question going to her room to make sure she looked just right should Orv stop by.

Orv did come by later, to drop off a book he had borrowed, Natalie did look cute, and he even told her so. She walked on air the rest of the evening.

If Orv can make her this happy all of the time, I wonder if the Burrells would consider adopting her?

THURSDAY, APRIL 11

So I'm chitchatting with Ed in math class today, and blame it on either my new-found attitude of maturity or male hormones running amuck, but I sort of blurted out, "Ed, do you want to go to a movie next week?"

"That would be nice, Wally."

Whew. One for one. My first time to ask a girl out, and she accepts. This is like hitting your first ever jump shot in a real game. Looks like I have my second date dead ahead. But hey, no big deal. I'm an experienced teenager now. No reason to break into a sweat. Under control.

Tomorrow is the first track meet, and I have set the following goals for my race:

1. Finish it.

2. Finish it without experiencing a lot of pain.

3. Look athletic when I cross the finish line, no matter where I place.

Goal #3 may need an explanation. Some guys look like wimps when they cross the finish line—chalky, panting, and looking as though they are in great pain, perhaps because they are. I, however, want to finish with dignity, my head held high, my stride fluid and graceful. I want to do this because I have self-respect and will not allow one lousy race to dictate my self-image, unless I win, in which case it will leap upward instantly.

I also want to do so because Julie might be done with tennis practice and could possibly be watching the last part of the track meet.

FRIDAY, APRIL 12

This is what one might call a bittersweet day.

First, the good news. My report card showed up with three A's and three B's, working out to a nice 3.5 GPA. Bless Perry Como. I got one of my A's in choir, and I'm sure that the mutual admiration for classic pop singers, not to mention our CD exchange, is what led Mr. Ashbury to give me the new, improved grade. For certain it wasn't my singing voice.

Third straight B in Mrs. English's English class. I may have to talk with her about what it takes to get an A, short of writing the Great American Novel or a sequel to *Moby Dick*.

The part of my day that wasn't so smooth was the track meet.

About eight guys lined up for the race. The starter raised his pistol and fired it. A rush of arms and legs darted off the line, and I immediately sensed trouble. With 790 meters left, I was already sucking air and feeling tired. I wanted to stop and shout, "Hey! You guys come back here! Let's all just stroll around the track for the first 600 meters, then we can sprint it in. No one is tired that way, the race will be more exciting, and the number of points you get for placing will be the same. Reasonable? Let's be mature and talk about this. Uh, guys . . . didn't you hear me?"

I had no other choice but to keep running. At least it seemed like running to me, although I kept falling behind. So I'm way behind, like one hundred meters after the first lap and not feeling well. All that stuff I wrote yesterday is haunting me. Bag the finish with dignity stuff. Just get the race over so you can collapse somewhere, I decide. If Julie is watching somewhere, maybe I can get some sympathy.

My legs turn to the consistency of tomato soup, my breathing sounds more like the swooshing of a locomotive in a tunnel, and I don't care how I look. Six runners have finished the race and by now are probably done sweating and are scouting the stands for good-looking girls. There's one guy left, about ten meters in front of me. How can I describe him? The word *chubby* comes to mind. Also the word *slow*. (Inquiring minds at this point will ask, "If he's chubby and slow, what does that make you?" Answer: Really slow.) I'm chugging into the home stretch and out of nowhere, I see a face leaning onto the track and shouting at me. It is Orville and his message is clear. "Take this guy, Wally! You're no weiner!"

Inspired by Orville, I begin my version of a sprint, which is barely faster than I am running anyway. Slowly, I gain on the fat kid. With about five meters left, I pull ahead slightly and lean across the finish line.

I edge the fat kid out by inches. I feel a strange kinship with him, brothers in sweet pain, and I turn and walk toward him after the race, two sportsmen, two gentlemen, brought together by the rigors of friendly competition. I'm still breathing hard, gulping for air.

"Nice . . . race (pant) . . . we really (wheeze, pant, gulp) put on a good show. You (wheeze) gonna run (gasp) the . . . 800 . . . (gulp, wheeze) all season (cough)?"

He looks up at me, hardly out of breath. "Naw. It's too much work. Besides, the only reason I ran it today was because I skipped practice Tuesday and the coach made me run it as punishment. I'm normally a discus and javelin man. I wasn't even hardly trying today."

My coaches all tell me never to go lie down or stop moving right after a race because it can make you feel ill. I'm sure it is good advice. However, after finishing my race and talking with the fat kid/discus thrower/javelin flinger, I felt ill anyway and decided it could not make me feel any worse if I were to lie down somewhere and think about the meaning of life, track, and running in circles.

SUNDAY, APRIL 14

Another small step was cleared today in my drive to drive. I presented my plan for my Eagle project to the other priests and they agreed to help me. Here's my scheme: I plan to let my mother's cookies sell themselves. To put it humbly, my mom is to chocolate chip cookies what Hank Aaron is to the home run, what Thomas Edison is to the light bulb, what Tony Bennett is to a good Broadway show tune. She is an artist, a pacesetter, the standard, the one that others will always look to as the measure of excellence.

My plan is simple. A half-dozen guys are going to station themselves at various businesses in a couple of weeks, shoving samples of Mom's cookies at people going by. One bite and they'll be hooked. I'll have a flyer made out explaining why we're selling cookies and what the money will be used for. Everyone will take orders on the spot, then in four weeks, we'll deliver cookies and have the cash to rebuild the shelter in the warm summer months. We figure that if we get fifty orders at five bucks a pop, then we'll have enough money, coupled with some donations from Aisles of Value that I've lined up.

The plan has the element of genius, I'd suggest most humbly.

Tonight I will devote at least five full minutes to studying my wallet, searching for the best place to put my license.

P.S. Sister Lawson's birthday today. We took her some flowers. She said it was the first time in years anyone had brought her flowers. I'm beginning to think that when you do something for someone else, it's hard to figure who gets the most out of it.

TUESDAY, APRIL 16

Today, Mrs. English and I had our little chat. She initiated it. Near the end of class, she asked me if I could stay an extra minute. "She's on to you, buddy," Orville whispered. "She's gonna haul you in front of the hangin' judge for rustlin' verbs."

As everyone else filed out of class, I grabbed my books and walked to her desk.

"I suppose you're wondering about your grade, Wally."

"Yeah, I am. But I figured you were just mad or

disappointed in me. And then you have a reputation, too."

"Is that so?" she said, smiling a little. "I hope it's one for fairness and being a good teacher. Wally, I'm going to tell you now that you will get an A next semester, barring a complete collapse in your performance."

"That's great," I replied, mentally calculating my new, higher grade point average.

"You have the talent to be a really good writer, Wally. It comes easily for you. You can make people laugh and you can make people cry by your writing. That's a gift."

"Thanks, Mrs. English."

"But . . . "

Here comes the hammer, I thought. I was right.

" . . . you don't work hard enough. You go through the motions sometimes, and because you are naturally a good writer, you do better than even most bright students. But you need to reach, to write about things that are important to you, to give more thought to what you are writing, to develop control and your point-of-view. You're like a baseball player who can hit .300 without practicing, and by most standards, that's very successful. But Wally, you can be a .400 hitter in writing if you really try."

I uttered a very meaningful, intelligent reply. "Oh."

"We have one more big essay due in class before school is out and the topic will be your choice. In your case, I want you to write with depth, write with intelligence, and most of all, write with feeling, Wally."

"I'll try, Mrs. English."

She stood up. "Trying isn't good enough. You keep at it until you succeed."

"I will." And I felt something inside that told me I could.

"Good, Wally. Start thinking now what your essay will be about."

"I'll kick it up a notch, Mrs. English."

I turned and started to leave.

"Are we still friends? All I want you to do is be a .400 hitter."

"Yeah. We're still friends. And I'll dedicate my first home run to you."

She laughed, and I went out into the hall feeling more like an adult than I had in a long time.

THURSDAY, APRIL 18

I know my sister. Give me a hypothetical situation, and nine times out of ten I can tell you exactly what Nat will do. It's not that I'm terribly smart, it's just a matter of programming "Me first" in your mind, and the rest is automatic.

Today was one of those rare occasions when she surprised me. It happened just a few minutes ago, as I was sitting down at my desk to do some homework. I have postponed my homework to record for posterity what just happened because it is an event of unusual magnitude, something like an unscheduled appearance by Halley's Comet or Lumpy passing up seconds on anything.

Anyway, Natalie poked her head into my room and asked if we could talk. I said sure, but we'd better keep it low since Chuck was asleep in his bed.

"I wanted to tell you something, Wally. I think you are very wise, especially, like, when it comes to human people, you know. Like, you understand a lot."

This came as a complete and utter shock. I tried to think of the last time that Natalie, without any prompting from our parents or with no hidden agenda, actually looked me square in the face and paid me a compliment. The last time I could think of was when a kid named Gilbert Zeilsky had a crush on her and kept calling her on the phone. Finally I stepped in and told Gilbert that Natalie had a rare, tropical skin disease and that in a couple of more years she would break out into permanent hives and facial blemishes. There was nothing that modern medicine could do about it. It was a lie, but it worked. Cooled old Gilbert right off. Natalie thanked me then, and told me I was a good big brother because Gilbert didn't exactly light her board.

"Why are you telling me this?"

"At school today, I sort of apologized to Lindy, like you told me to. I go, 'Lindy, I'm really sorry if I hurt your feelings or said anything that upset you. Seriously.' And it felt so funny inside to say that because I know I didn't, but I felt like I was being really sincere anyway, and then I started to cry a little, right there in the hall. I couldn't believe it. Seriously. And then Lindy looks at me and she goes, 'I thought you were mad at me and that's why we weren't doing anything together anymore.' Then she starts to cry, then we both start to laugh. It was, like, really neat. And now we're really good friends again, and we're going to the mall on Saturday, and we're going to get tans this summer together, too. I wouldn't have done all that if it weren't for you. And me and Lindy would still think we were mad at each other even though we weren't. So that's why I think you're really wise."

I vaguely followed what she was saying. "Glad it worked out for you, Nat."

"So am I. Well, that's all I wanted to say. I have to go now and think about what I'll wear tomorrow."

So my day ended on a positive note. I hope I can say the same about tomorrow, although I must admit that with the 800 meters staring at me in the meet, I can't say that I'm all that optimistic.

SATURDAY, APRIL 20

I had good news and bad news at the track meet yesterday. My time was two seconds faster than last week. That's the good news. The bad news is, I finished dead last. The really bad news is that Julie was in the stands watching me thud around the track.

She stayed until the meet was over. I started to walk toward the locker room and there she was. Maybe it was just my male ego, but I think she was hanging around waiting for me. I saw her looking at me, and my heart rate jumped to about the same level as when I was running my race. Make this good, Whipple, I mumbled. Don't go into brain lock.

"Hello, Wally."

"Hi, Julie. I didn't know you were here."

"I could hear the noise from the meet after tennis practice was over, and so I came down to see how it was going. I know Orville and Lumpy are on the track team, and so are you, and a girl in one of my classes,

Viola Barkle, is too. I thought it would be fun to see some of my friends. I got here just in time to see the finish of your race."

She looked really nice, dressed in dark blue shorts, a white top, and a red sweater draped over her shoulders. It was warm and a gentle wind was blowing. I felt a bit lightheaded, perhaps because of my oxygen debt from running, and momentarily forgetting my miserable race, I wondered if it was the right time to propose. Fortunately, her last comment about seeing my race humbled me, and I regained my senses.

"Yeah. The race. I had this tremendous sideache, and when that happens I normally just keep running, sort of mentally block out the pain. But I couldn't quite do that today, so I had a bad race. Half of running is mental, you know, and the other isn't."

Gray matter collapse, Wally. Half of running is mental?

"Oh, that's too bad. I see Viola and Orville won their events, though."

"Yeah. They're both really good. All they need to do is work on their grunts."

"Grunts?"

"Uh-huh. All good shot putters grunt."

"Oh, I get it. They grunt when they throw." She giggled.

"Guess I better go now. See you tomorrow in seminary."

"Tomorrow's Saturday, Wally."

"Saturday. Right. I knew that. Monday. That's what I meant."

We parted. I showered and dressed and slipped

out of the locker room before Orv had a chance to offer me a ride home. I wanted a little time to think. Yes, I'd made her laugh a couple of times, but I'd also stretched the truth beyond recognition. Why is it I say such dumb things around Julie? Why did I tell her I had a sideache when I didn't? Why didn't I just say, "Julie, I'm not a very good runner, and I'm not even sure why I am on the track team, and the reason I finished last today is that I am just plain slow."

I don't mean to say untrue things . . . it's more a case of this is how I want Wally Whipple to be and this is how I know he really is . . . and there's this gap, and maybe I'm trying to close it in my own way. Is this normal? Do we all look in the mirror and see what everyone else does? Do people like me for who I really am? Do I need to like myself better than I do now? This is all part of the search for Wallace Whipple, I think. Maybe it will take a few more months or a few more years even to find myself. Not a happy thought. I could be seventeen, maybe eighteen years old, a veteran of life, and not quite have finished The Search. Oh, well.

I worked at the store today, six hours, pocketing twenty-five big ones for my efforts. I haven't yet talked with Ed, but I think next Saturday will be the big night at the movies for us.

NOTE: Look at the newspaper and find out which movies are playing where. Call Ed. Arrange for transportation. ("Ed, we have three basic choices here. One, we can walk, even though it is three miles to the movie theater. Two, we can have my dad drive us, and because he is cool, he will probably ignore us, but this is not my preferred option. Three, can you drive us in your red sports car? PLLEEAASSSE? I'll even throw in a couple of bucks for gas.") Review date procedures and come up with date outline.

He who fails to plan, plans to fail, even on dates.

SUNDAY, APRIL 21

Brother Hansen gave a super lesson today. It was about the potential each of us has, how we all have unique gifts and talents, how we weren't sent to earth to fail. I need to hear that ordinary guys can succeed in important things. Brother Hansen also told us that we need to work on developing our talents, or they could be taken away from us. He said that we just can't expect success to come to us, that we have to pursue goals and always keep learning as part of our eternal progression.

Halfway through the lesson, I start to get this crazy idea. I mean, it's hard to even think about it. Be all you can be, right? I start to notice this swelling sensation, and what I am thinking feels right. It's like a message to me. And the message is this: **Wally, you need to run for class office.**

Class office! Let's see, I was senior patrol leader once in Scouts. And in the third grade, I was on the student council. Nobody has ever confused me with Abraham Lincoln. I'm not the political type . . . but look at my election base. The cross-country and track teams. The basketball team. The church kids, though few in number, will probably all vote for me and maybe be on a campaign committee. I can get Lumpy and Orville to help, and yes, maybe pull in my ace,

Joe Vermeer. Yes! And maybe Julie will help, too. This can be done!

TV Announcer Guy: "And tonight we have word that Wallace F. Whipple, well-known near-scholar, philanthropist, and athlete, is about to throw his hat in the ring for an as-of-yet unnamed political office at Benjamin Franklin High School. Let's go now to our ace reporter, Trixie LeBeau, at the Whipple home. Trix?"

"Check, Lance. I did get a chance to talk with Mr. Whipple earlier this evening, and while he would not confirm reports of his impending candidacy, he would not deny them. He did say to expect an announcement shortly, and that news has southeast Portland buzzing. Whipple, it is widely thought, would be a tough opponent for anyone. School officials said that they would welcome a candidate of Whipple's caliber. Tough but fair, Whipple is equally adept at negotiating delicate issues, such as dance lessons with his sister, or at taking a hardline stance, such as when he pummeled the school bully last year in a much-publicized incident. Whipple, it seems, has it all. Back to you, Lance."

Seriously, I may plunge in. What office shall I seek? President? No, that's too much. Vice-president? No, everyone makes fun of vice-presidents. One position stands out in my mind, a symbol of authority, calmness, and poise. It is the position I shall seek, the position where I can serve the best. Yes, I speak of the office of junior class, sergeant-at-arms.

Wallace F. Whipple, sergeant-at-arms. Has a nice ring, doesn't it?

MONDAY, APRIL 22

I'm a little behind in my plans with Edwina. Checked out the movie section today, and if you toss out the ones that are about gangsters, lust, drugs, lost dogs, or kids, there isn't much left.

But wait! Way down in the corner of the entertainment page, I see a Jimmy Stewart Film Festival advertised. Bingo. I know it's strange, I like music that is too old for my parents and I still think the best movies made were in black-and-white, fifty years ago. But my gut feeling is that Ed will like Jimmy Stewart, too. I'll give her a call and work out the details, especially the little matter of transportation.

One final note: More than twenty-four hours have passed since I think I was inspired to run for class office. During that time, I have given careful consideration to it, thought about the risks, the time involved, the commitment, the potential to be humbled by losing, and I have decided one thing.

I'm more excited than ever about being the next junior class sergeant-at-arms.

TUESDAY, APRIL 23

Today at lunch, I announced my candidacy for office to the closest group of friends that I have on the face of the earth, the illustrious members of The Posse. They listened to me with all the dignity, understanding, and empathy that one could expect from a mature, insightful group of young men. They made thoughtful remarks about my prospects and gave me valuable advice regarding the rigors of a campaign. Here is a sampling of their reaction:

LUMPY: "You're running for class office? You're out of your head!"

ORVILLE: "Jes' what is a sergeant-at-arms? Is he some big ornery dude who throws the rabble-rousers out of meetin's?"

ROB: "You'd better make campaign tags with candy on them because that's the only way you're going to win—you'll have to buy votes."

MICK: "No offense, but you don't seem the kind to get into politics. You're basically honest. Have you thought about the Science Club? That's more your speed."

ME: (realizing that this was a critical moment and I must say something articulate and firm to dispel any doubts about my candidacy) "Ha! Ha! again, to all of you!"

Saying it out loud commits me. I think I'll talk this over with Mom and Dad and see what they have to say. Oh, I know—sometimes when they think I'm about to do something stupid they let me know, but at least they are somewhat diplomatic about telling me.

Example: a couple of years ago, when I told my parents I wanted to buy a used motorcycle that didn't run from a guy named Rip Rammell who lived around the block, "Son, have you really thought this through?" Dad asked. "Wally, I think you should spend your money on something that works," Mom said, "even if Rip is telling you you'll be the only 14–year-old around with his own motorcycle." Translation of parental lingo: you will buy that motorcycle when pigs fly.

I have learned this lesson today. Politics is hard.

And running for office brings out things in people that you might have never known existed. And may never have wanted to know.

WEDNESDAY, APRIL 24

I sort of checked things out with Edwina today in math class, and she seemed excited when I told her about the Jimmy Stewart Film Festival. I've got to hand it to Ed. Not much fazes her. Most girls would probably rather bathe in axle grease than go to a film festival starring a guy who was old even before she was born, but not Ed. She's different that way, and it's a difference I like. And she is almost in the Joe Vermeer League when it comes to cool.

Like the delicate subject of wheels on our date. She handled it.

ME: (Trying to work my way around the delicate issue of transportation) "I guess, um, that we should, get together, uh, about, well, 7:30 since the flick starts at 8:00, and I was thinking a good place to meet was, well, somewhere like, er, close to . . . "

ED: "How about if I just pick you up. We can take my car, unless you wanted to drive."

ME: "That would be great. Yes. Super. My house. Sure. You bet. Good plan."

Teenagers can tell when someone their age has a license. Maybe it's the rosy glow on their face, the way they walk, the constant jangling of car keys, the way we have the ability to work the words "license" or "driving" into every other sentence, or maybe it is merely a sixth sense. *But we just know,* trust me on this one. Ed knows I don't have my license, even though we've never talked about it. But she saved me the embarrassment of asking her if she minds my dad tagging along as the driver on our date by offering her car. Now, that is cool.

Other things. Had a great day in social studies, got back a paper with a big A on it; did well on quizzes in math and health; then did something that bodes well for my athletic career. A couple of us were goofing around in the high jump pit before the distance runners started to torture ourselves, and just for the heck of it, I ran up to the bar and jumped over it. No big deal. But Mr. Leonard came up to me and said I looked pretty good at the high jump and that I'd just cleared 5'6", which would have placed me second in the meet last week. "Wally, you only go half-time with the distance crew today. Then come on over and work with the high jumpers. We may have found you an event."

It did not require much thought (like about .001 seconds) to say yes. I'd do anything to cut down on my distance running. And high jumping? What's so tough about running at and jumping over a stick?

THURSDAY, APRIL 25

Two more days until the second big date for Wallace F. Whipple. In order to improve my personality and bolster my self-confidence by megadoses, I need a quick review of what I learned on my first date.

1. Plan as best you can, but if things aren't going so well, know when to abandon your plan and be spontaneous.

2. You can talk about sports with some girls, which really surprises me.

3. Most dancing is just movement, and if you move long enough, sooner or later, you're going to catch the beat and look like you know what you're doing.

4. You should never write down on your wrists what your next topic of conversation will be. That's dumb and immature. A better place is on the inside of your fingers on your left hand.

5. Do not discuss politics with the girl's father. Even if you are going to grow up to be a Republican, and he has a framed picture of Ronald Reagan on his desk.

6. Do not talk about current events with anyone the entire evening. It kills the mood when you start talking about a huge earthquake in a faraway country or about a new disease strain that has medical researchers stumped or the fact that killer bees are expected to show up in your state next summer.

7. You have to be cool, but not too cool; you have to be friendly, but not too friendly; you have to be intelligent, but not too intelligent; and you have to be yourself, but not too much yourself.

8. Do not talk about adults whom you have not met, for example, Edwina's mom.

FRIDAY, APRIL 26

This day will go down in my journal as one of the most awesome ever. I mean, it's as if everything got together—my brain, my body, my personality—and said, "Okay, we've been pretty rough on the kid lately, not cutting him much slack. That trick last week of him needing a shave and having three new blemishes show up was not cool. Anyway, let's give him one really good day, before his ego sinks to below sea level. Let's try our utmost not to let him do anything dumb. If we work together, we can do it. Got it? Good. Now remember, team effort!"

How do I count the ways that this day went well? Got back a test in English and did well. I had several of your basic brilliant comments in social studies about the trade imbalance between Japan and the United States. And I indeed found my track event.

I am a high jumper.

Yes! I won an event! By clearing the bar at 5'7", I took first place in the sophomore high jump. *I belong.* I can look at the other guys on the track team and feel that I am their equal. I am no longer among the team nerds, guys who never do well. Instead, I am a real contributor. I can now joke around with the other guys, look cool before my event (rather than look like I am on the verge of getting sick to my stomach, which wasn't too far from the truth when I ran the 800), and can glance toward the stands and look totally unruffled when the announcer booms over the PA system, "Results of the sophomore boys' high jump: First Place, Franklin High, Wally Whipple." If Julie ever comes again to a meet, I won't have to fake sideaches and make up excuses.

"Super effort, Wally," praised Coach Leonard. "You now know what it is to think 'champion.' Wait until we teach you a little about technique. You'll be jumping six feet before the end of the season."

I basked in the glow of the locker room, soaking

up the smell of all things dear to me—sweaty socks, mildewed shower room, dirty running shoes, and smelly gym uniforms. It was glorious. I didn't want to leave.

"You was jumpin' like a cat with a burr under his tail," Orville said on the way home. "You found your place. Finally clenched that bit in your teeth and ran with it."

At home, I was very casual about my victory. I mean, at least three minutes went by before I told everyone. Dad seemed really pleased and said the only way to go from here was up. (Ha! I get it Dad! The only way is *up*, in the high jump. What a dad. What a sense of humor.)

Mom was pleased too, although she was unsure about what the high jump really is. "Do you run and jump, or just stand and jump, or do you jump by yourself, or with a lot of people? Be careful, Wally." Natalie was her usual sensitive, concerned self. "It figures that when you find something you're good at, it's a sport that nobody watches, but I'm glad for you, seriously. Did I tell you that me and Lindy are going downtown tomorrow?" Chuck was thrilled. "I knew you could jump high. You can almost dunk a basketball." Anyway, suffice it to say the whole Whipple family was pretty stoked about my success.

Tonight, I'll celebrate. Hamburger Bob's with most of The Posse. The second round of french fries and root beer might even be on me.

I feel that good.

SATURDAY, APRIL 27

Tonight was the second big date for me. Hey, I'm

getting to be an old hand at this stuff. No big deal. Just me and Ed, out for a good time in her sports car—a machine that most young male adults would commit a major crime to own.

I was ready. Had four topics of conversation neatly inked inside the fingers of my left-hand. On my pinky, that I worked today at the Aisles of Value hardware store, stacking boxes. Ring finger, my newly discovered ability to high jump, followed by how nice she looks, and on the little finger, should I sink to new lows in conversation, the weather, which had been what it always is in Oregon in April: very wet.

Ed came by for me a little after seven. The doorbell rang, and Chuck answered it.

"Wally, it's a girl! She's here!"

Now, even though I love my family members, I occasionally get this far-out vision of what my life would be like without them:

I live in an apartment, have my own car, eat out every night, and when my parents do call from some distant city where my father is a top executive of a major corporation, I greet them with a cheery, "Hello, Pamela. And how is business, Wallace?" Natalie, of course, is locked away in some expensive, all-girls school where she is learning good manners, how to show respect, and calculus. Chuck and I are still very close, and he jets out to see me every other weekend, plus holidays.

It's all just imagination and something I wouldn't really want to happen except for the part about my own car and Natalie in boarding school. Tonight, though, I had second thoughts. As soon as Chuck announced Ed was here, the other family members bolted to the living room to check out Edwina.

"You must be Edwina. We've heard so much about you," Mom said. "Isn't she darling, Wally?"

"Say, that's some nice car you've got out there," Dad exclaimed. "Someone must trust you a lot to let you borrow a car like that. Don't spill anything on the upholstery, Wally!"

Then Natalie. She came out and sort of sniffed around Ed, like one member of the animal kingdom checking out an invader on its turf. "You look nice," she finally said to Ed. (Rough translation: You're cute, but not as cute as I am, so it's okay if you go out with my brother. But just remember, this is my turf, so don't get any ideas.) Ed smiled at all of this, reaffirming her ultra-cool status in my mind. I wouldn't have blamed her if she wondered if she had by accident dropped in on a family that has somehow assumed the form of earthlings but who are actually from deep outer space and not yet used to the customs of planet earth.

Chuck probably did the least damage. "Do you like basketball?"

"Yes, Chuck. I like basketball very much."

"Oh, good. I hope you go out with Wally a lot."

"Where are you two headed tonight?" Dad asked.

"We're going to the Jimmy Stewart Film Festival. *It's a Wonderful Life* and *Mr. Smith Goes to Washington* are on tonight."

At the mention of Jimmy Stewart, both my parents nodded approvingly, while Natalie immediately searched for a hole that she could crawl into.

"You'll have fun. Got your key, Wally?"

"Right here, Mom."

"What time will you have him home?" Dad blurted out, in a rare lapse of cool.

"Before midnight," Ed answered, patiently.

"Nothing good happens after midnight," Natalie said, bouncing back to life at a most unfortunate moment. She owes her continuing existence on earth to Ed, because if it were not for her presence, I probably would have reached out for Natalie's throat and wrapped my fingers around it.

Instead, I channelled my energy into whisking us out the door, breezing right by my parents at a brisk trot, grabbing Ed by the hand, and shouting over my shoulder, "Don't wait up!" I got to the car, opened the door for Ed, then hustled around to my side. I thought of all the things that I might say, such as "Excuse my family, they are among the socially impaired and don't know what it's like to have a nice girl in the home because all we have is Natalie," but Edwina took the wind out of my sail before I could begin to utter the first apology.

"You have a great family. Natalie is very pretty. And that Chuck is a cutie. Do you really think he'll shoot baskets with me sometime?"

What could I say? For the first time in the whole school year, at least since I first saw Julie Sloan, I got this dry, fluttery feeling inside and realized that sitting right beside me was a girl I could really *like*.

SUNDAY, APRIL 28

Great date with Ed last night. She really liked the movies. J-j-jimmy S-s-tewart is cool.

I ran into the full-time missionaries today, and they

asked me about Orville. I said that I really hadn't yet felt right about asking him if he'd like to take the discussions, but I hadn't given up. They told me to pray about Orville, which I promised to do. They said that if I was really sincere about it, then a way would be opened for me to ask Orville.

I hope they're right.

TUESDAY, APRIL 30

Today is the last day to file for elections, okay? So I took care of it, right before school. I marched into the student activities office and asked for the form to fill out that would declare my candidacy. The girl who was working behind the counter gave me a long, hard look, one that fairly shouted, "You don't look like the kind to run for office. No dorks allowed!" Little did she know that she was sneering at Wallace Whipple, rising track star, almost mediocre basketball player, and soon-to-be honor student. Yes, she was dealing with a man of stature here, someone of importance. For a half-second, I thought about telling her these things but decided to let her find out for herself later and experience the pain of feeling foolish in her own private way.

I did ask if anyone else had filed for junior class sergeant-at-arms. She rattled a bunch of forms and couldn't find anyone at the moment. My hopes began to rise . . . what if nobody else had filed? I could start working on my acceptance speech right now.

"My dear fellow students . . . "

Nope.

"My fellow students . . . "

Bzzz. Wrong.

"My classmates . . . "

Yes, much better. I've got to start thinking like a politician, scary as the thought might be. I also need to practice being gracious in triumph, get used to the scrutiny of being in the public eye, and practice saying things such as, "I seek for the good of all, and not for personal glory," even if that is a tiny, white lie.

Note: Although I am only about eight months into my year-long diary, I am rapidly coming to the end of it. Who would've thought that I, Wallace Whipple, would actually enjoy keeping a journal as much as I have?

Note: Nail down the cookie sale details at Explorers tomorrow. Talk with Mel Pyne, who is the only guy I can trust not to eat all of the samples in the first fifteen minutes. Ask him if he will be in charge of the group at the mini-mall.

Note: Mother's Day is coming. Do not forget. This would be a major mistake, for which there may be no forgiveness. Not Mom, she would forgive me if it slipped my mind. I'm the one who would have a hard time forgiving myself.

Note: Continue to practice driving. Set up time with parents to take license exam. After acquiring license, immediately call up Julie and ask her out. Begin preliminary mission and wedding plans

CHAPTER 9

MaY

WEDNESDAY, MAY 1

Life is sweet at this moment, very sweet. I am on a winning streak. Everything is turning up roses, smelling good, looking good, coming strong and easy. The magic touch is mine. Whatever I do is going to work out super well. I have a strong suspicion that this is what it must feel like to be an adult.

School is great. My term paper for Mrs. English's English class is underway, and the words are flowing freely on the old computer screen. I have decided to write an autobiography of sorts, and it will knock her socks off.

Then there is my social outlook, which for the first time in many years—which is to say my whole life— is actually okay. Two good dates with Ed, Julie Sloan waiting breathlessly for me to ask her out, and the big one, my license, is only a matter of days away. FREE-DOM! It will be so simple after my license.

"Hey, Jules babe, you tired of being a wallflower? See ya' at seven on Saturday and expect the time of your life. Yo!"

Well, maybe I better put a grind on talk like that, but the old confidence is oozing from me these days, like thick mustard from a squeeze container. In the great salad of life, I am a crouton, sitting atop the whole heap. Maybe I've turned the corner for good.

Another excellent sign. Today at track practice, I high jumped 5'9". Couldn't help noticing three of the coaches clustered near the high jump area, watching me with very, shall we say, "pleased" looks on their faces. A natural, they were obviously thinking. Perfect form. So easy, so graceful. Like water flowing over rocks. "This kid may be our ticket to the Olympics someday," I could almost hear them say.

The Olympics. My face on cereal boxes. Posters of me leaping over the eight-foot high bar in the rooms of kids all over the country. "I want to be like him," they say, their cheerful little faces turned upward in admiration. "Maybe you will, if you work hard and honor your parents," moms and dads everywhere will encourage.

Then there is my new career in politics. I have competition for the sergeant-at-arms job. Okay, maybe that's a stretch. Dick Dickson is my opponent. *Dick Dickson!* Can you believe it? The biggest nerd in the school! A nerd's nerd. Pop-bottle thick glasses, high-water pants, top button of his plaid shirts always buttoned, a perpetually fuzzy upper lip which has yet to feel the touch of the cold steel of a razor blade. I mean, this guy could have written the book on nerds. The first guy in history to launch a career in politics with the computer club as his power base. Next to him, I almost look macho.

I saw Dick today on my way to the lunch room, as I walked with Orville. "So," he says to me, "I guess we're opponents." He is speaking in an unbelievably serious voice, which cracks me up. "I intend to campaign hard, Whipple. You'll find that I am very tenacious and will wage an all-out effort against you. Do not take it personally; it's just that when a Dickson decides to pursue something, a Dickson succeeds."

"Yo, Dick. Go get 'em tiger," I said, and he marched ahead, about fourteen textbooks scrunched under one of his scrawny arms.

"Who's that little feller?" Orville wanted to know. "Seems to have a wide streak of bulldog in him."

"That, Orv, is the guy I am running against in the election. Think I can handle him? He'll be creamed avocado. The only thing I worry about is that I may crush his feelings when I make bug juice out of him in the election."

Orville didn't look impressed. "Don't get too high and mighty just yet, Wally. You can't always judge a bronc by the way he sits in the chute. The most docile lookin' one in the bunch may turn into a terror once the gate opens."

"Orville, you are kind and wise and know a lot about horses, but in this case, you are worrying needlessly. I will humble Dick Dickson."

"Whatever, pard. But you might want to take two dallies around the saddle horn."

"What do you mean?"

"Be cautious, work hard, and don't count on good luck coming naturally."

"Gotcha, Orv. Dick Dickson. Too bad computers can't vote!"

Time to hit the rack now. Tomorrow brings a new day and I can hardly wait to see what puny challenges it throws at me. Yo, Whipple can handle them all!

THURSDAY, MAY 2

Life continues to fall into place for me. I know now what "having your act together" means. Today I came up with a foolproof plan for the big date with Julie. A feeling very much like inspiration came to me tonight, after dinner, while I was sort of being a couch potato in the living room. I picked up the paper and turned to the entertainment news. I saw an advertisement with the headline, "A Timeless Classic," and it really grabbed my attention. It was an ad for an opera by a guy named Strauss, called *Die Fledermaus*. It had a little picture of a guy sort of dressed up in some fancy clothes that looked like they came from a long time ago, holding his arm upward, and belting out a tune. I don't know much about Strauss, other than I think I remember when he died a few years ago, and my guess is that the plot has something to do with a mouse, but heck, if it's a timeless classic, it's good enough for Wally Whipple and his date. I got kind of excited thinking about taking Julie to the City Auditorium for this big fancy date. That would really impress her. I bet she and Joe never went to the opera. You just can't get any classier than that.

Then I started thinking about dinner. Why not go out and put the feed bag on? I was going to blow a bundle on her anyway. A nice restaurant, where the waiters speak a foreign language. Maybe Spanish would do. Like at Walt's Mexican World Buffet, where you can get an all-you-can-eat dinner for five bucks.

The more I thought about Walt's, the better the idea seemed. A foreign place that's cheap. Perfect. I could even leave a tip, you know, about seventy-five cents under the edge of my plate so Julie wouldn't think I was showing off. I could envision the response I'd get at the lunch table when I announced my plans.

ME: "Yes, Julie and I will be attending the timeless classic opera, *Die Fledermaus,* by Strauss, who only recently passed away, causing great mourning in the music world."

LUMPY: "Wow! You're taking her to the opera? What a guy—no, make that, what a *man,* Wally! The opera. She'll think you're really intellectual."

ORV: "Darn good idea, Wallace."

ME: "And that's only part of it. We're also going to Walt's Mexican World Buffet for dinner. Let it not be said that Wally Whipple doesn't show his date a good time."

LUMPY: "I hope Julie knows how lucky she is."

Okay, the event is in place. The restaurant is chosen. And now, the one big remaining question (aside from money, which I'll have to work out with my dad): Wheels.

I've been driving a lot. My skills are good. I feel really in control, and the driving test should be a cinch. *Die Fledermaus* is on May 23rd. If I start working on my parents now, I can take the driving test maybe a day or two before, just in time for the biggest date of this century. Perfect. Car. Food. Entertainment. Good company.

Julie will love it. "Joe Who?" she will laugh as we walk hand-in-hand to her door as The Perfect Evening comes to an end. "Oh Wally, Joe is such a nice guy, but he is merely a boy compared to you. Joe would have never thought of Walt's Mexican World Buffet and never have taken me to the opera. Why did I waste so much of my time on him? But we have our whole lives together." At this point, I will smile rakishly and say, "You are so right, my sweet. Our whole lives." Then I might plant one right on her chops. A kiss, that is.

Whoa . . . even by my standards, I'm getting carried away. But it's fun to think about. The opera. A fancy foreign restaurant. My driving the car.

It's a nice thought to sleep on. And that's exactly what I plan to do.

SATURDAY, MAY 4

This is sort of an odds and ends day. I was too busy after the track meet to write in my journal. Three of us went out last night and cruised around Foster Avenue in Orville's ancient pickup truck. Mostly we drove around the block and tried to act cool. Once, Lumpy leaned out the window and hollered something at a car with three girls in it. "This could be your lucky night, ladies! Three of the best-looking men in America are willing to share some time with you!" The girls started to laugh, one of them said, yeah, when Kansas floats, then they took off.

"I think that means 'no,'" Orville sagely observed.

"Well, it *could've* been their lucky night," Lumpy pouted. The truth of the matter is that we were probably all relieved to have gotten the big snub.

So we headed for home. Me, the new look Wally Whipple, confident, mature, suave, was in bed and snoring by 10 P.M.

Not that the day was a washout. I cleared 5'10" in the high jump, good enough for another first place. Coach Leonard was close to tears. "We have a genuine success story here, gentlemen. Whipple stayed with it until he found his talent, he worked hard, he is becoming the best he can be. Men, you need to emulate him."

I sat there and tried hard to look humble, my eyes directed to the floor, a self-conscious smile gracing my chiseled features, shuffling my feet a bit. I think I've about got humility down cold.

As Orville would say, one yellow jacket did show up at the Sunday School picnic. Three groups of guys from church camped outside the doors of various shopping areas and handed out samples of Mom's all-universe chocolate chip cookies to raise money for my Eagle project. I knew they'd sell, but maybe we overachieved. I'm worried that we did too good a job taking cookie orders. I haven't heard from Mel or Lumpy yet, but I know that Rob and I took in about sixty orders for a dozen cookies each. I hope that Mel and Lumpy didn't do that well—we're up to 720 cookies with my order alone!

Lumpy and his partner, Mickey, had a small shopping area staked out, but my guess is that Lumpy ate all of the sample cookies and we only sold a few dozen. Still, Mel is so conscientious . . . what if he sold fifty orders? Mom and I will be baking for three days straight. We're going to bake them and deliver them on Memorial Day, the 27th. Since we took a dollar deposit on each order, we're committed. I have this eerie feeling that I may never want to see a chocolate chip cookie again.

All the numbers will be in tomorrow. In the meantime, three things must be done.

1. Get my license.
2. Ask out Julie.
3. Pick up opera tickets.

Call these my goals for the upcoming week.

SUNDAY, MAY 5

I'm in trouble. Deep, serious trouble. You might say I'm up to my nose in chocolate chip cookies.

Lumpy stayed true to form and ate most of his samples and sold only fifteen orders. Fine. It was Mel who did me in. Eighty-three orders. I said, eighty-three orders! Add my sixty, Lumpy's fifteen, and I have to come up with 158 dozen cookies. Times that by twelve . . .

And I owe the world, one-thousand, eight-hundred and ninety-six cookies!

The kitchen will be my home for the remainder of my life. Friends will all graduate from high school, go to college, return from missions, marry, have three adorable children, and be captains of industry by the time I finish the last dozen cookies. "Great future that Wally once had," they'll say when my pathetic name comes up at social gatherings of which I am not a part. "Too bad about those chocolate chip cookie orders." I can't believe it. Done in by chocolate chip cookies, offered to the public for a noble cause. Is there no justice? Aren't things like this supposed to work out right? How do I break the news to Mom? What will this do to our relationship? "You're no son of mine!" she might snarl. Or she might ask which of the major armies of the world was I going to hire to help me with the project.

But this is my mom, so when I told her about our fortunes, she only smiled and said, "We have a problem, don't we? We'll figure out something, Wally." No fuss, no bother. That's my mom.

Natalie's comment was, as usual, to the point. "You sure are stupid sometimes, Wally. Why didn't you put a limit on the number that could be ordered?"

Even Chuck turned on me, sort of. "Natalie's right, Wally," he said.

How will I do this? Almost 2,000 cookies. HELP!!!

There is a bright side to all of this, though. When the money is in, we can make the shelter on Mt. Hood into a mountain chalet. Should I put in a spa? Walk-in closets? Cable TV?

Oh my. This is the only dark lining to my silver cloud of a life right now. But I need to follow through. If I don't, no license, no date with Julie, and Wally Whipple will regress to the state of dried spaghetti once again. I don't want that. Not now.

And all this, just as my life was going so well.

MONDAY, MAY 6

I had an uneasy feeling today at school. Dick Dickson, my unworthy little nerd opponent in the election, already has his campaign machinery greased. I mean, I saw about thirty kids (all from the computer club, I assume) wearing campaign tags supporting him. My campaign, on the other hand, isn't exactly off to a blazing start. Like, no committee, and I don't even have a slogan yet. Anyway, I saw Dick outside of school today, handing out campaign literature. A little flyer with his photo on it and a long list of ideas about what he would do if elected sergeant-at-arms. ("I pledge that only the best bands will play at school dances." Who does he think he is? Dick is one of the only guys who has been to fewer dances than I have.) Dick saw me on the way to track and sort of sneered at me. "How's your campaign going, Wally? Haven't seen anything from you, yet. The early bird catches the worm, or don't you know what that means?" Neener, neener, neener.

I wanted to take him by his scrawny little neck and tell him that he was going to be humbled in the election, but I decided that wouldn't be cool. Instead, I smiled, and said, "Just want to give you a head start, Dick. You'll need every advantage you can get." Then I turned and headed toward the locker room.

Grrrr. I shouldn't let people like that bother me. I know that I'm playing right into his hands if I get upset. I know that I should treat no class with class, no matter how difficult that is.

I also now know that Orville was right. You can't tell how much a horse is going to buck until you get him out of the chute. I've got to get my campaign rolling or face a trip to Humiliation City when Dick Dickson trounces me in the election.

TUESDAY, MAY 7

A boost, that's what I need. Not that my winning streak is over. But the encounter with Dick yesterday, the 2,000 cookies . . . and my bright star is dimming a bit.

Tomorrow. That's when I'll get my campaign on track. I'll have a meeting, explain my political philosophy (Note: develop political philosophy tonight before going to bed) to my throng of wildly enthusiastic and dedicated supporters. I will take statesman-like control of the election, forcing Dick to cough and gag on humble pie. Yes, that's my vision. For now. And who knows? Maybe it will get even bigger.

FAST FORWARD 25 YEARS

A gathering of people in an ornate conference room with a long, shiny table stretching down the middle. On one side, men wearing the robes of the desert sit, impassive, arms folded, scowling. On the other side of the table, sit men and women in business suits, looking ill-at-ease and also scowling. Dozens of aides stand behind the people on both sides of the table, waiting, at the beck and call of their leaders. Then, there is a commotion near the back of the room and excited whispers swirl around the table.

Wallace F. Whipple, ambassador-at-large for world peace, has arrived.

"Gentlemen and gentleladies," I say very formally, standing at the head of the table, with all eyes focused on me. "We have but one goal today. Peace. For all people. Everywhere. We have here the opportunity to make a statement that the world will long note and always remember. That you were the people who ushered in the greatest period of peace and prosperity ever known to modern society. That is my vision. That is your vision. Now, let's work TOGETHER to make it a reality."

The scowls disappear and the looks of scorn fade. A sniffle is heard. Then another. A man in a robe stands and says, "Mr. Whipple, we thank you. In your simple eloquence, you have helped us see what we all need to keep foremost in our minds."

He looks around his side of the table, and then says emphatically, "We are ready to talk peace. Seriously. Thank you, Mr. Ambassador. May your date trees always bear sweet and plentiful fruit."

I nod gravely and wisely and utter in a barely audible voice, "Thank you, my friend and brother."

On the other side of the table, a tall woman arises. "Thank you, Mr. Ambassador. We had a position marked for this meeting, but I for one—and I think I am speaking for my colleagues—have been touched by your appeal." Around her, all the heads at the table nod. "For the sake of peace, let the process begin," she says, somewhat emotionally. "Your presence alone, Mr. Ambassador, has made the difference. May all your stocks be bullish."

I look humble, but in control. "Thank you, your ladyship."

With a slight flick of my hand, I signal a trusted aide who steps up to my place at the table and clears his throat. Silently, I slip away, just as he says, "Let us now not only make friends, not only make memories, but let us also make history."

Someone at the end of the table pleads, "But where is Mr. Ambassador?"

"Off to another part of the world. A slight crisis in

Central America, I believe," my trusted aide says. "As you have all sensed, we have been privileged to be in the presence of greatness this day."

BACK TO THE PRESENT

Okay, okay . . . and it all starts with me blasting Dick Dickson into millions of pieces so tiny that only algae in the sea will be able to digest them. The campaign starts NOW.

WEDNESDAY, MAY 8

In my time of need, who can I turn to for help, encouragement, and guidance? Who can I ask to help me become the next junior class sergeant-at-arms? The Posse, of course.

Hmmm. At least it seemed like a good idea, until reality grabbed me by the throat.

"YOU WANT US TO DO WHAT? NO WAY!!!" was the immediate reaction when I asked for volunteers to help with posters and leaflets.

"Politics bore me," Lumpy sighed, looking . . . well, bored.

"You need some artistic people. We can't cut and draw. We're among the creative impaired," whined Rob.

"I'll help you out as best I can, but I ain't never done no campaign work and I ain't all that good at drawin', except for horses, which I can do fair to middlin'," Orville added.

"What would it take? Lobby for me. Talk me up. Tell everyone to vote for me. Say I'm a good guy. That doesn't take any skill. Talking is easy."

"Depends on the subject," Orville said.

"Yeah? I can say anything to anyone and feel really at ease," I said, temporarily forgetting my adventures in Swedish when I tried to talk to Julie.

"Prove it," Lumpy challenged.

"What do you mean, 'prove it'?"

"Go ask Julie out. Right now."

"I don't even know where she is," I said, suddenly feeling my throat drying up and hearing my voice go up about an octave. Scowling world leaders I can face. Julie Sloan, well . . .

"She's over there. Just sitting down at the table. If you ask her out now, I will not only campaign for you, I will be your campaign manager. We will have Dick Dickson begging for mercy from us by this time next week," Lumpy dared.

"Ha!" I said. "You don't think I can ask her out, do you?"

"Right. We don't," Rob quickly agreed.

"Orv, my pal. Do you doubt me?"

"You'd sit a little taller in the saddle in my eyes if'n you did, Wallace."

"You'll not only get a date, you'll get a campaign committee," Mel said. "You've wanted to ask her out for eight months now."

"Ha!" I said articulately.

"You're saying 'ha' again, Wally. That means you're nervous," Lumpy said.

"Me? No way. I can do it. I can walk over and ask her out. I just don't want to right now. She's with her friends and it's lunch. Lunch is sort of a sacred time. You just sit and eat and unwind and you shouldn't have tremendous life-changing experiences thrust upon you, like getting asked out by me."

"Just what I thought. He's chicken," Mickey sighed. Lumpy made the detestable chicken noise. My honor was on the line.

"Okay, I'll do it."

Bad move, I immediately decided. This isn't how I had it pictured. This is a day where guys in high school, no matter how idiotic it seems, hire telegram singers to ask girls out. Or rent billboards, or skywriting airplanes. And me? I'm wolfing down a cheeseburger. Nevertheless, I gave my word, sort of.

I rose stiffly. No time to plan. No time to work out just the right combination of words that would sweep her off her feet and make her wild with excitement. No time to practice being cool, which is a necessity for a date with Julie. No time to even check the basics—my hair, my clothing—to see if I have dribbled any mustard on my shirt. I began taking long, slow steps. I could feel the eyes of a half-dozen friends piercing my back. Man, I wished I had shaved this morning! And no aftershave, either! What she would get is Whipple in the Rough, not the cool, sophisticated version I had hoped to become by now. It will have to be my raw, animal magnetism that sees me through this crisis.

Ten feet. Seven feet. Five feet. Her back was turned to me. Three feet. I could reach out and place my hand on her shoulder now . . . I did, tapping her lightly. She turned and looked surprised. The girls at the table all stopped talking and eating. All of them gaped at me. Conversation and appetites were killed instantly by my presence. Dead silence. Her gaze met mine. This is the magic moment I had dreamed about for weeks . . . now it was here . . . and all I had to do was ask . . . a new and better life beckoned . . . speak, Whipple, speak!

"Erd, un girble en date to opera?" I babbled.

"Wally? Are you okay? Do you have vocalitis frigidalis again?"

"Uh-her. I . . . am . . . okay."

"Do you want something? Can I help you?"

I nodded as though my head were made of cork. She looked at me curiously. Her friends were all staring. And everywhere, cold, dead silence.

"Go out?" I finally mumbled.

"Oh, I get it! You want me to go out with you!"

"Yerrsss."

She looked around at her friends, then looked back at me. "Sure, Wally."

"Surrrrre? You mean . . . you will?"

"Of course."

My poise began to rally a bit. Not a whole lot, but enough to let her know that English was not a second language for me.

"How about . . . the opera . . . the one about the mouse by Strauss."

"Oh Wally, you're so funny! You mean *Die Fledermaus*. I'd love to. I saw the ad in the paper."

"Yes. It is a timeless classic," I managed to say in a nearly normal tone of voice.

She giggled. "When and where?"

"On May 23rd. It's a school night, so we won't stay out too late. Nothing good ever happens after midnight, like they say."

DUMB. DUMB. DUMB. Shades of Natalie!

"Sounds super. Why don't you call me and we'll work everything out?"

"Okay."

"This will be great, Wally. Thanks."

I began to feel really good. "Yeah. Really great." I was feeling fantastic.

"I didn't know you had your license."

I began to feel really terrible.

"Ah, well, yes. That is, I have my license. I'll drive. A car. With you in it."

"Super. Give me a call."

I turned and walked back over to the table where The Posse was watching me with nothing but pure admiration (or pure disbelief, I'm not sure which) in their eyes.

"So how did it go, Ace?" Orv wanted to know.

"Like falling off a slick log. You doubted me? You think I have no class?"

"I'm glad it worked out," Lumpy noted, "because you have a big piece of lettuce caught in your teeth."

THURSDAY, MAY 9

By the time I got home from school last night, I was feeling pretty good about the way I handled asking out Julie. Oh, a few rough edges. Got to get over my babbling. But overall, not bad, about a B minus. Mission accomplished. I mean, we are going out.

Although there is one slight detail I need to work out: My license.

Thinking it over, I have several options.

Option #1

I tell Julie the truth. "Uh, I don't have my license, so my dad is going to have to drive us. When I said that I had my license, I misunderstood you. I thought you said, 'Oh, I didn't know you had such good sense,' meaning that you admired my taste in opera."

Naw. Never work. It's only a half-truth, besides.

Option #2

I don't mention anything to Julie, just show up in the family station wagon with Dad at the wheel.

Even worse. Julie will think not only that I'm a liar, but that I don't have any guts, which may be true.

Option #3

Steal the family car. Walk out a few minutes before my date, sneak into the garage, and pull out of the driveway. Maybe Mom and Dad wouldn't notice.

Wrong. I'd get caught before I backed out of the driveway. Or even more humiliating, a police officer would pull me over and arrest me for car theft. Julie and I would be booked and sent to jail. And knowing how torqued my dad would be, I'd rot awhile before he posted bail. If he posted it at all. Also, getting arrested on your first date is not the best way to begin a relationship that might culminate in a temple marriage.

Option #4

Throw myself upon the mercy of my parents. Admit that in the excitement of the moment, I said something foolish. Tell them the only way I can save face is to arrange to take the driver's test before the concert. Promise them anything—mission, temple marriage, a life dedicated to good works, and perhaps even being nice to Natalie. Tell them how much I have admired their parenting skills. Let them know I am proud to be their son and bear the Whipple name . . . get on my knees and clutch their ankles, if needed. Anything!

Go with it. Really, it's the only practical thing I can do.

I hope Julie understands how much I'm going through for this date. I have risked the ridicule of my friends, will have to grovel before my family, and have been working Saturdays and at least one night a week to pay for dinner and the concert. I have thought, dreamed about, and planned for this date since . . . since . . . the first day of seminary. It has to be a perfect night.

Someday, when Julie and I are married, and we've put our six children down for the evening, and we're relaxing and reminiscing about the days when we were first getting to know each other, I may come clean and tell her how much I went through to win her heart.

I hope she will appreciate all the hard work that has gone into it.

FRIDAY, MAY 10

Another track meet. Another win. No big deal. (Ha! I love winning. I love hearing my name on the PA system. I love the way people who looked at me before as strictly a geek from the deepest part of outer space, are now giving me high fives, low fives, elbow bashes, talking with me, acting as though we were actually friends. I love to see Coach Leonard nod and smile at me after a good jump. I love watching all the distance runners churning around the track, gasping for oxygen, and I love thinking, save for my ability to jump over a slim piece of metal, there go I.)

Still haven't talked over with Mom and Dad how

my whole life depends on getting my license within two weeks.

Did get the concert tickets. Forty bucks! Love is expensive. No turning back now.

Chuck is on the driveway every day. No baskets yet.

Natalie and Lindy are now the world's greatest friends (at least until they wear the same outfit to school again). Natalie is spending the night at Lindy's, and in the morning they are going to launch an all-out assault against the retailers of Portland. Tomorrow, they are going "to do" three malls. (Note: Natalie's words, not mine.) Natalie said she feels that she has outgrown the mall closest to our house and that she wants to extend herself. "I need to grow. I'm stagnating," she told me before leaving for Lindy's. "Seriously."

Went down to Sister Lawson's house with Dad tonight and helped her plant a garden.

Mom and I made a list of what ingredients it will take for the cookies. Can you believe that it will take approximately twenty-five dozen eggs and more than one hundred cups of flour?

Still haven't approached Orville about the missionary lessons. I need to before mid-June arrives. That's when he is going back to Heppner for the summer, and I'm not sure of his plans for next fall. As much as I hate the thought, he may not return to Portland for school. The halls of Benjamin Franklin High will not be as pleasant if there is no Orville Burrell moseying down them next year.

Dick Dickson continues to irritate me. His friends somehow programmed every computer in the school to say, "Dickson's the One!" when they were turned on this morning. "Did you see my latest campaign maneuver?" he asked me today between classes. "Your problem, Whipple, is that you have no appreciation for technology."

He's wrong about my appreciation for technology. In fact, I'm working on a button that I can press and whoever it is that I'm thinking of will break out in zits and be transported to a medium-sized ice flow in the Antarctic. When my magical button is perfected, I will first try it out on Dick Dickson. Maybe then he'll understand my appreciation of technology.

SUNDAY, MAY 12

I decided that today was the day for me to talk over my driving dilemma with my parents. My thinking is, they've been at church all day, they have a nice feeling, they should be a little bit more in tune, a little more charitable, a little more generous, a little more willing to accommodate the needs of their firstborn.

One important alliance needed to be struck. I needed Natalie on my side for this one. I didn't want a snide comment from her to sink my ship. And Natalie has the finely honed ability to say just the wrong thing at the right time and turn the tide of popular sentiment against me. How many times, for example, have I been set to go shoot hoops with a friend and Natalie will seemingly materialize from thin air and say, "Gee, I thought it was Wally's turn to do the dishes tonight." My mom will look at me and say, "Yes, it is Wally's turn tonight. Put your plans aside until your chores are done, Wally." At that point,

Natalie will usually shoot me a quick glance of supreme triumph as she slithers back to her room.

Couldn't risk that scene tonight, though.

"Natalie, I need your help with something," I said,
as she slouched in a chair in her room after church,
flipping through a fashion magazine. "This is big, and
I don't want you to mess me up. I'm going to ask
Mom and Dad if I can get my license next week. I
really need it for something I have planned."

She carefully studied me. "You have your Eagle
Scout badge yet?" she asked with a wicked glint in her
eyes.

"No. But I've got all the plans made and it's only a
matter of time and 2,000 cookies."

"They won't do it."

"I think they will. Especially if you say something
nice at just the right instant. You have incredible timing, and for once I'd like you to put it to work *for*
me."

"Why should I? A deal is a deal, and you haven't
kept your end of it. Mom and Dad will see right
through you. You'll be dust."

"Maybe. But there is something in this for you."

"What?"

"A precedent."

"A what?"

"Precedent. Listen. Someday, you are going to
want something big. Maybe a job at the mall where
you can get a big discount, or maybe going out on a
school night, or maybe wanting your own license.
Mom and Dad are going to want to say no, and that's
when you pop this on them. 'But you let Wally have
his license before he got his Eagle Scout award!' See?

The stage has been set. This is to your advantage, too, Nat."

I'd struck something deep inside her soul: Natalie's motherlode of greed. "Yeah. That makes sense. Okay, you've got it. I'll be on your side this time and then you be on my side next time I need something big."

"Got it, Nat."

Most Sunday evenings, we sit around the oak table in the dining room and plan our week. This is the time I thought would be ideal to bring up the subject of my license. We went through all the business— church meetings, school stuff, work schedules—and then I cleared my throat. Dad looked at me as though he could tell something was on my mind. "Wally?"

"Remember our deal about my license? Well, I need it this week or next because something important has come up. It means a lot to me, Dad."

"What is it, Wally?"

"I have a date with a really nice girl, and I don't want to have to take the bus or have you drive us. No offense, Dad."

"Your date isn't with Edwina?" Mom asked. She really likes Ed.

"No. Her name is Julie Sloan."

At this, Natalie's eyes almost bugged out and the water she was drinking sort of spurted out of her mouth. "Julie Sloan? She's really pretty. And popular. Doesn't she go out with Joe Vermeer? What does she see in —" Natalie stopped abruptly, remembering her pledge. "Well, I know what she sees in you, Wally. You have many fine qualities. Seriously."

I gave her the most grateful look in world-sibling history.

"Wally has worked on his Eagle," Mom said, and I could feel the momentum building.

"Wally deserves it. He is a great brother and a really cool guy. Seriously," Natalie struck again, and I was almost moved to tears.

Dad was stunned by Natalie's show of support. I could almost see the gears of his mind briefly grind, halt, then lock in again. "I guess it's okay with me. What do you think, Pam?"

"We should support Wally now that he's showing more interest in socializing."

Dad drummed his fingers on the table. "Done deal, then. When do you want to try?"

"How about May 22nd? That's the day before I go out with Julie." I hadn't thought this part out, I just backed up one day from the critical Thursday.

"Okay. We'll arrange it. Can you get out of track for a day?"

"Yeah. The coaches will give me a workout to do on my own."

We went our separate ways. Natalie smiled sweetly and whispered, "You owe me big time, Wally. I put you over the top on this one, and you know it."

"Yeah, right, Nat."

I have only one word to say about the events of tonight, although I think I will say it several times just to make my true feelings known.

YES! YES! YES! YES! YES! YES!

TUESDAY, MAY 14

Coach Leonard reminded me today that the City Track Meet is coming on May 24th, the day after my date with Julie. He said that I had the best 10th grade high jump in the city and that I would have to be considered the favorite. "You've got 'city champ' written all over you, Wally."

City Champ. Whew. This is big-time stuff for me. City Champ. Sounds good.

Note: Casually mention to Julie on our date that the city meet is the next day, and if she would like, I would have no problem with her attending to cheer me on.

WEDNESDAY, MAY 15

Stuff I Need To Do Soon:

1. Practice being cool for my date with Julie. Talk in short sentences. Act as though I am very comfortable at the opera. Don't say "yo" too much because it will remind her of Joe. I need my own cool word that gives me my own distinct image. Possible candidates: wow, hey, nay, and several variations of the basic grunt.

2. Cheer Chuck on. He keeps shooting those hoops and none of them go in.

3. Practice for my driving test, although I have nothing to worry about.

4. Find out if Orville will take the missionary lessons. I know . . . I've been putting this one off for about three months. Dad has dropped some hints, too. "We could teach him in our home, Wally. I think he'll listen to the lessons."

5. My term paper for English. Time is slipping away. My autobiography isn't going so well. I can't really plug into what Mrs. English was telling me

about writing from the heart. I keep ending up trying to be funny or breezing through it. I need inspiration.

6. Get my campaign rolling. Every day I see Dick Dickson and his brigade of nerds out pumping hands, passing out tags, and looking extremely smug whenever I come around. My campaign is less than dynamic so far. The best slogan Lumpy has come up with is "Don't be a pickle, vote for Whipple." It doesn't even rhyme.

I bet Winston Churchill never had to go through this.

THURSDAY, MAY 16

Dickson strikes again.

Today he passed out pocket protectors with a silkscreen of himself and the words, "Fixin' to Vote Dickson" on the front.

Pocket protectors!

He's raised being a nerd to an art form. My first reaction was one of ecstasy. Political suicide. Handing out pocket protectors as a campaign gimmick has to be political suicide. Straight from the Planet of the Geeks.

At least, that's what I thought.

By the middle of the morning, I was seeing a lot of kids wearing them. And not just the computer nerds. Some very popular guys started to pop them on. Lumpy noticed, too. "I don't know how this is happening, but Dick is so uncool that he is becoming cool. He's a fad. I bet I've seen fifty of those pocket protectors around this morning."

"I know, I know. Dick is turning out to be a handful. A handful of warm sludge gathered from a toxic waste dump."

As the day wore on, the pocket protectors became even more conspicuous. Dick was starting to strut around like he was the principal or something. Pocket protectors! Who would've thought they'd be a hit?

"Whipple! Hey Whipple!" I heard Dick's irritating, screechy voice as I walked toward health class. "You may as well give up now and save face," he said, without the slightest trace of humility. "The pocket protectors have put me over the top. I've even got a couple of teachers wearing them. You know what, Whipple? You underestimated me. You should just face reality and give up. I've become a pretty popular dude around here the last few days. You don't have a chance."

I had continued to walk down the hallway, but when he started talking about how popular he was, it was a little more than I could stomach.

"Dick, you are not popular. You are a nerd. You were born one, you will die one. You can't be something that you are not. And I think you should at least call yourself Richard, which has a shred of dignity."

I turned and started into health class. Dick was fuming.

"You'll regret that!" he screeched. "You've made a serious mistake! No mercy now!"

I paused at the doorway. "Tell someone who cares, Dick." Then I ducked in.

I never expected all this from Dick. I thought he was a little different, but still an okay guy in his own way. Yeah, maybe he does go to bed at night and dreams about computers, but I didn't see this streak of arrogance in him until the election stuff started. If I lose the election, so what? I tell myself that I'm still Wally Whipple, and even if I'm not sure who he is, at least I know I'm not like Dick Dickson. I don't think I've ever done anything in my life to hurt someone on purpose. I can't do that.

It's got to be different when you're an adult. This competition stuff can't last beyond high school. It's so immature. A couple more years and my generation will have outgrown it, and I'll never have to deal with it again.

I hope.

FRIDAY, MAY 17

Mom, being the organizational genius that she is, lined up a school cafeteria, complete with baking equipment, for our 1,856 cookies. "Industrial strength," she said. "We'll have a regular production line going." I have faint hope now that we actually will get our cookies baked and delivered.

Another best in the high jump today, cleared 6'2". "Unlimited potential," Coach Leonard gushed. I love that kind of talk. City Champ. Unlimited potential. I'll get the chance to prove it next week.

SATURDAY, MAY 18

Six more days until the first day of the rest of my life begins. Does that make sense? What if . . . Julie and I really hit it off? I mean, what if we're taco chips and salsa, pizza and pepperoni, scrambled eggs and ketchup?

We will become the Barbie and Ken of our day. We will be asked to speak at firesides and teach classes on how to conduct a successful courtship. She will write to me once a week on my mission, and I will ask her to marry me the day I get home, soon after she greets me at the airport. Then, we will join our lives, two beings devoted to one another, serving all, a shining light, a tower of strength, a wonderful example of what life is about.

We will also be ideal parents to our perfect children, especially during their turbulent teenaged years.

Whoa . . . I think I'm getting way ahead of myself here. First I need my license, which is merely the key to my eternal well-being.

I was mowing the lawn this afternoon, thinking of how I need to act when I pick up Julie. We have a big fir tree in our front yard and I pulled the lawnmower over as I cut a swath close by. I decided to practice on the tree. Sounds dumb, I know, but *like* can make you crazy.

"Yo, Julie. You look good. You ready for the evening of your life?"

NOT. A little too greasy.

"Jules, babe. Lookin' good. Are you ready for the magnificent tonight?"

Naw, too much like they talk in the movies.

"Hey, Julie. Glad you could make it out tonight."

Nope. Something an elders quorum president would say to a less active member at the ward banquet.

"Julie. Hi."

I like it. Simple. Direct. Not much of a message though.

It was about then that I got the eerie feeling I was being watched. I turned around and there, wide-eyed, mouth drooping open, was Marshall Phelps, one of Chuck's buddies.

"Is your tree named Julie?"

"No, it is not named Julie."

"Why did you call your tree Julie?"

"I did not call the tree Julie. I said, 'This tree is a beauty.'"

"No you didn't. You called the tree Julie. You told the tree that it was lookin' good. I heard you."

"Marshall, your mother is calling you."

"No she isn't. She's not at home."

"Marshall, go away."

"I don't want to. I'm going to tell Chuck that you called the tree Julie."

"Chuck won't believe you. He'll believe me because I'm his brother."

"Why did you call the tree Julie?"

I could tell I wasn't going to win. You can't argue with little kids, English teachers, or nerds running for office. I pulled the starter on the lawnmower and its roar blissfully drowned out further questions from Marshall. I trudged away, once again cutting the long, green grass. Looking over my shoulder, I saw Marshall knock on our front door. Chuck answered it, and I could see both of them staring at me as Marshall pointed to me. He was mouthing the words, "Your brother is weird."

Considering that I was talking to a tree, trying out my opening lines for the big date, maybe Marshall is right. I am weird.

SUNDAY, MAY 19

Orv and his dad came over for dinner. It was nice to see Mr. Burrell again.

Natalie, as expected, was charming. "Hello Orville. So nice to see you again. And Mr. Burrell, you are looking well tonight. Seriously." She looked cute in a new outfit that she had purchased yesterday, approximately sixty minutes after she learned that the Burrells were coming to dinner. She was cute with Chuck, she laughed her winning little laugh at just the right moments, and she even offered to help with the dishes, which hasn't happened since Ronald Reagan's second term as president. I've got to face it, Natalie can really turn on the old charm when she wants. And she has cute down cold.

"Old Chuckwagon is quite a kid. Makes me wish I had a little cub to follow me around. And that's some little sister you've got," Orville allowed, after dinner, when he and I decided to go out in the backyard and sit on the grass in the cool, early evening air.

"Yeah, some sister. She actually might be the same species as the rest of us."

"Well, she's jes' a little more than a kid. You got to give her some time. She'll likely turn out to be a mighty nice person someday, and you might even start to feel a tad bit proud of her," Orville said. "Say, you're fixin' to make big medicine this week. You got the date with Julie, the city track meet, and if I remember right, you're gonna whomp on over and take your drivin' test."

"Yeah. Big week, Orv." We were silent for a moment. It was really pleasant outside, the temperature was just right, and a few crickets were starting to chirp. The grass, which I had mowed yesterday, smelled fresh. Orville looked peaceful, almost content. For a moment, I saw him as he must be back on his ranch, at ease, in his element. I knew for all of his cowboy-cool exterior, Orv had weathered some tough changes in the last year, adjusting to the loss of his mom, moving to the city, getting used to seeing asphalt and powerlines instead of meadows and hills. True, some people would say he had the touch of gold, but they couldn't know the price he had paid. Maturity was forced on Orv. Grow up in a hurry, or sink.

"You aren't coming back to Portland next fall, are you?" It was a statement more than a question.

He didn't say anything. Then he sat up a little. "I been wrasslin' with that decision for a time now. Some things, you can run from and they won't catch up to you. Other things, you can never leave them behind because they're too much a part of you. Where you were born, your family, what you stand for, and what you know how to do. I guess that's what me and Dad have figured out. We're country people, and while neither of us regret comin' to the city and seeing how other folks live, we're a little bit like worms on a hot asphalt road. Out of our element. We decided just last night, that come July or so, we'll head back to Heppner. We'll help my brother with the hayin' through the busy time of the year, and I think we've both about figured that we'll stay on. That's our home, y'know. Even cowboys need a home."

"Yeah. I know. And maybe you can only call one place home."

"Yup. You got it. You can't get too far away from

the pea patch without feeling those home pangs pinchin'."

"If you go, I'll miss you, Orv." I was surprised by what I said. But, it was true. Orv had become a great friend, and I had learned a lot from him. I wanted to be like him in many ways.

I started to get a sensation inside my stomach. I got this incredible feeling: a swelling, a shakiness, a sense that something good was about to happen. *I should ask him about the Church.* July! Not much time. I tried to ignore the feeling, but it wouldn't go away. Was it the Spirit? Brother McNair and the missionaries both told me I'd know the right time . . . it must be now.

"Orv . . . " Can I go through with this?

"Would . . . you, like to, um . . . " He looked me straight in the eye. My confidence began to melt like an ice cube in the August sun. "Would you like some dessert now?" I blurted, a sagging feeling already coming over me.

He looked at me as though he expected me to say something else. "Sure, Wally." And we went back in, ate some strawberry shortcake, and the Burrells were back in their truck and on the way home thirty minutes later.

The moment had come and passed. I had failed. Definitely not the way Ammon would have handled it. I'm sure, thinking about it now, that tonight was the right time to ask Orv about taking the lessons. I felt it. Will I get a second chance? I blew it. Why did I chicken out? If he'd said no, so what? We would still be friends, life would go on, and I wouldn't feel as if I'd messed up big time on the most important thing to come along in months. But I couldn't get the old brain and tongue together to ask him the question.

The brain, tongue, and maybe the heart. If it happens again, I will not blow the chance. That much, I'm promising myself.

MONDAY, MAY 20

Okay, we're down to the wire. Let me put it in basic terms. This may be the biggest week of my entire life. Am I nervous? Well, let me put it this way. I wasn't able to do much more than pick at my sub sandwich at lunch today. That is a first.

I've got to get my act together this week. Thursday must be perfect. I've got to be cool and make a great impression on Julie. I can't be the Wally Whipple who talks in strange languages when he gets nervous. I can't be the geek who wears his suit to school because a coach told him to. I can't be the guy who slogged through cross-country season at the back of the pack, the teenager who did the hokeypokey at his first dance.

And there's more I can't be. I can't be the person who tried to lip-synch through choir and who asked Ed's dad if he were a Republican or a Democrat. I can't be the dork who sends his friends Christmas cards or asks Joe if it's okay to go out with Julie. No way. Not this kid. A new image, a total retooling.

The version of Wallace Whipple who knocks on Julie's door will be poised, polished, confident, and smooth. I will look good. I will be witty and charming. I will make good conversation without the assistance of a cheat sheet scrawled on my wrist. Wally

Whipple will emerge! Julie may not fall head over heels for me, but at least she'll know she's been out with a class guy, and see a side of me that was hidden before .

Come to think of it, maybe I haven't seen that side of me, either.

My campaign committee, such as it is, met tonight at our house, and we made a bunch of tags, posters, and whatever. We'll hand them out tomorrow. The election is one week away, and I know it's going to be an uphill battle. I'm still unsure how Dick Dickson, hero of the highwater pants brigade, overtook me and became a cult figure at school. Maybe he's right. Maybe I should have withdrawn gracefully and avoided the humiliation of being trashed by the pocket protector platoon.

Oh, well. I've got other things to worry about. License. Julie. City meet. And come next Monday, spend the holiday in a sweltering kitchen baking about a zillion cookies. For now, Dick Dickson is just going to have to wait.

TUESDAY, MAY 21

Got the campaign tags out today. Not exactly an overwhelming response, except by my closest friends, to wearing a tag in the shape of a pickle. Someday, I'm going to write a book about the things this election has taught me.

Dick Dickson went out of his way to taunt me again today. This guy, who I thought was sort of a humble, sweet, shy nerd who was running for office only because it would look good on his application to M.I.T. or Cal Tech, has all the sensitivity and compassion of a piranha at feeding time.

"Saw your campaign tags, Whipple," he snickered. "Pretty pathetic. A pickle. Well, maybe it fits after all, considering your personality."

"Dick, go home and feed your pet rats. Be with your own kind," I suggested.

The other event of the day: Man of the Year. We had a school assembly, the last one of the year. The seniors are all coasting now because they get out a week before the underclassmen. The assembly today is the one where they pass out all the awards—most likely to succeed, most athletic, most humorous, most this, and most that. Scholarships are also announced. But the biggest awards are "Man of the Year" and "Woman of the Year." Everything is taken into account: Grades. Activities. Character, and a bunch of other intangibles. The selection is made by a group of student leaders, faculty, and the principal. It's a big deal to be chosen number one out of a student body of two thousand kids.

One award went to Wendy Del Rio, who has perfect grades and was student body president this year. And the other went to . . . drum roll, please . . . will the audience please hush . . . our very own, JOE VERMEER!

It was awesome. Joe ambled up on the stage, looking surprised and happy. As soon as his name was announced, everybody stood up and started to applaud. Then came the chant . . . Joe! Joe! JOE! JOE!!!

Shivers went up my back. True to nature, Joe was so cool about accepting the award. He thanked the principal, his parents, the students, his church leaders.

He thanked just about everyone, as though he didn't do anything himself to win the award. He held the plaque high over his head, then slowly walked back to his seat.

It's something to be a legend and not yet nineteen years old.

Tomorrow is the first big one for me this week. The driving test. I've heard that parallel parking is where most people mess up, so after track tonight, Dad stuck some milk cartons next to the curb and I practiced parking between them. Tried it four times and left all the milk cartons standing.

I am ready. Call it Phase One of the New and Improved Wallace Whipple. In less than twenty-four hours, I will be licensed by the State of Oregon to operate a vehicle on the public highways and byways. No longer will I have to suffer in shame when my peers talk about driving. I will actually feel like an official, bona fide, genuine teenager. I will have this tremendous sense of responsibility as I carefully turn the key, gently put the car into gear, and then lay rubber all the way down the street where I live!

And most of all, I will be FREE. Free to let the true personality of Wallace Whipple come boiling to the surface. Free to go places and do things. Free to leave the old Wally behind and become . . . me.

Julie Sloan, you are a lucky woman, indeed. You are going to be the first to witness the metamorphosis of Wallace Whipple in his transformation from caterpillar to butterfly, from ungainly chick to soaring eagle.

Twenty-four hours to go!

WEDNESDAY, MAY 22

This is the worst day of my life!

TRUE STATEMENT: Got out the atlas today and started to scout out new places I could live, somewhere far away from Oregon. A place where I could establish a new identity, where no one would ever know how close I came to beginning a new life before having it shattered by cruel fate.

I finally settled on a little island far away in the South Pacific, where life is simple . . . fish for a living, eat coconuts, where home is a thatched hut, nowhere near anything resembling a high school and other things that have immensely complicated my young life—such things as automobiles and dowdy old license examiners named Officer Clayton.

I hate to even write the words. Everything is still so painful, so fresh in my mind . . . as if it all happened only a few hours ago. Which it did. But here are the wretched words: *I flunked my driver's license test!*

Flunked! I can't believe it yet. I'm still in a daze. I checked for signs of shock, based on my first aid merit badge, and I exhibited four of the five. Flunked! My life is ruined. What will I do about tomorrow night? I feel miserable enough right now to call Julie and with a certain amount of justification, tell her I am sick, and sorry, we'll have to go out some other time. Flunked! It's my worst nightmare. Where did I go wrong in life? Why is this all so difficult? Why can't life be a series of simple, easy choices with no major consequences no matter what decision you make? Where did the days go when my big choice was whether I would have a tuna or peanut butter sandwich in my lunch box? How do I get back to that time? Get me a ticket, fast!

Flunked. It will be on the front page of the morning newspaper. "Dumb Teenager Flunks Driver's Test, Date with California Beauty Up in Air!" I won't be able to bear it. I won't be able to look at the tabloids in the supermarket checkout line for fear that I'll see a picture of me with Officer Clayton. She'll be scowling and shaking her finger at me while I feebly attempt to park the car. I'll be right there with the singing pigs from Mars, the frozen dinosaurs found atop the Himalayas, and the group of clergy who sighted Elvis on a fishing boat in the Gulf of Mexico during a cruise with their wives.

Officer Clayton. I'll remember those thick glasses, the long scraggly gray hair, her dingy gray skirt and yellowed, white blouse, the corners of her mouth perpetually turned down, the look in her eyes that said to every teenager taking the test, "Make my day, punk. Do one thing wrong and you're navel lint."

I passed the written test, no problem. Two examiners were giving the driving test. One was a fairly normal looking man in his late 20s, almost bald, but who seemed nice. The other was Officer Clayton. I wanted the bald guy to be my examiner but had the creepy, sick feeling that it wasn't meant to be. A few other people were ahead of me in line. The bald guy would come in and announce a name, then take someone on the road test. Officer Clayton would come in and bark a name, then do the same. This went on for almost an hour, and then I knew that I was up next. Mom reached over and patted my hand.

If she only knew! Please, Bald Guy, come in and speak my name!

No such luck. Officer Clayton came in and boomed, "Whipple, Wallace F.!" in a voice that would make a Marine drill sergeant envious.

I had a sick feeling in my stomach, like the time I was in the 8th grade play and spaced out my only line in the whole production while three hundred people stared at me, except for Natalie who was doubled up with laughter on the floor.

Officer Clayton led me to the car. "You're the driver," she growled, grimly motioning me in. "Pull over to the parking pylons and execute parallel parking."

Execute? Why that word? This was not a good sign.

I put the car in gear and gingerly drove to the parking area. Cautiously, I flipped my turn signal, hoping to pick up brownie points for my effort. I checked the rearview mirror, looked over my shoulder, eased my foot onto the accelerator—and promptly shot forward. I'd forgotten to put the car in reverse!

A crooked smile began to play around Officer Clayton's mouth. I began to sweat, perhaps as no other human being has ever done before. I remember Mr. Catton telling us in health class that people have up to five million sweat glands. All five million of mine instantly performed their ordained function. "Why don't you try again, Mr. Whipple?" Officer Clayton oozed. "This time, remember that the little 'R' on your transmission indicator means reverse. You need to know that before you can make the car go backwards."

I tried again. I tipped over one of the pylons. Officer Clayton looked at me with scarcely concealed delight, sensing the kill was at hand. "You have one more chance, Mr. Whipple. Three strikes, and you're out, in this league."

I was so nervous by then that my hands were trembling and I would have had a hard time tying my shoelaces. A vision of Thursday night, with Julie and my dad sitting in the front seat of the station wagon with me cowering in the back, flashed into my mind. But to the task at hand . . . I did everything right . . . my signal . . . checked in back of me . . . eased the car inside the pylons. I sat for a second or two, breathing heavily and trembling. "Guess I'm done. What's next?" I mumbled.

"Not so fast, Whipple. I need to check out your distance from the curb," she sneered.

She jumped out of the car and pulled out a tape measure. She got down on the ground and did some measuring. Then she came back with a wicked look of glee. "You're nineteen inches away from the curb, and the law says that you have to be eighteen inches or less. Come back when you're better prepared."

"You mean . . . I flunked?" I stammered. "Flunked by an inch?"

"That's the short of it, sonny."

"But . . . but . . . I can't. Tomorrow. My date with Julie. Oofer un Fielder mouse and then upmpen eat . . . see? Must have license . . . it's mine." My voice trailed off in a pathetic and unheard plea.

"Sorry, buster. You have to wait a week, then you can try it again." Officer Clayton smiled, drawing a heavy line across my application. "Take the bus on your big date. Do something for the environment." I had this urge to ask her if she were related to a guy named Dick Dickson. In my mind, I could envision her carving another notch on her gun.

MR. CLAYTON: "Have a good day at work, dear?"

OFFICER CLAYTON: "You bet, honey. Flunked four teenagers, one traveling salesman, and two little old ladies. Even had one kid crying. Gosh, I love my job."

I walked back to the waiting area. Mom was sitting there with a book. "Back so soon?" she asked, looking up. Then she read my face. "Oh, my. I'm so sorry, Wally."

What now? My date with Julie is less than twenty-four hours away. I guess Dad can drive us . . . a taxi is out because of the expense . . . I'd have to work until my next birthday to pay it off . . . How do you handle a situation when you don't like any of the choices you're presented with? Is this life, or is this just a bad day in life?

Why can't I say, "Peanut butter," kiss my mom good-bye, and trundle off to the first grade, where my main challenge that day would be to recite the alphabet?

Why ask why? My social life is over. I've lost Julie, even before our first date. The children who would've been ours are weeping in the pre-existence, all because of Officer Clayton.

It saddens me to think what might have been.

THURSDAY, MAY 23

I thought yesterday was the worst day in my life. I

couldn't imagine anything being worse. Rock bottom.
The pits. Operating on maximum humble. Down to
zero. That was me.

Then came today, and I found out how low you
can really go.

In the great computer of life, my hard disk
crashed.

My date with Julie was a disaster. Pure and simple.
No excuses, no rationalizations, no attempts to dismiss
how things went. The bare truth is that I bombed.
And I'm talking major league bomb, the kind that will
be felt clear across the Pacific. The best thing that can
be said for it is that Julie will never forget her date
with Wally Whipple. Never. No matter how hard she
tries.

The license part was tough. All night I tossed and
turned, seeing the face of Officer Clayton and her in-
fernal tape measure. One inch! That's all that sepa-
rated me from success. Why couldn't she have had a
heart? Why didn't the bald guy call my name?

But as Orv would say, that part of the trail is behind me. I had a problem. After agonizing, I decided
to ask my dad if he would drive us tonight. I worked
it out with him that he would drive us to the restaurant, sort of hang out in the parking lot while we ate,
then drive us to the opera. Then, more hanging out
for him, after which he'd take us home. My whole attitude has changed about tonight. Remember how I
wanted to be so cool? Doesn't fit now. "Hey Jules. Get
ready for the time of your life! Just hop in the car and
my father will drive us anywhere we want to go!" And
how can you be cool at the doorstep with your date
when you know your dad is parked in a car twenty

feet away? Should I ask him to drive around the block a couple of times so that he won't cramp my style?

No way. I'm afraid Julie is going to get the plain old Wally Whipple tonight, not the new and slicker version. It isn't my idea of really bowling over Julie, but what choice do I have? None. Dad, I think, understood my predicament, even if he is a parent. "Wally, don't worry. I'll be a ghost. You won't even know I'm along. I work until 5:30, but I'll be home in plenty of time."

Okay, so it won't be a pretty sight. But I'll handle it. At least that was my thought. Then disaster number two struck.

I'm at home, putting the final touches on. I'm wearing a sportcoat and my dad's best tie and his best socks. I'm looking in the mirror, hoping for a sudden outbreak of rugged handsomeness. The aftershave is on, every hair in place. Natalie, who for some reason is very concerned about my date with Julie, even gave me a thumbs up. "You almost look like you aren't a geek," she told me. "Seriously." I took it as a compliment.

While I'm fidgeting around waiting for Dad and thinking of a reasonable explanation to Julie about why my father is along on our date ("We're very close. We like doing everything together," is my current best line, which I realize isn't very good), the phone rings. It's fate—as soon as the first BBR-RRNNNGGGG! I know it is for me and that the news will not be good. Sure enough, I hear Chuck's voice. "Wally! It's Dad!"

Dad! Why is he calling me? He should be pulling into the driveway now!

"Wally . . . I've run into a problem. I'm still at the store. I went out to the car about ten minutes ago, and I can't get it started. I think it's the alternator but there's no way I'm going to get back in time to take you and Julie out to dinner."

True to my cool nature and newly found maturity, I handled this news with all the grace and aplomb that I've come to expect of myself. "DAD!!! YOU CAN'T DO THIS TO ME!!! THIS IS GOING TO RUIN MY ENTIRE LIFE!!!"

Yessirree, you can't ruffle a Whipple, I always say.

"Is Mom around? Can she drive you?"

"No. Mom is gone. She just left for the store. She won't be back for at least forty-five minutes, and by then, IT WILL BE TOO LATE AND MY LIFE WILL BE OVER!!!"

Steady as a rock, that's Wally Whipple.

"Son, I'm sorry. I'll be there as soon as I can. You may just have to call the girl and tell her that you're going to be late, or that you'll have to get a bite to eat afterwards."

"I CAN'T DO THAT!!! IT WILL CHANGE THE WHOLE EVENING!!! I CAN'T HANDLE ANY CHANGES AT THIS STAGE!!!"

"I'll hurry home, I promise. Got to go. You can think of something, Wally."

"HA! HA! HA!"

I hung up. My head was spinning. There's got to be a way to handle this. Keep calm. I stumbled over to the couch and sat down.

"Are you okay, Wally?" asked Natalie. "You look like you just ate some bad pizza."

"Uhhhhh. Awwww. Ohhhhh."

"What's wrong?"

"I'm supposed to be to Julie's house in five minutes. Dad's car is broken down. Mom just left. My life is over. I will never date, never marry, never progress."

"Don't be stupid. Call Orville and ask him to drive you."

Orville! Why not? "Natalie, you may have just saved my life. You are a genius."

She blushed. "It wasn't much, Wally. If you'd only stopped acting so panicky, you would have thought of it, too. Seriously."

I am somewhat reluctant to admit this, but I jumped off my couch and gave my sister a hug. Call it temporary insanity.

"Don't be all slobbery, Wally," she complained.

"Nat, thanks." I ran to the phone, and with trembling hands, dialed Orv's number. I was never so happy to hear anyone's voice as his when he answered. I quickly explained my problem.

"I'll be over like a scalded dog. You jes' sit tight and think cool cowboy thoughts, Wally."

Lickety brindle, Orville was at my front door. "You look like you jes' found a hair in your biscuit batter. You're all pale, Wally. Things will be okay, you can bet your best horse blanket on it, pard."

We drove to Julie's and before I had time to think, I was swinging open the door to Orv's truck and walking to her front porch. I was hoping that her parents wouldn't be around because I didn't feel up to making small talk with adults. In fact, I didn't feel like making small talk with Julie. I said a little prayer to the effect of, "Please just help me get through this without any more major goofs. All I want tonight is to survive."

It's funny how much I think about death while I'm on dates.

I reached out and rang the doorbell. This was supposed to be my magic moment, the crowning act of my entire social life, the instant when Julie would look me in the eyes and know that I was hers and she was mine and that we were each other's. Instead, I was trying to not feel so dizzy and saying silent prayers about survival. This is not the way fairy tales begin.

Julie opened the door. She was in a long, white dress, her light brown hair pulled back and tied with a black ribbon. She looked so . . . so . . . beautiful. I'd seen her practically every day for the last eight months, yet I was stunned at how gorgeous she looked. I stood there, speechless, my mouth open.

"Hi, Wally," she greeted me. "Are we ready?"

"Ready . . . yeah, like, for our date, right?"

"Right."

"Do I get to meet your parents?"

"If you want to."

The episode with Dr. Purvis flashed into my mind. "Maybe not now. We're a little late." I turned around and began to walk with her down the steps. I looked up and then experienced a severe anxiety attack as Orville's truck came into full view.

Let me explain it this way. Orville says there are two kinds of trucks. There are working trucks and strut trucks. Strut trucks are those that are painted some glossy color, waxed until they shine like the noonday sun, and have all sorts of what Orv calls "beautifiers"—cd decks, racing stripes, tinted wind-shields, and so forth. Orv holds strut trucks (so named because the people who drive them look like a pea-cock strutting around) in something very much akin to pure contempt. "Ya wanna truck or do ya wanna prissy sports car," he is wont to mumble as a strut truck roars by.

Needless to say, Orville's rig is a working truck, used for pulling trailers, hauling hay, a place where a hound or two can perch on the seat next to the dri-ver. His truck is two years older than I am, has never known the silky feel of wax. And its colors are so faded that it's hard to tell exactly what they originally were. For entertainment, there's only an AM radio and about 10,000 squeaks and groans. The floorboards are mostly held together by rust. The other distinguishing characteristics of the truck are that the odometer stopped working at 168,000 miles, and there are at least two inches of dog hair on the seats.

And now I was about to ask Julie, vision of loveli-ness personified, to climb into Orville's working truck and go to dinner and then to the opera. You've got class, Whipple. Third class, that is.

Julie looked up and saw the truck. "Are we going in this?" she asked politely. "I thought you had your license and we'd be going in a car."

Face life, Whipple. Square up like a man and be bold. "So did I. But yes, we are going in this. Orville is our chauffeur."

"How interesting," Julie murmured. "I've never been on a date with two guys in a truck."

I opened her door. Orville smiled and greeted her. "Howdy, there, Julie. Climb on in and let's go to supper. I put a fresh plastic garbage bag down on the seat for you to sit on so that you wouldn't get dog hairs all over your dress."

Julie looked at me as if to ask if this were all a joke. A slight sideways shake of my head told her it was not a put-on. She meekly got in the truck.

"Next stop, Walt's Mexican World Buffet," Orv breezily announced. "Dang good chow there, I hear."

Julie looked very nervous. *"A Mexican buffet?"*

I nodded.

Ten minutes later, we were in line at the restaurant. I told Orv on the way over to Julie's that he might as well join us for dinner, since the all-you-can-eat buffet was only five bucks. Orv and I went through the line, piling our plates high with enchiladas, burritos, tacos, chips, and other goodies. Julie shied away from the buffet and ordered a salad and a soft drink. Girls are weird when it comes to eating out, I mentally noted.

"She must not be hungry," Orville whispered as I handed a $20 bill, representing my entire net worth, to the cashier. We carried our trays and sat down at a long table, next to a family with three little kids, each of whom had decided that they really didn't want to be there with their parents and were letting the whole world know about it at the top of their lungs, roughly at the decibel level of a jetliner taking off.

"Ain't exactly magical, is it?" Orv said quietly to me between bites.

"No. This is a horror show. It can't get worse."

Julie picked at her salad and kept an eye on the three-year-old next to her who was lobbing mini-tacos in her general direction. She appeared somewhat tense. In a feeble attempt to salvage my big date, I tried to be suave. "So, Julie, do you know much about opera? I understand they have big drums in the orchestra part."

She looked up at me and started to say that she knew a little about opera and was looking forward to learning a bit more, when it happened.

No, "it" doesn't mean that our gazes locked in a sudden understanding that true love was ours. "It" meant that a huge bite of enchilada that I had balanced carefully on my fork slid off and dribbled its way down my white shirt and onto my lap, leaving a greasy trail of red sauce all along the way.

Julie stopped in mid-sentence. Orville looked over and between chomps said, "You dropped your food, Wally. Did you pack along a spare shirt tonight?"

"No, Orv, I do not make a habit of packing along a spare shirt on a date."

"Maybe we can get some hot water on it and take out the stain," Julie suggested with hope. I stood up, revealing a scar of grease on my shirt roughly the size of Michigan. "Oh. Maybe we can't," she said limply.

For the first time since we sat down to eat, the children at the adjoining table were quiet, with the exception of a boy about five who said, "He needs a bib, Mommy."

The rest of our meal was consumed in near silence. You might say the enchantment of the evening was disappearing fast.

I left a dollar tip at the table and didn't care who noticed. We got back in the truck and drove downtown. We traveled in absolute, dead silence. Julie carefully picked dog hair off her dress, trying to do so without us noticing. It was hopeless. My world was caving in.

The City Auditorium has a nice, circular driveway in front of it. One by one, the vehicles pulled up and people dressed to the max climbed out and went in. Orville's truck was in line between a European sports car and an American luxury sedan the size of a cruise ship. We finally got near enough to the sidewalk and Julie and I hopped out. "I'll find a place to park, then hang around until the show's over," Orv said. "Don't fret about me, you two jes' go in and have yourselves a good ol' time. I'll be in the lobby."

With that, he gunned the engine, which, true to the nature of the evening, backfired.

I had discovered on our way over that if I took my sportcoat off and sort of hugged it to my chest, you couldn't really see too much of the Great Enchilada Stain. Julie and I walked in, and I had to fish for the tickets to get inside. Naturally, they were in my sport-coat pocket, and I sort of had to double over to get hold of them so that my shirt wouldn't be noticeable. Anyway, I managed to find them and hand them to the usher, who seemed a little snooty for a guy wearing a black and red uniform that was four sizes too big for him. I hoped that the inside of the auditorium would be dark, but no luck; in fact, it seemed that everyone in the place turned around and looked at Julie and me coming in. Gratefully, I found our seats and we slid into the obscurity of the crowd.

Ten minutes later, the opera began. Fifteen minutes later, I made a social blunder of such proportions that it will, I predict, be written up in world record books.

Biggest Social Faux Pas Ever Committed: Wallace F. Whipple, Jr., age 16, on May 23, at a performance of *Die Fledermaus.*

I need to ask a question. It is not an accepted practice in our society to clap for a singer? Yes. It manifests approval, displays gratitude, it is a form of recognizing a high degree of skill and talent. No problem, right?

Operas are different, however. The lights were low and the music began. I put my coat down next to me in the chair, relieved that the Great Enchilada Stain could not be seen in the cover of darkness. The music was pretty good, certainly not Torme or Bennett, but not bad. Looking at the spectacular scenery and wondering what the story would be, I began to think that something might be saved from this evening, after all. Maybe Whipple would made a comeback. Perhaps Julie and I could engage in some scintillating conversation later on, laugh at the rocky start to the evening, and maybe the Great Enchilada Stain would fade away from her memory. Yes, I was feeling a trace of hope. But then, the fat lady stopped singing and smiled pleasantly at the audience.

So I started to applaud.

Suddenly, I realized that I was the only person out of a crowd of 2,000 who was clapping. And I'd forgotten to cover up the Great Enchilada Stain, meaning that it was visible to anyone looking at me.

And that included everyone. There were 4,000 eyes in the audience, not counting the singers, the conductor, and the orchestra members. About 3,996 of those eyes were focused on the kid in the middle of the auditorium with the big stain on his shirt who was applauding. The only eyes not focused on me were (1) mine; and (2) Julie's. She was slumped down in her chair with her eyes riveted to the floor, as if hoping that a crack would appear in the earth's crust and swallow her up.

The room temperature soared to about 112 degrees and I could feel myself turning the color of hot lava as it flows down a mountainside.

I halted my one-man show of appreciation, my clapping trickling to a pathetic, sporadic patter, noticing that even the object of my adoration, the fat lady, was glaring at me. I also slumped deep in my chair. My head, in fact, was lower than Julie's.

"It wasn't the right time to clap," Julie whispered from six inches above the floor.

"I figured that out, Julie," I croaked back. "I'm really sorry."

"It's okay, just make sure that other people are applauding before you do. That's safe, Wally."

What else can I say? The rest of the night was pretty uneventful, at least compared with everything else that had taken place. Disaster? Yeah, that's a fair description of my big date with Julie. Calamity? That fits, too. Tragedy? Of course. Catastrophe? Why not? Comedy? No. Net yet. Maybe someday it will seem funny, but not now. Julie could have been out with Joe Vermeer, Man of the Year. Instead, she went out with Wallace Whipple, Geek of the Century, who proved in every way that he's worthy of the title.

Oh, yeah. I almost forgot. The big door scene. This was going to be the perfect way to end the perfect evening in my original plan. I was going to tilt my head so that my most ruggedly handsome angle was toward Julie, the manly fragrance of my aftershave lightly scenting the spring night air. I had intended to say something clever and intelligent, something that would cement our relationship forever. (Granted, I hadn't thought of what that might be, but I was going to rely on the mood of the moment to come up with something. Sort of like relying on inspiration.) Instead, I walked up to Julie's house at a brisk pace. (She set it, not me. I think she wanted to get inside the door safely before something happened that might leave permanent emotional scars.) She turned to me at the doorway, key in hand. "Good-night, Wally. Thanks. See you around."

"Right. See you around."

Then she shook my hand.

The most dreaded words on the doorstep are "See you around." It's like, "Well, I'm sure we'll bump into each other again sometime in the next decade, if only because we both happen to be in the same relative location on the planet Earth, but I will certainly do nothing to trigger the event."

"See you around" is miles away from, "I had a great time, let's do something again soon," and isn't even in the same league as, "I had a super time. Are you busy Saturday night?"

Nope, just a plain, old, vanilla-flavored, "See you around." The old romance killer, the aorta smasher. Of course, if I were Julie, I probably wouldn't have even given me that much of a farewell. I probably would have fled into the darkness long before and called my father from a pay phone and begged him to come and pick me up.

I got back in the truck. Orville looked at me sympathetically and sort of punched me on the shoulder. "You played your rope out tonight, Wally. You might've got rope burns on your hands, but you haven't hung yourself. Remember that, buddy."

I got home. Chuck was in bed, but everyone else was still up. Nat spied the Great Enchilada Stain and blurted out, "Wally, did you embarrass the family tonight?"

Pitifully, I nodded my head.

FRIDAY, MAY 24

Well, it didn't happen. And it didn't happen in the worst possible way. Does that make sense? Yeah, it makes a lot of sense, given the way my life is going right now. I'm not only blowing things, I'm blowing them royally. If it's true that into everyone's life some rain must fall, then the monsoon season has hit me.

Even with all the events of this week swirling around me, I tried really hard to focus on the city track meet. I needed to experience some kind of success. I needed to win the high jump competition. I worked extra hard on my technique and concentration. I listened to every word that Coach Leonard had to say. Some things I can't control, but that's not the case with high jumping. How it would turn out was squarely on my shoulders.

"You'll have competition," Coach Leonard warned. "A kid named Green from Jefferson and a guy named Winslow from Benson look tough," he told me on the way to the meet.

We arrived at the track. I warmed up, trying my best to be cool. My family was in the stands—I could hear Chuck yelling hello to me. Even Natalie came, which surprised me. The emotions were really churning. All I wanted to do was get started, hoping that competition would chase away the butterflies. City Champ! It was my only shot at self-respect in the next few months.

Orville was over in the shot put area, flinging and grunting. His grunt really had improved during the season and he was a shoo-in to win the 10th grade shot put championship. He was walking around and shaking hands with all of his competitors, saying, "Pleased to meetcha," and wishing them the best of luck. That's Orv.

After what seemed like thirty-six hours, the call came for the high jump to begin. The bar was set at 5'6" and I chose not to enter until it moved up. Very cool. Some of the jumpers began to wash out right away and by the time I made my first jump, there were only six of us left. I marked my steps, concentrated on the bar, took my funny jumper's stride toward the pit, flung up my hands, and cleared it with no problem.

The butterflies didn't disappear, but they did find a flower to land on. On it went. Five-nine. Five-ten. Five-eleven. Six feet. Two more guys clanged the bar and only three of us remained. One of them was Winslow, the guy Coach Leonard had told me about. The wind was starting to kick up, making the jumps a little tricky. The bar went to 6'1", and it was my turn.

Concentrate, Whipple. Focus. I closed my eyes, and in my mind pictured myself clearing the bar. I opened my eyes, let out a couple of puffs of air and made my approach. For a split second, I thought my trailing leg might knock the bar off, but I heard happy shouts from the direction of my family and knew that I had made it as I settled on the foam cushion.

The next jumper missed. It was Winslow's turn. He cleared the bar, but not by much. For the first time, I really *believed I could win*.

The bar went to 6'2" and both of us cleared it. Up it went by a half-inch. We both jumped again and both cleared it—a new personal record. Now it stood at 6'3". We had three chances. Both of us missed badly on our first two tries, the bar bouncing on the foam mattress in the pit. We each had one jump left. Winslow went first. He eyed the bar, began his approach, and took off . . . He barely nudged the bar and it bounced on the standard. My heart—and my life—bounced right along with it—but the bar stayed in place. "Winslow! Cleared!" droned the field judge. "Whipple up!"

Lucky. How lucky can a guy get? Winslow should be out, and the worst I could do was tie for the city championship. I could live with that. Co-City Champ. Not bad. But Winslow had made it over, and now, I *had* to do the same.

One-half inch, Wally, just one-half inch. Pull everything together now and do it. No excuses, it all comes down to this.

I look around and see my dad and mom and Natalie and Chuck in the stands. Dad gives me a thumbs-up signal and Chuck is hollering something I can't understand. Natalie was staring at me, not at her friends, not at the good-looking guys on the field. Mom is holding both of her hands and looks nervous. Mr. Leonard is off to the side of the pit, pacing.

Orv comes over to watch. "How'd it go?" I ask him.

"Won," he says with a shrug. "Now it's your turn, pard. You got it in ya, Wally."

I mark my spot and do my routine. I block out everything except the bar. I stare at it, and tell myself that I can get over it and again mentally picture myself doing so. I wriggle my fingers and take a few deep breaths. I rock back and forth and start my approach. I jump—pumping with energy—and barely clear the bar!

Success! Whipple comes through. Finally.

It all seems in slow motion. I start down and hit the cushion. A gust of wind rattles across the field. It whips at the bar, wiggles it, wobbles it, and it comes tumbling down, thwacking me on the shoulder as I lie in the pit. The cheering slides into a heartsick groan.

"MISS!" shouts the field judge. "Winslow the winner! Event over."

I can't believe it. I make it over clean, and the wind does me in. Winslow, City Champ, and he hit the bar but got lucky. For the second time in forty-eight hours, I am done in by an inch or less. At this moment, I understand the meaning of the phrase, "Life is not fair."

Why me? I'm a good kid. Don't I deserve better? Isn't that what they teach you at church?

Why now?

What do I have to do to get it right? I mean *anything* right.

This is harder than it should be. Not just the high jump, but being a teenager.

How can you be yourself when you're not sure who yourself is?

I closed my eyes and stayed there, lying on my back in the pit. The last few minutes symbolize my whole life since the first day of high school. Good intentions. Good form. No breaks. Think of it. The whole year, and what had I accomplished?

I went out for cross-country and on my best day might have been mediocre.

I tried to lip-synch my way through choir.

I got tongue-tied when I tried speaking to Julie.

I got in a fistfight and all I could do was slap a guy's ankle.

I had to ask my sister for dance lessons.

I wore a suit to school.

I sat on the bench almost the whole basketball season.

I sent out Christmas cards. No guy my age sends out Christmas cards.

I thought Julie might ask me to the Anything Goes Dance, and when she heard about it, she laughed.

I made an impression on Edwina's dad that probably left him wondering if all the mortar between my bricks was dry.

I asked Joe if I could take out Julie.

I flunked my driver's license test.

I haven't been able to write my paper from the heart for Mrs. English.

I was responsible for the worst date known since the earth stopped spewing molten rock and continents stopped drifting, and that's not an exaggeration.

I will spend Monday, a holiday, baking almost 2,000 chocolate chip cookies.

And I'm not the 10th-grade-city-high-jump champion.

That's the short list. I'm a failure. I can't do anything right. I feel like a loser. My life is collapsing on me. I will move to Wyoming and become a cowboy, far away from this life I now lead. I will change my name. Lance. Brian. Matt. Joshua. Jason. Anything other than Wallace. Is it just a coincidence that I'm lying in a pit thinking these thoughts? Get something right. Anything. And soon. Please make it soon.

Can anyone hear me?

"Wally, you okay?"

I opened one eye. I stared into the face of Orville Burrell, a face filled with concern. He was bent over me, the blue sky above, framing his head. I got a funny little sensation in my stomach, and I knew something that I could do right, then and there.

"Yeah. I'm okay. Orville, will you take the missionary lessons?"

SATURDAY, MAY 25

Sleep is a wonderful thing. I crashed Friday night and for twelve oblivious hours, got away from this world of misery. It was almost ten o'clock in the morning when I was awakened by two sounds: Chuck, bouncing his basketball on the driveway and my mom coming upstairs with a small tray of food.

"Good morning, Wally. I was wondering when you'd wake up," she said cheerfully.

"It felt good to sleep in a while."

"I'm sure you're disappointed, Wally. We all are.

We know who is the real champion and that's what counts most."

"I suppose. It just doesn't seem fair."

"It's not," Mom said. "Your sister sure doesn't think so. You should have seen her after your jump. She went down to the field and almost attacked the judge. She was so upset she was in tears. Nobody pushes her brother around."

I was shocked. "Natalie did that for me?"

"She sure did. For all the bickering and teasing, Natalie does love you, Wally."

Maybe she does.

"And Chuck's worried, too. He made you some toast and orange juice and asked me if I would bring them up to you when you woke up. Then he told me he was going out to shoot some baskets and think about how he could make you feel better," Mom said.

Toast and orange juice. Chuck is awesome. A superstar.

"I know how you're always talking about moving to somewhere like Wyoming or Tibet whenever things get tough, Wally, and I know you're just kidding, but part of growing up is staying and facing things the way they are and learning how to handle adversity. When you can learn to work through difficult situations with poise and class and a little humor, then you're really starting to mature. And as bad as things got for you this week, I never heard you grumble. For that, Dad and I are really proud of you. You're a champion to us, dear."

For once, I was enjoying an FBL.

I took a bite of toast and sipped some orange juice. "Mom, does it get any easier when you're an adult? Can you control your life better? Is it like you just wake up one morning and know you're an adult and everything that happens will work out okay?"

She smiled. "Not quite, Wally. Let's get you through teenagerhood first. Then we can talk about what it's like to be an adult. But there are more similarities than you might imagine. In some ways, we're all kids forever, and that's not necessarily a bad thing."

The phone rang and Mom left to get it. I was there with my toast, my orange juice, and my thoughts—the whumping of the basketball the only sound. I heard a car pull up in front of our house but didn't think much of it. A minute later, the door slammed, and I heard Chuck's feet flying up the stairway.

"Wally, somebody's here to see you. It's Joe Vermeer," he panted.

Joe? Come to see me? What on earth for? I could think of about five thousand other people I'd rather face, including most third-world dictators and Les Lorris. Maybe Joe heard about the flop Thursday night with Julie and had come by to tell me to never ask her out again. Just as I was sort of pulling a few pieces of my life together, Joe is in the living room waiting for me. Well, I might as well get it over with. Mom says that handling adversity with poise is a sign of maturity, so why not do some more instant maturing? I'd hold my own with him, even in my pajamas with crumbs of toast all over me.

I started downstairs. Joe was draped on the couch, looking as natural as if it were his home.

"Hey, Joe."

"Hey, Wally."

"What's up?"

"Heard about the high jump yesterday. Sorry."

"It's okay. I've got two more years to win it."

"That's cool. Doesn't surprise me, though. In fact, the reason I stopped by here this morning is to tell you that I think you're one of the coolest guys I know, Wally."

He might as well have punched me in the stomach. Joe Vermeer, telling me I was among the coolest guys he knew? That's like Rembrandt saying you're a good painter, or Chef Boyardee saying you make a good plate of spaghetti. It's like Michael Jordan saying you've got a decent jump shot. It's like . . . like . . . Natalie saying you are a good dresser. I was stunned. After about thirty seconds of complete silence, I finally managed to squeak, "Me? You think I'm cool? I'm about as uncool as they come. Look at me . . . "

Joe held up his hand. "Naw. You are cool, trust me. Thinking you're not is part of it, if you get me. I saw Orville this morning at the car wash. Funny, but he was scrubbing that old pickup of his. He told me that you'd asked him to take the missionary lessons. That's ultra-cool, Wally. Being a missionary. Not everyone can do that. And I was also thinking about the time in the library when you talked with me about Julie. At first, I didn't get it. I couldn't figure out why you were sort of asking me if it was okay to take her out. It hit me, later. You were worried about our friendship and didn't want anything to come in the way of it. That's cool, too."

"Yeah. I guess that was cool."

"Then, there's the seminary Christmas party. You organized it, and that was the best thing I did over Christmas. It felt great to see all those gifts around the house. I heard that we were pretty much that family's whole Christmas. You think of other people, Wally. That sets you apart. Not a whole lot of guys our age do."

"Well, naw, I guess not. They're not as mature as we are."

"Then there's the Eagle project you're working on. What you're doing could save someone's life. And if you need help with the cookies, let me know. I'm an Eagle Scout and can get some guys in our ward to help you."

"I may need some help, Joe."

"And the election . . . "

"But I'm going to get creamed by Dick Dickson . . . "

"Don't think so. Yesterday after school, while you were on your way to the track meet, Dickson started handing out these little campaign flyers with your picture on them. They said something like, 'In November, my election opponent was involved in a fight at school and was disciplined by the administration for it. Is this the kind of boy you want to be your sergeant-at-arms?'"

"Dick did that? That's low even by his standards."

"Yeah. But it backfired. Everyone remembers it was Les Lorris that you and Orv took out, and he was the biggest loser in the school. And nobody thinks you picked a fight with him. So I think the novelty of Dick is wearing thin. Kids see he's a jerk. So I think he tripped himself up."

"What goes around comes around," I said.

"Right. And I think I can help you with your campaign next week. I'm pretty sure I can deliver some votes. I'll do some talking around for you. You'd be good in student government."

Suddenly, my political prospects brightened.

"I've got to go now. Due at the hospital to read books to little kids."

"No way! And after that, you help little old ladies across the street, leap across tall buildings, stop locomotives with your bare hands . . . "

"I only like to help."

Joe got up from the couch and moved over to the front door.

"Wally, you are cool. I really mean it."

"So are you, Joe. Yo."

We gave each other a high-five, a low-five, and an elbow bash. Hey, it seemed like the cool thing to do. You've got to go with your instincts. It's part of being cool.

Well, my day was definitely looking up, and it got even better. After lunch, Chuck came running in from outside. He grabbed my hand and said that I needed to come out to the driveway. "What's up, Chuck?"

"Just come. You'll see."

Now, I guess that I've watched Chuck shoot at least 10,000 times in his life, and he's never made a single one. But something told me this time might be different. It was his attitude. He seemed more confident. He picked up the old, worn ball, smoothed by countless bounces on the driveway, and stood about three feet in front of the hoop on our garage. He looked at me and said, "It's going to go in." He eyed the rim, and pushed the ball up with both his hands. It bounced up and off the back rim, then nestled through the net. Chuck and I both let out a holler that you could probably hear clear to Seattle. He jumped into my arms and knocked me over. We sat on the edge of the driveway, laughing and giggling and punching each other. Chuck's first-ever basket, and it was kind of dedicated to me.

"May this be the first of a zillion more, Chuck. You can't believe how happy I am."

And I meant it. The memory of the last few days was starting to dim.

By the way, I couldn't get to sleep tonight, maybe because I slept twelve hours last night. Then maybe I'm a little wound up about the way things went today, too. So I started thumbing through my journal, then I picked up a pen and a stack of notebook paper. I started writing . . . writing about everything in my life, the way I feel . . . about my family, my home, my friends, the Church. About being a teenager, about confidence, about maturity. About my dreams, my hopes, and what I want to be like. About Chuck's first basket and Natalie arguing with the field judge. About Joe, Julie, Ed, Lumpy, and of course, the one and only, Orville Burrell. I wrote about running slow and jumping high and what it's like to miss being a champion by an inch. I wrote about baking cookies and wearing a suit to school, and how friends are friends because they like who you are and not how you look or what you do or whether you are in or out.

And somehow, twenty-seven pages later, I tied it all together and made sense out of this life I'm leading, if only for a moment. I read what I had written, and I liked it. I finally connected, reached inside, and put it down on paper. Maybe I will be a writer someday. Now I know what Mrs. English has been talking about. You've got to *feel* what you're writing.

And she's going to have a pretty interesting term paper to read from Wallace Whipple, who, I've decided, ups and downs and everything in between, is a WINNER!

SUNDAY, MAY 26

And here I am, on the last page of my journal. It's hard to believe that I once wondered if I'd ever be able to fill it up. My journal was supposed to last a year, and I'm down to the last page in only nine months.

Writing in this journal has been awesome. Bishop Winegar was right—you don't have to be a rock star or a big-time someone to have an exciting and important life. Maybe it depends on how you define exciting, and figuring out that you can learn something from both good and bad experiences.

I need to buy another journal and start this all over again.

You see, the search for Wallace Whipple isn't finished. There are a few things more I know about him, a few things more I like about him than when I started my journal last fall. But there's a whole lot more left to discover about Wallace Whipple. And for the first time, I'm looking forward to it, not wishing it would all be over quickly.

And you know why?

Because I've grown to like the guy.

ABOUT THE AUTHOR

Donald Smurthwaite is a 1977 graduate of Brigham Young University where he earned a bachelor's degree in communications. He works for a government agency as a public information and marketing specialist.

A freelance writer, Donald has written many stories and articles for publication. *The Search for Wallace Whipple* is his first novel.

Though he has served as a counselor in the bishopric, a stake missionary, and a high counselor, Donald says his favorite calling was to be a Sunbeam teacher. He currently serves as president of the Young Men in his ward.

Donald is married to Shannon McClary Smurthwaite, and they are the parents of four children.